FLIGHT

KATIE CROSS

KCW

CONTENTS

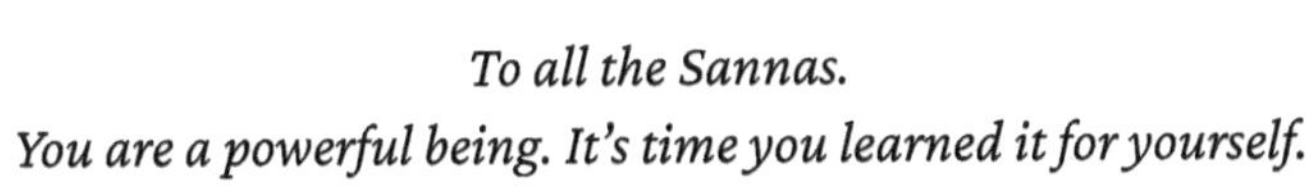

To all the Sannas.
You are a powerful being. It's time you learned it for yourself.

CHAPTER

ONE

The chilly fingers of winter crept into Isadora Spence's carriage through gaps in the door. She frowned at the wide cracks and pulled her cloak more tightly around her shoulders.

Winter was *so* intrusive.

The carriage wheels creaked with every jolt, both seemingly threatening to collapse and announcing their exact location. Could the traveling box be any louder? Or older? Maximillion likely chose it on purpose—just to make her more uncomfortable. Any minute now and the faded cushions beneath her would break their last string and split in half.

Still, it was safer than being out there.

A thick band of darkness stretched across the horizon, no doubt teeming with Defenders waiting to attack. The Defenders' steep hatred of Watchers seemed mandatory. As if they knew this was her first raid, her first attempt to save an innocent Watcher from their famed interrogations, as a member of Maximillion's rogue force that protected Watchers—the Advocacy.

Unable to bear the darkness anymore, she glanced at her hands. Enough gauzy moonlight slanted through the windows to highlight thick, ropy veins under her translucent skin. Her back curved into a hump. In the reflection of the window, an old woman stared back through different-colored eyes. No matter what kind of transformative magic she attempted, her eyes remained distinctively off. Like Maximillion's—only his were far subtler. Indistinguishable, really. Much like his emotions. Only now, her eyes were rheumy, red-rimmed.

Terrified.

A girl in her early teens sat across from her. Bright, wide eyes peered out of a heart-shaped face. Unassuming. Naive, even, with her perky nose and bowtie lips. No one would imagine she was a powerful witch beneath layers of meticulous transformation spells. The girl caught her eye and winked. Lucey, Isadora's mentor, hid beneath the disguise.

Next to Lucey trembled a young man—a boy, really—with olive skin and pools of umber for eyes. Alessio. His fingertips tapped an uneven rhythm on his bouncing knee. Isadora swallowed her questions for Alessio. *How did it feel when you transitioned? Is anyone else in your family a Watcher?* The strange Watcher magic operated on unknown rules. Not even Maximillion's intensive study had formed conclusions on how one became a Watcher, or where the magic originated.

Was Alessio silently saying goodbye to the Eastern Network and the only home he'd ever known? Lucey had said he was a musician once destined to work with the Eastern Network High Priest in Magnolia Castle—and that he was now headhunted by his own witches. The Defenders in the East were ruthless. Not a week ago, they'd captured a new Watcher, violently interrogated her in front of her family, then burned their house, and abducted her. Before Lucey could get to the seventeen-year-old girl, the Defenders had whisked her into Carcere, an ill-reputed prison from which there was no escape.

Isadora turned the thoughts away.

Your focus on the mission must be meticulous, Maximillion had said with a hint of irritation in his voice. *Never waver. They won't.*

She studied the unchanging landscape again.

Rolling hills, separated by stone hedges and copses of trees, passed by. Humidity lay thick in the air. Two days farther east and they would have seen the ocean. Isadora tried to picture the expanse of water in her head until an unusual flash in the distance caught her eye.

Lucey tensed.

For Isadora to ask about the strange light while maintaining their deception, she would need to use *Ilese,* the Eastern Network language. While the last six months of dedicated study since she joined the Advocacy made her speech passable, it was a halting mess. Her tongue wasn't used to the language's gentle nuance and soft edge, so she hesitated. Was it worth breaking the silence?

Lucey's young face furrowed. Her brow creased. Isadora lifted an eyebrow in silent question, but Lucey shook her head and leaned back again.

Not yet, she mouthed.

Magic hummed bright in Isadora's chest. She let it hum through her body. The momentary reprieve of energy granted her a bit of courage. Lucey gave no indication she noticed. Eventually, Isadora calmed.

Alessio's tense shoulders remained taut. Isadora tucked the magic away again. It flared, as if impatient, then settled.

Minutes passed. Alessio closed his eyes while he muttered under his breath, hands clenched.

Embrace the uncertainty of whether you'll live or die, Maximillion had said. *You'll pay more attention.*

Isadora kept her mind focused on the biggest question of all—what was the purpose of *any* of this? Why did magic have to be so beautiful and so dangerous?

"We're almost there," Lucey murmured in *Ilese.* "Just an hour to the Central Network border."

A chill swept through Isadora. Her eyes darted back to the darkness. She fought off a shudder. Lucey shifted ever-so-slightly to the left to peer out the window.

What could have been a simple extraction—requiring only Lucey's help—was complicated by Alessio's young age. At eleven, he was one of the youngest Watchers Maximillion had ever heard of. He hadn't learned to safely transport before he transitioned into his powers—and certainly not to an unknown location. He would have to be smuggled into the safety of the Central Network.

The bitter stench of rotten eggs wafted into the carriage. A metallic taste filled her mouth.

Lucey's eyes brightened, gleaming in the still night.

"Palude Marsh," she whispered in delight, still using *Ilese* for Alessio's sake. "Wonderful."

Prepare yourself. Defenders will be waiting in the marsh, Maximillion's voice said, an echo of his instructions early that morning. *If all goes according to plan, you won't even have to see them. Avoid the bog if you can help it.*

Alessio squirmed.

"Never fear." Lucey grinned, a twinkle in her eye. "Letum Wood awaits."

At that, Isadora's tension faded slightly. If nothing else, she could look forward to the protection of her forest home.

A wispy blue bird with yellow-tipped wings fluttered into the carriage. It alighted on Lucey's shoulder and leaned toward her ear. No sound came from its beak—no one else could hear the message it carried. An update from Maximillion, no doubt. The bird dissipated into smoke.

Lucey squeezed Alessio's arm with a reassuring smile that seemed to ease him, no doubt in part because of her transformed, youthful face. The putrid scent intensified—the driver had taken the carriage on a road alongside the marsh. Isadora nearly gagged.

"All is so quiet," Lucey said.

The words Isadora had been waiting for. She closed her eyes and slid into the waiting magic.

At first, darkness encased her vision.

Then Letum Wood blossomed before her, filled with thick vines and a canopy that soared so far overhead she couldn't see where it ended. No sound stirred in the twelve sprawling trees that formed a circle around her, as wide as several houses put together, so tall their closest branches were barely visible in the high canopy. Light seemed to infuse their trunks, their leaves, the ground where their roots stood taller than she did. Flowers bobbed in lazy coils along the trunks, draped with vines and ivy. Not a breath stirred here.

Twelve trails appeared in front of her.

"Twelve," she murmured. When in the magic, possibilities for the future of whomever she was with showed themselves through paths. The paths populated on their own, shifting, betraying possibilities of the future. Only her twin sister Sanna's paths and her own were always present. Exploring the paths posed a legitimate danger—Defenders could sense Watcher magic at work. In nearly all cases, Watchers helping the Advocacy refrained from using their magic on a raid. Tonight, however, was different.

Isadora was different.

The Defenders already knew Watchers were there because Lucey had carefully sculpted their plan. She *wanted* the Defenders to ambush them.

They won't expect it, she had said. *And we always have to take them by surprise. Otherwise, they'll guess our next move. Their magic is the opposite of yours. You see future possibilities; they see the past. Their advantage is seeing what you've already chosen, or not chosen. Cecelia trains them to analyze our decisions to learn our weaknesses.*

Isadora turned her mind and focused on the forest. The twelve paths formed a complicated map of ethereal wisps, some of them as vague as smoke, some so articulated she felt the witch stood in front of her in the flesh. Only six of the faces were familiar to her. Lucey, Alessio, Sanna, herself, and the two drivers. That meant six Defenders awaited them.

"Show only my path," she commanded the magic. Her clear voice rang through the forest.

The others faded away. Her paths spread over the area. Almost immediately, the main trail broke into two sections; each moved opposite directions. She frowned. That had never happened before. The possibilities had always split away from the main path, which remained mostly solid.

Perhaps danger also toyed with fate.

Isadora brushed past it—there was no time to study or guess. On either side, her paths branched out five different ways. Each segmented out, spreading through the forest with wisps of light that meant ... *something.* Isadora hesitated. If only the future were more concrete.

All the immediate paths showed her in the marsh, or in

Letum Wood, except one strange one showing her on a dragon. The trail was faint—which meant it wasn't a strong likelihood. Isadora shook her head, forcing herself to focus. If not careful, she'd get lost in the paths again, which happened every time she tried to make sense of her future.

With a heavy sigh, she stepped back to the top of the trail. Already, the possibilities had shifted. Trails had moved. Some disappeared. New ones sprang up.

The temptation to stay nearly overwhelmed her. Following the paths to see endless possibilities was always interesting—the future led to amazing, wild places. Like a toddler with a paintbrush and blank canvas. Time was easily lost here. Not to mention her powers were … different.

She closed her connection to the magic.

Lucey and Alessio waited. A glint of something—impatience—reflected in Lucey's eyes for a moment. Isadora's breath hitched. Egads, but time passed differently in the paths. She'd likely been there too long. Her cheeks burned.

"Sorry. Six Defenders," she whispered, avoiding *Ilese* to spare Alessio the anxiety. "I recognize none of them. From what I could tell, they were all waiting in the trees."

"Near the marsh?"

Isadora shook her head. "Not that I could tell."

Lucey's brow furrowed. No doubt the Defenders had a single scout who would summon them to the ambush the moment success seemed certain. "Only six," Lucey murmured. "So few? A bit insulting, if you ask me. They sent fifteen last time, and I still managed to avoid them."

"Cecelia isn't amongst them."

"She never is."

If Cecelia, leader of the murderous Defender force and Ambassador to the Eastern Network, wasn't here, why did

Lucey frown? She peered outside again. "No matter," Lucey murmured. "More may transport in as soon as we get going." Lucey looked at Alessio and asked both him and Isadora in *Ilese*. "Do you remember the plan?"

Isadora nodded. Alessio gulped, nostrils flared, and nodded.

Lucey grinned.

"Then I shall go break our axle and proceed. Good luck," she whispered.

She disappeared into a transportation spell.

Alessio straightened, eyes wide, as he studied Isadora for what seemed like the first time. He looked so much like a little boy right then. Frightened, vulnerable. His own Network would interrogate and kill him for something he had no control over—being born with powers that gave him a glimpse of future possibilities. She ignored his uncertainty and put a hand on his arm.

"I'm going to take good care of you, Alessio." Despite the terror of knowing what awaited them, certainty filled her tone. "Let's get ready."

"It's a dead belua."

Sanna Spence's nose wrinkled as she stared at a decaying carcass. The mottled skin of the gigantic, blue forest creature had turned a pinkish hue as it lay on the ground. The sightless face—beluas had no eyes—was slack, the jaw half-open. Decaying, cracked teeth filled the inside. She grimaced.

They stink even worse in death. Her dragon Luteis lifted his nose to the air and sniffed. His powerful wings folded against his back as if he were at ease, but tension rippled through his taut, serpentine face. This part of Letum Wood —so far west of where they lived—was unfamiliar. Pockets of deadly strickenine moss had overtaken once-healthy trees. The score marks and holes in the trunks indicated no lack of beluas here—perhaps even some trolls.

Not good things.

Sanna straightened. "What could have killed a belua so violently?"

A troll. I stumbled upon one when I was a hatchling, but it left me alone. They're not that intelligent, thankfully.

She frowned. "A troll kills with its hands. They don't have claws. The belua would have bruises or something. Besides, trolls hunt to eat, and they don't eat beluas."

Luteis snorted. *Nothing with any sense would.*

"Then what gave it those wounds?"

Dried blood stretched across the belua's legs, staining the dirt around its back a thick ebony. If they rolled it over, Sanna suspected they'd see deep gouges there as well. Something had slashed it to ribbons.

A mystery.

"We better tell the other Dragonmasters."

What purpose will that serve?

Sanna scowled at the thought of approaching grouchy Finn yet again. Recent confrontations with the other Dragonmaster hadn't gone very well. Disastrously, in fact. Arguing with Finn over the next best steps for their small dragon community only served to isolate her further in a world of witches who already thought she was lower than scum.

Than beluas, even.

"Warn them that we're not safe?"

That would certainly not surprise them. We could be safer, you know. Luteis gave her a sidelong glance. *If you would just accept the fact that you're High Dragonmaster and access the magic it grants you.*

"Or we could just move back to the circle of the Ancients."

He snorted. *You will do neither, stubborn witch.*

He said it with some affection, but Sanna still squirmed. The circle of the Ancients—twelve massive trees in the heart of Letum Wood—was different. Sacred, perhaps. The idea of dragging the Dragonmasters there to live shot a prickle of annoyance through her spine. It would likely be safer, sure. Creatures tended to avoid the deepest heart of the forest. Fresh water ran through it. Luteis had kept the deadwood cleared out of that area.

But was it the right thing to do?

"When a troll or a foe greater than beluas disrupts our camp, I will take the Dragonmasters to the circle. For now, this is manageable enough. Let's go."

Luteis remained silent as they trekked back toward the only spot open enough to land in a world so cluttered with vines, fallen branches, and dead trees. Sanna grabbed his tail, hauled herself up, and scrambled up his back to the spot on his shoulders where she always sat. Their magic merged so instantly now she didn't even notice it—like the beat of her heart.

We go?

"We go."

Luteis sprang off the ground, wings spread. With some difficulty, he navigated the long stretch of canopy overhead, dodging branches as wide as several houses, chattering tree gnomes that threw moss, and vines draped in complicated tapestries. By the time they burst out the top of the expansive, emerald world, his lungs heaved with exertion. Once airborne, his wings sliced through the sky without hesitation, calming his breath. Sanna closed her eyes, relishing the wind on her face. The ample forest flowed beneath her.

The delicious feeling of wind rippling through her hair—even if bitterly cold—roused Sanna from her spiraling thoughts. Luteis's sweltering body undulated below her with every beat of his wings, heating her chilly legs. Ancient Dragonmaster magic protected her from falling off. It happened automatically. She couldn't control that magic, nor would she want to. Her nose wrinkled at the thought of magic, which she quickly dismissed.

Dawn lingered on the horizon—a mere sliver of light. The tangy air pressed into her cheeks, stinging like the kiss of nettles.

It seems it shall be cold today.

"Says the giant lizard with fire in his belly."

Witches are inherently weak. We have discussed this. Again, if you would just—

"I know, I know. Magic, and all that."

She snorted, amused despite herself, and lay on his scales. Witches didn't need magic, and just because the forest goddess Deasylva forced her to be the High Dragonmaster for one day didn't mean she was that *now*. Nor, did it seem, that the magic wanted her to be. Heat pulsed through Luteis's scales, warming her skin, her muscles, even the bones in her arm. He dipped, soaring away at a surprising speed. When a little chill skimmed her back, Sanna turned around, pressed her spine to his scales, and watched the burning clouds overhead.

You are quiet today, he said.

"Thinking."

Would you want to think out loud?

Sanna hesitated. Luteis was in her head, but he didn't hear anything except what thoughts she directed to him.

Even then, she mostly spoke out loud because it was easier to keep track of what she'd said. When she spoke with her mind, sometimes it jumbled amidst her thoughts and confused both of them. She wondered if dragons had more organized minds than witches, because Luteis never tangled his communication.

"Do you want me to think out loud?"

I would prefer it if we planned a time of day for us to communicate about your thoughts, but I have learned that spontaneous communication is also enjoyable.

Sanna rolled her eyes. Their daily flights helped Luteis keep the edge off his energy, but not his obsession with planning. Since the death of the previous dragon sire, Talis, there had been little to plan. Both of them had devoted almost all their time to helping her daid right the Dragonmasters. Frightened dragons. Livid mams. Traumatized hatchlings. What felt like an eternal trek of arguments between Elliot, Finn, and Daid filled her mind.

Daid had bonded with the new dragon sire, Rubeis, but had only flown with him once, two months before.

"My legs were made to be on the ground," he'd said after the flight, then not uttered another word about it. Rubeis had disappeared for four days.

She frowned.

"Where's Deasylva?" she asked.

The question bubbled out of her before she knew it was there. Luteis drew in a deep breath, his chest billowing beneath him before he began a steep climb toward a stray cloud. This would be his last climb for the day, before settling back in at camp and pretending that all the dragons didn't fear him. They'd spend the final chunk of morning soaring close to the forest, near the treetops, hunting as they went.

Sanna couldn't be sure, but based on how far north and west they'd flown, they had at least an hour flight back. It would tire him enough to stay settled, though she knew he longed for a solid eight-hour flight again.

Deasylva has retreated.

"Where?"

I have not been told.

"Why did she leave?"

To maintain her strength.

"For what?"

She did not say.

Sanna's frown deepened. How convenient that the goddess of the forest could retreat as needed. Deasylva's warning rang through Sanna's mind. *War,* she had said. Sanna shivered. War with whom? She thought of the belua.

Or with what?

Is her absence what's bothering you?

"No. Not really. I just … I tried to talk to her a few days ago, but she didn't respond."

Your questions about the dragons, perhaps?

"Yes."

We should check the ruins again. She often responds faster when I speak with her there.

"Maybe."

I perceive that something else is bothering you?

Sanna hesitated, wondering if Luteis could even understand. Finally deciding that telling him would be better than not, she said, "Isadora has been gone for a long time."

Her cheeks burned, but she pushed down the embarrassment. Likely, Luteis already knew she missed her sister. His sprawling, thick wings beat the air with a gentle, even cadence. For several seconds, he said nothing.

Sanna let herself breathe. Saying that hadn't been easy.

You mourn this?

"I think so."

Is she ill?

"No, but she's ... different."

Why?

His voice betrayed no judgment, but she felt an annoyed prickle at the back of her neck all the same. "I don't know. It's just ... it's almost like ... like ... she doesn't want ..."

Yes?

"She doesn't want *us*."

How so?

"She's distant when she's home, which is less and less. She's always lost in thought or studying the paths—whatever that means. It's like ..."

Your sister has a magic that I am not familiar with.

"So she says."

Has she not told you?

Sanna hedged. "Well ... I think I just don't get it. What in Halla does it mean to see the future, anyway? How can you pinpoint that? We haven't really been able to just ... talk the way we used to."

Is this your fear?

"That we don't talk?"

Yes.

Sanna rolled the question around in her mind. "No. I think ... my fear is that she's different. She's not the sister I've always known."

You are different as well.

"Not that much!"

Are the old ways good enough for you?

Something hot welled up in Sanna. She hurled it away before she learned what it meant. "No, I suppose not."

Then change is inevitable.

"You're wiser than you sound, you know."

Dragons are surprising creatures.

They fell into silence while Sanna chewed on those thoughts. It wasn't just about Isadora being different—Sanna knew *she* was as well. At least a little.

After what happened with Talis nearly destroying the brood, refusing to make things right, and then dying at Daid's hand in a fire that wiped out all of Anguis, it would be impossible not to be changed. But Isadora was *so* different that there seemed no way to come back. The other families were even more uneasy around Isa than they were with Sanna. Isadora didn't seem to notice. Or care.

Even Mam seemed on edge around her; although, Mam had taken Talis's death harder than anyone.

Luteis dipped his left wing down, the tip of his right wing skimming the foggy underbelly of a cloud. The cool breeze whipped past her face, inundating her with ice crystals and mist. She closed her eyes, enjoying the bracing cold. It roused her from her frustration with her sister. From deeper thoughts of freedom, loneliness, and witches who wouldn't listen.

Your meeting with Finn occurred last night.

She scowled.

I take it by your silence that it didn't go as you had planned? I understand that frustration.

"No."

He is free to choose as he wishes. If he chooses to live apart and isolate his dragons and family, that is his decision.

"I know. I just don't like it. The families haven't separated in ..."

Her voice trailed away. Thanks to Talis, she didn't know how long it had been. He'd wiped out their history to create his own tyrannical society, making choices for the entire brood and eliminating their agency.

Why don't you like it?

A hint of something laced his voice. She sensed a trap but didn't know what it was. Sanna fidgeted. So much for a relaxing flight in the clouds.

"Let's talk about something else."

You always want to talk about something else when the subject of your being High Dragonmaster is broached.

"No one said anything about that!"

I was just about to, and I believe you know that.

"Let's just go home."

As you wish. But heed my warning: you will have to face up to the truth soon. You lead these dragons, whether you like it or not. The sooner you embrace that, the sooner the magic will be available to you.

"It's not just me who doesn't like the idea of a High Dragonmaster," she muttered. "It's the dragons. They weren't too happy about it, remember? Besides, we don't need one more leader to guide us astray. Not to mention that the magic is dangerous and fickle."

Luteis said nothing, just dropped closer to the ground. Not even the thrill of flight or the gentle burn of his heat on the back of her legs could comfort her today.

Hold on.

He dove. Sanna lay down, tucking her arms and legs close to his body. When they stood next to each other, Luteis loomed at least six times taller than her. She couldn't wrap her arms around any part of his massive body, but the magic of their merging kept her close to him, and safe.

Branches whipped past them. She buried her face closer to the scales of his neck. A shriek, a roar, and a puff of fire followed. Luteis alighted on the ground, a massive forest lion in his teeth. The animal struggled. He pressed his talons farther into it, and the beast stopped moving. Sanna slid off his back.

"Take your time," she said with a yawn. "I'm going to nap. By the way, when are we going to—"

A piercing noise rent the air, startling Sanna. She whipped around. Luteis peered to the left. His nostrils flared. Beneath her, his back expanded as he held his breath. He gently dropped the forest lion.

Step down.

"Why?"

There is a witch—several I think. I don't recognize their scent.

"Witches?"

He rolled his neck to the left, eyes tapered. Slight movement snapped Sanna's attention to the right.

There. Luteis nodded to the left. He darted through the trees with agile movements despite his rolling muscles. Sanna followed, ducking to avoid branches. He veered to the left, winding around a sprawling oak. She glanced behind them. There had been something on the right as well.

I still smell them.

They paused, listening.

Luteis slipped between two house-sized trees. Sanna stood, peering through the bracken and fallen wood, back toward the other movement she'd seen. Witches by themselves, in this part of the forest, were unheard of. Trees, undergrowth, old vines, and logs congregated so thickly here. Luteis stopped, blocked by several fallen logs.

Straight ahead. The scent is strong.

The vague *crack* of a stick followed.

Sanna's head jerked up. She stole through a drape of ivy,

toward a sliver of motion on the other side. The cluttered undergrowth seemed to embrace her as she ventured forward, able to move more easily than Luteis. Behind her, Luteis dug his talons into the bark of a tree and started to climb, his wide body hidden by the massive trunk.

The close growth gave way to a small, open space between trees. Movement to the left caught Sanna's eye. She turned and saw streaming blonde hair, slender shoulders, and dark brown skin dart behind a tree. Sanna took off after the woman, her sandals digging into the loamy earth for traction.

"Stop!"

The woman darted back through the trees, heading toward Luteis. A bow dangled from her back, but she had no quiver. Luteis snarled, slinking back down the tree. Branches waved in the canopy behind him.

And also—

Thwack.

Sanna ducked. An arrow slammed into a tree off to the right, not far beyond them. Luteis growled, shooting fire. Boughs rustled. A shadow disappeared into the underbrush near the arrow. Sanna ran to inspect the bolt. Charcoal-colored feathers stuck out from the shaft, which was as thick as her wrist. Runes, glowing a bright silver, glimmered around the shaft. They faded as something from the inside leaked out, spilling down the tree in rivulets.

Silver-filled arrow, Luteis hissed. *Poachers!*

That dreaded word sent a cold chill through Sanna.

She ran, hurtling through the forest toward the witch, shoving aside branches and leaping over waist-high tree roots. Luteis slipped along behind her with a growl, but Sanna worked through the underbrush and smaller saplings faster than he could. The witch darted through the trees with surprising speed. Ahead of her, something else seemed to be running.

Two of them, Luteis said. *I cannot see the one ahead of us. They are invisible, perhaps? No, they appear to … to blend in. The scent is strange. I do not recognize it.*

"Hey!" Sanna screamed. "Stop!"

The flap of the woman's cloak seemed to mock Sanna as she gained ground, sprinting almost out of sight. A flash of a bright-blue tattoo on her neck caught Sanna's eye. Was that a dragon tattoo? Sanna pressed harder, her chest burning for want of air. Behind her, Luteis roared. Heat rushed past her in a long wave, stirring her hair. The ground trembled underneath his steps.

The woman slipped behind a tree just before Sanna caught up. Sanna skidded to a stop in the rich dirt to find an empty forest. The spot where the witch had disappeared was empty. Sanna panted, glancing around. Nothing.

No one.

Not even a footprint in the muddy soil.

CHAPTER

TWO

Seconds after Lucey disappeared, a *crack* rang through the air.

The carriage lurched to a stop. Horses whinnied. The driver muttered under his breath. When he moved from the top of the box, it shifted. Isadora's stomach reeled with the gentle sway. Outside, a strange, insidious fog crawled from the marsh, toward their stopped carriage.

Isadora drew in a deep breath and murmured the right incantation.

A vague shimmer filled the air next to Alessio, and a second version of him appeared. Lucey often used ancient, complicated spells to prevent the Defenders from knowing when normal magic was in use. Older magic, because it was unfamiliar, was more difficult to detect, even for the most sensitive witch. Likely, the Defenders would anticipate her using something from the Declan magic, but Isadora doubted they'd expect such a simple deception spell.

The real Alessio's eyes widened as he studied the mirror image of himself. Isadora held up a hand.

"Do not touch," she whispered.

He nodded once. Isadora cast a second deception spell, duplicating herself. "Now," she murmured. "Remember—be very quiet. Keep the invisibility incantation active."

Alessio swallowed hard and nodded. After a nervous murmur, his body disappeared.

Step one, she thought, fading into her own invisibility incantation. She rapped once on the top of the carriage with a knobby knuckle. "What seems to be the issue?" she called, infusing a purposeful croak into her voice. The shuffle of the driver's footsteps sounded outside right before the door swung open. Isadora paused for a moment to allow Alessio to leave ahead of her. Meanwhile, the two deception spells remained sitting in the carriage, strangely unmoving. After one last glance at the eerie representations, she slipped outside.

The driver's eyes darted around. "Just a few minutes," he said into the carriage with near perfect *Ilese,* as if they were waylaid on accident. "We broke an axle. Not sure I can fix it."

He shut the door before the lack of movement from the deception spells gave them away.

She couldn't see Alessio, but felt him near as they moved away from the carriage. The horses pranced, tossing their manes, no doubt unnerved by the strange fog rolling off the marsh. A mat of stars sparkled overhead, mute in the distant sky. The cold drove into Isadora's fingers with foreboding promise, intensified by the cool rush of her invisibility incantation.

Palude Marsh lay on the other side of the trees, hidden in shadows and blunted moonlight. She reached out, blindly, until her fingertips grazed fabric, and she clasped Alessio's elbow. She tugged him toward the marsh, along a barren patch of ground that wouldn't betray their steps in the still night. They both stumbled in the strangeness of walking without seeing their own feet.

The night pressed on them as they slipped into the thin, brittle trees. No sign of Lucey. *Always,* Lucey said. *Always change what you do. Make no decisions until you have to. Surprise yourself, if you can.*

Isadora saw a more open area of trail and resisted the urge to move toward it. Instead, she plunged them closer to the swampy waters. No doubt Lucey was working through the marsh now, attempting to find and distract the waiting Defenders—who would be well hidden themselves—to give Alessio and Isadora a head start once the Defenders attacked the carriage.

The sound of the driver shouting broke the air.

Isadora whipped around just in time to see the driver disappear with a transportation spell moments before a witch, dressed in a black cape and mahogany shirt, attempted to grab him. The carriage lurched. Several witches shouted, surrounding the carriage. A chill raced down her back when she recognized the *Ilese* word for *halt* over the shriek of the horses.

Step two.

She shoved Alessio ahead of her, toward the brackish waters.

"Go."

They darted into the marsh, invisibility spells at work. Another shout. Isadora glanced over her shoulder as the horse and carriage tore away, flames licking the wooden box. Two Defenders sprinted toward the marsh—no doubt they'd already figured out the game. No matter. They had the advantage now.

Lucey appeared off to the right with a delighted giggle. She waved to the Defenders with an impish, girly hand.

"Over here," she sang.

The Defenders growled. Isadora pulled Alessio through a cluster of trees and into deeper shadows. His incantation was beginning to wear away. His legs appeared to run by themselves as he dodged spindly trees and low scrub. Murky water splashed at their feet. An orange cloud charged them from the amassing Defenders, racing toward them with ruthless speed.

"Run!" Isadora hissed. "We can't breathe that in."

The ground dampened, sucking their feet like a living thing and slowing them until the mist overtook them, clogging their throats. Isadora coughed. Alessio wheezed, a hand on his chest. Drawing in air felt like breathing through a small hole. Her head spun. Alessio stumbled.

Isadora slowed, studying the burbling water, barren trees, and broken sky. They wouldn't be able to outrun the Defenders, and the trees were too skinny and naked for refuge. They should escape along the edge of the marsh, where the ground was still firm, and they could make better time. But the Defenders would be able to catch them there —certainly now that they could hardly breathe.

Dread made her stomach heavy as she glanced at the burbling bog.

Only one thing for it.

She grabbed Alessio's arm and yanked him into the freezing lake. The slimy water splashed her face as she sank. It squelched along her back, oozing in a flood against her skin. She grimaced. Alessio heaved. Isadora pulled them farther in, behind a moldering log, until the icy water lapped at their necks. After a moment's hesitation, she leaned back, covering her hair with the same muck. Tears filled her eyes at the stench.

"Over there," someone shouted in *Ilese.*

Isadora slapped mud on her cheeks and forehead and indicated for Alessio to do the same. Faces smeared with the foul muck, they stilled behind a floating log, submerged to their jaws. Something brushed against her leg. Alessio's jaw tightened as he pressed his teeth together to keep them from chattering. The vile bath sapped all her heat, leaving her to tremble.

A twig broke.

Isadora froze.

Defenders whispered only ten paces away, hovering near the edge of the swampy waters. The invisibility spells had completely faded now—a good thing. The Defenders wouldn't be able to feel the magic.

Alessio silently fought the urge to retch again. She put a hand on his shoulder, ready to dunk him if she had to. Her powers remained tied within, as if locked in a chest deep inside. Her heart pounded. She sank a little lower when one Defender stepped back, sweeping the swamp with a piercing gaze, while the other stood unmoving.

As if he'd come out of a trance, the second Defender turned, then pointed along the edge—where Isadora would have run. They stepped onto it, then paused, murmuring in *Ilese*. The Defenders lingered, waiting for movement, no doubt. Lucey had warned her about their patience. Alessio's wide, frightened eyes met hers.

Another twig snapped, this time behind them. Isadora's low, raspy breaths faded. The foggy incantation began to weaken its grip on her throat. An explosion hurled a burst of yellow fire through the trees. The Defenders recoiled.

Pieces of bark and tree whipped through the air, landing in the water.

Another explosion.

Isadora shoved Alessio deeper into the brackish waters,

and they began to move. Tongues of fire licked the dry trees overhead, driving away the pervasive mist. The Defenders howled.

She thought she heard Lucey giggling until the sounds faded into the distance. Isadora forced Alessio to keep going. The lake gave way to slick banks. The deeper marsh became thick mud as high as their knees. The mud froze to their skin as they pressed on, winding through the trees, hidden by the dark flakes of drying mud.

"N-n-next?" Alessio whispered, gazing into the darkness with soulful eyes. The Defenders were minutes behind them. For now, there was some room to breathe and walk and plan. Lucey would continue to work against the Defenders. Unless Isadora wanted to be locked in Carcere or killed by Cecelia, she had to get Alessio to Letum Wood.

Both their lives depended on it.

Isadora calmed her chattering teeth and pointed west.

"We walk," she said.

ALESSIO SAID nothing as they trudged through the mud, slogging around fallen trees, past slushy pits, and into the occasional stretch of shoulder-deep swamp water. Isadora kept as close to the tree line as she dared. Hours seemed to pass, filled with paranoid imaginings, unfamiliar sounds, and the pull of dried mud on her face. If possible, the night chill deepened.

Letum Wood appeared like a band of midnight in the distance. Eventually, the watery marsh gave way to firmer, cluttered ground. Saplings. Young trees. Shrub brush. The stench faded—or perhaps she'd just gotten used to it. At her side, Alessio clung to his arms. His teeth chattered like a bag of old bones.

"Soon," she murmured.

He said nothing.

Mud froze on her dress. Flakes scraped off her arms, falling to the ground in petals. Although they pressed hard, the landscape didn't change much. Marsh. Bog. Letum Wood in the distance, as if it would never get closer. She paused, holding out an arm to stop Alessio.

"Wait," she murmured.

She slipped into the magic.

Letum Wood proliferated around her again—oddly comforting. This time, only three paths remained. Hers, Sanna's, and Alessio's. No Lucey, but also no Defenders. She fought the temptation to check on her sister and returned. The magic settled inside her like a sigh.

"Just us," she said.

Alessio's shoulders relaxed a little bit.

"For now. Let's keep going."

The first fingers of dawn hinted on the horizon when Isadora and Alessio skidded to a stop an hour later. The marsh had ended. An open field, at least a thousand paces across, lay between them and Letum Wood. It would take several minutes at a full run to cross, but neither of them had the energy. She hesitated. The distance didn't bother her.

It was the lack of Defenders.

Moving through the marsh and toward Letum Wood was their obvious path—the Defenders would have known. But the odds were good that the Defenders didn't know when or where they'd pop out of Palude Marsh. If Isadora entered the paths again, she'd draw them to their location, something they likely hoped for.

"Running is our ... *ah* ..." Her mind skipped around, too numb and tired to remember the right words in *Ilese*. "Only, ah ... *chance*. Can you do it?"

Alessio blinked, eyes bleary. The bone-deep cold had long ago shifted from misery to numbness. Finally, he nodded once.

"Fast," she said, searching for the right words. "Er ... *really* fast."

She reached out and grabbed his hand. He sucked in a sharp breath but didn't pull away. Isadora nodded.

"Go."

They sprinted together. Clumps of weeds tore at her feet, reaching up to trip her. Rocks covered the ground. Saplings, struggling to grow so near the marsh, clogged their path. Isadora's aching legs burned with the exertion. Her lungs, still tight from the orange fog, cried out for more air.

The air next to her shimmered, and something slammed into her side. She stumbled with a cry, caught herself before skidding to her knees, and clambered back to her feet.

"Go, Alessio!"

Alessio pulled ahead of her, eyes wild. Within seconds, she tripped over her own feet. When she attempted to stand, she fell onto her head, scraping her right ear.

A tripping curse.

She wracked her mind for the counter-curse. She only had a few more seconds to counter it before it took hold for four days.

Alessio grabbed her arm, jarring her back to reality. Isadora muttered the counter-curse and shoved back to her feet, fistfuls of dirt in her hand. She threw out a shield that would survive three curses. Attacks pinged off the invisible magic with dull *thuds.*

Four Defenders appeared in front of them, teeth bared.

Isadora threw the dirt. One of the Defenders recoiled. She cast another protective spell around Alessio and herself, then attempted a blindness curse. The Defender transported before it hit its mark, opening a space for them to dart through. The others disappeared, transporting not far ahead. Isadora threw a second and third curse. She struggled to replace a protective shield that broke under an onslaught of magic.

Alessio managed to stay at her side. Less than two hundred paces left. The Defenders fanned in front of them in a half circle now, shooting curses in a flood. Her chest ached—she thought her heart would pound through her ribcage. She couldn't keep replacing her magical shield *and* outrun them.

She slowed. If they focused on her, Alessio could escape. Isadora wrapped an invisibility spell around him. He disappeared. The Defenders scowled, peeling away. Four toward him, two toward her.

A Defender appeared next to her, reaching for her dress. She ducked, avoiding his hand, and sent a rock flying at his face with a spell. He stumbled. The magic of the shield wavered. A curse slammed into Alessio. The invisibility spell disappeared. He reached up for his eyes, slowing.

"I can't see!" he screeched and stumbled over a bush. He fell, skidding on his shoulder with a cry.

Isadora lurched toward him, grabbed his arm, and hauled him to his feet. She started a fire on one Defender's shirt. He howled and backed away. Another transported away, appearing close at her side. She threw a blighter—a magical ball of energy—at him.

"Do the counter-curse!" she called to Alessio.

"I don't know it!"

The forest loomed thirty paces away.

"Just keep running!" she said. A Defender swiped for her arm, but she dodged. Her shield wavered underneath another barrage of curses.

Twenty paces.

Isadora focused all her mind on the shield just as a burst of magic slammed into it. The shield shattered into a gauzy mist, throwing them forward. She fell, rolled, and leapt back to her feet. Alessio shouted, arms flailing. She couldn't do the counter-curse for him.

Ten paces to Letum Wood.

Where was Lucey?

Maximillion?

Isadora shoved Alessio as hard as she could into Letum Wood just as a Defender grabbed her sleeve, grunting as he lunged. The fabric tore. Isadora whirled around, maintaining her balance by sheer luck, and kept running. The other Defenders lingered back, eyes on the forest, which loomed tall and terrifying.

A vine whipped out from the forest. It grabbed a Defender by the neck and tossed him into the air. His scream stopped when he landed fifty paces away, head bashed into a rock.

Two Defenders transported away.

One advanced.

The crack of magic hitting a tree trunk exploded in her ear as Isadora sped into Letum Wood. Alessio fell to his knees, hands on his eyes, sobbing. Isadora grabbed him and yanked him back up.

"Come on," she said.

"I'm blind!"

She pushed him through the trees, ignoring his terror for the moment. It didn't matter *where* they went in Letum Wood as long as they went deep enough. The sound of following feet still stalked them.

A burly Defender, all muscle and brawn, sprinted after them. His eyes darted around. He ran distracted, gaze swinging from the floor to the trees, no doubt scanning for vines.

There were far worse things here than vines.

Something tall, thin, and precariously built on an old stump caught Isadora's gaze. A fairy house. They were rare enough—especially this close to the edge of the forest—but unmistakable. She skidded to a stop. The Defender did the same, only a few paces away. His chest heaved.

"This is my home," she called in *Ilese*, panting. "Get out."

"You will die with the rest of the Watcher scum!"

"I *am* a Watcher scum," she hissed, then smacked the fairy house. Bright colors boiled out of the tree with hysterical shrieks. The cries of at least ten livid, bloodthirsty fairies cut through the air. Isadora cast an invisibility spell and disappeared. The fairies came face-to-face with the Defender. A moment of silence lingered in the air.

"Get him!" a tinny voice bellowed.

"He harms the fairies!"

"You. Must. Die!"

The entire stump shifted to the left from the sheer force of raging fairies as she and Alessio sprinted away. The Defender's screams faded as they plunged deeper into Letum Wood, leaving the bog and the Eastern Network far behind them.

~

AN HOUR LATER, a young boy with bright eyes and long blond hair stood in the middle of a weak animal trail. He wore ragged clothes and no shoes, but he peered at Isadora and Alessio with a sharp gaze. He couldn't be older than ten, although the sheer lack of light in this part of Letum Wood made it difficult to tell for sure.

"Ya stink." He plugged his nose. "Did ya roll in troll dung?"

"Not now," she snapped.

"Ya here for the lady?"

"Yes."

"Prove it."

Isadora opened her hand, palm up. A swirl of bright-blue magic coalesced into smoky, glowing lines. The criss-crossing design blended into a smooth tapestry that tilted on its side and turned to face him. The boy frowned.

"That's not it!" he cried.

"That's it!"

"The lines are drooping. It's supposed ta be neat and even."

The edges of the design *did* tilt where they were supposed to be flat. And, the final color in the scheme was violet; though, it was supposed to be sapphire. She scowled.

"It's a work in progress."

"I should send ya to the bog again."

"Let us through!" she muttered, scowling. "We made it this far."

Alessio slumped against a tree. The young boy glowered. "Come on, then," he muttered as he spun around. "She's waiting."

Only a few more steps brought a small cottage into view —or perhaps the disappearance of a powerful transformative incantation that hid the cottage. A kind, old woman, with a crooked smile and bright-white hair twisted into a braid, waited in the doorway. She raised a hand.

Isadora stopped walking. This wasn't the woman's real appearance—no one in the Advocacy ever showed their *real* face. Not even to other witches in the Advocacy. Though the transformative magic had long since left Isadora, at least the dried mud protected her fair features and blonde hair.

Isadora motioned to Alessio.

"They hit him with a blindness curse. It will be a few days before he can see again."

The woman glanced at the high canopy, then back again. "Sometimes that's better," she said.

Isadora turned to Alessio, a heavy hand on his shoulder. "You're safe now. You'll stay with her until we can find you a new place to start your life."

"Here?" He gulped, still touching his eyes. "In the forest?"

"For now. It's safest. Once things settle down, we'll bring your family to you."

He hesitated, then nodded once. "Thank you." The woman advanced, taking him by the arm. Together, they disappeared inside the safe house.

The young boy followed Isadora as she turned and moved farther into Letum Wood, lost in thought. The aftermath of their escape burned hot in her veins, as if she were on fire. She'd transport back to the castle eventually, but only after putting distance between Alessio and herself, just in case.

A familiar voice broke her reverie.

"And where in the name of the good gods is Lucey?"

Maximillion strode next to her where the young boy had been. Instead of his usual ironed clothes and pocket watch, he wore a faded pair of pants and a simple white shirt rolled above his elbows. On him, the simplicity, taken with his disarrayed hair, was ...

Oddly wild.

Isadora turned away, swallowing a lump in her throat.

"I haven't seen Lucey since the ambush."

"Something went wrong," he snapped.

Isadora pressed her lips together with a frown. "Nothing outside our plans." But something surely *felt* wrong. She recalled the strange split in the paths that she saw in the magic. The lack of Defenders throughout the marsh.

She recounted everything she remembered while Maximillion folded his hands behind his back, his glacial blue eyes contrasting with the thick locks of chocolate hair on his forehead. He never could contain his hair when he transformed. It about drove him mad.

"Interesting," he murmured. "Well, no doubt Lucey will be fine. It was a ... decent first run, despite a plethora of mistakes."

"Don't choke over the compliment," she muttered.

"Regardless of your many failings, you still managed to save Alessio's life. That's something, at least."

"I'm glad of that."

She waited for a *well done* or *I'm proud of your work*, but when it didn't come, realized that was as good as she'd get. She sighed. It had been a long night. Real concern for Lucey filled his gaze despite his forced ease, distracting him. Lucey's absence for such a long stretch of time wasn't unusual, but still gave cause for concern.

"Go home," he said. "Take a bath. Get some rest. I won't expect you for the full report until tomorrow morning. Lucey will have contacted me by then."

"Send me word when Lucey returns, will you?"

He was already gone.

Sunlight grazed the far horizon in shades of yellow, violet, and burgundy when she transported back to her predesignated spot, and then to another location, just to be sure. Through the trees, not far from where she landed, loomed Chatham Castle. Night shadows still clung to the facade. Fatigue consumed her to the marrow of her bones.

Isadora stifled a yawn, walked fifty paces into the forest for extra insurance against being followed, then transported back to Pearl's home in Berry.

THREE

Sanna doubled over, her breath coming hot and fast as she stared into the trees. A poacher in Letum Wood.

"Mori."

Witch magic bore that poacher away.

Sanna clutched at the stitch in her side. There was no doubt that arrow contained liquid silver—the only thing that could kill a dragon. Silver paralyzed dragons, allowing witches to hack them to death or drain their blood. Eventually, the silver would stop their heart. It was the exact weapon Daid had used to kill Talis and stop his regime, and what poachers used over one hundred fifty years ago to massacre the forest dragons.

She leaned against a tree, head spinning. Her ribs ached. "She had a tattoo on the back of her neck. Did you see it?"

Yes.

"A dragon, wasn't it? Maybe? I-I couldn't tell."

His eyes narrowed. *Yes.*

The questions choked her. Too much concentrated fear

coursed through her like fire to allow her to think clearly. She didn't even know where to start. *Poachers* again. She had to warn Daid. Jesse. Elis. All of them. If poachers were already here ... *It might be too late.*

We must be on alert.

"We need to warn Daid. We have to go back. Now."

He hesitated for just a moment—a moment long enough for Sanna to comprehend his pause. If she ran back and told everyone there was a poacher in the forest, they'd stare at her. Finn would laugh. Daid would listen—but he'd want to know for certain. Without proof, she was the last witch they'd trust. Never mind that she'd saved them from Talis's tyrannical reign and, given time, the almost-certain destruction of the forest.

They'd never see it that way. Six months had passed since Talis died, and they still hadn't accepted it.

You would induce panic before we have enough information. I do not agree with this plan.

She couldn't believe he could be so calm about this. A leaf drifted down from the spires of trees, sliding past her cheek with a gentle caress. For half a second, she thought of pressing her hand into the nearest tree and trying to speak with Deasylva. The fickle forest goddess came and went as she pleased, but sometimes she was around. Sometimes she answered questions.

Sometimes she didn't.

The unknown behaviors of a vague goddess weren't high on her priority list. Besides, she'd taken pains to avoid Deasylva ever since she'd forced the title of High Dragon-master on her—for one night, at least.

Now, it seemed more sensible for Daid to take the title. Everyone followed him anyway, even though he had killed

Talis. Sanna bore the burden of upending life in the forest for all the Dragonmasters.

Sanna sucked in another deep breath, forcing herself to calm. Luteis was right. Panic on any level wouldn't serve them right now.

There is already much panic. His ears perked up. Not even a dragon of his behemoth size could hide his ideas. *But Deasylva can help us.*

Sanna scowled. Why did he have to think of it too?

"Do we have a choice?"

Always. She may have returned.

With a sigh, Sanna let her thoughts untangle, winding through the paths of her frustration with Finn, Daid's lacking desire to fly with Rubeis, and the strange fracture of the brood. Although Rubeis had stepped up as the new dragon sire, not all of the dragons wanted to follow him. Sanna could feel their anger simmering in the darkness as she walked by.

Besides, the night Talis died, Sanna had been able to hear all the dragons' voices in her head. A probable sign that she was High Dragonmaster, although they couldn't know for certain thanks to Talis erasing history.

But now?

The voices were gone.

"Fine. We'll ... ask Deasylva. But not until tonight," she said. "We'll go farther away and speak with her."

Luteis stared at her through a wide, yellow eye. *As you say.*

Feeling better, she nodded once. "After talking to Deasylva, let's look around. See if there are any camps or other signs."

Tonight.

LATER THAT NIGHT, Sanna climbed up the last few branches of a familiar, ancient oak and settled back on her haunches. It was the same tree, the same branch, where she'd first met Deasylva the previous year. Luteis lurked just behind her, his globe-like eyes peering through the thick tangle of trees. Sanna glanced at him over her shoulder.

"Do you think she'll talk to me?"

Why not?

"I've tried, and she doesn't answer."

Perhaps you aren't really listening.

She reached out and stroked the tree trunk with the tips of her fingers to avoid responding. True, Sanna had approached Deasylva mostly out of obligation in the past. Talking with the goddess felt weird. At this time last year, Sanna didn't even know she existed.

A sliver of light illuminated under her touch, flaring to life like a miniature spark of sun. As quickly as it came, the light faded, leaving a pit in Sanna's stomach. She frowned.

She is there. I can feel her more than I have recently.

"Now?"

The thin scales above Luteis's eyes drew together, creasing his forehead. *Well ... I am not certain. But she is in all things in the forest.*

Sanna quirked an eyebrow. "How long has it been since you last spoke with her?"

I cannot recall.

"Weeks?"

At least.

"Hmm."

Sanna straightened, grabbed a vine, pressed her feet into the trunk, and used it to walk to the other side of the tree, where another sprawling branch jutted out. She used the uneven edges to stair-step her way higher, then pressed her palm to the rough bark, but no light flared this time. Her brow furrowed.

"Do goddesses die?"

I've always imagined her immortal.

"I always imagined her male and a lot less forgiving," Sanna muttered, craning her head back to peer into the canopy. "It's amazing how reality changes so swiftly. Can she leave?"

No. She is Letum Wood. He paused. *At least, that's what I have always imagined, but I may err in my assumptions, for she isn't always here. You pose a worthy question for once.*

"I'll let that one slide. Do you remember last time I spoke with her, after Talis died?"

Briefly.

"She said we needed to prepare for war."

This I remember.

"Could she be preparing for war, somehow?"

I don't know how to answer. I am not used to witches asking such astute questions.

"Har har."

I'll think on these.

They sank into another silence. Sanna dropped her feet from the tree trunk and grabbed the vine. It swung back around. She alighted gently on the first mossy branch. A flicker of light caught her gaze. With it came a faint surge of heat in the tree, a strange new *swish, swish,* like a beating heart of sap. The swoop of a letter in a line of light appeared on the umber branch.

"Ah," Sanna muttered. "There you are."

Letters appeared in the mossy bark one at a time, so painstakingly slow Sanna almost couldn't handle it. The threads were gossamer thin, as if Deasylva scratched with the tip of a needle. Sanna pressed close to the tree.

"*Avay*, Deasylva," she said.

I am always here, the words said.

"I beg to differ."

Luteis bumped her with his snout. She scowled at him but continued. "There are poachers in Letum Wood again, and … that's all." Luteis nudged her again. Sanna swatted at him. "Fine," she growled. "And I can't hear the dragon voices anymore. Luteis wants to know why."

Luteis's answering growl rumbled in his throat. New lines appeared in the tree.

They also prepare.

Sanna's brow furrowed. "What? Prepare for what? Who is 'they'?"

The light faded, giving way, yet again, to the three letters Sanna feared most.

War.

"I know that already. Why are they preparing for war with silver arrows?" Something cold trickled through her. "Is this a poacher war?"

You have what is required.

"We don't *have* anything. We can't even get proper houses built."

You have my trust.

The light ebbed.

Sanna floundered, at a loss. What good was Deasylva's trust? They needed weapons. Certainty. More food.

"But that doesn't mean anything!" Sanna cried. "That doesn't make any sense!"

Soon. The word faded, barely legible. *Soon.*

"But what about the dragon voices?"

No response came.

Sanna rammed her hand into the trunk once, scowling. Soon, what? The gentle stir of the air faded. The scent of honeysuckle went with it. An edge laced Luteis's tone.

That was ... unexpected.

"This isn't good, Luteis. We have poachers, lazy dragons, dissenting Dragonmasters, and an apparent war on the horizon that we know nothing about. What exactly are we supposed to do next? She wasn't any help!"

We plan for war and care for the dragons.

"Talk to Finn. He has some radical ideas on how to take care of dragons."

Then we must do the best we can to prepare ourselves.

"But prepare for what?" she growled, shoving away from the tree. "What good is a goddess who only stirs up more questions?"

She made that clear. We're preparing for war.

"Yes, but the war is here now. Poachers have come. That makes it personal."

She said that they also prepare. Perhaps they aren't poachers.

"Then why the silver-filled arrow?"

He gave no response.

Her chest tightened at the thought of what a silver-filled arrow could do to Luteis. Sanna grabbed a vine and plummeted down, branches, leaves, and mossy clumps whizzing past her in the dull wind. She landed in a crouch, glanced around, and straightened. With a glare at the canopy, she clapped her hands, shaking bits of vine free. Luteis landed next to her, and the two slinked through the forest without another word.

CHAPTER

FOUR

T he stench of the marsh lingered in Isadora's nose, though she'd scrubbed her body for an hour with rough salts and heavy soap.

Late winter sun streamed into the room with a blunted light when she woke up after a heavy sleep. Her entire body ached, but especially her calves, which had borne the brunt of slogging through the murky water. When she slipped out of bed, she grabbed *Daily Incantations for Busy Mothers* from the shelf, flipped to the back, and found a *smell removal* incantation.

After working the magic, she stumbled into a dress, wrapped her hair in a bun, and left her room. The smell of coffee permeated the air as she advanced into the kitchen. Sunlight streamed through the tall cottage windows, illuminating frosty designs.

Isadora yawned and sat at a rickety wooden table. Three skinny windows overlooked a section of rolling fields that eventually led to Letum Wood in the distance. She soaked the beautiful sight in, lost in the undulating lines of field and grass. Something about the openness of the world outside Letum Wood thrilled her.

"She awakens!" Pearl cried, bustling into the kitchen. Her apron bow, large as ever, bounced with every movement. "How are you feeling?"

"Tired."

"As you should be."

An edge of … *something* bothered Isadora. She couldn't name it. She slipped into the paths to find the answer there. The magic stirred with a sigh inside of her, as if pleased she'd returned.

Something was different.

She studied the wide sprawl of the familiar, ancient trees. Was the landscape brighter? Maybe a little, but it was … humming. As if she could hear the magic. Her blood buzzed. She felt saturated with magic. This had happened before. Her power had seemed to grow by the day since she joined the Advocacy and began using it, but sometimes it exploded, expanding by massive amounts.

Three paths appeared on the ground, infused with strands of light. Herself, Pearl, and Sanna.

"Show only my path."

Now only two paths disappeared into the quiet, lush forest. A meandering trail cut through the trees, populated with colorful wisps. The most distant of them—an untold number of days, weeks, or months away, she could never tell—seemed innocuous enough. Letum Wood in the spring. Smelling flowers. Standing on top of a building, peering at the edge of an expansive, rippling body of water. A storm lingering on the distant horizon. The ocean.

The wisps were mere representations of future possibilities that never ended. Future-gazing was a capricious art. Some paths revealed the strangest things, like Isadora wagging her finger at a troll or Maximillion grimacing—perhaps attempting to smile and failing magnificently.

She reached out, touched one of the trees, and felt a thrill zip through her hand. Power built inside her, then eased. She closed the magic and blinked out of her daze. The powers were a bit different, but nothing concerning. She put it off to think about later.

"Any plans for the rest of the day?" Pearl asked when she returned, unbothered by Isadora's minutes-long mental absence.

"Meet with Maximillion. Then study *Ilese*, I suppose."

Pearl's gaze darted to a pile of laundry, then hastily looked away.

Isadora reached for her teacup. "Of course, it will feel so good to do the laundry when I return. There's nothing quite like it for relaxing."

Pearl beamed. "Lovely idea!"

A copy of the *Chatham Chatterer* newsscroll lay on the table. It shifted as its articles updated, sometimes with more sentences, sometimes fewer. With so many battles in the Networks and so much political tension, the scroll never calmed.

War left little breathing room.

"It's a wretched time, isn't it?" Pearl asked, as if reading her mind. "Maximillion so busy he can hardly exhale. Berry in ruins. Things escalating against the East. The Southern Network building a wall to keep everyone out. Madness, I tell you. I've never heard of such unrest."

Isadora pushed the newsscroll out of sight.

"I've been reading like a madwoman to distract myself." Pearl gestured to piles of books and scrolls all over the floor. "Can't get myself to stop. Those romances are so ... whew ... exciting. Better than focusing on what's happening here, anyway. Or what's not happening here. Oh, I almost forgot. A letter came from your sister last night. It's, ah ... *quite* unconventional."

She hadn't visited her family in a month. Lucey had been teaching her transformation, which proved to be distracting magic. A leaf the size of her hand, folded into four, fell into Isadora's palm. Purple ink covered the velvety backside. Babs's ink, no doubt, made from the boiled remnants of a rare mushroom. She recognized Sanna's awkward handwriting immediately.

WHERE ARE YOU?

Isadora sighed. Pearl stared at her, eyebrows high.

"That is a—"

"A leaf? Yes."

"Hmm."

"I should go visit them after I report to Maximillion," Isadora murmured with a pang of guilt. "But I'll probably go before, just so I have an excuse to leave if I need one."

All the strange stares she'd drawn at home the past six months returned to her mind. Her shorter hair, no doubt, caused some of them discomfort, even though she tried to pull it into a bun. Never mind that she'd chosen to live away from Letum Wood but still returned to visit frequently. Something else unheard of unless she was learning a trade to bring back to the families.

She wasn't.

Pearl motioned to a plate of bread with a wave of her hand. The plate rose into the air. Five slices of bread flew into the napkin, which folded over itself, and zipped to Isadora's side.

"Take the bread. I'm sure they're still quite hungry."

Isadora almost refused. Pearl was as hungry as they

were, but seeing the challenge in the older woman's eyes, Isadora accepted the gift with a smile.

"Thanks. I better get going. I'll be back this evening."

"Mam, you must eat."

Isadora set a cooling bowl of mashed tubers on the table, next to the bread. Without the bread, the meal would hardly have been big enough for Mam and Daid both. Mam stared out the window at the faint rays of the waning sun. Daylight diffused through the thick canopy overhead.

Mam sighed and reached for a spoon with her thin fingers. Isadora nodded once.

"Thank you."

Mam's bony shoulders stuck out from her long-sleeved dress, which hung on her like an old rag. Some of the color had come back into her cheeks, banishing the pallor that had appeared after Talis's death. Months later, it still seemed as if the life had ebbed away from Mam's countenance. The drastic changes had taken a ragged toll on many Serv—Dragonmasters, and Mam was no exception. Every time Isadora returned home, the change seemed starker than before.

Perhaps the change was really greatest in herself.

"Where is Sanna?" she asked.

"Meeting with the other Servants," Mam said.

"Dragonmasters, you mean."

Mam frowned.

The dishwater had cooled by the time Isadora dunked her hands in it, rubbing bits of food off a plate. Daid opened the door and stepped inside. Their crude, makeshift hut had been thrown together five months ago, before winter settled in. She hadn't told them she'd used magic to rein-force several gaps in the walls. Mam wouldn't appreciate the help.

Isadora drew in a deep breath, forced a smile onto her face, and turned around. Soapy water dripped from her hands as she faced Daid.

"*Avay*, Daid."

He sank into a chair without looking at her. "*Avay*."

She set a bowl of food—and two slices of bread from Pearl—in front of him. "Eat up. You'll need your strength."

"Sanna already gone?" he asked Mam.

"Yes."

Dinner passed in strained silence while Isadora bustled around the kitchen. Mam and Daid said little around her anymore. What could be said? Her hair was shorn like a wild thing. She wore dresses more elaborate and wasteful than any they had ever seen—even though they were considered modest and simple in the Network. And she actively practiced magic.

A confirmed heathen.

A gentle knock sounded on the back door. She grabbed a towel and dried her hands on it as she crossed the dirt floor. Babs Chandler stood outside. She glanced at Isadora's hair, swallowed, and extended a basket.

"I brought this for your parents."

"Thank you, Babs."

"Can't stay. Tell your mam I expect her for tea in the morning."

With that, Babs spun on her heel and headed back into the trees. Isadora watched her go with a sharp pang in her chest. Babs probably would have stayed if Isadora weren't there. Sanna and Isadora had been effectively cast out.

Socially, at least, because no one dared attempt to send Sanna away. Not with Luteis at her side.

Despite everything changing, not much had changed at all.

The sound of a distant roar, followed by a grumpy shout, made her lips twitch. Sanna was on her way home. Isadora shut the door against a brisk wind.

"From Babs," she said, setting the basket near the table. "She would like you for tea tomorrow."

Mam nodded once, weakly.

Silence descended again as Isadora finished the dishes. Just as she'd dried the last plate, set it in a wooden bin on the floor, and turned to hang up her towel, a tiny bird appeared above her. She caught her breath. Mam and Daid hadn't noticed, lost in their own thoughts. Daid frowned over a slice of bread. Mam pushed her mashed tubers around.

"I need to grab some more firewood," Isadora said.

Her parents said nothing as she stepped outside, bird following. Bright, turquoise wings beat so fast they hummed. The entire body had a strange, gossamer appearance. She could see right through it. It looked like a hummingbird but much smaller. It dove toward her ear. Isadora held her breath. The command that issued from the delicate bird made her jump.

"My office," Maximillion barked. "Now."

She straightened with a scowl. She most certainly would *not*—

"Yes, you will."

Isadora rolled her eyes.

"Lucey has been taken by the Defenders." The bird dissipated into smoke.

Lucey captured? She forced her racing heart to slow.

Lucey had been captured by East Guards plenty of times. The Defenders had captured her once, but she'd escaped by sheer luck thanks to a well-placed bridge and a homeless vagrant willing to give her some clothes. Surely this time—

Sanna dropped in front of her with a *thud*. Leaves filled her hair. "So much for Finn listening to reason," she muttered. "He's irrational; did you know that?"

"Expecting anything else from a witch like Finn is bound to disappoint. *Avay*, Sanna."

Sanna's eyes tapered. "What are you doing?"

"Standing here."

"Something's wrong."

Blast having a twin. She never could lie to Sanna.

"I came to see you."

"But now what?" Sanna asked, batting away a twig that dangled in her hair. "Why do you look so concerned?"

Isadora sighed. "I came to see you, but ... now I have to go."

"You *literally* just got here."

"I've been here for a few hours."

"Not for me!"

"I just received news from Maximillion. L—our friend needs my help."

"Maximillion has friends?"

"Shocking, I know."

Aside from one cursory meeting, all Sanna knew of Maximillion was what Isadora had told her, and that wasn't much. For some reason, describing Maximillion in all his curmudgeonly glory seemed impossible.

Behind Sanna, the trees rustled. Isadora eyed the shadows. Despite Sanna's undying affection for Luteis, Isadora still didn't feel comfortable around him. He was eerily hot, seething fire and calm at the same time. All the dragons avoided him. Isadora did too.

"What is so important that you have to go now?"

Because Lucey helps run a secretive operation that saves Watchers from the tyranny of the Eastern Network. That's what.

Isadora bit back the truth. She still hadn't told Sanna everything. For some reason, sharing that much about her new life felt ... wrong. Intrusive. Strangely too much.

"It's complicated."

Sanna's frown deepened. "When are you coming back?"

"I don't know."

"We need you!"

"Do you?"

Sanna opened her mouth, then closed it again.

Isadora shook her head. "Even with Talis gone and the old ways abandoned, Mam and Daid *still* barely talk to me."

"Of course we need you. I know you fixed parts of the house with magic, and the only reason I didn't tell Daid is because we're desperate. I'm not stupid. Besides, you're a Dragonmaster too. Just because you don't want to be doesn't change the fact that you *are*."

"I know, Sanna. I just ... I have to go."

"That's right," Sanna snapped. "You have a life outside of us now."

Isadora closed her eyes and drew in a deep breath. When she opened them again, Sanna stared at her with the same recalcitrant expression as before.

"A life where I have obligations," Isadora said calmly. "Sanna, I know it's hard to understand, but I can really make a difference out there."

"You shouldn't have obligations outside your family!"

"*You* do."

"I didn't make a life away from them," Sanna shot back.

"You lived in the forest with a dragon!"

"Note the *with-a-dragon* part," Sanna cried. "That's what we're supposed to do. We're Dragonmasters! Besides, I had to."

"So do I."

The rage in Sanna's eyes seemed to cool all at once. Her shoulders slumped.

"I'm sorry. I'm just ... I wish you were here more."

Isadora smiled softly. "Me too. But even you have to see that I'm not welcome here. No one wants me. Everyone treats me like a ... troll."

"Me too."

A laugh bubbled out of Isadora. "Maybe we are."

Sanna snorted. "You, maybe."

"You're the one who took over a brood of angry dragons."

Sanna's expression turned distant. Her smile faded into a frown. "I didn't *take over*. I liberated. Big difference."

They stood there in the silence until Isadora couldn't bear it. Maximillion barked incessantly from the depths of her mind. "I have to go, Sanna. I'm sorry I couldn't see you more this visit."

A reluctant forgiveness came into Sanna's gaze.

"I know."

"You won't hate me?"

"Hate you? No. Be annoyed with you? Indefinitely."

"*Amo*, Sanna."

"*Amo*, Isa."

～

Isadora disappeared.

Sanna scowled at the empty space.

Before she could head inside, a cry sounded a few paces away from her, drawing her gaze. Rosy and Junis, Sanna's favorite hatchlings, tumbled into a clearing between the massive trees, followed by their mother, Cara, a beautiful mauve dragon. Talis had broken her wings as punishment and turned her out of the brood. Luteis had burned her infected wings off to save her from dying. Now she walked with a little stumble—her movements weren't so graceful without the heavy wings—but neither did she seem as weighty. An affectionate glimmer always shone in her eyes when she saw Sanna.

Cara was alone in that respect.

Luteis slipped out of the forest, ears perked up when Cara appeared. He sniffed gently, tracking her as she eased back out of sight. Her two hatchlings tumbled behind her. Junis shoved Rosy away, nipping at her shoulder, but she ran, leapt off a log, and took to the sky. Seconds later, both hatchlings twirled in a wild air dance.

Sanna grinned.

Rosy dove toward Junis, nearly sending Sanna's heart into a panic. But Junis, his wingspan bigger by several paces, dodged away. He blew fire at her. Rosy hissed in a good-natured way and spun a circle in the air. Sanna smiled. The hatchlings had picked up flight quickly.

Very quickly.

Beyond them, the forest glittered with pockets of emerald and ebony. Color winked every now and then as a forest dragon passed by. *The hatchlings are skilled beyond their years,* Luteis said, gliding back into the forest. She sensed him more than saw him there.

They've always been eager to fly, she said, preferring to speak to Luteis in her mind while her parents were in earshot. Mam still couldn't stand the sight of Luteis.

Sanna's gaze slipped back to the dragons lurking in the shadows. *At least* they *like it.*

Rubeis as well.

A dragon with marbled crimson running through sheer black scales sat on a high branch just above the meadow where Daid had built their shack. Rubeis. The hatchlings called it the *jumping tree* because Luteis had all of them jump off the branch to learn how to glide. The exercise strengthened their wings as well. Rubeis, after eighty years of never flying or using his wings, had more muscle to build than the hatchlings, but he'd been working steadily for the past six months. He didn't fly high but could stay airborne for more than an hour now.

He did well yesterday, she said to Luteis. A beat of quiet passed, then Rubeis's head swiveled to look at her, as if he'd heard.

His crash into the tree left a dent in the trunk, Luteis said with some amusement. *Such is the fate of any who get in his way, he says. Amusing.*

A pillar of smoke blew out of Rubeis's nostrils. Sanna laughed. Rubeis, a solemn leader, had proven to have more spunk than she'd expected. Daid had taken to him quickly —until he progressed to flight. Then Daid seemed to shrink away, curling up within himself.

Rubeis said he would like to hunt with us tonight.

Luteis communicated with the dragons on her behalf ever since the dragon voices faded away, not long after Talis's death. Luteis and Rubeis had formed a sort of half-truce. Luteis avoided the brood, and Rubeis managed the dragons. Daid had taken over as a sort of go-between for the dragons and witches. Rubeis told Luteis what was needed from the dragons, and Sanna told Daid.

Slowly, they'd started to introduce the idea of dragons

flying, even hunting, for themselves. Aside from Rubeis, the hatchlings, and a young dragon named Elis that could nearly match Luteis for speed, the others hadn't cared enough to attempt a hunt. Finn continued to hunt for them, making the transition even more difficult. Even Elliot hunted for his dragons every now and then. Only Daid had given it up entirely, and some of his dragons had defected to Finn.

Rubeis opened his wings and leapt free of the tree. He soared between the trunks, slipping out of sight.

Your sister—

"Time for dinner," Sanna said, whipping around. "Talk to you later."

Luteis growled as she hurried into the house, letting the door slam shut behind her.

CHAPTER

FIVE

That night, Sanna lay on her back and stared at the ceiling.

Her thoughts ran in wild, rampant circles. Flashes of the poacher's blonde hair. The shadow moving ahead of her—what had it been? Should she tell Daid?

Unbidden, Isadora filtered back through her mind.

She rolled onto her side with a huff and wished she could turn her thoughts off. A rock dug into her shoulder. She flipped onto her stomach, but another uneven edge on the ground cut into her ribs. Just before she threw her pillow into a wall, a whisper at the wall caught her attention.

Jesse.

"Are you still awake?" he asked.

She peered toward the sound. Two fingers wiggled near the floor, under a loose log at the bottom of the makeshift wall.

Sanna crawled forward.

"Yes."

His fingers moved out of the way, revealing an eye.

"Want to get some air? Elis is just about ready for our nightly flight."

"Yes," she said with relief. "Let's."

JESSE MET her outside with a rueful grin.

"It's hot in there," he said, motioning with a jerk of his head toward his family's house—more like a shanty—not far away on the other edge of the small meadow. Only Finn lived far enough away they couldn't see or hear him. "And the kids are loud, even when they're asleep. Did you know that five-year-olds can snore as loud as a dragon?"

"Not as loud as your daid."

He grimaced. "You hear it?"

"I think everyone does."

"You're probably right." He eyed her, his face barely visible in the low light. Cool air had settled over the night, twice as chilly as it had been during the day and more keenly felt along her arms and deep in her bones. Still, it felt good. Refreshing. Brisk. A gentle breeze brushed her face. They fell into step together, heading away from the houses.

"Isadora was here," he said, glancing at her from the corner of his eye.

Sanna scowled. "So?"

"You're always annoyed after she shows up."

Surprise rendered her momentarily speechless. *Annoyed?* She wasn't *annoyed*. She was ... pensive. He shuffled toward a foot trail, leading them away from the shanty.

"You're always a little ... off after Isadora comes."

"What does that mean?" she snapped.

He lifted his eyebrows.

She frowned, recognizing the annoyance in her voice,

and blushed, flooded with sheepish shame. "Oh. Right. I hear it now. Sorry."

"What did she do to make you mad this time?"

Sanna rubbed her arms with her hands, grateful they were walking away from the dwellings. Luteis was out hunting. She could still hear him in her head, though. It seemed as if distance mattered less the more time they spent together.

"Isadora didn't do anything to make me mad. Just ... it's different with Isa, that's all. And, it's weird when it's different. I don't like it. It's like ... everything else has changed. Why does she have to as well?"

"Things are definitely different."

She grabbed his arm to stop him from walking. "Do you blame me?" she asked.

His brow furrowed. "What?"

"Do you blame me for this?" Her hand gestured to the forest around them. "Do you think it's my fault we lost everything?"

"No. Not at all."

"Be honest!"

"I blame Talis, if I blame anyone."

"Yes, but there *was* peace when Talis was in charge, wasn't there? Food? Shelter? Clothes? Now we have nothing." She turned away, releasing him. Mam rose up in Sanna's mind. Her stoic silence. Lack of eye contact. "I feel like it's all my fault."

"We were enslaved, with no choices. Besides, we didn't have food, remember? Things were starting to get bleak. We couldn't have stayed in Anguis forever. And now we can save the forest. Can you imagine if another ten or so years had gone by?" He cast a long eye on Letum Wood. "This would have all fallen apart. Maybe we wouldn't have had a home after all. You'd probably blame yourself for that."

Sanna dragged her bottom lip through her teeth. "Yes. You're probably right."

"Don't give yourself so much responsibility, Sanna," he said with a light nudge of his elbow. "Some of us didn't like being slaves to the dragons, either. We just didn't have the guts to do anything about it. You pushed us into action. Which means you'll push us toward something better."

She held up two hands. "Whoa. Not my job."

He sighed. "You're still fighting it?"

"There's nothing to fight. I can't even hear the dragons anymore. Deasylva obviously changed her mind and removed me as High Dragonmaster."

Jesse sighed. Sanna ignored him.

They continued to walk for several steps, crunching their way through the snow and the carpet of long-dead leaves and twigs. Sanna drew in a deep, appreciative breath. Being back in the trees, even though she'd only been inside a few hours, calmed her thoughts. Her wild turmoil eased to a simmer.

"Elis and I need your help," Jesse said.

"I—"

"I'm not asking you for help as High Dragonmaster. Just as the only other witch who has really ridden a forest dragon."

She stalled, mouth half-open, before snapping it closed again.

"Fine."

"We're able to fly for over forty-five minutes now. Feels good, too. No heat. Just being in the air. Kind of scary at first, but we've improved a lot."

"Where are you flying?"

"We haven't ventured much above the trees."

A shuffle and snort sounded on the other side of a curtain of ivy. Elis. Rivers of slate gray rippled through his ebony scales, winking in the darkness. He was a fifty-five-year-old dragon with one of the mildest temperaments in the brood. He and Jesse had bonded a month before—apparently, Elis had always been one of Jesse's favorites. Jesse never admitted it with Talis looming around all the time. Elis had a broad profile—even for a dragon—with meaty shoulders, a short tail, and unusually small legs.

Amusement flickered through Sanna. Jesse, too, had always been short and brawny.

At first, it seemed odd that a dragon should be motivated on its own to bond with a witch the way Elis had. Luteis took weeks to trust Sanna. Even then, he only capitulated after dire necessity forced him to. Then again, Luteis hadn't lived with her. Elis had seen Jesse grow up. Had eaten from his hands.

"Don't rush it," Sanna said to Jesse, thinking back to her first flight with Luteis, who had already been skilled in the air. Why did Jesse and Elis expect *her* to know everything? Still, Elis did seem a bit cumbersome. It took him ages to turn around.

"Have you been practicing in the canopy?" she asked.

"Every day. He keeps slamming into trees."

Without warning, Elis shoved off the ground. His wings unfurled from his back, the thick membrane marbled with veins. Several mighty wingbeats bore him higher, raising him into the tangled expanse overhead. He landed on a tree limb instead of crashing. This time.

"His form is stronger," Sanna said. "He's learned when to reach out with his hind legs to land on a branch."

A puff of pride rang through Jesse's tone. "He's doing

great, isn't he? I think it's because he trusts his instincts more these days."

Elis soared down from above before crashing into the ground, legs first, digging up several ruts. Both acted like they hadn't noticed. Elis nudged Jesse with his stubby snout.

"But after we've flown for more than an hour, the magic starts to, I don't know … get kind of weak?"

"Weak?"

"I start to slide around." Jesse wiggled in place. "It feels like I'll fall off."

"Have you?"

"On every landing."

Sanna frowned. That couldn't be right. She'd never once even *felt* like she'd fall. *Luteis? Any ideas on helping Jesse and Elis have a stronger bond?*

His reply came from the back of her mind.

None.

You're no help.

Agreed.

"I'm not sure," Sanna said to Jesse. "It's never happened to me."

Elis's wings drooped, and Jesse's hopeful expression deflated. She chewed on her bottom lip. What *could* it mean? Thanks to Talis, the legacy the Dragonmasters had passed down was long gone. She had no idea what *normal* was.

Unable to bear their disappointment, she asked, "How much time do you spend together outside of flying?"

"A few minutes here and there."

Escaping Talis meant that Sanna had been with Luteis nonstop. Maybe that had contributed to the strength of their connection. "Try being together more often? It may strengthen the bond."

I have returned, Luteis said. The low, baritone purr of his voice filled Sanna with relief. Her tight fists relaxed. A shadow passed overhead, drawing her gaze. Luteis circled. These days, he had to fly farther than ever to find food. Two days before, he'd gone as far as the ruins before he caught something. She didn't like him being that far away, alone.

Luteis alighted in front of her. The ground trembled when his massive, muscular body landed. She reached out a hand, receiving a gentle nudge from his muzzle in return.

Sanna frowned at Luteis.

"You were gone a long time."

I had a taste for boars.

"Even after the cohereo tree incident?"

He snorted. *I didn't chase them far. Is Jesse going to fly with Elis tonight?*

Luteis peered past her to where Jesse and Elis stood not far away. Jesse held out his hand, keeping it on Elis's flank, facilitating communication. Their merging, like Daid and Rubeis's, was tentative. Sanna and Luteis had merged like a dropping boulder. Everyone else seemed to be easing into it.

Do you think it's common for witches to look like their dragons? she asked. Luteis followed her gaze. His head tilted to the side.

Perhaps. Does your hair gleam as bright as my scales?

I was thinking more along the lines of powerful and occasionally grumpy.

You are definitely one of those things. Luteis's head whipped around, searching the area. *Is there no one else to fly?*

"No."

No other witch has come forward with interest today?

Her back stiffened. "No. Or dragon, either."

Curious.

"Is it?" She scowled. Luteis nudged her with a wingtip.

Indeed. You are ready to change and improve. The rest want to hide. Very curious.

Frightening, Sanna wanted to say, but didn't. Elis remained one step ahead of Jesse as Luteis joined them on the forest floor. Luteis ignored his distrust. Elis extended a wing, allowing Jesse to step up and slide onto his thick shoulders. Sanna tilted her head back to watch.

They are fully merged, Luteis said. *I can sense it.*

Then why isn't it working? Sanna asked.

Luteis blinked. *That is the mystery. You are the witch. The use of magic belongs to you.*

Sanna pushed aside a wave of concern. She didn't know what to tell them—she'd only just figured this out with Luteis herself, and she felt lucky at that. Clearly, she didn't lead the brood.

Sanna turned to Elis.

"Do you trust Jesse, Elis?"

He says he does, Luteis replied.

Elis wants to know if you know how to help them, Luteis asked. *He's doubtful that you know enough.*

He inquired so dispassionately that Sanna couldn't even feel annoyed; she really *didn't* know what their problem could be. She had no way to find out. The more Jesse worked with Elis, the more she began to suspect that it had less to do with Jesse, and more to do with the dragon.

Or, more precisely, *her* dragon.

Luteis seemed to be the exception to everything she'd observed in the others. He was faster. Stronger. More agile.

His intelligent mind worked as quick as a whip, leaving the rest scrambling to keep up.

Let us fly, Luteis said. *It will be easier to discuss this after we've expended some energy. Rubeis will meet us in the air.*

Sanna sighed and followed him a little farther into the trees. Elis joined them. Between the two dragons, the ground trembled under Sanna's feet. The tree trunks here stood a little farther apart but were larger in size than those near Anguis. Moss, vines, and deadly flowers wound up their trunks, disappearing into the seemingly eternal heights of the canopy.

"Fine," she said as she climbed on top of Luteis. "But we *will* figure it out."

We will, Luteis agreed, voice eager. *But first—flight.*

He shoved off the forest floor, his gigantic talons tearing into the dirt and leaving nothing but a whisper behind.

CHAPTER

SIX

Ten minutes after receiving his message, Isadora stood outside Maximillion's office. The cold confines of the hidden passage hugged her, wrapping her in a dank smell. At his insistence, she never walked into Chatham Castle and asked to meet with him. Instead, she entered through various means of trickery and subterfuge, preventing anyone from knowing who she was or what she did.

No one can know we work together, he said often. *Not just for the sake of my reputation, but to protect the Advocacy.*

His barb for his reputation left her rolling her eyes, but she let it slide for the sheer challenge of it. Today's entrance: the servants' quarters.

No one questioned her—or recognized her beneath a layer of freckles and a near-perfect replica of the maids' outfits—or her hasty entrance. From there, she snuck down back halls, entered the hidden passages, and knocked at the back door disguised by a bookshelf in his office wall.

Except he didn't answer.

Isadora rolled her eyes. She'd rather endure the bog

again than a stressed-out Maximillion. She lifted her hand to knock a fourth time, but the door opened.

Maximillion glared. His cravat hung loose around his neck. He wore a sharp sapphire vest over an impeccably pressed white shirt fitted to his wrists. His hair shone as if it were wet. His brow dropped over his eyes.

"A servant?" He stepped back. "That's new."

"Good to see you, too, Maximillion."

"Your magic is weak. I can hardly sense it."

"My recovery was fine; thanks for asking. I slept most of the day."

"You're late."

"I'm not."

He pointed to a clock. "One minute past the hour."

"You didn't summon me for a certain time. You just *summoned* me."

"It's courtesy to show up on the hour. Some witches have schedules."

He whipped around, coattails flapping, and strode behind his desk. Isadora followed. The door wheezed shut behind her.

Maximillion sat in his chair, jaw tight. Then he stood up and paced the space behind his desk, near a massive glass window that occupied the entire wall. Letters scattered his desk in a mad array of parchment.

"Have you had anything to eat today?" she asked. "You're in a surly mood."

"I'm not surly."

"No, you're delightful."

Isadora crossed the room to a tray with a teapot, two boiled eggs, and two slices of bread. A rare treat to receive eggs these days. She felt the teapot with her hand. Cold, as expected. She warmed it with a spell and tipped the brew into a cup. She poured cream inside, then floated it to him with a spell.

"Drink."

He scowled. "I don't need a mother."

"Drink."

He shot her a scathing glare but obeyed. Once finished, he flicked it aside. The cup and saucer winged back to the tray, settling with a gentle *clink*. Then the plate flew to Maximillion.

She lifted one eyebrow and waited. He scowled, but grabbed a piece of bread and tore into it. Isadora leaned back against a shelf.

"Better?" she asked when he swallowed the last bite.

He scowled. Like most in the Central Network, Maximillion had grown leaner. His face was borderline gaunt.

She motioned in front of her. "Go ahead."

"First, an update on your powers. Have you been successful yet?"

"Well, yes. I helped the mission."

"But were you successful using the powers in the way I instructed?"

"Ah ... I *did* as you instructed."

His perpetual frown deepened. "You sought the paths, tried to feel which one was right, and waited?"

"Yes."

"What happened?"

"Nothing."

He frowned. "That's not right."

Isadora rubbed her hand over her forehead. She rarely had headaches because of the magic now—but she had them whenever she worked with Maximillion.

"We've been working on this for six months, and

nothing has changed, Maximillion. I think it's safe to say my powers don't operate like yours. I can't *feel* my way into a decision. I see them."

He opened his mouth to protest, then closed it again. "It's how the power operates for every Watcher. You go in, wait in the darkness, observe the paths that appear, and then return."

Isadora hesitated. There was still much about her powers she didn't know. "As we've discussed," she said, "I do not see darkness."

"There's no other way for it to work. Yes, I know!" he snapped, anticipating her corrective remark. "I know there's no *darkness* for you. You're in that blasted forest, or whatever."

"My powers work differently."

His face pinched. She paused, giving him a moment to work through it. No doubt he hated the idea of not being in control of something. "And there's nothing to feel?" he asked.

"No."

"What do you see?"

She described the first two paths.

His brow furrowed. "That much detail?"

"Yes."

"The wisps are solid?"

"They appear so, but are vapor when I touch them."

His eyes bugged out. "You can reach out and touch them?"

"I always have been able to."

"You failed to mention that before."

"I didn't know it was pertinent."

"Is there anything else you haven't told me?"

Isadora fought the urge to squirm—countless facets of

her magic were unknown to him, the greatest of which was the fact that the magic showed her witches. She didn't know how else to describe it. She saw their strengths. Sometimes their weaknesses. But even that wasn't predictable. She swallowed hard. "Why would I hide anything?"

His gaze tapered, as if he suspected her half-truth. "Can you see yourself there?"

"I *am* there, just as I am here."

His nostrils flared. "I see."

"Do you ever wonder why we have these powers?"

"What do you mean?"

She shrugged. "What's the purpose of this magic? Why would I stand in a forest and ... see what could happen, but doesn't always? Seems a little ... I don't know ... strange?"

"To serve."

"Whom? Not us."

He scowled. "And why doesn't it serve you?"

"I lived happily without it for years," she said. "It gives me access to future possibilities, but even those aren't concrete. At best, it's distracting and inconvenient. And where does it originate, anyway? All magic comes from *somewhere*. How are we chosen? Why does the magic come to us?"

Spilling her questions gave her a sense of relief. She paused, waiting. His mouth opened, then closed. If possible, his scowl deepened. "You're asking questions that have no answers."

"I don't believe that."

"I don't care," he snapped. "We don't have time for a philosophical discussion on the purpose of magic. It's here; you have it; deal with it. On to more interesting news."

A beam of light sped across the room, slammed into the

doorway, and zipped around the doorframe. A silencing spell to be sure their voices weren't overheard. Isadora stumbled to keep up with the quick subject change, even as he started talking.

"Lucey has been taken by the Defenders."

"So you said."

Several things had gone wrong at the beginning—before they'd taken a turn for the worst at the end. Isadora had been late to their original rendezvous point due to confusion on where to transport. Once there, she'd nearly forgotten the sign to give Lucey. Her transformative magic had worn off at the end—unforgivable in his book—which meant the bog had been her only saving grace. The sheer scope of what Maximillion had set up in the shadows to save these Watchers was overwhelming enough. Executing it perfectly was even more over-whelming.

Still, he expected perfection.

"I'm sure Lucey will return soon," she said. "Hasn't she escaped the Defenders before?"

"Once. But the Defenders don't have her now. Cecelia does."

Icicles slid through Isadora's veins. Cecelia Liam, the Ambassador to the Eastern Network, was notoriously known as one of the most eccentric witches in history. And, to those who knew her well enough, the leader of the resistance against Watchers. Rumors circulated that Cecelia had attained her position as Ambassador in the Eastern Network solely by killing innocent Watchers—something the fearful witches of the East turned a blind eye to.

"Where?" Isadora asked, voice raspy. "Is she already in Carcere?"

"A fantastic question," he snapped. "One I've been

pursuing all day, thank you very much, with no help from you."

"Max, I'm sorry. I—"

He slammed a fist into his desk, eyes blazing. "Never! Never shall you call me Max."

"Sorry! I meant Maximillion."

He dragged a hand through his hair and turned his back to her. For a long time, he stared out the window without saying a word. Isadora, heart hammering, left him to his silence. He and Lucey had a strange friendship. Beneath all his hauteur, Isadora had always believed he cared deeply about Lucey. She seemed to share the distant affection. She was the only witch in the Advocacy unafraid of him.

Maximillion turned around. He drew in a deep breath, shoulders lifting and falling. His eyes were hard as flint.

"An inside witch close to Cecelia confirmed it just before you came. Lucey is in Carcere."

Isadora sank into a chair. "The good gods," she murmured. Maximillion set both hands on his hips.

"Apparently, the Defenders are all quite proud of themselves." His nostrils flared. "Some of them believe Lucey is the Advocate."

"Does Cecelia know it's you?"

"Who said it was me?" he murmured. "I need you to search your paths. To see whatever you can."

"I can't see her paths if she's not with me."

"Have you tried?"

"I ... no. I suppose I haven't."

"Time to try something new, then. Into the paths. Now. This is precisely the kind of thing for which I brought you into the Advocacy."

"What am I looking for?"

"Lucey. Now that we have you, she'll attempt to position herself in a way that will reveal where she's been taken. She'll make decisions to stir up the paths. To do ... *something* that may get our attention."

"But—"

"Try it!" he snapped.

Isadora hesitated. When his scowl deepened, she closed her eyes and opened the magic. The ease with which she slipped into the paths was like turning from one thought to another.

The twelve ancient, massive trees instantly surrounded her with their sprawling bodies and massive limbs. Graceful, drooping vines inundated the soaring canopy. Emerald swaths of moss climbed the tree trunks, filled with patches of pink-and-white petals. The scent of honeysuckle drifted by.

Isadora let out a long, easy breath. Letum Wood and *this* version of Letum Wood were very different places. While it was still thick and dark, no fear of trolls, beluas, or forest lions stalked Isadora's heart here.

Her trail, Sanna's, and Maximillion's populated in front of her. They shifted constantly, revealing new witches. One of Maximillion's Assistants appeared. Another wisp showed Isadora talking with Maximillion. In brief moments, she saw Pearl, and in others, a man with auburn hair and a prominent Adam's apple.

"Remove Sanna's path."

The wisps faded. Maximillion's paths expanded to fill the extra space, nearly crowding out hers like a bristling porcupine.

"Show only the paths that occur away from the castle."

Half of the options faded.

"Oh," she murmured. She'd never been so specific

before. "Lovely. Show me only the paths that occur outside of the Central Network."

Now only several paths wound into the trees. She slipped past trails with strange backdrops in the wisps. Leaves the shape of diamonds. A sticky, tenacious mud on Maximillion's shoes. One path showed the two of them standing together. Isadora's eyes were wide, his grim and narrowed. He held onto something—or someone. An arm, perhaps? She couldn't be sure. Isadora studied it, then moved on.

The more she trailed away from the base of the great trees, the more the paths split. Wild wisps awaited, as if magic had an imagination it put to use through possibility. She paused in the midst of the gauzy, ethereal things, the circle of ancient trees far behind her now.

"Show me Lucey."

Nothing happened.

Isadora turned around to find all the wisps she'd passed still there. They shuffled in a gentle breeze, changing form entirely until Isadora didn't know where she was. New trails snaked through the ground.

"Lucey Chandler," she called. "Can you show me her?"

Nothing.

She eased her shoulders back, slightly relieved. There had to be *some* end to her abilities. Isadora strolled down the middle of two divergent paths until they split too far to see both at the same time. She walked for what felt like days, taking the brightest paths while watching for clues about Lucey. None came.

Maximillion's world was filled with witches she didn't know. A ballroom. A fine dinner. Glasses of wine. She stared at a wisp of him sitting at a desk—not his, and not one she recognized—and peered over his shoulder, unable to make out the words on the paper.

One branch of his possibilities intersected with another distant branch of hers, leading to strange roads. An ocean. A creaky cottage in the trees lined with porcelain cups. Fire in the distance. Isadora doubled back, checked the closest wisps that had already changed.

Finding nothing, she closed the magic.

"W ELL?"

Maximillion's cutting voice welcomed her out of the magic with a jerk. She opened her eyes and sat up. He paced with sharp, jerking movements, his heels striking the floor with definitive *thuds*.

"Your life is quite complicated," she said. A weak feeling flooded her body, and a yawn threatened to overtake her. She glanced at the clock on the wall, which ticked the evening steadily away. "The good gods. I've been gone for two hours!"

"And nothing to show for it." Maximillion stopped pacing. "Did you see Lucey?"

"No. I tried to see her amongst our paths."

"Nothing?"

She shook her head. He swore under his breath, jaw tight with tension. No doubt his frustration was twofold— they couldn't find Lucey with such a haphazard approach, and he had no idea *why* her powers weren't like anyone else's.

He stopped pacing to loom over her, fire in his eyes. Tiny threads from his intricate, velvet vest waved in the air.

"Lucey's life—and the life of all the Watchers in the East—may rest on your ability to do this."

"No pressure," she mumbled.

"There's a prodigious amount of pressure. I'm applying it for a reason."

Isadora folded her arms across her chest, maintaining her calm resolve by sheer willpower. He tried to rattle her all the time, just to test her temper. She'd learned an impressive amount of control from him.

"I cannot change what I don't know."

He muttered something under his breath and returned to his desk. Isadora pulled in a deep breath, forcing herself to maintain her patience. Behind Maximillion's cagey pacing and cutting responses was hidden fear. He worried for Lucey, though she doubted he'd ever admit it.

"We must monitor Cecelia," Isadora said.

He glared at her. "Don't insult me. It's already been done."

"Then there is nothing to do but to send the Advocacy in after Lucey."

His expression hardened, but his eyes gleamed with a terrible light. "So it would seem." He spun and faced the window, dismissing her with a single wave of his hand.

Before she could go, a quick rap on the door broke the tension. Maximillion glanced up, murmuring under his breath. The light sped back around the edge of the door. Maximillion whipped around.

"Yes?" he called.

A soft, lyrical voice said, "Max?"

Maximillion rolled his eyes but issued no correction. He straightened his vest, cleared his throat, ran a hand through his hair, and said in a clear voice, "Come in, Your Highness."

The door slid open. The High Priest, Charles Dauphin,

stumbled inside. He tripped over a crack in the doorway and caught himself on a sculpture of a half-nude witch. Isadora reached out, snatching the sculpture before it plummeted to its certain demise.

The High Priest's pale skin clashed beautifully with his carroty hair and abundant freckles. He had a rounded face with pouty lips and a quick smile.

Maximillion forced an even edge into his tone. "What may I do for you?"

"Just stopping by to ask about—oh! Merry meet."

Charles jumped when he saw Isadora standing there. A wide grin stretched across his surprised face. His curls spiraled all over the place as he extended an arm. Isadora accepted, shaking it.

A shot of nerves jolted through her. She'd met many witches before, but never the Highest Witch. By all accounts, he wielded more power than anyone in the Central Network—although most would argue that Maximillion truly ran the Network.

"Merry meet." She curtsied.

"Oh, none of that. We're not formal all the time." Charles's smile widened. "Exhausting stuff. What's your name?"

"Isadora."

A broad back and a crisp, white shirt broke their arms apart. Maximillion stood between them, forcing Isadora to step back or be crushed.

"She's a pupil of mine." Without turning around, he said, "You may go, Miss Spence."

Isadora stilled her rage. Pushing Maximillion wouldn't be wise when he was under so much pressure. Then again, the temptation was all-too-strong. She sidestepped him with a bright smile.

"It's a pleasure to meet you, Your Highness. I'm sorry for the mess you've inherited."

Charles beamed. "A lovely girl. Thank you."

Maximillion gritted his teeth.

Isadora deepened her reverential tone. "I have full faith in your ability to serve the Network and prevent war," she murmured, smiling. "I know you'll save us."

The giddiness in Charles's bright eyes faded slightly. His smile became wooden. "Er, yes. Right. Of course. Greta was a strong-willed witch, you know. But we'll come 'round, no doubt, with witches like Maximillion at my side."

Charles clapped Maximillion on the shoulder. Maximillion's nostrils flared. "Please respect my boundaries, Your Highness," he murmured.

Charles withdrew his hand. "Right! Sorry, Max. Forgot you don't like to be touched."

"Maximillion, if you please."

"So, Isadora," Charles said, turning his full attention to her. "How is it being one of Max's pupils?"

"Enlightening."

Charles smiled. "Yes. He's that, if anything." His eyes narrowed. "Are you from the area? I don't recognize you, and I never forget a pretty—"

"That's enough of that." Maximillion shoved her into the hall. "Keep trying. Return in the morning."

The door slammed behind her. Isadora stared at it for a full minute before gathering her wits and transporting away, her thoughts spiraling around Lucey, Cecelia, and the awful prison stronghold, Carcere.

SEVEN

S anna, Luteis, Daid, and Rubeis soared above Letum Wood together.

Rubeis's elegant, glittering wings stretched out like flapping war banners, glinting ruby in the moonlight. Luteis flew at a leisurely pace next to him. A gentle wind tugged at Sanna's clothes as they cut through the cold air.

Daid held on to Rubeis with both hands, his knees clinging tightly to Rubeis's neck. His pale face had a sheen of sweat, and his eyes darted to the ground every other second.

"Daid, you all right?"

"Fine," he snapped. Sanna stifled a grin.

He came, Luteis said. *That means a great deal.*

I'm extremely proud of him.

Considering Talis' abuse of your father's trust, your Daid is a courageous witch to try this.

The respect in Luteis's tone surprised her, but she agreed. Talis's rule had been strict; there were lasting beliefs she knew Daid would never discuss. Things that would prevent him from truly trusting dragons—and prevent the dragons from trusting him. Still, the fact that he'd climbed on Rubeis tonight to test flight a second time meant something in him stirred.

"Is Mam afraid of the dragons now?" Sanna asked, leaning back on her palms. Her legs hung lazily over Luteis's shoulders, barely a third of the way down his neck. At her back, the first ridge of his spine shot up, providing natural support.

She'd be a fool not to be, Luteis said.

"She's afraid of many things. The unknown." Daid's brow furrowed. "The memories that Talis's betrayal stirred up for her."

"Of her daid?"

Daid pressed his lips together and nodded once. Mam had rarely spoken about her life before coming to Anguis to handfast Daid—after meeting him in her village during one of his yearly resupplying visits. When Mam did mention her childhood, her voice choked, but not with tears.

It was more like hidden rage.

"Does she blame me for what happened?" Sanna asked. "If I hadn't chosen Luteis, none of this would have come out."

He paused for half a breath, just long enough to tell her that Mam did, in some way, blame her. Despite the fact that Daid had delivered the fatal blow to Talis, the blame rested on Sanna, who had stirred up trouble to begin with. She'd suspected that Mam agreed with the other Dragonmasters, but the blow stung all the same.

All the more reason not to lead, she said to Luteis. *To disappoint and rule as a tyrant? I can't.*

"It's not your fault," Daid said, preventing Luteis's response. Daid's nostrils flared as he looked down, gulped, and said, "She blames Talis. The truth flies in the face of everything we once thought we knew. It's hard to trust anything now, much less ourselves. It will take her a lot more time to understand this. I only ask you to give her the extra space. She'll find her way. Eventually."

"Yes, Daid."

He turned his face to the wind and clung to Rubeis.

She sank into her thoughts for a moment. The families seemed to walk around in a sort of daze now. Mam, who had clung to Drago—Talis's false god—with such dedication, had taken it harder than anyone else. Her mind, already delicate, seemed crushed under the blow at first.

You have had more time to understand and mourn this, Luteis said. *Your daid has lived more years than you under Talis.*

Sanna stroked his neck in response.

The fuzzy night sky stretched in front of them like a dark carpet. Only the moon shed any light that Sanna could see—the indistinct stars blurred into a thick canvas. The beat of dragon wings was the only sound. Sanna let it be. How much of Daid's uncertainty stemmed from the same doubt they all felt inside themselves?

Luteis's head snapped to the left. His nostrils flared. Rubeis followed suit.

A pack of forest lions, he said. *And ... something more.*

Rubeis's chest rolled with an assenting grunt.

Without another word, they banked left, tilting their bodies until they pivoted ninety degrees, then dropped lower into the cloud cover. Sanna's broiling thoughts fell silent while the dragons cut into the canopy.

Rubeis struck a few boughs with his wings, slicing leaves off in chunks, as he descended. Luteis alighted on a wide branch forty paces from the ground without making a single sound. He tucked his wings into his sides and lifted his nose.

The smell is ... strange.

A hint of uncertainty lingered in Luteis's tone. Rubeis, despite being leader of the dragons, still knew so little of hunting. He hung back, not far from Luteis, waiting for him to act first.

Sanna sniffed the air. She smelled nothing.

It's animal, Luteis said, *but ... new. I may have smelled it before. Perhaps with the poacher the other night?*

Is the poacher with it?

I cannot tell. Perhaps I am paranoid.

Rubeis rolled to the right while Luteis forked left. Sanna grabbed her knife. Hints of a troll had been lurking in the shadows for weeks now. The gigantic, hideous creatures were more dangerous than beluas, but not so prolific. Most lived in the North and came down only during times of famine. She and Luteis slipped between the trees. Letum Wood wasn't so dense in this area. But the upper canopy proliferated as a separate world, with branches the thickness of dragons. The dizzying height of it loomed so far above them, it was seemingly eternal.

Are you ready? Luteis asked. *I shall hunt first, investigate second. Cara is needing more food.*

"Always ready."

Only a few minutes followed before the shriek of a forest lion sounded from just above. Sanna dodged a branch that fell as a lion sped away, yowling when Luteis threw fire. Brief flashes of mottled yellow and strands of shaggy fur darted through grooves in the bark. Luteis wrapped his neck around a tree and snapped, stopping one lion mid-bellow. He released it. The lion whirled head over foot toward the ground. Another lion attempted to skitter away, but Luteis smacked it in the middle of the spine with his tail. The lion shrieked, and its back legs went limp. Sanna winced when it fell, head smacking on a branch twenty paces down. The lion fell silent, giving way to a distant *thud*.

"*Mori*," she muttered, "you're violent when you hunt."

Hungry. There's a difference.

A *thud* and a scream sounded just behind her.

Sanna leapt to her feet and whirled around. A forest lion stood on Luteis's back, talons slipping on the scales. Luteis shifted to the left with a growl. The lion compensated by leaning to the right. Sanna tensed, gripping her knife.

"Here kitty, kitty," she sang under her breath. "We could always use one more lion."

The lion hesitated, growled, and leapt. Sanna ducked, then stood just as she felt the velvety underside of its belly passing over her. The lion's stomach slammed into her shoulder, knocking her off her feet. She rolled onto her back, swung her arms up, and jammed her knife into the soft flesh under his jaw. It tore through the skin, cracked into the skull, and silenced the lion. Blood stained her hands as she wrenched the knife free and kicked the mangy cat off Luteis's back. The dead lion plummeted to the ground, a spray of blood trailing in its wake.

Well done.

Sanna wiped the blood off on her shirt. "That's disgusting."

You aren't injured?

"No. I think I'm getting used to it. Remember when—"

Another bellow came from the south, only this time it wasn't a lion. Sanna's blood turned cold. "What was that?"

Rubeis.

"Daid!"

Luteis plummeted to the ground, wings folded against his body. He used his feet to push off branches and the closest tree trunk, sinking his talons into the wood to control their descent. Not twenty seconds later, they landed on the forest floor.

Sanna's heart stopped.

Rubeis lay on the ground, jaw snapping at something above him. A shadow. Rubeis attempted to stand but couldn't move. The lumpy, broad shadow disappeared. Rubeis struggled to his feet and crouched over Daid, who lay on his back. Heat flooded her body in torrents, sweeping through her.

Sanna slid off Luteis's back. "Daid!"

She sprinted to his side, heart in her throat. Blood bubbled up from his forehead. Three slashes across his chest cut through his shirt, tearing into his ribs. Lines of crimson seeped up from underneath. He blinked slowly, eyes like glass. His chest made a strange, sucking sound.

"Daid?"

"S-sanna."

Blood tinged his teeth as she grabbed his shirt, hauling him into her lap.

"Rubeis! Your blood! Give it to me, quickly."

Daid choked, coughing. Rubeis, back leg hanging at an awkward angle, attempted to stagger his injured leg closer to Daid. Luteis reached out, using his neck to stabilize Rubeis's weakened body. Sapphire blood poured from a wound in Rubeis's neck. The scales had been torn free. Rivers of blue flowed from it, scorching the ground.

"Daid, don't you dare—"

"Your mam—"

"Rubeis will give you his blood. It will heal you. It's going to be—"

Daid's eyes fluttered open and closed. Sanna tore Daid's shirt open as Rubeis approached, eyes pained. He panted. Steam billowed from his nostrils, turning the air sticky.

The deep gashes in Daid's chest revealed slices of bone. Blood flowed out, so thick and rich it appeared nearly black. Daid's chest arrested for a long pause. His face turned pale. His lips moved, but no sound came out. Sanna reached up, touching his face, her fingers on fire. Something hot swelled in her chest.

"Daid?"

With a grunt, Luteis moved Rubeis's front body until blood dribbled onto Daid's chest and sizzled.

"Mam—"

"Stop, Daid!"

Luteis's voice rang through her mind, filled with strength, authority, and something else. *He may not make it. Not even with dragon blood. We heal. We cannot always save. Give him what comfort you can. I am here to catch you when you fall.*

Daid stared at her, eyes half gone, sinking into a different place, as if he crossed the shadowy veil into a different world. Sanna choked back a sob and grabbed Daid's hand. Tears burned hot in her throat, but she swallowed them back.

"Daid, I'll take care of Mam. Sh-she'll be fine."

Even as she spoke, Rubeis dropped his precious blood onto Daid's chest. His breathing eased, losing the wet rattle that hung in the back of his throat. Sanna held her breath. The moments passed like years. Rubeis tottered, then fell. He slammed into the ground behind them, sending a tremor through the trees.

"No!" Sanna screamed. "Break your merging. Break it!"

Rubeis's eyes rolled back in his head. Daid's breathing

evened out, but the life did not return to his eyes. He stared at her, his pale face drawn. When he reached a hand toward her face, the fingers trembled. Sapphire stained the portions of his shirt not already claimed by blood. His hand, weak and bloody, rose, as if to touch her. She clasped it in hers.

"Daid?"

"*Amo*, Sanna," he whispered.

"Daid, please!"

His shoulders slackened. The tension released out of his neck. His head leaned back, turning slightly to the side. The rattling ceased. Sanna stared in horror at the blood seeping out of his chest, onto her hands. Her legs.

"No," she whispered. "Daid, no. Babs!" she cried, straightening. "We have to get him to Babs! She can fix him. Where's Lucey?"

Sanna—

"I won't give up!" she snapped. A sob wrenched from her throat. "I won't. Daid ... I won't—"

Sanna of the Forest, Luteis murmured. He nudged her gently with his snout. *My heart mourns for you.*

Sanna doubled over Daid with a wail.

SANNA MOVED AS if through water.

The world around her seemed to chatter, moving so fast it bent into eerie whirls. She heard witches talking to her. She answered their questions. Embraced Mam, who collapsed, pale-faced, and frighteningly still. Elliot spoke to her about the dragons. Finn about honoring Daid as a Servant. Someone washed the blood off her hands.

She spoke to them with serene calm that radiated from

the midst of her chest, where a little voice darted in circles, saying, *This is all a bad dream. This is all a bad dream.*

Sanna stared at the darkness that night. She'd have thought Daid's death would have taken her voice. Her mind. Her personality. She imagined it whisking her away to the darkest place imaginable, a place of burning torment and bitter regret. But it felt strangely hollow. Distant. As if she were staring at herself from afar, wondering why she looked so confused.

Sanna wrote a letter for Isadora, putting it in the old fairy house as they'd agreed.

Then she wrote another.

Where was Isadora? Why hadn't she come back? How couldn't she *know*? The powers would show her soon ... wouldn't they? The entire world spun on a different axis now.

Surely, Isadora would come soon.

Soon.

∼

"You did it wrong."

Isadora ground her teeth and fought the urge to throw something at Maximillion.

She stood in the middle of Maximillion's office, half her hair purple, the other a rainbow of yellow, blue, and green. One look in the mirror floating between them made her want to vomit. Maximillion stared at her in unrestrained disgust, his lip and nostrils twitching.

"Yes," she muttered. "I *see* that it's wrong. But why?"

"You have no conviction at all." He turned his back on her, surlier than ever.

A darkening winter sky unfurled outside. She longed to

step into the cool air, or at least open one of the stuffy windows. But she didn't dare suggest it—Maximillion had been on a rampage all day after meeting with Charles that morning and receiving no updates on Lucey. They suspected Lucey was in Carcere, but until it was confirmed, they clung to hope that they could intercept or find her.

Her magic flared with unusual agitation this evening—no doubt because she'd been ignoring it to practice more accurate transformation skills. She tucked it away.

Later, she promised. *I cannot right now.*

"What am I doing wro—"

A rap sounded on his door. "Ambassador Sinclair," said one of his three Assistants. "You have a visitor."

"Who is it?"

"Miss Cecelia Liam. Ambassador—"

"I know who she is," he snapped, but he paled slightly. Isadora met his gaze, a bolt of fear curling in her stomach. Cecelia coming here?

This wouldn't be pretty.

He pointed to the wall where his bookcase hid the seamless crack in the stone. Isadora backed up, pressed her hand to the second shelf, and murmured an incantation. The stones swung into the dank, empty landing of the hidden passage.

Isadora ducked into the damp hall.

"Let her in," Maximillion said, voice fading as the bookshelf swung toward Isadora. The door slid shut, encasing her in utter darkness.

Isadora closed every connection to her Watcher magic she could possibly find, imagining herself tucking away hot, white ropes. The magic responded after a momentary struggle.

The air in the secret passage lay thick and cold, muggy

with death. Without the warmth of the magic in her body, chill emptiness flooded her. A thousand questions rolled through her mind, but she couldn't shake the most important of them: just how *much* did Cecelia know about Maximillion?

Unable to bear the silence, Isadora cast a simple spell to amplify sounds, one that Cecelia could detect—if she were randomly looking for functional magic that no one cared about. Isadora pressed her ear closer to the chilly stone, detecting a quiet, melodic voice.

"Always right to the point. Maximillion, you never change."

"I'm as reassuring as the tide."

A long pause. Isadora almost recast the spell, but Cecelia spoke again. "I come on official business."

"We had no parlay scheduled."

"Do we have to?"

"It's preferred. Some witches have schedules to keep."

"Speaking of witches, one of yours is in Carcere."

Isadora sucked in a sharp breath, and a creature in the depths scurried past with a screech. She shuddered. Carcere was located on the famed La Torra island, where the Defenders trained. The captured Watchers all died there, often burned on a star-like structure meant to represent fate.

Isadora's stomach twisted. Lucey had only managed to free one witch from La Torra, and it had been almost accidental. She'd dressed as an East Guard sailor, then intercepted the witch when he walked off the boat and onto the island.

But she'd never been able to get *inside* Carcere.

"There are likely many witches in your horrific prison," Maximillion said with unrivaled calm. "I hardly think they warrant a special trip from someone as busy as you."

"You flatter me."

"I never flatter anyone."

Isn't that the truth, Isadora thought.

"Even after ... extensive persuasion, I haven't been able to get a name out of her. Her own, or that of your ridiculous Advocacy. She's quite powerful that way, even without the ability to use magic. Impressive lot you've recruited to your little tribe."

"You say that like it's mine," he murmured.

"Isn't it?"

A long stretch of silence passed between them. Cecelia broke it first, as unbothered as Maximillion.

"Don't you want her back?"

"How do you know she's from the Central Network?"

"She was fleeing into Letum Wood. What other witch in their right mind would go into that awful place?"

He scoffed, voice crisp. Cool. Flawlessly uncaring. "Hardly proof. Let's not act like we're friends, Cecelia. You cannot harm me here, and you've never found me anywhere else. What do you want?"

Isadora pressed the shell of her ear so hard against the stone it ached from the cold. Cecelia continued as if Maximillion hadn't asked, her voice as unyielding as ever.

"I want to know how many paths she sees."

"Paths?"

"I already know your secret, Maximillion. You cannot fool a Defender as powerful as me. How many paths does your henchwoman see?"

"It's so hard to keep track of all the Watchers ..."

"Fine. What of you?"

"I have no idea what you're talking about."

"Your own paths? The fate of the entire Network, perhaps? Give me an idea of just how powerful you are, oh-mighty-Ambassador."

Silence reigned.

Cecelia broke it first. "I see. Not powerful at all. This witch is quite plain, with no great beauty to speak of, and she's been a thorn in my side for some time now. I recognize her paths, you know. No disguise can hide those—not from me. She's had many, many run-ins with Defenders. In fact, I've seen her with you often enough. Do you love her? I'd always imagined you lonely for the rest of your life. Well, with this witch in the mix, perhaps not. Does she also love you? It may be that—"

"Don't waste my time, Cecelia."

"Of course, you're not a romantic."

"Neither are you."

At that, she laughed, a low, rolling sound. "Tell me more, Maximillion, about your powers. Or her powers. Perhaps we can come to some kind of arrangement."

"Why did you come here to tell me all this? A letter would have sufficed and wasted less of my time."

Cecelia didn't waver. "Dante wants to speak with her. It's the only reason she's still alive."

Isadora's heart thumped. Dante, the High Priest of the Eastern Network. Why would he want to speak with Lucey?

A known Defender sympathizer, Dante had put Cecelia in power as Ambassador years ago, inaugurating the bloodiest regime against Watchers of any High Priest in known history. He'd turned La Torra island over to her as a stronghold, furthering its reputation as one of the most powerful and unconventional castles in Alkarra.

"I couldn't care less about your ridiculous High Priest,"

Maximillion said, voice cold. "Your time here is done. You may leave."

"Nervous, are you? You've never kicked me out before."

"Not as nervous as you should be," he murmured silkily. "I'm not afraid of you or your misguided notions about Watchers. Shall I mention that your Defender dogs must have been in the Central Network if you were near Letum Wood? A clear violation of edict number—"

"Quick, as always. I'm not afraid, Maximillion," she hissed. "Of a Watcher? Never."

"No one ever said you were afraid. Are we finished?"

"Your shameful prisoner will remain on La Torra until Dante comes to interrogate her himself. You know he gets what he wants under stressful circumstances. No reason to make her passing too easy."

"I've never known you to pass up an opportunity to torture anyone. Even those within your circle of influence. Such as the beloved High Priest you torture frequently, I hear, by reminding him of a specific evening six years ago."

Another tight silence. Isadora plastered her body to the wall in an attempt to hear better.

"You know not of what you speak," Cecelia said, a hint of sorrow in her tone. "Farewell, Maximillion. I always have enjoyed when Watchers and their sympathizers burn at the stake. Her death is scheduled for three months from now, the day after Dante interrogates her. If she survives. Perhaps you could come watch? Or invite the witch hiding in your secret spot in the wall. No doubt she must be some kind of Watcher as well, running from the nasty Defender."

Isadora sucked in a sharp breath but resisted the urge to drop the spell. Maximillion's voice didn't break stride. "Will you be burning next to the witch?" he asked. "I would like to watch that."

"One day, Maximillion, you and I shall face off. I very much look forward to it."

Isadora's heart squeezed. Lucey. Sweet Lucey caught in Carcere, slated for death by fire after an interrogation by the powerful High Priest, Dante. Cecelia may have already subjected her to horrible torture already.

"Get out of my office," he said with resounding finality. "I have work to do."

~

THE AIR SEEMED to swallow Isadora.

Her thoughts knitted into a tangle of disbelief, questions, and fear while she waited in the darkness. Lucey was alive, at least, but in what condition? Cecelia's lack of fear, her chilling tone, turned Isadora's stomach into a fist.

What felt like an eternity later, the door opened.

She stepped back, wincing at the bright flash of light. Inside, Maximillion paced, nostrils flared, brow heavy. Isadora slipped inside and folded her hands in front of her. The door closed.

A full minute passed before she spoke. "How ... ah ... interesting."

"Interesting," he spat. "Not *interesting*. A game. Definitely a game. She wants me on La Torra. They're waiting three months to bait me."

Isadora paused in the middle of the room, still blinking. "She sounded surprised that you didn't care."

"Cecelia is rarely surprised."

Another full minute passed while he paced.

"Do you want to talk about it?" she asked.

Maximillion drew himself up, shoulders back. The flickering firelight threw his cheeks into sharp contrast. He stared hard at her with a distant expression—and not the one that indicated he was using his powers. A flush of cold rushed through Isadora.

"Oh, no," she murmured. "That's your planning face."

"You must know what I'm thinking."

"I haven't the foggiest idea."

His eyes gleamed. His lips twitched as if he'd considered, for a half a second, a smile. The look disappeared, fading into the flinty lines of his usual sour expression.

Isadora fought back a groan and ran a hand over her face. "You want to put someone on La Torra and break Lucey out."

She stared at him for a long moment, lost in the strangeness of knowing his mind so well. Of agreeing with him on something so fundamentally risky that she could hardly reconcile herself to it. In the six months she'd been working directly with Maximillion, she'd never heard of a mission planned without Lucey.

"Precisely," he said.

"Without Lucey? That's madness."

"Not as *mad* as leaving her in there to die. Not only is she the best witch for this job, but Dante will torture the information out of her. We must do it to protect ourselves, the Advocacy, and everyone else involved."

"I agree," she said.

"That was more than just a visit from Cecelia, you realize." He wagged a finger, head shaking. "It was a threat. An invitation. She *wants* us to go after Lucey. She wants … something. She's prize focused. She likes to be the winner. The most powerful. She hates a long-term game." He shook his head, clucking under his breath. "There must be something else she wants."

"Insight into your powers."

His shoulders stiffened.

Isadora moved toward him, warming to it now. "She wanted to know the number of paths you saw, right? That Lucey saw."

His gaze narrowed. "Yes."

"But why? What could she learn?"

"No idea," he muttered. "Perhaps to gauge the strength of my power against hers?"

"Does it work that way?"

He paused, staring at a map of the Southern and Eastern Networks unfurled on his desk. His brow furrowed.

"I don't know."

Like most Watchers, the nuance of the magic was lost on Maximillion—Isadora wondered if any of them really knew the details of the magic they wielded. The tip of his finger tapped a spot on the map near the far eastern border of the Eastern Network along the ocean. A spot lay underneath his fingernail. If not for a grouping of words that pointed to it, she would have mistaken it for dust.

"La Torra," he said.

"That?"

"Indeed. Almost invisible from the coast. Breaking Lucey free wouldn't be so hard if it weren't for Carcere's ability to suppress magic, its sheer lack of windows, and an entrance none of my contacts have been able to find."

"It's imbued?" she asked.

"Not sure. It's inherently magical in the way it operates, but it's also a suppressor. Strangest castle I've ever heard of."

"Sounds like a lovely place," Isadora muttered.

Colors bled away from the painted map beneath his finger. Its lines faded, reshaping on a different part of the parchment. Several moments passed before she comprehended that he'd moved in on the map; now she stared only at La Torra.

"Goodness."

"It's a godless island. Small as can be. You could probably walk the entire perimeter in thirty minutes—without trying very hard. It used to be a royal prison for high-society witches. Plenty of High Priests' mistresses have been banned to this island and then killed. Or died a long, lonely death in the endless halls of Carcere. Some have said it never ends—that it could house entire armies if it needed to."

The ragged edges of the island looked like teeth. In the middle, what appeared to be a circular castle occupied most of the space. A round courtyard broke up the middle of the castle, as if the whole structure had been designed around the circle. Green slashes indicated strange trees scattered throughout the island. Aside from a vague reference to a sea dragon with the end of its tail in the water, Isadora saw nothing else.

"Bleak."

"Death traps often are," he murmured.

He rotated the map around so the castle faced her. Another section of the map gave a grounds-eye view of the structure. Even as a painting, the barren shore felt angry. The circular mainstay stood seven stories high. The first five floors were made of reddish stone imbued with yellow veins, but the top two were gray stone. In these upper floors, there were no windows. No doors. Like a giant trap sitting on top of something that would otherwise have been beautiful.

"Carcere." He rubbed a hand across his forehead. "This will be the hardest extraction we've ever done."

"But you're going to do it?"

His head snapped up so fast it startled her. Isadora stepped back.

"What kind of question is that?" He growled. "Of course, I'm going to send someone after her. If not go myself," he added in a mumble.

"Surely *you* can't!"

"I can."

"But you're the Advoca—"

"Just because I can doesn't mean I *shall*. We cannot lose Lucey. Until she came along, nothing worked. Most of our missions failed. Her transformational skill and quick mind are irreplaceable. Something about her working with us made everything different. I'll find our way in. Probably through the *lavanda*."

"What?"

"No one wants to work in a *lavanda*. Don't you know anything?" He tapped his chin. "Marguerite. She would be perfect. She moved to the Central Network from the East fifteen years ago. Not married. No children. Fifty years old. If the current *lavanda* maid were to become unexpectedly ill and need to leave ... "

"Is Marguerite a Watcher?"

"Volunteer in the Advocacy. Her father was a Watcher, burned at the stake before Cecelia's reign."

Isadora swallowed. Marguerite would walk right into the lion's mouth. Such a dangerous mission. Such potential for failure. Isadora had only been under Lucey's tutelage for a few months—nothing near what she'd need to undertake such a mammoth assignment. She shuddered, grateful the mission wasn't hers.

Maximillion lifted one eyebrow. "You thought I'd ask you to do it?"

"It never crossed my mind."

"Good. See that pile of books? Read them. I want you to be rock-solid on the advanced conjugations of *Ilese*. Then we'll start to work on the *Yazika* language of the Southern Network."

"Can I help in a different way? To study books while Lucey is in a prison cell seems so ..."

"Never question me," he snapped. "Start reading."

THE NEXT MORNING, Sanna stood in the midst of the slight, open meadow.

Luteis, Elis, Cara, and Selasis circled Daid on the pyre, flying in low circles. Isadora was nowhere in sight, despite four letters set in the stump she was supposed to check. Sanna's desperation for her sister had turned to panic, then to fury. Now, she felt the emptiness beside her with deep resignation.

She'll come, Sanna told herself, clenching her fist. *She'll see it with her magic, or whatever.*

All the dragons amassed, looming in the forest with flickers of color, soundless. She could feel their curiosity and was grateful she no longer heard their voices. Dragons didn't mourn the same way as witches. At least, she didn't think so. All six hatchlings lay on the ground, their heads pressed to the dirt, keeping a wary eye on Daid's still form.

Next to them, Cara keened low in her throat, reaching down to nudge Sanna, who put up a hand to trace along her scales. They cooled immediately after she touched them.

"*Amo*, Cara."

Cara closed her eyes, sent an affectionate, warm breath to dance around Sanna's ankles, and withdrew. Jesse watched with a furrowed brow.

Dried bundles of sticks and weeds filled the space beneath Daid's makeshift bed of rocks. His face lay inert. Pale, if not peaceful. Only a few traces of blood remained near his neck, around wounds that Adelina and Babs couldn't hide.

Mam stood next to Babs, clinging to her. Babs kept a firm arm around Mam's too-thin waist. Mam stared at the ground. A lone tear streaked her face.

"Sanna," Elliot whispered. He held onto her arm, near the elbow. "Can you release your daid?"

Sanna sucked in a sharp breath.

She shouldn't have to.

Mam should do it. Elliot *could* do it. Isadora should have done it. At the very least, Isadora would have been part of it —had her new life not intruded so much. The tradition of releasing a loved one to enter the fields of Halla usually fell to the spouse, parent, or oldest child.

Isadora wasn't here.

Neither was Mam—not really. She hadn't spoken since Luteis returned with Sanna clinging to Daid on his back and Rubeis hanging inert in his talons. The flight back had threatened to be too much for Luteis. A dragon wasn't meant to carry the weight of another, older dragon. But somehow, he did it. Sanna drew in a deep breath.

She would also.

Sanna looked at Elliot. Her eyes required several moments to truly see him, and then she turned to the body. "Release him to honor and glory in the fields of Halla," she said to Luteis. "May he live there as he could not here."

Luteis wrapped his tail around her legs none too soon. The moment she said the words, her knees gave out. Only his gentle warmth kept her upright. Gently, Luteis turned to the pyre. Flames issued from his mouth in licking tongues, consuming the dried sticks and branches beneath Daid.

One at a time, the other dragons slowed, landed, and joined in. Their heat scalded the backs of Sanna's hands. She stood in the curling heat instead of looking away. Each second that passed as Daid disappeared into the hellish flames seemed to awaken feelings that had been dead, lost to shock. Numbness. Sheer disbelief.

Hadn't Daid just been flying next to her? Talking to her? Experiencing flight again, even if reluctantly?

Sanna turned away when she couldn't stand the heat anymore. Mam sobbed, and her knees went out from underneath her. Babs caught her, lowering her to the ground. Sanna forced herself to watch, grim-faced, while Mam wept in Babs's arms. Babs swallowed hard. Elliot reached out and put a hand on Sanna's shoulders as the crackling began to subside.

"He's at peace."

His body burned away in what felt like minutes, flying skyward in coils of smoke and tendrils of bright flame. Only ash remained, piled on the rocks, dusting the ground. It was the way of things, and it brought Sanna a little sliver of peace.

Smoke filtered through the trees. Sanna felt a firm, heavy emptiness all the way to her chest.

It was over now.

There was no going back. Daid was gone.

Once the dragons finished, they retreated, except for Luteis. Rubeis had disappeared sometime in the night, reclaimed by the forest, nothing but a bright-red heart scale and a brand-new sapling left behind. By default, she supposed the scale belonged to her, but she left it near the tree, unable to bring it home.

"It's finished," Elliot said. "Rian can go to his reward with—"

His sentence choked off. The Servants—when they were that—used to say *go to his reward with Drago*. No longer. What was beyond now? Where was he going that she could not visit? The questions flittered in Sanna's mind. Did Deasylva claim him?

She stood there, staring at the charred remains, with no thought in her empty mind except one.

Gone. Gone. Gone.

The Dragonmasters slipped away. Soon, only Sanna, Babs, Elliot, and Mam remained.

"Roxy," Babs whispered, holding Mam tight to her side. "Let's get you some rest."

Mam blindly followed as if she weren't present in her own body. Her face had turned an unearthly shade of white. Elliot's hand dropped from Sanna's shoulder.

"And you?" he murmured.

Sanna tilted her head back. Unbidden, a vine dropped from the great heights, landing just a few paces away.

"I'll be back. Eventually."

Sanna grabbed the vine, twisted it around her ankle, and began to climb. Luteis scrambled up the tree behind her, digging his talons into the trunk. She stepped onto the first branch, then climbed higher. To the next. And the next. Tears dropped down her cheeks as she worked past hanging vines and old animal bones left by beluas. The world seemed to pass her as if she wasn't really in it.

Once she was far enough away from the ground that it didn't seem to exist, she stepped onto a mossy branch and began to run. She darted through the canopy, leaping from one vine to the next, crossing great spaces in a single breath, then finding another branch and running as fast as her legs would carry her. Her calves burned, and her chest ached. On any other day, she never would have thrown herself from limb to limb, risking such great jumps.

Luteis soared through the canopy, dipping in and out, sometimes below her, sometimes above. Sanna pressed harder, comforted by his heavy, glittering shadow. Her bruised heart would burst out of her chest any moment now and join Daid. When her toe snagged a dead sprig of ivy, catching her mid-stride, she fell forward, skidded on her chest, and dropped off the mossy branch. She braced herself for the hard edge of the branch below, but a soft cushion of dragon wing embraced her instead.

Sanna curled into a ball, sliding onto Luteis's back, where she stared at the dull, olive canopy. All signs of life had vanished. Not even birds rustled in the background. Her heavy breaths subsided. The agony of watching Daid's body burn eased into the low, heady simmer of pure rage.

"He's gone, Luteis."

He is.

Tears welled up in her eyes.

"I *will* figure out what took him."

We will.

Her resolve hardened as a hot tear dropped out of one eye. "And they will pay."

CHAPTER

EIGHT

Isadora rested her hands behind her head and stared at the ceiling early the next morning.

Rain plunked against the window, racing down the murky gray pane. She shivered. The foggy in-between when winter turned into spring was always strange. Frigid mornings with rain instead of snow and a bone-deep chill that led to days with warm rays of sunshine and budding flowers.

Her mind spun with magic and memories and deep thoughts. Despite the fatigue of searching for Lucey in the paths for hours, the magic still tugged, beckoning her back. She mentally tucked it away.

Later.

"Lucey," she murmured. "Where are you?"

Her lack of firm conclusion only frustrated her more. What was the point? Why train? Beyond assisting raids, the magic had to serve *some* purpose, surely.

For a brief second, she thought of going home. Cuddling up to Sanna in the chilly night, the way they used to. No. Sanna slept so fitfully these days, she didn't want to wake her. She shoved out of bed, wrapped the blanket around her, and rummaged around her armoire for a wool dress.

Lying in bed wouldn't solve any of her problems.

A FRUSTRATED SIGH ESCAPED ISADORA.

The absolute stillness of Maximillion's office rang around her. She longed to throw the windows open … but he'd probably stroll into the room, snap at her for letting the chilly air inside, and proceed to grill her with impossible questions. With a spell, she commanded a single candle to flame. The light bounced to life, the only cheery aspect of the dreary day. To have more light, she lit several others.

She grabbed her *Ilese* book from his shelf and settled into his chair to wait.

The distant sound of new recruits training outside in the lower bailey—a meager contingent of small boys likely lying about their age—rang through the window. The Network was so desperate for Guardians, she doubted they even screened them anymore. She stared at the words on her book's pages, forcing her thoughts to the awaiting verbs.

Her brain stuttered and stopped.

"Come on," she muttered, pressing a fisted hand to her forehead. "The word for disaster. What is it?"

She paused, so close to the answer it taunted her, just a breath away. The moment she thought she'd remembered, it slipped away, lost in the eddy of her mind. With another insistent tug, the magic swirled in her chest. Isadora sighed and dropped her head onto the desk.

Honestly.

The idea of Maximillion storming in and finding her in a less-than-composed state was mortifying. She was no Lucey, who seemed to take everything in stride. His temper never fazed Lucey's cool exterior. In fact, the two of them together—

A *slam* echoed through the room.

She jumped, startled to see a thin, ragged witch in the doorway. Clumps of blonde hair spilled out of a rag tied in a swatch around her head. Dirt marred her gaunt cheeks and the backs of her hands, which stuck out from an old, wrinkled blouse. The smell of salt and body odor filled the space.

"Where's Ambassador Sinclair?" the young witch cried, whipping around. "I must find him now!"

Isadora stood. "He's in a meeting with the High Priest, I believe. Can I help you with something? Who are you?"

"No!" the witch moaned. She shoved her hands through her greasy hair. The familiar, light accent of the East tilted her words. "He can't be!"

"He is, I assure you."

The girl wrung her hands. "Oh, this is a mess. He's going to have a fit when he finds out."

"When who finds out?"

"Ambassador Sinclair!" she cried. "Aren't you listening?"

Isadora frowned. Maximillion was no saint, but he rarely *had a fit* that Isadora hadn't caused. "What's happened?"

"Marguerite! She's not there."

"Who?"

"Marguerite."

The name rang familiar in the back of Isadora's mind. "Where is she not?" Isadora asked.

"At the wharf!"

Isadora's head spun for just a moment before the words sank in.

Marguerite.

Maximillion had mentioned her just yesterday as the witch he wanted to search for Lucey. Isadora's eyes widened. "Oh!" she breathed, moving out from behind the desk. "Marguer—"

"Yes! She's supposed to be boarding the boat for"—the girl glanced around, then whispered—"*the island*, and she's not there. No sign of her. I've stalled them, but they're about to leave!"

"Wait. What is his plan?"

"Who are you?" the girl growled. "Don't you know anything?"

"I don't know his plans!"

All the blood drained from her face. "Oh no," she whispered. "I've done it. He'll destroy me. I-I-I shouldn't have—"

Isadora held out a hand. The blue, woven Advocacy sign—the same she'd created in Letum Wood—wavered above her hand. "It's all right. I'm part of this."

The girl relaxed. "Oh. Thank the goddess mother Prana."

"Tell me everything."

The girl buried her face in her hands. "He'll kill me!"

"It's not your fault," Isadora said, reaching out with a warm touch, but the girl didn't seem to notice. She'd already collapsed into sobs. Isadora bit her bottom lip. Maximillion would be utterly livid if he knew how sloppy she'd been on Advocacy business. The girl had a right to be frightened, but she was lucky Isadora knew what she was about.

"Ah, what's your name?"

"Might as well tell you, because you'll need it for my grave." She sniffled, wiping an arm under her nose. "I'm Sera. I help Ambassador Sinclair gather the …" She glanced around again, then stopped. "Is this a test?"

Isadora almost sighed. Sera's paranoia wasn't unfounded. Maximillion had tested her many times, creating false situations just to see how Isadora would react under pressure.

"He is not testing you right now."

"Fine. I gather his … *friends* in the East when they're needed."

"And Maximillion is sending Marguerite to La Torra?"

Sera nodded. "The *lavanda* maid fell sick last night. Violently so. Marguerite is on Fiona's list as a back-up."

Setting aside Fiona and the not-so-strange "coincidence" of the maid *falling sick*, Isadora forced the puzzle pieces together. Maximillion must have acted immediately after Cecelia left—no doubt putting things in place before Cecelia even returned to La Torra, so it seemed less suspicious. His ability to command the Advocacy never ceased to amaze her.

"This can't be all that bad," Isadora said, using the same soothing tone as she did with Sanna. "I'm sure Marguerite will show up soon. And if she doesn't, Maximillion can hardly blame you for it."

"They're leaving for La Torra in a few minutes." She shuddered, tears brimming in her eyes. "I was supposed to see her off and report back, but what if she doesn't show up? Everything could fall apart." Sera leaned forward with a dramatic whisper. "Everything."

Isadora sucked in a sharp breath. This was, decidedly, the most important mission in the world. If things went badly and Cecelia murdered Lucey, dozens of lives would be lost. That alone could set the Advocacy so far back it never recovered. Not to mention the horrid fate Lucey would endure.

"How about I come back with you?" Isadora asked. "I'll see if there's something I can do. Stall them further, perhaps?"

Sera's eyes widened. "Really?"

"I can do that without much danger."

"And you'll tell Ambassador Sinclair what happened when you return?"

Ah. There was the rub. Sera likely wasn't as worried about the mission or Marguerite as she was about her own hide.

Well, Isadora couldn't blame her.

"Yes. I'll tell him."

Sera brightened considerably. Her tears stopped, and terror took their place. "Then we must go now!"

Before Isadora could get out another word, Sera disappeared in a transportation spell.

"Wait! What wharf?"

But it was no use. Only the empty room heard her call. Frantic, she ran back to Maximillion's desk and scrubbed through the parchment there. Nothing. No letter. No description of where she was supposed to follow Sera.

Of course there wasn't. Transporting to a place she'd never been before was too risky—she'd almost died doing that last year. She didn't know how to follow magic yet. Isadora huffed. "What am I supposed to do now?"

Sera didn't return. Isadora paced, her thoughts

whirling. "Think," she murmured. "There must be another way. Think about what it would look li—"

She gasped, her head popping up. Seconds later, she opened her powers and slipped into the magic. Wisps populated before her, no doubt responding to the frenzy of her emotion, tripling in front of her with unusually high numbers. Sanna littered most of them, but Isadora ignored them for now.

"Show only my path. And only the Eastern Network. And only immediate possibilities."

The powers obeyed.

Wisps disappeared, leaving four trails that wound into the bracken. Isadora rushed up to the first wisp she saw. A wharf, indeed. Teeming with people and populated with unwanted fish guts. She scoured the image for details, closed the magic, and returned fully to Maximillion's office.

"Please," she murmured, lacing her fingers together in an icy ball. Transporting to a place she'd never been was a dangerous art—at least, this time, she'd seen something of the wharf. "Please work."

Isadora reimagined the picture of the wharf, whispered the words to the transportation spell, and let it wash over her in a long, cool brush.

Magic whisked her away.

An eternity of darkness and discomfort followed, as if she were swimming in a tunnel that pressed upon her. Her chest—which wasn't really there—ached for air. The pressure bore down on her face as if it would peel her skin away. She wanted to scream but had no voice. Finally, when she thought she'd die, the pain stopped.

She landed on her feet in something soft.

∿

"My dragons have spoken."

Finn said the words with a finality that sent sparks of annoyance up Sanna's spine. She stood near a makeshift window of Elliot's house, peering past a lion hide and onto a wet world. Cold crawled into the room, slipping between the cracks in the walls, twining into her bones. She ignored it, comforted by the dismal sound of the rain, and whipped around.

"Your dragons have said nothing."

Finn hesitated, his expression twitching as if he held back a sneer. "They've clustered around my house!"

"They're scared. The leader they've always known was just killed, and the next leader died as well." Sanna maintained an even tone by sheer willpower. "They're seeking reassurance."

She let the lion skin fall back into place, then stepped deeper into the room, shoving thoughts of Isadora aside. The last place she wanted to be was in this haphazard structure Elliot and Jesse had cobbled together with thin flakes of bark the length of her body, but she couldn't avoid this confrontation any longer.

Finn watched her movement with beady eyes. Despite every attempt to hide his fatigue, the signs showed on his face. Baggy skin. Bloodshot eyes. He grimaced and reached for his leg stump every few minutes—Sanna wondered if he even realized what he was doing anymore.

"My decision remains firm," he said. "I'm leaving."

"You can't just leave," Elliot mumbled, rolling his eyes. "We have to stay together. We'll only weaken ourselves if we split up." Elliot stood near the fire. His baggy clothes hung off his shoulders—once meaty and strong, now lean and gaunt—and were tucked into his pants, which were tied with a rope. He held a fist to his lips as he stared into the distance. Jesse lingered on the other side of the room with a perpetual frown.

"The dragons will throw a fit," Sanna said. "Not that ..."

Not that it really matters, she finished silently. Weren't the dragons always having fits these days?

No. Not all of them.

Elliot sent her an assessing look, then glanced away again.

Finn scowled and waved his hand. "You know as well as I do that this isn't going to work," he said, twirling a finger around at their new home. "Our dragons don't know *how* to be wild. How can you teach a one-hundred-year-old dragon to sneak through the forest after a boar? We've been trying all winter. All of us are almost dead, dragons included." He hesitated for half a second, long enough for another shot of annoyance to pulse through Sanna's body. He continued without apology but in a lower mumble, "We have to create a new Anguis."

Elliot opened his mouth, then hesitated, a flicker of uncertainty in his gaze. In that pause, the entire world shifted.

Did Elliot agree with Finn?

Finn will be the downfall of us all, Luteis growled. *You must put a stop to this, lest the race of forest dragons fall extinct from his stupidity.*

"Finn, you just want to bring back a system that didn't work," Sanna said, dragging a hand down her face. "Dragons aren't meant to stay in one area. They're meant to prowl the forest and ..."

"Be slaves to a supposed goddess?" Finn barked. "Right."

Stinging animosity rang in his tone. For that, Sanna could hardly fault him. She recalled all the nights she'd spent scrawling her prayers to Talis's false god Drago in her prayer book. Falsehoods, all of them. Had Deasylva been any more receptive than Drago? Not really. She'd allowed awful things to happen. She just hadn't been as restrictive as Talis. Playing in the world of goddesses left Sanna feeling burned.

A swelling silence filled the air.

"Besides," Finn muttered, "if our dragons were hungry before, they're positively starving now. Our only option is bringing back the old ways, when we all worked together." He sent her a dark glare. "Before some of us decided *not* to hunt for the dragons."

"They can do it themselves!"

"They can't!"

He pounded his fist on a makeshift table—really a massive flake of bark she'd found on the forest floor. The table cracked all the way down the middle.

Elliot growled. "Calm yourself, Finn. Getting angry won't help anything."

"I'm not angry," he barked. "I'm hungry! So are the dragons. This one"—he jabbed a finger at Sanna—"has done us no favors by killing Talis and burning Anguis to the ground."

Sanna bit the inside of her cheek until she drew blood. Another pause, and Sanna realized they were all waiting for Daid to jump in with his usual wisdom.

Elliot blinked and shook his head. "It wasn't like that, Finn. Rian killed Talis, not Sanna."

"She started the revolution, didn't she? And now that Rian's gone, who is our leader now?" Finn threw his hands in the air. "The dragons follow no one! Certainly not our supposed High Dragonmaster, whatever that means."

Elliot glanced at Sanna, but she ignored it.

"We'll have to figure that out," Sanna said. "It's why we're here."

"Then we need a leader." Finn raised his arm. "I volunteer."

"No," Sanna said.

Elliot echoed her. "No."

"Never," Jesse muttered.

Finn sneered. "I'll do a better job than any of you."

"You will not," Sanna said.

"Not a good idea," Elliot said at the same time.

Finn scowled. "Then we remain at an impasse," he snapped at Elliot. "Your son can't vote. He isn't the head of a Servant house."

"Sanna?" Elliot asked quietly, turning to her. "One can't deny that Deasylva made you High Dragonmaster the night you defeated Talis. What of it now? What can you tell us about High Dragonmasters or the magic?"

Her irritation gave way to uncertainty. Like Elliot, she had no certain knowledge. Her goddess hadn't given her that advantage, either. Memories of Talis whispered back through her mind. Oppression. Power. Pain. What was leadership if not that?

"I can't tell you anything else," she murmured, flashes of fiery rage broiling in her mind. "Maybe I was the High Dragonmaster then, but I'm not the leader anymore. I can't even hear the dragons. I don't ... I don't even know what it means to be High Dragonmaster."

"Is that something that just goes away?"

"I don't know."

"You know more than anyone about the dragons," Jesse said. "How to fly them, and how to merge. It makes sense that *you* would lead."

Sanna shifted on her feet. Lead now? Her chest ached at

the thought. Waking up in the morning was difficult enough. "I'm eighteen years old. Nothing about that makes sense. Elliot, what about you?"

Elliot's cheeks flared. He still hadn't chosen a dragon—though Sanna suspected he had Melaris in his sights. Unlike Daid, Elliot had put off attempting to merge and fly, no doubt out of fear. Sanna turned away, thinking all the damage Talis's regime was still causing. Maybe Finn was right. Could one hundred and fifty years of beliefs be erased?

"… I don't know," Elliot finally whispered. "I just …"

"Without Rian or Talis here, I won't stay." Finn stood. "There's no food here. We'll have better luck moving north."

"You're a fool," Sanna snapped. "We can't go north. Signs of mountain trolls have been popping up everywhere. You're just putting yourselves in greater danger."

"It's a choice I've been forced into." Finn lifted his chin. "You think I like it? You think I enjoy that Talis lied to all of us? That Drago isn't real? We're all going to starve if we don't find another place and resume life as it was before! Unless *that* one agrees to constantly hunt for them."

He gestured outside to Luteis. *He cannot leave without meeting greater dangers,* Luteis replied. *He will only sentence his family and the dragons that go with him to almost-certain death. He may want to ignore the greater problems at hand, but he only dooms himself.*

I know.

"We'll figure something out," Sanna said to Finn.

"*We* won't." Finn gestured between Sanna and himself, teeth bared. "I'm taking my family and my dragons. We're leaving. We'll establish our own Anguis, thank you very much, and avoid the certain death about to fall on all of you."

Sanna turned away, throat burning with all the unsaid words. A deep fatigue washed through her, robbing her of her fire. Finn didn't matter anymore—and maybe on some level, he was right. Their functional system had been wrenched away. Perhaps going back was the only way forward for these dragons. They could teach the hatchlings the new ways, but let the rest live out their lives as they chose.

All that really mattered now was finding whoever —*whatever*—killed Daid.

"Finn," Elliot said quietly. "I am concerned you don't understand the gravity of what you're suggesting."

"That I go against Rian's precious daughter?"

"That you want to break up the Ser—Dragonmasters. We're far stronger together than apart. If you leave, that doubles the chance that danger could fall on the dragons. Not to mention all the work required of you and your boys to feed your dragons alone."

"We feed them alone now."

"It will be far worse with no back-up. As much as you're loath to admit it, Luteis *has* hunted for your dragons this winter."

Finn stared at him for a long, hard moment. Sanna's breath caught. If Finn did leave, the poachers would go after him. The dragons he took with him would die.

"Come, Elliot," Finn said in a harsh whisper. "Could things really get any worse than they are now?"

Something filled Elliot's eyes. Something like wrath and fear and desperation in a bundle of black.

Do something, Luteis hissed. *Or we perish.*

Sanna blurted out her next words without a moment of forethought. "I think it was a poacher."

Lines creased Elliot's forehead. His eyes narrowed. "What?"

"That killed Daid and Rubeis. It's the only thing that makes any sense, really. Luteis and I saw her before, but there was something else there too. She shot an arrow filled with silver at us, but missed. The same sort of unexplained … *something* was also there when Daid died."

With halting breaths, she relayed the incident. Elliot's expression darkened.

"You have no proof it was a poacher. A monster killed him," Finn said without inflection or a hint of concern. "Based on your initial recounting, no single witch could have done it."

"Something *else* was there. Both times. We couldn't see it clearly, but that doesn't mean it wasn't a poacher."

"Magic, perhaps. An animal. Do you really think a witch could fillet Rubeis open? No. Your father's death was tragic." A pained expression flashed across Finn's face. He pressed on, nostrils flared. "But not at the hands of a poacher."

Sanna hesitated. She didn't have any firm proof. In truth, a poacher wasn't likely. At least, not one working alone. The shadow had been nearly indistinguishable from the rest of the forest and had disappeared—almost as if it could do magic. She knew so little about magic. But it seemed even less likely that *creatures* could do it.

So, what was it?

"No," she finally admitted. "I don't think a witch could have done that damage to Rubeis. But Luteis will agree that it wasn't just *any* creature. He's lived in wild Letum Wood all of his life. He's never seen or heard anything like it, and he's seen just about everything."

Before she could pose her own argument, Elliot drew in a deep breath and said, "Until we have more definitive proof, there's no reason to alarm the rest of the brood or the witches."

"If there are poachers, you'll lose, Finn. You can't fight them alone."

"You mistake me," Finn said quietly. Resignation, perhaps exhaustion, leaked through his voice. He ran a hand through his ragged hair, face pale. "I feel that aligning with Sanna and her supposed *goddess* is far more dangerous than recreating the safety we had under Talis's reign. The choice is mine to make. You cannot stop me. The dragons have no leader anymore, Elliot. Their only loyalties lie with the old ways. Those that wish to go with me, I shall gladly take."

She's not my goddess, Sanna wanted to mutter, but she bit her lip.

Can you stop this? Luteis said.

How?

Luteis fell silent. Finn leaving wouldn't directly affect him, outside of the possible extinction of his race. He'd been a pariah since the day he dropped into Anguis and was tolerated now only out of fear and necessity.

Sanna tried to untangle her viscous thoughts. She longed to think of nothing. To lie back in her trees. To sleep through the nightmares, the fits of rage and burning tears and pangs of loneliness for her sister. Or Daid. For *something* solid that couldn't be taken away.

No. She couldn't think of nothing now.

She had a killer to catch.

Elliot stared at Finn, rendered speechless. "No," he

finally said. "I cannot stop you. That is the power of choice you received in Talis's death. If you choose to leave and create your own village, that is your decision. You must make it. But your dragons also get a choice of whether they want to stay and learn how to fly, or run away with their tails tucked between their legs and possibly get themselves killed."

Finn hesitated, then shrugged with one shoulder.

"Fine. But they'll choose me. I know they will."

He ducked out of the structure, his wooden leg *thump thumping* on the ground. Sanna sank into a chair with a weary sigh. She wanted to duck back under Luteis's wing and sleep for days.

"We have to call the dragons now," Elliot said. "Finn can't be left alone with any of them. You know he'll lie to them. Try to convince them that he's right."

I gather them as we speak, Luteis said.

"Yes," Sanna murmured to Elliot, rubbing a hand over her eyes. "I know."

Elliot put a hand on her shoulder. "C'mon," he said. "Everything's going to be all right."

AT FIRST, Sanna couldn't see the dragons along the perimeter, but she felt them staring at her back.

She stood between two massive oaks with Luteis at her side. Finn, Elliot, Jesse, and a few of Finn's oldest sons stood near. She swallowed the lump in her throat. Daid would be furious. Livid that Finn would turn his back and leave.

Hurt that she didn't try harder to stop him.

Elliot turned to her. A sense of helplessness lingered in his gaze. He lifted a hand, motioning to her. She frowned.

Luteis, though not trusted by the brood, was the closest thing to a dragon leader they had. By extension, that meant she should do the explaining.

"Finn wants to leave and recreate the old ways of Anguis," she called. She paused, uncertain of how to proceed, but a glance from Elliot and the feel of Luteis looming next to her gave her courage. "We are not a dictatorship. If any witch or dragon desires to split the brood into factions and go with him, that is their right. But consider yourselves warned! There are poachers out there."

"Debatable," Finn called, arms folded across his chest. "We've seen no proof except for a single arrow that anyone could have found and used to kill Rian and Rubeis."

"That's absurd!" she snapped.

Finn glanced at her from the corner of his eyes. "*You* found one," he said quietly.

His rebuttal silenced her. With a shudder, she relived the moment Daid shoved the silver-filled arrow into Talis's chest.

"Breaking up the brood will weaken us, undoubtedly. We are stronger together. But the choice is yours. It should have always been," she continued, though she wasn't entirely sure of that. All the dragons were so ragged and untrusting, even she wondered if she'd done them any favors by setting them free.

"Whoever will stay with me, Luteis, Jesse, Elis, and Elliot, please stand behind us. Those who want to go with Finn, please stand behind him."

An interminable amount of time seemed to pass while she waited for the shadows to shift out of the forest. The last time she'd seen them sweeping toward her in that way was at her Selectis, which felt like a lifetime ago. Four dragons fanned behind Finn.

"Food!" Finn called, one arm raised. "I promise you a new forest, just as remote as this one, teeming with wildlife. There will be enough to eat. And I promise you safety, away from witches."

"You can't promise that," Sanna cried.

Finn ignored her.

"Life is not the same out in wild Letum Wood as it is here," she said, snarling. "There are dangers you cannot comprehend. There are creatures and magic that not even Luteis has seen. *Trolls* have come down from the northern mountains!"

He snorted. "Nothing that a whole brood of dragons couldn't defeat, I'm certain."

"You who claim they cannot hunt for themselves?"

Finn ignored her. Three more shuffled to his side. Seven now.

Cara came out of the trees, moving behind Sanna and Luteis. Her hatchlings followed. Sanna growled as more dragons walked over to Finn, but Luteis wrapped his tail around her waist, holding her back.

Your rage will not help. They're frightened.

I can't promise them anything. Neither can Finn, she said. *He's lying to them!*

Then they must learn that the hard way. Like you, they can make whatever choice they desire.

I thought you were just as angry about this as me!

Deasylva has spoken to me.

What did she say?

That choice must be honored.

Why hasn't she spoken to me?

He paused, allowing her a moment, before he said, *Perhaps you have not listened.*

Sanna frowned, watching shadows shift through the forest as dragons moved around. *We'll lose everyone.*

Not everyone.

The dragons, like a river, funneled into channels. Most streamed to Finn. Three shuffled behind Elliot, then four. Only Elis, Luteis, Cara, and her hatchlings remained anywhere near Sanna. By the time the dragons settled—six adults and three hatchlings with Elliot, three adults and two hatchlings with Sanna, and fifteen adults and one hatchling with Finn—Sanna braced herself for Finn's inevitable gloating. But something like sorrow filled his face instead. It disappeared as quickly as it came. He spun, turning to face her, his expression as solid as rock.

"The brood has spoken. I am the new leader."

Sanna clenched her hands into fists. Only Luteis, Elis, Cara, and the hatchlings remained on her side.

Her heart stung.

Elliot reached out, briefly touching a dragon before the heat burned him. The dragon sidestepped with a grunt. Elliot's hand fell to his side.

"So be it," Sanna said to Finn. "Take your dragons. I shall hold you responsible for the end of the dragon race, should the worst happen."

He hesitated.

"We'll welcome you, if you ever want to join us."

With that, he turned around and walked away, an army of dragons in his wake. Sanna watched them go, heart beating a raw, visceral rhythm.

No, she thought, finding comfort in the rage. *I don't need dragons to avenge Daid.*

CHAPTER

NINE

Sounds accosted Isadora all at once.

A crowd of witches surrounded her in a rolling cacophony. Scrounging, mangy dogs slinked amongst the chaos, feasting on the innards of dead, discarded fish. The ocean, wide and tangy and smelling of brine, stretched all the way to the horizon. Her mouth dropped open.

"Egads," she murmured, straightening. "It worked."

Not only had she made it in one piece, but she was standing at the *ocean*. The sapphire blue waters expanded endlessly, fading into the horizon. Sera's frantic shriek drew Isadora back to the present. She whirled around to find the lean girl standing in front of an oblong boat near a rickety, ocean-drenched pier. Two East Guard sailors stood in front of her while she yelled at the top of her lungs.

"Can't go!" she screamed in *Ilese*, stomping a foot. Isadora could just make out the words. "My friend is coming. She needs the job, she—"

"Too late!"

They grabbed Sera by the arm and shoved her back.

Sera stumbled to her knees on the wooden dock with a bellow.

"You cannot leave!"

"*Ceasa!*" Isadora shouted as she shoved through the close press of bodies. White shirts, oilskin boots, and salt-stained pants brushed past her as she moved. "Stop!"

On the boat, a thickset woman with ruddy, round cheeks and thin, graying hair tied into a limp braid caught Isadora's gaze. She stood at the front, hands folded in front of her, observing the commotion. Sera attempted to stand, but the East Guards shoved her back down.

"Leave her alone," Isadora said in halting *Ilese*. "She's a ... a harmless young girl."

"They're leaving!" Sera whispered in the common language as Isadora crouched next to her, a reassuring hand on her back. "They won't be coming back for another six weeks."

Isadora straightened. "You can't leave yet. Our, ah, *friend* just needs a few more minutes before she ... ah ... arrives."

"I can leave," a sailor barked. "And I will."

"Five minutes?"

"No."

"Four?"

Isadora's mind raced to translate the words he rattled off as he waved a hand through the air. Maximillion's relentless grilling her *Ilese* knowledge had helped, but these witches possessed supremely thick accents she hadn't expected. Not to mention the blur of quickly spoken words.

"It won't work. No more *suchransa*. We leave! You've delayed us long enough. One more word and—"

"La Torra needs her!" Isadora blurted out. "They have no, ah, *lavandoor* worker. Cecelia will, er, not be pleased."

The woman on the boat lifted one eyebrow.

Sera pressed her lips in a tight line. "*Lavanda*," she hissed. "And she is called The Great One."

"Er ... right. I mean *lavanda*."

The chatter on the wharf quieted when the sailors looked at the quiet woman on the boat. Her brow had furrowed. She murmured a reply Isadora couldn't make out. For a time, no one spoke.

"You," she called to Isadora. "You know Marguerite?"

Seconds passed while Isadora worked through the woman's lilting accent. She hesitated. No, she didn't. But the question bought them time.

Come on, Marguerite, she silently pleaded. *Please arrive!*

"Ah, yes. We are ... good friends."

"Is she coming?"

"Certainly."

"And if she doesn't, can you guarantee her?"

Isadora paused. Had she conjugated that word correctly? *Guarantee.* Yes. Maybe. If Maximillion had assigned this Marguerite to a mission, she would show. Isadora had never heard of anyone in the Advocacy *not* coming through, and with so important a mission? Guaranteed, yes.

Isadora pulled her shoulders back.

"Yes."

The woman glanced at the sailors, speaking just low enough that Isadora had to strain to hear. She patched the words together phrases at a time.

"Ten minutes ... girl will find this woman ... milady would not be pleased ..."

One of the sailors turned to Sera, barking something Isadora didn't catch. Sera disappeared with a squeak.

"Ten minutes," he muttered. "And we leave."

The sailors stared at Isadora with unrelenting annoyance. She ignored their unwavering gaze. Silence filled the dock. Isadora kept her arms hanging at her sides—another thing Maximillion demanded—in order not to betray her nerves. She tried to act bored, but kept her eyes on the ocean. The massive, enchanting ocean that seemed to never end.

A thought struck her, sending terror through her body.

She was in the Eastern Network. *That* was a ship to La Torra. One of these sailors could be a Defender in disguise. She clamped down on her powers, wondering if she'd already betrayed herself accidentally. The magic often moved within her on its own when she wasn't paying attention to it. In the rush to help, she hadn't considered what she might be getting herself into.

She could be caught. Or locked up with Lucey. Maximillion would froth at the mouth if she inadvertently caused her own demise. Or maybe he'd laugh and say it was inevitable. Either way, he wouldn't appreciate her dying after he'd sunk time into training her.

How would her family react?

No.

She couldn't think that way.

Isadora swallowed hard as another minute ticked by. Where was Sera? What did it mean to *guarantee* someone, anyway? Dozens of possibilities whirled through her mind. Before she could settle on one, the sailor called out, "We go!"

The sailors scrambled onto the boat.

"Wait!" Isadora called.

One sailor with dark brown skin grabbed her by the neck and shoved her onto the boat. She kicked, hitting him in the knee with her boot. He leapt back with a cry, fire in his bright, umber eyes. Another sailor grabbed her arm and jerked her forward.

Her shoe slipped on the wet floor when she attempted to fight back. The woman inside grabbed her by the arm before she pitched into the water and then stood between her and the sailor. The scowling sailor backed away from her hot glare.

"Come," the woman said to Isadora. "The time has passed, and you have guaranteed her. You will work in her place now."

Shock froze Isadora like a winter icicle.

"What?"

Sera reappeared—alone—just as the sailors shoved away from the dock with a grunt. A silent scream filled her eyes.

"Miss!" she called. "I cannot find her!"

Isadora's mouth opened, but no sound came out. Sera mouthed, *I'm so sorry* and disappeared. Hopefully to tell Maximillion.

By sheer willpower, Isadora kept herself from transporting away or hurling herself into the water. She'd only draw more attention if she made a bigger mess out of this already-sticky situation.

The wharf grew smaller, then disappeared into the coastline as they lurched away on choppy water. In the distance, on the edge of the horizon, lingered a foamy slate cloud. The robust woman sat next to Isadora, face turned to the sea breeze and eyes closed.

"This goes to La Torra?" Isadora asked.

"Yes," the woman said. "You are the new *lavanda* maid."

Watcher or not, Isadora was going to live with Cecelia.

There was no going back now.

~

SANNA LAY on her stomach on the branch of a young tree—although it still stood as tall as Luteis—with her limbs splayed out on either side. She studied the forest floor with relentless determination. Her vision kept blurring from the intense scrutiny, so she shifted her gaze to another spot. More mulchy loam, thick with leaves that hadn't broken down from last season. Little sunlight reached the forest floor here, casting shadows that seemed to play tricks on her. A bump in the log burrowed into her ribs. She readjusted, sliding to the right.

Luteis hid on the forest floor beneath her, in the shadows. If she hadn't known he was there, she would never have seen him. In a tree forty paces away, Elis hunkered on a branch at the same level as Sanna. The shadows hid Jesse from sight where he watched from another tree. All of them waited, listening.

I hear something in the trees, Luteis said. *A faint rustling.*

Let's hope it's something, Sanna said. "Come on, poacher," she sang under her breath. "I'll have my revenge."

Last night's vigil had been all but useless—except for the excuse to lay in her trees, sleep during the day, and use the cover of darkness to stay awake with her thoughts. Still, she persisted. Elliot said nothing, but his clamped lips seemed to suggest he thought it a waste of her time. Sanna frowned and dismissed the thought.

This hillside here and thick, clotted brambles along the floor, would naturally funnel witches along the paths below. Given the thickness of the forest, anyone would mistake it for dragon territory.

Luteis luxuriated in the strange new routine that kept them up all night. Though tired, Sanna didn't fight her desire to sleep all day. Daid's death drained her of all sense of energy and normalcy. And Mam didn't notice—she'd moved in with Babs and had been sleeping or weeping ever since. Sanna left her to it and tried not to feel rage toward Isadora, from whom they still had no word.

I hear it again, Luteis said.

At first, Sanna heard nothing except the low shuffle of forest life. Then a subtle shift from the right caught her ear. She tried to sink into the tree limb. Leaves shifted on a sapling far to her right. Something was walking below. Could be a burrowing gnome family—or a witch.

A shadow crept along the ground, shifting from tree to tree with blithe, easy steps. A willowy figure. Witch, for sure. Most likely a female with shoulders that slender. Sanna's chest burned. By sheer willpower, she forced herself to remain on the tree branch when she saw a swatch of blonde hair and dark skin.

You are calmer than I expected, Luteis said.

Sanna gripped the trunk tighter.

By necessity.

The witch crept ever closer, this time with slower steps. More than a shadow now.

Sanna could make out just enough to see that she was the same witch as before. Blonde hair around her shoulders. Dark skin the color of the forest floor—rich as umber. The witch paused for at least a minute between her movements. She'd clearly practiced stealth. Only the bright color of her almost-white hair gave her away.

What is your plan? Luteis asked. *Or should I ask whether you even have one?*

Drop on her.

You may kill her before you can gain any information. She's of more use to us alive. I have already planned several ways we could question her.

Sanna scowled. Of course, he'd planned it. She should have anticipated that. *I'll drop next to her, then tackle,* she conceded.

Better. Your planning skills continue to improve, although they remain meager.

The witch's gaze focused on a spot closer to Elis, ahead of them on the trail. From what Sanna could tell, the witch never looked up. Her first mistake. Forest lions always dropped from the canopy.

She hasn't looked away from that spot for a while, Sanna said. *Can you see anything there?*

No. A faint movement of trees, perhaps.

Do you hear anything?

He paused. *Nothing we weren't hearing before.*

Smell?

No.

Another ten minutes passed while the witch approached Sanna's tree, her gaze still intent on whatever lay beyond. For a witch who survived in Letum Wood, stalked with utmost patience, and had managed to kill Daid and Rubeis, she certainly didn't *seem* self-aware.

She's not using magic to hide, Sanna said to Luteis. *Do you think that means something? Isadora said all the witches in the Network use magic.*

She said all the witches in the world use magic. And yes, I do think it means something.

The last thing she wanted to think about was magic.

But what does it mean that she isn't using it?

Another mystery to discuss later. She approaches.

A snort in the distant bushes made Sanna's stomach catch. The witch had slipped behind the tree Sanna waited in, her back pressed to it. Although it was painfully clear she was stalking something, Sanna couldn't imagine what. Nothing lingered in this part of the forest. Luteis straightened, as silent and imperceptible as a shadow. Sanna slowly stood.

Now, she said. *I have to go now.*

Before he could protest, Sanna grabbed a vine, clenched her knife in her teeth, and stepped off the branch. Something hot woke in her chest, spreading through her shoulders, crawling into her arms.

The tips of her fingertips prickled as she plummeted toward the ground. The brush of wind across her face sent a thrill through her. In mere seconds, she landed on her feet two paces away from the witch, just as she'd planned. A pair of deep-brown eyes rimmed with shock met hers. Sanna grabbed the knife, thrusting it into the gap between them.

"Don't run, or you'll die, you murderous troll. I have excellent aim."

They stared at each other for one heartbeat.

The witch swallowed.

Sanna lunged.

The witch dodged just as a scream issued from the copse of trees the witch had been stalking. Sanna threw herself at the woman. Her hands closed around a scrap of fabric—the edge of the witch's sleeve. She wrenched the witch back. The witch braced herself at the last second, swayed slightly, and darted under Sanna's arms. Sanna tackled her, and they toppled to the forest floor, knife knocked aside by a swift kick to Sanna's wrist. Her knife tumbled away. Another scream came from the forest, this time closer.

For several breathless moments, Sanna grappled with

the witch in the undergrowth. Roots burrowed into her spine. The witch gasped as Sanna rolled off her back and slammed her into the ground. They struggled, equal in strength, until the ground shook. A roar of fire bellowed overhead, illuminating the darkness with sharp lines of yellow-and-orange light.

Cease! Luteis hissed to Elis. *Something is out there. Something—*

You deal with out there! Sanna replied. *I'm a little occupied down here.*

I cannot help, Luteis said calmly. *Not without hurting you. This fight is mine.*

Another scream pealed through the air.

"Let me go!" the witch cried. "I wasn't here to hunt you. You'll regret it if you don't."

Sanna barely maintained her grip, rendered almost speechless. The strange witch with the tattoo across her neck spoke her language, although an accent thickened the words. For two breaths, they stared at each other.

The witch panted, shoulders heaving, then slammed an elbow into Sanna's ribs. Sanna grunted, strengthened her grip, swung the witch around, and rammed her shoulder into the tree trunk. The witch shouted.

"Surrender," Sanna hissed. "You murderer."

Another roar came from not far away, just over Sanna's left shoulder. The witch paused, muttered something under her breath, and reached for her waist. A braided whip came away in her hands. Words flowed out of her lips in a strange, foreign tongue. A shriek followed, cut short by a burst of bright light. In her shock, Sanna released the witch.

The witch darted around the tree, nearly disappearing. Seconds later, the crack of the whip broke the air.

Sanna followed and skidded to a stop with a cry. The

witch held out an arm, forcing her back. "Don't ruin this," the witch cried. "I've been hunting him for ages."

Sanna sucked in a sharp breath. At the end of the whip was a dragon—the likes of which she'd never seen before.

The dragon snarled, revealing two rows of bloodstained teeth on the lower half of his jaw. He was half Luteis's size, with no forelegs. His arms stretched out into wings that were longer and thicker than those of a forest dragon, though smaller in overall size. His scales were a deep slate, almost charcoal, and seemed to change to lighter gray as he moved. Something green and sizzling filled the air. Acid? It foamed with a silvery smoke from his mouth, coiling from his nostrils.

The witch chanted something under her breath. She held an arrow filled with silver in her left hand. The other hand grasped the braided whip that had latched around the dragon's neck. The dragon writhed, shrieking, but couldn't break free. Tense muscles strained in the witch's arms and shoulders, but she didn't break her grip.

"Stay back," the witch commanded. "It can still break free."

Sanna swallowed hard, and for the moment, obeyed. The almost unbearable heat in her body seemed to fade, cooling slightly. "*Mori*," she muttered.

What is this, Luteis?

I have never seen or heard of such a creature.

With a tug of her hand, the whip yanked on the dragon's neck. He twisted onto his back with a shriek, spewing fluid onto the trunk of a nearby tree. The bark burned and sizzled, dropping to the ground in chunks. Acid thickened the air. Sanna recoiled, her throat burning at the back.

The witch darted forward, dodged one of the dragon's flailing wings, and slammed the arrow into the middle of its chest. The dragon screamed and snapped, but she disappeared and then reappeared behind him. She freed the whip with another tug. It snaked back, following her into the trees.

Sanna threw her hands over her ears when the dragon shrieked again, but its limbs stopped flailing, and its neck drooped. Pinpoint eyes turned, staring right at Sanna, before it screeched one last time and then fell limp on the ground.

A heavy shadow moved behind her. Luteis. She backed up until her spine touched his face. He sniffed at the dragon, growling deep in his cavernous chest.

A dragon, Luteis said.

Not one of ours, she replied. A flicker of movement came from overhead. Elis descended slowly, wings outstretched, with a wide-eyed Jesse on his back.

"This was an unexpected twist," Jesse murmured.

Sanna said nothing. The witch appeared again and shoved the arrow farther inside the dragon. His wings lay limp on the ground, fanned like veiny paper. Blood flowed out of his chest. Her eyes seemed sorrowful but wary when she looked at them.

"It's dead?" Sanna asked.

"Lucky for you." The witch climbed on top of the dragon, then crossed over it and dropped to the other side in front of Sanna. "There are thousands of others where he came from, and all of them just as motivated to kill you."

Her ease of movement, so strangely self-assured, set the hair on the back of Sanna's neck on edge. Luteis growled deep in his throat. The witch ignored him.

"Come," she said, striding past them. "Now that is done, we have much to speak about and not much time to do it. Selsay is not going to be pleased that I killed her spy."

"THEY CALL ME TASHI."

The witch sat across from Sanna, features illuminated by the warm glow of a fire. Luteis and Elis hovered close by. Jesse kept glancing at Tashi, then looking away. Only Tashi seemed at ease as she turned a spit with a dead marmot on it, her long, brown legs draped in front of her. The light shone off her skin.

Elis growled low in his throat but remained in the shadows. Tashi stared at the spot where he lingered with a deep, steady gaze, as if she were curious about something. Whatever she thought remained hidden. She glanced away, elbows propped on the wood, and stared into the flames. The flickering firelight gave Sanna the opportunity to study her in greater depth. A necklace of lumpy, white objects hung around her neck in a perfect circle, a sharp contrast to her dark skin.

"You've never seen any of my people, have you?" Tashi asked, startling Sanna out of her thoughts. She jumped and blushed, embarrassed to be caught staring. She'd never met *anyone* outside of Anguis.

"No."

Tashi touched her own skin, as if amused by the difference between them. "Bet you didn't know witches could be brown instead of pale."

Sanna shook her head.

Tashi laughed again, then turned the spit. "Well, now you know."

"How do I know you're not here to kill us?" Sanna asked.

Tashi laughed. "Would I have killed that dragon? He

was about to kill *you*, you know. You were so focused on me that you forgot to watch for other dangers."

That dragon wasn't there. I would have smelled him. Luteis snorted a burst of fire and shuffled his wings.

"He wasn't there before," Sanna said.

"He wasn't. He had just transported there. It's long been a favorite place of his because it's so hidden in the brambles."

Sanna's eyebrows rose. Transported. That's what Isadora did—it gave her free rein to travel as she wished with ease. But a dragon doing magic? Absurd. And ... spying? Her questions seemed to double at every word that came from Tashi's mouth. Tashi readjusted the roasting critter. Beads of fat rolled down its side and dripped onto the fire with a bright sizzle.

"What do you mean he *transported*?" she finally asked.

Tashi's level gaze met hers. "You heard me."

"Dragons can't do magic."

"*Forest* dragons can't."

"What was he?"

"A mountain dragon."

Sanna rolled that idea around in her head. *Mountain dragon.* "There are others?"

"Many, many others. If you didn't know that, you have lived a sheltered life. Thanks to Deasylva, no doubt."

To Sanna's surprise, Tashi maintained a surprisingly neutral tone.

"How would we have known?" Sanna snapped. "We live in the forest, not the mountains."

"One doesn't have to see the sea to know that monsters live there."

Sanna felt a shudder down her spine. Hadn't Isadora alluded to something like that on her last visit? Insinuating that they knew less simply because they didn't know the whole world? Sanna didn't need to go to the rest of the Network to know she wanted nothing to do with it.

"Who are you?" Jesse asked. He'd been quiet for so long that hearing his voice was a shock.

"An emissary," Tashi said, leaning back against a fallen trunk. "I came to kill Selsay's scout and bring you to Yushi."

"Who is Yushi?"

Tashi's hooded gaze sent a chill down Sanna's back. "You'll find out soon enough," she said after a long pause. "It's not in my agreement to tell you."

"So, you won't?"

She shook her head in an easy back-and-forth. Sanna rolled her eyes.

"I'm only supposed to kill the scout, Thranall, and deliver the leader of the forest dragons to Yushi. That is you, isn't it?"

Sanna hesitated.

"It's her," Jesse said.

Sanna scowled at him.

Tashi lifted one eyebrow. "Aren't you?"

"Let's just say there's been differing opinions on that," Sanna muttered. If all the dragons followed Finn, but Sanna once spoke directly to all of them, who was the leader?

"Who communicates with Deasylva?" Tashi asked.

"I do—when she'll speak."

"Then that's the extent of it. You're the leader. We leave tonight."

"If I refuse to go?"

Tashi motioned with a tilt of her head toward the dead mountain dragon.

"Then you may want to prepare for their invasion. And good luck doing it alone."

Tashi pulled the marmot off the fire and dug her fingers into it. She pulled away with a little hiss and then used her teeth to tear into one of the back legs. Sanna's stomach grumbled, but the memory of the mountain dragon's smell made it churn again. She'd smelled that sulfurous stench before—when Daid died.

"Did that mountain dragon kill my daid?" Sanna asked.

Tashi paused.

"The witch and the red dragon?"

"Yes."

She nodded once. "Aye. Tried to stop it, but they're buggers when they transport. Faster than a witch. And their scales blend into their surroundings. They're almost impossible to detect, except for their smell."

"I thought *you* were a poacher," Sanna said. "I never dreamed ..."

An invasion of mountain dragons had far-reaching implications beyond the obvious fact that Sanna didn't know everything. Thanks to Talis, she really knew *nothing*.

"I'm not a poacher," Tashi said. She stood up, roasted animal in hand. "I'm here to stop the real problems. Besides, you want to know why your father died, don't you?"

"Yes."

"Then you must follow me. Poachers are the least of your worries. C'mon. Let's ride as far as we can before first light. We have a couple days' flight ahead of us."

CHAPTER

TEN

"I'm Fiona."

That much Isadora understood, despite the woman's thick accent and the splash of the ship cutting through the water. Isadora forced a smile that felt more like a grimace.

"Isadora."

Fiona nodded, then turned her face back to the wind.

The white-capped waves hissed, rousing Isadora from her shock. Cold sea spray, intermingled with tangy, warm air, woke her powers. They shifted in the back of her mind. She imagined clamping a hand on their bright forms, tucking them into a box and setting it aside in a hidden drawer, in a dark corner of her mind.

Sleep, she said.

Their restless power faded, giving way to a thousand questions. What would she do now? Would Maximillion find her? Would she have to meet Cecelia? What was a *lavanda,* anyway?

She was on the ocean.

Alone.

In a new world that, by all accounts, would destroy her the moment they found out the truth.

She folded her trembling fingers and set them in her lap. Aside from the crates, corded piles of firewood, and a prowling, mangy cat, only Fiona and Isadora waited at the front of the boat. Fiona nudged her with a meaty elbow, pulling her back from her thoughts.

"Nervous?" Fiona asked, thin eyebrows raised high.

Isadora managed a wan smile and nodded, managing to stutter out the words for *a little* before she realized she'd accidentally said *a lot*. With a sigh, she let it go.

Fiona rattled off a few more sentences, speaking so quickly Isadora only caught a word or two here and there. When Fiona stopped and peered at her expectantly, Isadora realized she'd asked a question. She frantically worked back. Had she said *seta* or *pita*?

"Ah ..."

"You don't speak *Ilese*?"

Isadora held up two fingers close together. "A little?"

Fiona's words slowed, her enunciation growing more precise.

"Where are you from?"

When lying, Maximillion always told her, *stick to the truth or nothing like it. There is no safe middle ground.*

"I'm from the Central Network."

"How do you know Marguerite?"

"Distant cousins."

Her gaze tapered. "You said friends."

"Ah ... better friends than family."

"Marguerite has no family. She has worked for me before."

Isadora cleared her throat with a sheepish smile. "They don't claim me. A bit too ... free-spirited for their taste."

"Is that why you are in the East instead of your Network?"

"Yes."

Fiona seemed to think that over, then nodded. Rogue witches traveling across borders wasn't unheard of these days, although all the skirmishes at the Network boundaries had caused a lot of travel to slow. "You've heard of La Torra?"

"A little."

Fiona tilted her head to the side. "It's ... odd."

Isadora held her breath, waiting for more of an explanation or to be called out as an imposter, but Fiona fell quiet. What felt like an eternity passed in silence.

Overhead, a distant screech caught her ear. Isadora craned her head back. A bird of prey with broad, pearl-like wings, speckled a deep umber, swooped past them. The unfurled wings were twice as long as she was. She'd heard of them, the *aquila*. Sharp, intelligent predators. Not unlike dragons, in some respects, though these reminded her more of magnificent, enormous eagles.

The aquila plummeted into the white-capped waves, talons extended, then burst away with a silvery fish in its grasp. It turned, headed for the horizon, and disappeared into the sky.

Isadora shuddered.

"Frightening birds," Fiona said, watching it disappear. "They can use a little magic and become smaller or bigger and fool their prey. One never knows what an aquila will do. They love La Torra. It's quiet."

"Ah," Isadora said, unable to fathom how an aquila would need to be any bigger.

Sailors chattered in the background, providing a soft backdrop of noise against the crashing waves. Isadora used the quiet stretch to translate in her head, recognizing *delivery* and *schedule* and *The Great One*. They hadn't come far, but the distant storm seemed to have tripled in size. Fiona pointed to the water. In the distance, the edges of a castle were barely distinguishable from the rolling waves.

"La Torra. We'll arrive soon." A rueful smile swept her blocky face. "Goddess mother Prana willing."

Isadora gulped as she glanced at the broiling clouds, which seemed to race over each other. They'd left the shore probably thirty minutes before, which meant the island wasn't far from land.

Something in the water caught her eye. She leaned forward. A flash of light glinting off scales turned into a fathomless darkness. Whatever she saw had been deep red, almost burgundy. She shook her head. Almost like ...

A dragon.

"How long have you ... ah ... worked here?" Isadora asked Fiona.

"Twenty years."

"A long time."

Fiona shrugged.

"Do you like it?" Isadora asked.

Fiona hesitated, a flicker of something moving in her gaze. "Yes. It's ... mine."

"Yours?"

She pressed a palm to her chest. "It lives here. It's tethered to me."

"Oh."

Fiona gestured back to the water. "My husband is out there."

"The water?"

"A sailor. Sometimes, when La Torra seems so small, as

if the ocean will eat me, I ... feel him closer. It's why I sleep on our boat."

She gestured to a boat bobbing in the thick waves on the other side of the now-visible island.

"Oh."

La Torra was a little thing. Anguis, before it burned to ashes, had been greater in size than the whole island. In the middle stood the stone castle she'd seen painted on the map. The main body of the castle was a wide circle seven floors high and at least as wide. Spindly trees with only high branches ringed it, stark against the pale, sandy beach. The windows were tapered to points at the bottom and the top, and colors stained individual glass panes, which sparkled despite the approaching storm. The castle walls had warmth. The stones were a lovely, reddish hue laced with veins of butter yellow. Windows dotted every floor except for the top two levels, which were a solid ring of dirty stone, as if they'd rotted from the inside out.

"It's ... lovely," Isadora said.

Fiona shrugged. "Made for vagabonds. You will fit."

Isadora let that go.

Three Guardians stood on a short, wooden pier when the boat pulled in. Fiona cut a sharp glance to Isadora.

"No flirting, speaking, or looking at the Guardians."

Fiona stood, and Isadora hastily followed. They stepped onto the island together. The Guardians gazed past her, as if she didn't exist. Overhead, an aquila soared, calling out. Fiona marched down the pier with a determined stride.

"Come," she called over her shoulder. "Much to do. First, I will show you to the *lavanda*."

Several wooden crates dropped to the pier. The three Guardians stepped toward them, chatting with the sailors unloading armfuls of firewood bound by twine. Barrels of liquid sloshed on the back of the boat. The word *vino* was painted across most of the barrels, and the others read *acqua*. Wine and water.

Fiona led Isadora through a side door. Open windows spilled sunshine into the hallway, casting puddles of light on a well-worn stone floor lined with rugs. Isadora fought the urge to cringe. She hadn't even worn her best shoes. She didn't have clothes to wear or her hairbrush. Did witches dress up here? Where would she sleep?

They swept down a long hallway circling the outer wall. Windows and paintings and a thick, busy wallpaper decorated the space. Isadora stared at it in fascination. Paper on walls?

"Cecelia's maids work upstairs," Fiona said, "on the third floor. You'll know them by their cuff links. Don't speak with them. They should not leave their floor, and you shall stay in the *lavanda*. If you see them, act as if you don't, then report them to me immediately."

"Why?"

"Don't question the rules."

Fiona plucked at Isadora's sleeve, pulling her out of the hallway and into another room.

"Here's the *lavanda*."

Piles of clothes, sheets, dresses, aprons, and what appeared to be uniforms covered the floor. The square room boasted more cabinets than floor space, and two glass doors against the far wall opened onto a courtyard stretched with ropes. Aside from the sheer number of clothes, not much was here. Fiona sorted through a few cupboards. She spoke slowly.

"Everything you'll need is here." She cast her gaze around the seemingly endless piles of laundry. "If I were you, I'd start now."

Laundry was scattered like the dirt piles of burrowing gnomes. Isadora lost count at fifteen, with one pile as high as her head. With this much laundry, weeks might pass before she could venture out to find Lucey.

"So much?"

Fiona scowled. "The previous *lavanda* maid drank too much *vino*, and the resupply was late. We're out of linens." Fiona gestured to the empty cupboards. "It's why I had you guarantee your friend. The Great One would have gone *pazzo* if no one caught it up soon, and the last maid couldn't keep up. No one was sad when she fell ill."

"Can no one else do it?"

Fiona scoffed. "We know our place. None would stoop so low again. Your room is up those stairs." She pointed to a set of spiral stairs outside in the courtyard. "Dinner is at 7:30 every evening, breakfast at 5:00. See that little bell on the wall? It will ring when we're ready for you. Your lunches are brought here. Don't wander the castle, don't speak with any Guardians, and don't use magic."

Isadora choked. "What?"

Fiona jabbed a finger at her. "No. Magic. The Great One forbids you to use it. Break the rule, and you'll drown."

"But ... why?"

"The Great One's rules. This book may help."

How many rules could Cecelia have? Fiona reached into a nearby cupboard, extracting an old tome with brittle paper and a flaking exterior. Like most books in the Eastern Network, the title was an entire sentence.

The Book of the World's Greatest Laundry Secrets and Other Things You Never Knew About Silk.

"May Prana be with you."

Fiona left, skirt swaying. Isadora stared at the door with

a surreal sense of disbelief. Her eyes grazed the piles of laundry. She tipped her head back and groaned.

What had she gotten into now?

SANNA TOSSED her only other piece of clothing into a blanket, tied it in a roll, and slung it over her back. Jesse did the same. She gave him a quick nod, and he returned the gesture. Some of the tightness in her chest relaxed. If she was making the wrong decision to leave Letum Wood and go with Tashi, at least she was making it with Jesse.

Tashi wore a narrow object on a strip of leather around her neck. It was as long and thin as Sanna's pinky, with holes down the side. Pearlescent, too thin to be wood but too thick to be paper. Sanna could only guess at what it was. Tashi pressed her lips to it and blew. No sound issued.

Then another dragon glided down from the sky.

Dusty brown wings and a small body—compared to Luteis and Elis—landed gracefully on the ground. Standing straight up, he barely reached the top of Luteis's leg, possibly only two or three times taller than Sanna. Broad shoulders and wide wingspan with a short torso made this dragon seem ideal for speed. Beady black eyes and a longer snout, tapering to a point, locked gazes with her. It shrieked and pranced back, surprisingly lithe on its feet. She almost swallowed her tongue.

"There's more?" she cried.

"Halloa, Tenzin." Tashi turned to Sanna. "This is Tenzin, my escort back to the West. He's a desert dragon. I'll explain later. We shouldn't stay here long. Yushi awaits."

Tenzin snarled at Luteis but allowed Tashi to touch his

wing. He didn't glimmer like the forest dragons. His scales were a murky tan without luster, and they bristled along his neck when Luteis sniffed the air. Around his belly and shoulders was strapped a square piece of leather and a rope that looped around the top of his neck but avoided his face. Tashi grabbed a rope ladder and climbed up it, settling onto a square patch of long haired, ebony fur.

"Although you'll see it yourself soon enough," she said, grasping the rope, "desert dragons aren't as intelligent as forest or mountain dragons. They have to be trained to fly with witches. They can't communicate through speech or thought. They have no language except desperation. They're as feral as your forest lions."

When Tashi tugged the rope in her hands gently to the right, Tenzin shuffled that way.

Luteis remained uncharacteristically quiet. Sanna pressed a hand to his foreleg. He nudged her back.

"Come," Tashi called. "Let's get this ride over with. It may get bumpy over the desert."

Tenzin coiled back, then sprang into the air. His lithe, nimble size made it easy for him to navigate the gargantuan trunks of Letum Wood. Within seconds, he disappeared in the complicated canopy.

This, Luteis said, *will be an interesting flight.*

Luteis lowered his tail, and Sanna scrambled all the way up, running along his spine. He took to the sky.

You've been quiet, she said to him.

Deasylva has never spoken of any of this to me.

I've always thought she's trying to hide something.

For once, Luteis didn't defend her.

The wind caught Sanna's hair as they flew over Letum Wood, heading directly west. The refreshing, cool air roused her thoughts, clearing her head. Sanna sank into the silence, grateful Luteis seemed as tentative as she. Jesse and Elis also ventured no words. Deep grooves of concentration lined Jesse's forehead. Tashi flew ahead of them and slightly higher, her hair flapping behind her like banners.

By dawn, they reached the edge of the forest. Sanna sucked in a sharp breath. Ahead of them sprawled nothing but desert and sand as far as she could see. Only the whip of the wind and the unbroken silence below rang in Sanna's ears. She met Jesse's gaze, but his eyes revealed nothing of his thoughts. By the time morning broke on the distant horizon, Letum Wood lay too far behind to see. Still, Sanna kept searching for it.

Tashi pulled on the rope around Tenzin's back. He slowed, banking alongside Elis, whose head drooped dangerously low. Elis lifted it again, eyes flashing, but it soon began to droop again.

"Do you need a break?" Tashi called.

"Yes," Jesse said. "He's new to flying. This is too much for him."

Surprise registered in Tashi's eyes.

"Is he young?"

"Fifty-five."

Tashi blinked. "We've been flying less than six hours. He cannot maintain?"

Jesse's shoulders straightened, and his nostrils flared. "He's only been flying for four weeks. This has been monumental for him."

"Four weeks? You jest."

"A break," Sanna called. "When can we have one for him?"

Tashi pointed ahead.

"There's an oasis not far away. We'll stop there for a

short rest. Tenzin's getting restless. I think a storm is coming, so we can't stop long."

Tashi nodded once, to a vague spot Sanna couldn't see in the distance. Sanna nodded while Luteis spoke to Elis.

Can he make it? Sanna asked Luteis.

He will try.

Elis's wings beat with determined ferocity. Even if he *could* make it to the oasis, what would they do during the storm? Sanna kept her thoughts to herself but exchanged a concerned glance with Jesse. Whatever they had to fly in or through, Luteis could likely manage. His wings were broader and longer than Tenzin's, with one wingbeat for Tenzin's three—but he couldn't carry Elis. And one short reprieve wouldn't restore Elis's strength.

The edge of something emerald glimmered not far away. Though it was only early morning, the heat would be intense once they dropped below the clouds. Waves of heat shimmered on the ground.

Tashi ordered Tenzin lower. Elis gulped the air greedily as they dropped, which seemed to restore some of his vitality. Before Sanna knew it, they had reached the ground. Elis collapsed, shuddering as he pressed his body into the sand with a limp *thud*.

Tashi pointed to a grouping of scraggly bushes along the ground. "Water is over here."

Clumps of greenish-yellow fronds sprouted in a wild array that gave shade to the sand and leafy undergrowth. The smell of water thickened the air. Luteis nudged Elis, who struggled through the sand toward a small pond hidden in the thick cluster of leaves. Without the wind, sweat ringed Sanna's armpits almost immediately. Luteis motioned her to the water.

"No," she said. "You, Elis, and Tenzin first."

Tashi listened, eyes narrowed.

Sanna ignored her, allowing the dragons to drink first. Then she splashed herself with the water and drank deeply from cupped hands. It tasted brackish and mossy, but the liquid restored her parched throat. Jesse dropped to his knees and dunked his head into the pool.

After drinking, Tashi peered to the west with a frown. "We'll rest an hour; then we must leave."

"Elis won't be able to fly again that soon."

Elis lay with his eyes closed near the edge of the small lake. His wings drooped limp on the sand, twitching, a testament to his already-deep sleep.

"It's another eighteen hours of flight," Tashi said. "There are two more oases we can stop at for breaks, but the next one is ten hours away."

"Then Elis needs a long break."

Tenzin lifted his snout toward the west, then shrieked. His scales stood straight up along the ridge on his back. Sanna followed his gaze. A smudge clouded the distant horizon. Was that a brown cloud? With nothing to obscure the sky, she felt open. Exposed.

Such an unnerving, barren place.

"Storms are fine," Sanna said. "The water will be good for them."

Tashi's gaze darkened. "This is no forest storm. If Elis needs a long break, then a long break he shall get. It's time to drink your fill and then prepare. The storm will be here within the hour."

Sanna frowned. "But there are no clouds."

Tashi looked at Luteis, who watched her with his glittering, intelligent eyes.

This is no ordinary storm, he said. *I can smell it. It's changing the air.*

"If you have a covering of any kind, now is the time to get it ready." Tashi reached for Tenzin. "The sand is almost here."

~

THE STORM DESCENDED EXACTLY as Tashi predicted.

It grew on the horizon like a living thing, filling everything in sight and howling with a deep burr that rattled Sanna's teeth. Brushes of wind flapped at her hair only minutes before the sandy wrath descended with full strength.

Luteis lay on the ground near the oasis and spread his wings wide, enfolding Sanna, Tashi, and Tenzin. He coiled his neck and tucked his head inside the circle. Sanna briefly caught a glimpse of Jesse's bright eyes before he disappeared in a cocoon of Elis's making. Seconds later, the entire world became a gritty blur.

Sand infused the air, filling Sanna's nose, mouth, and lungs with its tenacious grit. Luteis's wings held off the buffeting wind, but sand skittered underneath in piles.

Does the sand hurt your scales? she asked, pulling her knees into her chest and leaning into his foreleg. The scales were smooth and warm, but the air soon felt stifling hot. Tashi and Tenzin gave no complaint—they were no doubt used to heat far worse than this—but sweat rolled down Tashi's face.

No. But it is not very comfortable. Like someone scratching too hard. Already it begins to weigh on my wings.

Sweat trickled down her back. At first, they sat in the silence, unable to hear over the wild, portentious winds. Sanna thought she heard a scream every now and then. A wild, horrific sound.

Thank you for shielding me.

He nudged her with his nose. *We should have tried to fly above it. You will have to ask Tashi if it's possible.*

If it's this wild, it may be a very high storm.

I have flown above thunderstorms before.

Elis couldn't have made it.

Perhaps not.

The thought sent a shiver through Sanna. Streaking lightning. Booming thunder. How much louder would it be if she were flying through the thick of it? She drew her arms tighter around her legs, cognizant of just how far from home they'd come. Tashi curled in a ball in the very center of the circle and closed her eyes. Tenzin stared at them, yellow eyes slitted. His gaze never wavered, not even to sleep.

Do you think we made a mistake following Tashi? Sanna asked. *What if she's lying? Perhaps she's taking us away from Letum Wood for other reasons.*

I thought of this myself.

And?

Why would she have this other dragon? What could her motivation be?

Sanna sank into this question with relief, grateful to have something to chew on that stifled her fear of the howling storm.

I can only think that she works for poachers and is going to attack the rest of the brood, Sanna said.

That would certainly be possible without taking us away from Letum Wood.

Sanna thought of Daid. It wasn't Daid's fault that a mountain-dragon spy had descended at the wrong time. And why did she bear the burden of his loss? Her mind wandered to Isadora.

She turned that thought away, throat aching.

It could mean the downfall of your race, if Tashi and Tenzin do have nefarious plans, she said. *I think we shouldn't trust too easily.*

He said nothing but seemed to fall into a deeper, brooding silence. Sanna thought of Cara and the hatchlings and hoped they were safe. Briefly, she thought of Mam. Then, with Daid on her mind, she slipped into a restless sleep filled with dreams of witches screaming and dragons plummeting from the sky.

CHAPTER
ELEVEN

In Isadora's new room, a round, old table stood against one wall, near a narrow cot she presumed to be a bed.

The walls were white, bare, and riddled with holes along the bottom. A suspicious scuttling echoed in the inner walls—she hoped it wasn't some form of island rat. Her door opened to an uninterrupted view of the ocean and the stormy sky beyond, which helped.

Overall, she had little more space than a closet.

On the floor stood an oak chest. Isadora pried open the heavy lid to find clothes inside. Marguerite's, no doubt. Most were made of light linen, perfect for such a mild climate. They were several sizes too large, but she could fix one or two with a tailoring incantation Pearl had taught her.

No magic, Fiona had said.

Or not.

Isadora sank onto the bed, lost in the silence. It certainly wasn't the first time she'd lived without magic— but now that she'd gotten used to it, curbing her use would be difficult. Only the occasional, high-pitched shriek of an aquila outside interrupted the eerie quiet. Two of the giant predators soared in a strange, circular dance, changing size and color with every spin. Foamy clouds had moved in overhead, then floated on toward the horizon.

For a long time, she fell into thought, eyes on the distant, churning sky. Amidst all her questions—and intense fears—she thought of Sanna.

What was she doing?

What would she think of the ocean?

Hate it, probably. Isadora had gotten used to the openness of life outside the trees since moving to Pearl's, but this felt different. A pang of sadness for her sister struck her. How small Sanna's life must feel without wild adventures in distant places.

"What in the good gods happened?"

Isadora shot to her feet, eyes wide. Maximillion stood in the doorway, silhouetted by the light behind him. His hair stood straight up, as if the wind had slapped him from both sides at once. Her heart skipped a beat—so Sera had told him after all. His glacial eyes burned with chilling fury.

Now he'd kill her.

He stalked into the room. She lifted her hands. "Wait!"

He grabbed her arm, wrenched her away from the window, and shut her door at the same moment. "What happened?"

"I have the exact same question."

His hand gripped her arm above the elbow. His nostrils flared. "Now is not the time for your clever games. Tell me why you're here."

"It was an accident."

"Clearly."

Isadora backed up a step. He pressed his lips into a thin

line and drew in a breath. He calmed, but flames still flickered in his cold eyes. "Explain yourself."

Isadora related the events in full, starting with Sera appearing in his office and ending with Fiona leaving her in the *lavanda*. For a long time, Maximillion said nothing, staring hard at the ground with a hand over his mouth.

"This wasn't supposed to happen," he said.

"But it did. Why didn't Marguerite show?"

"Sick. Not sure what it is. I found her in her house when Sera came to tell me what had happened. By then, you were long gone."

Isadora sank back onto the edge of her narrow cot.

"Oh."

He stepped toward her. "Come. You're going back home."

"But—"

"You are not staying here where you are going to get yourself—and possibly others, including me—killed."

Emotions flooded her. Relief, for one. Confusion—even annoyance—for another. Sure, she didn't *want* to live in the lair of her greatest enemy ... but she didn't want to leave Lucey, either. Maximillion had made it seem like this was their best option when Marguerite was prepared to come here. That wouldn't have changed.

Isadora pulled her shoulders back. "No."

"What?"

"I'm not leaving. I'm here. I've already met Fiona and received my room. I want to stay and help Lucey."

"You're not competent."

"I can be."

"You are the worst witch for this job. Your execution of the language is passable, at best. You have no experience as a spy. Not to mention your lack of knowledge of how to work your own magic."

"I can work my magic!"

"You know it so well, do you?" he snapped. "Why do you see in a forest? Why is there no darkness? Why can you not see Lucey now? What limits do your powers have?"

Her reply stalled. Functionally, she *could* do the magic, but she didn't understand its depths, nor its purpose. Isadora scowled. Not that he had any room to brag about understanding the purpose of their magic!

Livid, she put her fists on her hips.

"I can do this!"

"You want to stay, do you? You think you're so ready?"

He said something in perfect *Ilese*, speaking so fast she only caught a word or two. If she hadn't known any better, she would have said he had grown up here. Fury bubbled under her skin. Of course, Maximillion would only see what she *couldn't* do. She couldn't even protest the unfairness, because he'd throw that in her face, too.

No, she'd have to take an entirely different tack.

"You've already half-poisoned a witch to death," she said.

"We did her a favor. There's no joy in being the *lavanda* maid. Besides, she did half the job herself. Her sickness wouldn't be so bad if she didn't drink so much wine."

"If you pull me out now, you're going to draw suspicion."

"You think that debacle at the dock didn't already? The Defenders will be investigating you. Cecelia won't let just anyone on this island."

"What will they find? That I grew up in Letum Wood as a forester? That I live in a small town with a sweet old lady who's obsessed with coffee?"

"They'll find out I mentor you."

"How? You've never told anyone. Only my family and Pearl know. You always make me go to elaborate means to avoid being seen near your office."

For another breathless moment, he said nothing. Isadora wondered if she'd actually been able to silence his qualms.

"Besides, what East Guard—or Defender—will travel deep enough into Letum Wood to research me? Far enough to find out about the dragons? None of them. Their own superstitions prevent it. Besides, they'd never be able to talk to my family. Luteis wouldn't allow it."

He turned away, driving a hand through his hair. "This is madness."

"Perhaps it's fate."

"Fate isn't real, you ingrate. How am I supposed to justify sending *you* into this?"

"You've never justified anything."

"That's beside the point," Maximillion snapped.

"Is it?"

He shot her a sharp glance. His mouth opened, then closed. He turned away with a growl. Being on La Torra, though terrifying, seemed better than spinning in circles at home, hoping Lucey didn't die a horrid death. Besides, how could she turn away so much ocean and sky?

He paced the small room. Surely, he could see the bitter truth. This was the only way to save Lucey. He stopped. His eyes had hardened into discs of ocean-blue flint. He drew himself up, chin tilted back.

"Fine. You want a chance to prove yourself? Take it."

She quelled her rush of excitement—and terror. The good gods. She hadn't thought he'd actually acquiesce.

"There are rules. One: you're not to use your powers.

Ever. Magic only if it's absolutely required to preserve your life."

"You used magic to come here."

"But not *on* La Torra."

"Then how did you get here?"

"That's no business of yours. Besides, I can afford a little risk because I'm not living here and Cecelia knows what I am. You can't."

How in the name of the good gods could he be here without having used magic on the island? A thousand questions rushed to the tip of her tongue, but she forced them back.

"Of course not."

"No magic. Not even a breath of it. Not a hint. Cecelia is rigidly strict about it."

"Why?"

"No one knows. Can you maintain that for weeks at a time?"

She thought of the restlessness of the powers, her need for Letum Wood. Her certainty waned.

Could she do this?

"I think I can."

"You better know it."

He paused, staring hard at her. She swallowed. "I can."

"Two: never breathe a word about your real life."

"Obviously."

"Witches in the East don't clasp hands. They kiss each other on each cheek. No bowing. Don't ever thank a superior verbally, simply avert your eyes. They don't drink tea here but have wine at every meal and sometimes between. It's a weaker version of the wine you know, but they get raving drunk often enough. No one should care that you're from the Central Network, not with borders as porous as these, but do your best to blend in anyway. Because of the prohibition against magic, they have a hard time staffing this place. Your rank is the lowest of all of them."

He pulled a book from his pocket. She almost cried in relief. Her *Ilese* study book! She'd be able to study the language in the evenings, now. When she reached for it, Maximillion held it back, forcing her to meet his gaze.

"Notice everything you can about this place. Details. Facts. Observations. Nothing is wasted."

"Should I try to find Lucey?"

"No. Observe. Do nothing without my authorization."

"How do I—"

"You don't. I'll find you. Be careful." His lips twisted, as if he'd sucked on a lemon. "With Lucey incarcerated, we can't afford to lose someone with your potential."

"Don't trip over the compliment."

"Do you understand?"

"Yes."

A flicker of something else moved in his eyes. Something vulnerable and raw. Isadora accepted the book, stuffing aside the urge to ask him why he had it on him in the first place. As if he'd planned on her staying all along. Maximillion yanked his hand back before she could touch him. His expression returned to its usual stoic indifference.

"No communication with anyone. I will be in touch with you. If you're in danger, transport to Letum Wood, as deep as you can. Transport again to four different spots before walking for thirty minutes in an unorganized fashion and then transporting to Pearl's. I will come to you."

If she transported, they could follow her magic. But if she transported around Letum Wood several times, they probably wouldn't follow. Walking in an unpredictable way would prevent the witches from finding her magic immediately when she transported a final time.

Such an elaborate scheme.

He eyed her.

"Good luck, Isadora. You'll certainly need it."

"I can do this."

He peered outside, then stepped out and closed the door behind him. Isadora ran to the window, but by the time she'd made it, he had already disappeared, leaving her with a hollow feeling in her belly and a stomach full of fear.

THE BOOK *of the World's Greatest Laundry Secrets and Other Things You Never Knew About Silk* became Isadora's best friend.

And worst enemy.

Explicit instructions on the laundry process filled every page, requiring elaborate, headache-inducing translations—not to mention hand-brewed potions. At least she could translate most of it, thanks to her study book, but it consumed hours of time. Isadora spent the rest of the day in the laundry room, alternately reading the instructions and staring at the piles and piles and *piles* of laundry.

Had the other *lavanda* maid really done nothing? Was it so hard to staff this lovely place—the horrific prison overhead aside?

The sun sank closer to the horizon as she leaned against a counter and turned a page that detailed the temperature of water based on color and type of fabric. The options ranged from lukewarm to warm to hot to boiling. How could she even tell? Her mind spun with instructions on dye creation, types of fabric to iron based on relative humidity, and potions for the perfect soap base for dense wool. All the information entered her mind, then vanished again.

"Find one thing to do," she murmured, reciting advice Mam had given her when she was a little girl, staring at the teacups, unsure where to start. "Then do it."

Isadora gazed around.

Exploring the *lavanda* seemed a better place to start. She set the book aside.

Irons hung from the wall in various states of disrepair—some of them wider than she was. Odd contraptions that must have been drying racks stood along another wall, near mounds of driftwood, firewood, and massive cauldrons. Wooden barrels were stacked along another wall—they hadn't been there before when Fiona first brought her in, nor had the firewood. How could she use such massive barrels? No doubt all the freshwater had to be shipped in—she doubted there'd be any here naturally.

The back door opened onto a small courtyard surrounded by a high stone wall. Yards of twine hung a little higher than her head. Another drying area, no doubt. In the far-right corner lurked an old well, which smelled as briny as the outdoors. Could she wash clothes in sea water?

There wasn't much more to discover. How was she supposed to find Lucey? Her eyes trailed up, above her, but she couldn't see the strange stones of Carcere.

"Sorting next," she said, clapping her hands.

The book specified that everything washed together had to be the same color, so she shoved her sleeves up. Deciding it would be safest to start washing the whites, she grabbed several sheets, towels, and grungy Guardian shirts and tucked them into one spot. An hour passed, and she'd created twenty new piles. The torches sprang to life when she lit them with a piece of flint, casting shadows in the corners.

Isadora stepped back with a satisfied sigh.

"Not bad."

Strands of the sunset colored the sky as the sun sank to its watery grave. The sound of approaching footsteps came from the hall, drawing her from her thoughts. She straightened. A slender man stood in the doorway. His crisp, raven hair shone in the light, cut so it tapered around his ears and face. He'd rolled the sleeves of his white shirt halfway up his arms, exposing muscular forearms.

"You did it wrong," he said.

Shock flooded her. Her eyes widened. Had he just spoken in the common language?

"What?"

He advanced, moving with an easy finesse. He wore a pair of loose linen pants that flapped around his legs. No shoes, which seemed odd. She swallowed when he motioned to the piles surrounding her in colorful mounds.

"Magic isn't allowed here," he said, his voice lightly accented, almost lyrical. Hesitation lingered in his gaze. His dark skin and hair stood in stark contrast to his white shirt.

"I-I didn't use magic to sort them."

"Good."

He strode across the room, shoving and kicking all the piles into one great lump, leaving open space around the new central pile.

"Stop! I just spent an hour—"

"You wasted an hour."

A shirt flew to the top of the pile with a quiet flutter.

"Wait, please. I just—"

"You sort wrong," he said, *tsking* under his breath. "Not

just by color, but by fabric, too. See this? It's silk. If you wash it with cotton?"

He clucked, throwing a filthy apron into a corner with other kitchen towels. All her questions dissipated.

"I—"

"And no soap on the whites."

"But why?"

He motioned to a cupboard. Vials of a pearlescent, filmy solution waited inside. "The potion you use with whites is finicky. Water must be a certain temperature, but it's almost impossible to nail down. If you don't, the whites will turn gray. If that happens? I suggest swimming home, particularly if the mistake is made with one of The Great One's dresses."

Isadora studied him as he sorted through the laundry. He must be some kind of servant here. A butler? No. No one visited here, and Fiona seemed to rule the castle. No one with his poise and deep eyes would be a servant.

"How am I supposed to get into the barrels?"

"Pry open the top." His eyes darted to the wall when footsteps sounded in the hallway. He froze, then resumed sorting—albeit faster than before—when the noise faded.

Her faint echo of his instructions faded in the air. "Pry open the—"

How did one pry those open, anyway? He gestured impatiently toward the wall, where a metal crowbar leaned against the stone.

"With that. Use the bucket to put water into the cauldron. Don't waste any. We only receive water every six weeks."

"There are spells that—"

"Never speak of magic again."

The coldness in his voice arrested her suggestion. Isadora clamped her mouth shut.

He frowned, and the expression softened his face. "That firewood and water has to last at least six weeks, until the next resupply. Don't waste a twig or a drop. Reuse the water if you can. Wash the filthiest things together."

Ah, that explained it. The previous *lavanda* maid must have been out of water and firewood, which accounted for the ridiculous amount of laundry strewn around the floor.

"The driftwood burns in different colors, too, so beware."

"I—"

The sound of a deep gong rippled through the air. He stopped and glanced over his shoulder toward the hall. When he turned back to Isadora, he seemed hurried.

"When it comes to silk, always by hand. Cold water, and no potion except the light blue one in the far corner."

"The book says there's a spell that works beautifully for silks."

"Don't use it."

"Then why even read the book?"

"There's good information in there."

"Which is good and which bad?"

"Trust me on the silk."

"Why should I?"

He glanced at her, eyes widening. Isadora fought the temptation to apologize. She hadn't done anything wrong, and she didn't know him at all.

His shoulders relaxed a little, although his gaze remained sharp.

"Because I worked the *lavanda* last year, when I had no place or honor."

"What do you do this year?"

"Cleaning. Fiona runs the castle, I clean, and three cooks work in the kitchen. The Guardians staff Carcere. The Great One has her own staff of maids who are kept separate from us. She doesn't like them interacting with us."

"Why?"

"The Great One has many rules."

Isadora's rank on the bottom rung implied restrictions, no doubt. Like not being allowed to wander the castle, which Fiona had alluded to, but Isadora had hoped been a formality. Even if she snuck out from under Fiona's studious gaze, others would recognize her.

A problem.

"Cleaning is better than laundry?" she asked.

"Oh, much. Much, much better. You are compared with the lichen on the stones. The, uh, waste of the fish in the sea. A *lavanda* servant is—"

"I get it. I get it. Why are you helping me?"

He paused. "Because I'm from the West, and I understand how it feels to be here. They're obsessed with class, and it's odd. Rich. Poor. Servant. *Lavanda*. Without social strata, they fall apart. The sooner you learn, the better."

"Thanks. I think."

"Best of luck to you."

He spun on his heels and headed for the door. Isadora rushed after him. "Wait!"

He stopped just outside the door, eyebrows lifted.

"What's your name?"

"They call me Lorenzo."

Lorenzo turned around and left, the sound of his gentle footfalls echoing in his wake. The words *place* and *honor* rang in her ears. With determination, she shoved her sleeves farther up her arms, turned around, and faced the piles yet again.

ISADORA DIDN'T LEAVE the lavanda the next day.

Lighting the fire, lugging the heavy cauldron into the dry fireplace, and filling bucket after bucket of water occupied most of her day. Not to mention scrubbing the shirts on the washboard, wringing out the clothes, hanging them to dry, ironing them once the hot breeze whisked the moisture away, and folding them. She didn't dare venture into the castle to put the finished laundry away but left it in neat piles. Fiona's command not to wander rang in her ears.

When she woke the next morning, the finished laundry was gone. Only a note remained.

Work faster.

She pitched it into the fire.

Without the monstrous pile of bedsheets clogging the floor, the towels, servants' stockings, washcloths, and elegant silk garments that frightened her to death could occupy her attention.

Meals—and not bad food at that—had shown up for her the day before. Most of it was dry, with too much salt, but it satisfied her ravenous hunger. The meals arrived again on the second day, which passed in hours of backbreaking work that reminded her of spring planting in Anguis.

The morning of her third day, Isadora held up a mousy brown apron with a groan.

"Too cold," she cried, rubbing a hand over her face. What now? The once-white apron looked like the hairball of a screaming gnome. She shoved the ruined garment back into the bucket and grabbed *The Book of the World's Greatest Laundry Secrets and Other Things You Never Knew About Silk.*

There had to be some sort of instructions for whitening

fabrics. While she frantically shuffled through the pages, footsteps sounded in the hall. Her gazed flicked up just as a tall body filled the doorway.

"*Idiota!*"

Isadora shrank back, clutching the book to her chest. A wiry man with a mop of dark hair and fire in his eyes advanced on her, clutching what appeared to be a chef's hat. She swallowed hard. She hadn't washed any hats ...

... had she?

He shoved it in her face, knuckles white. A single, round tomato stain splattered the top of the hat. Words flew off his tongue at an alarming rate—she couldn't decipher a single one.

"*Regretta*," she stammered. "So sorry... er ... *mucha regretta?*"

He hurled the hat onto a pile—of shirts, which wasn't even kitchen laundry—threw his hands in the air, and stalked out. Isadora blinked and swallowed hard to force the tears back.

"Two mistakes," she said, soothed by the sound of her own voice. "Of course I'm going to make mistakes. Two is ... n-nothing."

The logic didn't comfort her.

Before she could sink too far into her frustration and self-pity, Fiona's head popped into the *lavanda*.

"Breakfast." She waved her hand. "Come. I will introduce you to the staff now."

Spurred by curiosity and relieved she didn't have to go alone, Isadora followed her into the hall and to the right. The hallway flowed in a circle, illuminated with beams of light from the long, colored windows. They walked into another hallway that branched away from the main circle.

Two words hung above the door mantle on an elegant, dried piece of driftwood.

Solo coraggioso.

"Servant?" she asked Fiona, then immediately shook her head. The first word meant ... licorice? *Ilese* had a strange habit of reversing sounds on any given word. She could never remember which ones. "No ..."

The corner of Fiona's mouth lifted. "You'll figure it out one day."

They turned down a new hall, which branched right and left. The smell of porridge drifted on the air, along with several loud, laughing voices. Her palms began to sweat. If she could help Daid fight Talis, she could walk into a dining room and eat breakfast. More laughter rang out.

At least they *sounded* friendly.

Fiona nudged her to the right, then grabbed her arm to stop her. Isadora froze in the doorway. Five witches stared at her from the dining room. All laughter immediately ceased. Like Fiona, nearly all of them had the same warm skin and rich, black hair like shimmering coal, so unlike Isadora's dark blonde waves.

The moments that passed seemed interminable. Lorenzo stood at the far end holding a pewter mug. His eyebrows lifted with interest, but he said nothing to save her from the heavy awkwardness. Between them lay an irregular dining table cobbled together from pieces of driftwood.

Fiona broke the quiet with a calm, even voice.

"This is Isadora." She stretched her name out to *Eesadorra.* "She's running the *lavanda.*"

Based on the dismissal on most of their faces—two of them turned back to plates full of food, and two rolled their eyes—she imagined Fiona hadn't needed to announce that much.

The voice that had been laughing the loudest—the cook who had screamed at her only minutes before—patted a new hat and glared at her. Two other cooks sat around the table. Someone said *The Great One*, and the rest laughed uproariously. Snatches of *Ilese* floated to Isadora here and there, but she struggled with their rapid-fire speech.

"Better than I expected," Fiona mumbled under her breath, then tapped Isadora's elbow. "Go. Before the wine turns cold."

Fiona shuffled toward the far end, near Lorenzo. Before Isadora could step up to the table, the cooks rose. Their chairs grated against the stone floor as they shoved back, casting Isadora wary glances before exiting through another doorway. The good gods, but they acted like they couldn't leave fast enough.

Only Lorenzo and Fiona, who spoke quietly together at the end of the table, remained. With a piece of white chalk, Lorenzo wrote on a long wooden board hanging on the wall. Fiona glanced at it often, also writing with a piece of chalk. The duties of the house, it appeared.

"Help yourself," Lorenzo called without looking at Isadora. He waved a hand toward the sideboard but continued to regard the wall.

"Ah, thank you."

Fiona sent her a quizzical glance, and Isadora realized her faux pas too late. *Never say thank you to a superior,* Maximillion had said. Lorenzo cleared his throat, a hand in front of his lips. Isadora turned away, cheeks burning.

Sunlight warmed the room, highlighting aprons hanging from the wall. A vase of flowers decorated the middle of the table. Broken remnants of what appeared to have once been crackers filled a pewter bowl. Next to it was a jug of warmed wine and a crock of jam.

After scraping the cracker crumbs into her bowl and topping them with a dash of jam, she pulled her translation book out of her pocket and set it on the table. Grumpy cooks or not, the change of scenery felt better. The well-creased pages flopped open to the middle. In between saccharine-sweet bites, Isadora murmured verb conjugations.

Fiona called over her shoulder as she bustled by, "*Lucere* is said as *loo-sare*, not *looser*."

Isadora repeated it. Fiona nodded. Instead of voicing her thanks, Isadora averted her eyes. Fiona bustled off with a *tsk*.

"It will come to you; don't worry," Lorenzo said as he leaned against the table.

"They don't like ... ah ..." She flipped through the book, consulted a page, then said, "Foreigners?"

He pointed to the book. "Foreigners are fine. We are all a bit ... strange. It's the *lavanda* maid they don't like. But it's good you are trying to learn. The others will eventually warm up to you if you just try. Because you are nothing, that means they are something. They rank above you. To them, that feels good."

Odd logic.

Lorenzo waved a hand. "The East." He shook his head. "They love their rules."

Isadora cast a sidelong glance toward the kitchen. "I suppose accidentally missing a stain on a hat hasn't helped my reputation."

He winced. "Certainly not. It was Ernesto's favorite."

"It's not my fault he stained it!"

He shrugged. "You are the *lavanda*."

"No. I work *in* the *lavanda*."

"There is no difference."

Isadora fought the urge to roll her eyes. What was so bad about doing laundry, anyway?

Lorenzo straightened. "You are young. One day, you'll advance and be a little less despised. Take courage. Have a good day, yes?"

"You as well."

He folded his hands behind his back and walked away. Isadora hesitated, saw other bowls left on the table, and decided to leave hers. She gathered her book, tucked it in her pocket, and rubbed her soon-to-be-pruney fingers together. At this rate, she'd never gather any information to help Lucey.

With a sigh, she returned to her laundry.

CHAPTER

TWELVE

The wind stopped all of a sudden.

Sanna woke up, startled by the quiet. Sand carpeted her like a layer of fine silt. She sat up and shook it off, the top of her head grazing Luteis's wing, which drooped from the weight of the sand. Luteis stirred. A downpour of sand cascaded off his neck.

It appears we survived, he said, musing.

"Come on," Tashi called, her voice muffled by his wings. Somehow, she'd slipped out.

The thick, stifling air created by the heat of Luteis's body cleared as soon as he withdrew his wings. A rippling red sun rose on the horizon in a bright-orange wash. Had the storm lasted through the night?

The oasis lay scattered in ruins. Leaves were completely ripped away, leaving shreds in the sand. Dirt muddied the water now—not even Tenzin would drink it. A small trickle bubbled up from below.

They wouldn't be able to drink it now, even though her stomach grumbled and her dry throat longed for a cool drink. She wondered if the oasis would survive. Tashi rubbed the sand from her thick hair. Dust coated her nose and forehead.

"Welcome to the West."

A monstrous pile of sand next to them shifted, then shook. Elis straightened up, his scales peeking through layers of dust. His head popped free, his eyes groggy. He stood slowly, Jesse at his side, the same dusty color as all the rest.

"Get a good rest, then?" Tashi asked Elis with a laugh.

Elis grumbled.

Will he be able to fly? Sanna asked Luteis.

He must, mustn't he?

Sanna hesitated. What option did they have? Tashi grabbed Tenzin's rope, then climbed on the saddle.

"Let's get going," she said. "It's another ten hours to the next water, and I don't want to waste another minute getting there."

The heat posed no problem for Luteis and Elis—they were creatures of fire. But long distances and a lack of water would challenge their wings. Sanna stuffed her fears away. No use dwelling on it—whether forward or back, they had to fly. She climbed up Luteis's tail before standing on his shoulders and stretching her arms far overhead. When she glanced over, Jesse gave a quick nod, still brushing sand from his hair.

"You all right?" she asked.

He squinted one eye—the sun was already punishingly bright against such a white, unchanging vista.

"Think so."

"Then let's go," Sanna said. "I want to find out who's responsible for Daid's death."

~

"THEY SAY that the desert god, Saren, ruled over the West with his twin, Sarena," Tashi said at the second oasis. She touched the tip of a blooming purple cactus with bright pink flowers and long, foreboding spikes. "Legend says Sarena and Saren abandoned this land thousands of years ago. That when the mortals left to cross the ocean, banished by witches during the Mortal Wars, they took with them the gods."

Sanna's brow furrowed. She knew of the Mortal Wars, when witch and mortal fought against each other. Almorran magic was destroyed, so they said, and the forest dragons were saved by the pleading of her distant ancestors, who convinced Esmelda they were not traitors. But she'd never heard of *gods* being involved.

"Really?" Jesse asked.

Tashi nodded once, then straightened. Behind her, Elis gulped hungrily at the water, his wings trembling.

"I don't believe it, though," Tashi said. "It is one thing for a god to leave with the mortals he loved. But no goddess would abandon her desert or her land. Not Sarena. I think she hides and will return."

Sanna glanced at Luteis, who had the same questioning, uncertain gaze. He returned to drink at the pool—twice as large as the last one—leaving Sanna to her thoughts. Tenzin sniffed toward the west again but turned away, seemingly bored.

"Tomorrow," Tashi said, lying on a long leather roll on the sand. Tenzin curled up twenty paces away, tucked into a neat little ball. "We'll arrive then."

"Where, exactly, are we going?" Sanna asked.

Tashi yawned. "The ocean, of course. Yushi wishes to meet you."

"Right there!" Tashi shouted. "Land in the open sand field."

She pointed to the right, where the edge of a vast body of water—presumably the ocean—met giant mountains, creating sharp cliffs that soared above white-capped waves. The undulating desert landscape still loomed to the west, but signs of life cropped up here and there as they approached the ocean. Hints of green. Bushes amidst the mountains of sand. Red-rock cliffs littered the vista now, breaking up the monotony.

Elis's wingbeats were staggered and halting. Even Luteis drooped with fatigue, the ravenous cry of his belly like a song. Luteis normally ate every three days. Sedentary dragons ate less often. To fly this far with nothing except an occasional desert lizard had pushed him to his limits. Elis flagged again.

Fatigue is no reason to lower our guard, Luteis said. *We must be more alert than ever.*

Agreed.

The sandy knoll quickly approached. Luteis descended in a slow, gentle swirl. Far to the north, high, purplish peaks loomed as a backdrop to the looser, silt mountains here.

Beasts littered the fields below. More desert dragons, or so it appeared from their tawny colors. Amongst them were fluffy white creatures, running like wild things within expansive pens blocked off by walls of dark-red rock. Elis dropped like a boulder; he flew too slowly to take it carefully. He crashed with a moan near a pond, then stuck his head into the water and began to drink.

Luteis landed gently. Sanna slid down his foreleg, hand

on her knife. Tenzin landed thirty paces away, seeming almost … pleased. As soon as Tashi alighted, he bounced back into the air, flying fast for the craggy hills. He disappeared in the rocks.

Tashi joined Sanna, who watched a group of witches huddling together near a red-and-yellow rock outcropping. They stared at Luteis and Elis with wide eyes. Sanna thought she saw hints of other dragons stirring in the rocks above them. A flicker of tail. A distant grunt or a flash of wing. Too difficult to tell—their scales blended with the rocks.

Tashi called to the witches in a different language, then motioned for Sanna to follow.

"Come. We have a tent, a bath, and food for you," she said. "The dragons can hunt in the mountains just behind us."

I will be fine, Luteis said when Sanna turned to him.

Elis—

I will hunt for him, Luteis said, shaking off his wings. Water dripped from his lips. Elis peered back at the witches, his eyes flickering to the distant, craggy hills where Tenzin had disappeared.

"I'll go with Sanna," Jesse said before Luteis could ask. Luteis snorted.

I'll return shortly.

Elis let out a little croak—no doubt to say thanks—and lowered his head. His eyes remained open. By the time Luteis was a dot in the sky, Jesse and Sanna had turned to follow Tashi toward a cluster of tents not far away. The smell of roasting meat lingered in the air, making Sanna's stomach grumble.

"What do you think of all this?" Jesse whispered.

"I'm not sure yet."

"Trust her?"

Sanna frowned. "I'm not sure of that, either."

Looming above all her other questions—particularly about Yushi, whoever that was—lingered the greatest questions of all: Why were the mountain dragons spying on them?

And why had they killed Daid?

"Whistle," Jesse said, "the way the falling gnomes do if you're in danger or suspect it."

"Same."

Feeling marginally better, Sanna turned her attention to their new world.

A field of sandy tents stretched through an open space three or four times wider than the old meadow in Anguis. The sprawling canvas homes had flaps that fluttered open and closed. Large spaces, at least forty paces across, separated each tent. Brightly colored rocks, set in patterns, lined most of the areas—as if marking off boundaries.

It wasn't until she followed Tashi along the edge of the small, makeshift city that she realized the yards were for dragons. A young desert dragon curled up next to a tent, snarling as they passed by. A sloping forehead and slender shoulders made it seem more feminine. A metal chain anchored her to the ground.

In between blocks of homes were lanes where witches —and desert dragons—walked. Sanna eyed a young hatchling trailing a girl who couldn't be older than ten. The girl spoke quietly to the dragon, giggled, and ran. The desert dragon followed, bound by a chain.

"Are they all feral, you think?" Jesse murmured.

"Must be. She said they weren't as intelligent."

Witches spilled out of their tents, chattering in another language. Warm lamplight illuminated the tents from within, casting long shadows and heralding the night. The open tents showed few belongings. Cots. Blankets in bright colors. An open, red-rock box with clay plates or cups spilling out. Some of the tents were wide and tall, large enough to encompass her old house. The snorts of dragons blew open a few tent flaps.

Ah. That was why.

"This is the city of Aztal."

"It's …"

"Transient. We go where the food is, as our ancestors did before us. Right now, Yushi and the other sea dragons supply us with fish. It's not safe for us to be near the mountains."

Sanna peered at the craggy hills that surrounded the sandy valley. Weren't those enormous rocks mountains?

A young boy with a string of white beads around his forehead passed Sanna, eyeing her askance. The unfamiliar sounds of their language made her feel closed in, disoriented. What was she supposed to do here, anyway?

She already wished that Luteis hadn't left. But the thought of another minute in the air—and Elis's desperate state—made her think differently. Luteis wouldn't stay away long.

"I would take you into the city, but there's no space for your dragon to walk or land." Tashi motioned ahead of her with a wave of her hand. "You'll stay here."

Sanna skidded to a stop.

A cave loomed ahead of them, fading into a deep-black recess. For a moment, she thought she heard Junis and Rosy crying. The sound of metal grating on stone as they tried to escape.

She shook the memories away. Talis was gone. This wasn't his cave.

Inside the cave waited two pads, two blankets, a basin for water, and several piles of clothes.

"Put your dirty clothes out here, and someone will take care of them."

"Someone?"

She shrugged. "Someone always does. They'll bring it back. Although I'd hold onto your shoes. They'll go quick."

"Er, thanks."

"There's no hot water unless you want to start a fire and heat it up yourself. We're in the valley now, so Selsay likely won't find us here for a week. Or you can go to the ocean. Just the other side of the hill. Wait until it's dark, and no one else will be there. They don't like nighttime here. In case Selsay attacks. If you need something, just stop someone outside. They'll help."

"That's very … kind."

"They owe it to you."

With that, Tashi strode away, leaving Sanna and Jesse at the mouth of the cave. "Odd," Jesse murmured. "Why would they owe you anything?"

"We'll find out, I'm sure."

Sanna glanced around. The cave would fit Luteis and Elis. When she ventured farther inside, the light followed. She paced across the cavern, dropped to her back, and lay down. Having *something* over her head helped her feel less exposed. She forced herself not to check on Luteis.

Jesse said nothing, just peered outside with a frown.

"Sanna?"

Her eyes opened moments later, and she realized she'd started drifting off.

"Hmm?"

"I don't like leaving Elis alone. He says he's fine, but I'm going back to get him. He needs to rest here."

"Agreed."

Jesse shuffled away. Sanna glanced out, surprised to see that night had almost fallen. She thought of Daid. The dark blanket of Letum Wood on their house. The shuffling sounds as Daid moved around the house, speaking quietly to Mam.

A snort brought Sanna out of her memories.

I have returned, Luteis said. His bulky shadow filled the entrance to the cave. Sanna sat up. His heat rushed over her in a comforting wave. She already missed the friendly weight of the forest air. It seemed so dry here. The air was almost ... thin, and laced with the coppery smell of blood.

"How long do you think we'll be here?" she asked as he settled in, licking his lips.

Until we have answers.

"The rest of the Dragonmasters are in danger." Her heart sank when she thought of Finn and everyone else heading farther north. "You heard Tashi—it's not safe to be near mountains. But Finn is going north. We can't stay here long."

We cannot.

She reached out and touched his snout. The slickness of his scales on her palm calmed her.

I left a carcass with Elis, but someone had already brought him food. There was enough for Jesse.

"Good."

A reluctant desert dragon showed me to the cave. I heard some other witches talking, saying that there would be a summit in a few days. What is a summit?

"I don't know."

They also said that we would meet Yushi tomorrow. I don't understand what a yushi is.

"More like *who*, I think."

This should prove interesting.

"Are Jesse and Elis going to come here?"

No. Elis asked to stay where he was. Jesse will stay with him. It appears that Jesse enjoys seeing all these new things.

Winks of his burnt-orange scales glimmered in the darkness of the cave. The yellow-moon orbs of his eyes glowed. Sanna lay on the floor near him with her back to the cave opening. He wrapped his tail around her. She closed her eyes and rested her head on her arm.

Time to rest, he said. *We can ask our questions in the morning.*

Luteis settled his wing over her again. The dying sounds of the camp at her back faded. Cocooned in darkness, Sanna fell into a fast, deep sleep.

CHAPTER

THIRTEEN

A headache slammed into Isadora with a walloping *smack.*

She pressed her hands to her neck with a groan. Light wheeled through her mind, demanding release, like white, hot, burning ropes of magic. They wriggled and writhed, unusually agitated and bright and searing.

Acknowledge me, she imagined it would say, if magic had a voice. She commanded it to obey her, then stuffed it away again, imagining shoving the bright filaments in a closet and closing the door.

The headache ebbed. Slowly. It wouldn't be much longer before she had to use her magic or bear the pain of it —and eventually, death.

Still wincing, Isadora rubbed her neck and peered over a stack of recently folded pillowcases, through the open doors, and into the empty hallway.

Silence.

She quietly crossed the *lavanda* in slippered feet, then pressed her back against the wall near the door. Still quiet.

Breath held, she leaned out and looked right. An empty hallway. To the left, the same.

No sign of Ernesto.

After breakfast the day before, the surly cook had shown up with a bucketful of dishes and demanded, in rapid *Ilese*, that she clean them. After several shouting rounds, she figured out that the last witch to eat was supposed to clean up the meal. Not long after she finished and returned *those* dishes—which barely passed his intense scrutiny—Fiona showed up, demanding fresh towels she didn't have.

Ten blankets hung from the ropes in the courtyard outside the *lavanda*. A warm draft blew by, stirring them. Lightning streaked down to the ocean from the clouds in the distance. For the hundredth time, Isadora forced her gaze away from the rolling waves. She longed to wade into the ocean. Run in the wet sand.

Ignore all this laundry.

The sound of shouting drew her attention to the hallway. Who would be shouting? Lunch had long since come and gone, and La Torra usually lay in sleepy repose at this time of day. Despite housing, supposedly, tens of Defenders, she'd seen no one but the servants so far. Which also meant she had little to report to Maximillion, and even less confidence on her ability to help Lucey

There was no sign of Lorenzo or Fiona in the halls, which meant she *could* attempt to deliver the linens to Cecelia's maids. It would give her a chance to see something, at least. Visions of finding Lucey in some obscure room instead of Carcere danced through her mind as she slipped down the empty hall.

Wouldn't it be lovely to rescue her?

The circular layout of the castle led her past the

servants' hallway—marked *solo coraggioso*, which she still hadn't translated—and to the other side. According to gossip she'd overheard from the cooks, guest rooms populated the second floor, Cecelia occupied the entire third floor, the Defender trainees lived on the fourth with the East Guards, and the permanent Defenders inhabited the fifth. Carcere consisted of the sixth and seventh, she deduced, although no one had confirmed because no one spoke of it.

Like killing innocent Watchers, the inhabitants of the East seemed to think it easiest to act as if horrible things or events didn't happen.

She passed velvety divans, tiny porcelain figures on curved shelves made of driftwood, and breezy curtains. Every few steps waited a new standing screen covered with elegant paintings. Some historic, no doubt. Outside, crashing waves stretched onto the shore in a foamy line.

The shouting continued, louder now. No, it wasn't shouting.

Cheering.

Isadora slipped into a nearby staircase she'd found the day before and headed up—all the less likely to run into Ernesto, who never left the first floor. The sounds of celebration continued once she left the winding stairwell on the third floor. Open windows let sunshine into the halls. Three aquilas circled overhead, calling out with shrill screams, morphing from burgundy to white to sky blue and nearly disappearing.

Isadora stopped and peered into the circular courtyard. The gold sheets she carried slipped to the floor.

Her blood ran cold.

Six witches, likely Defender trainees wearing black, stood in a circle in the middle of the courtyard. Cecelia walked amidst them in an elegant gown with a skirt like a bell. Its layers of fabric rustled in the breeze. She stood next to a prostrate, crumpled body. Thin through the shoulders, with a frail frame. A woman, for certain. Her coppery hair shielded her face. A metal manacle glinted in the sunlight where it clasped her willowy neck. She rested on her knees, her entire body trembling.

"Finding a Watcher with your powers is a simple matter of darkness versus light," Cecelia said in the common language. Her shoes clicked on the stone floor as she walked a lazy circle around the prisoner. Rumor had it that Cecelia recruited Defenders from all over the world—her use of the common language seemed to confirm that.

Some of the trainees clutched whips, but others stood by whips that lay on the ground, next to scattered shards Isadora thought had once been porcelain vases. Untouched vases perched on benches not far away. The Defenders had been practicing, no doubt. Lucey had told stories about those whips—and bore a few scars herself.

"We are the past," Cecelia continued. "We are that which knows all. Who can hide from what is done? No one. We see what witches have chosen, and what they have not. That power resides within each of you. It is a gift. A defense. An honor. Be worthy of it."

Most of the Defenders stood stock-still, only their clothing flapping in the wind. Cecelia stopped to sneer at the witch on the ground.

"With such power comes a calling. We protect others from the *power* of the Watchers. From their interference with fate. We are that which protects the future from the greedy eyes of those who would alter its course."

Cecelia paced away from the girl. She was no different here at La Torra than she'd been when Isadora first saw her at Chatham Castle. In fact, she was every bit as terrifying. Cold. Calculating. Elegant and refined in a gaudy way. The gems she wore—eccentric earrings that dangled all the way to her shoulders—felt out of place against such a simple, serene backdrop.

The prostrate witch glanced up through her curtain of hair while Cecelia circled.

"Ages ago, beyond memory, Watchers and Defenders worked together, in pairs. They used their powers to bring justice to a failing world, to foresee difficult times, and to stop wrongful tyranny and oppression. As often happens, the power went to the heads of the Watchers that held it. The Watchers began to murder their matches in their sleep. Thanks to the unusual connection between us, Watchers began to exploit our abilities. They would anticipate our moves, what protective lies we would tell to keep ourselves safe from their power. Imagine that ability in the hands of the power-hungry."

A ripple of voices murmured back. Animosity ran thick in their accented tongues.

Cecelia cast a disgusted glance at the girl.

"We underestimated their talent and overestimated their goodness. We gave too much to our Watcher matches. Watchers are ruthlessly intelligent and cunning, but one should never expect them to be trustworthy. They are steeped in the light—blinded by it. All they know is interrupting fate and bringing about their own will. We, the Defenders, preserve fate in all her righteous causes. We use the past to allow fate to take her course unrestrained."

The Watcher shifted, revealing scabbed blisters along her wrists. Her hair parted in the back to show chafed skin along the neck manacle, flecked with dark, dried blood.

What appeared to be clumps of hair had fallen—or been torn—from her scalp, leaving bloody patches behind.

Isadora dug her nails into her palm. "No paths," she murmured, distracting herself from the overwhelming desire to enter the magic. "No paths. No paths."

Outside, one of the Defenders growled.

"Now, milady!"

"Hold yourself!" Cecelia barked. The crack of a whip followed a subtle motion from her wrist. Seconds later, one Defender reached for his face. A bright-red slash marred his cheek.

"I alone speak right now."

Isadora clenched her teeth. The magic beckoned, taunting her with a swirl of light. She could save the girl, couldn't she? Her mind raced. Likely, it wouldn't work. So many possibilities would converge on the path.

But maybe ...

A *snap* broke the air.

The Watcher lay sprawled on the ground, Cecelia's foot pressed into her back, a length of whip around her neck. Blood oozed from its edges. The Watcher screamed. Cecelia used the whip to lift the girl's head off the ground and then drop it again.

Blood sprayed.

The Watcher stilled. Her eyes closed. Cecelia grinned, alight with pleasure and passion. Her diamond earrings glinted. Below her feet, the Watcher's life bled away onto the cobbled courtyard floor.

Terror overcame Isadora, but she forced it down. Fear drove terrible decisions. She forced the panic back so she could think clearly. If she could just *distract* Cecelia, the Watcher had a chance—albeit a slight one. Jumping out of the window would draw their attention. While falling, she could use a spell to cast a protective bubble. No—she might be too late.

The hiss of the ocean caught her ear. She brightened. A wave. If she could bring a wave onto the beach and—no. A spell powerful enough to bring a wave over the castle would cost her too much energy. A horde of bees? Unlikely out here. With no one else using magic, they would surely track it back to her. Only one thing would get their attention for certain.

Another Watcher.

Just as Isadora called for her own magic, Cecelia reached down. Her thin, pale fingers gripped something on the back of the manacle, then twisted. A strangled sound emitted from the girl before she slumped forward.

Dead.

A clatter startled Isadora. She shoved away from the window and whirled around. One of Cecelia's personal maids appeared. She frowned.

Isadora pasted on a smile. "*Goffo,*" she said, scrambling for the cloth she'd dropped on the floor. "So ... ah ... clumsy."

The maid rolled her eyes, muttered something about *idio lavanda,* and strode away. Once clear, Isadora rushed back to the window. Blood pooled around the Watcher, blending with her bright hair. Her eyes lay closed.

"Unless we continue to defend fate and our own lives, the Watchers will take over," Cecelia continued. "They'll create whatever glorious hell they choose. Who is to say that isn't why our world is at war?"

"That is our mistress, The Great One."

Isadora jumped and squeaked at the same time, sending the sheets toppling back to the ground. Fiona stood behind her, lips pressed in a thin line as she peered past Isadora into the courtyard.

"You scared me!"

Fiona sent her a dirty scowl. "That's your fault."

Isadora's hands trembled as she tried to collect her scattered wits. "Er, right. Sorry."

"Cecelia," Fiona said, her voice low and brow furrowed. She shook her head. "Nasty business."

"A Watcher, is it?"

Fiona folded her hands behind her back. "Yes. New Defender recruits. They come from everywhere."

"How often does this happen?"

"Monthly. Depends on how many Defenders she finds and how many Watchers she has from the raids. She collects Defenders often, trains them, and sends the weaker ones back to their own Networks to be available when she needs them. The more powerful stay here, with her."

Something lingered in the words, *the more powerful stay here, with her*. A thousand questions assaulted Isadora at once, jumbling in a tangle. How did Cecelia find the trainees? How many Defenders were there? How long had this magic been around?

Isadora forced her thoughts back to the present. "You've watched this happen before?"

"Cecelia forced us to watch in the past. With a more ... rowdy staff."

"But ... why?"

"Control, of course. She cannot lose discipline on an island such as this. Besides, it's just a Watcher. They are dangerous. Very dangerous. Some think that a hidden Watcher is responsible for all these wars. They like to pull the strings of fate, you know." Fiona shook her head. "Not good."

Isadora wrestled back the words she wanted to say. Instead, she maintained eye contact through sheer force of will.

"So I've heard."

"Anyway, what can be done? They believe that Watchers must be culled for the greater good; they act on that with the full support of the High Priest. It is the way of things." The words sounded wooden and strange and too easy all at the same time, as if she'd detached from what they meant long ago. "And, as you see, The Great One is known for strong emotions."

"Her temper?"

Fiona said nothing. Isadora hugged the sheets to her chest.

"Is she gone much?"

She shrugged. "What is much?"

Isadora blinked. She'd never realized how nuanced language could be until she'd tried to learn a new one.

"Does she live here?"

"No."

"Where does she go?"

Fiona's eyes narrowed. "Why do you ask?"

"I wish I had her dresses—and a place to go in them—that's all. I've never worn something so elaborate or beautiful before."

"The *lavanda* girl wants more than laundry?"

Fiona seemed amused but also waited for a response. Maximillion had described the balls that Greta, the old Central Network High Priestess, had thrown once. Extravagant. Lavish, well-planned events with elaborate menus and countless scores of witches in silk and *linea* and sparkling gems.

"Perhaps just to try a life such as that. Only once."

Fiona nodded toward the linen room, then motioned to the pillowcases. "Well, you are not The Great One. You only wash her clothes. Don't mistake yourself. I will take these from here. Do not attempt to leave the *lavanda* again without permission. It is not for you to roam these halls."

Isadora cast one glance back at the dead Watcher and her copper hair.

Fiona stepped back, *tsking*. "Sad that it must be done for the good of all. We are better without them."

"I am proud of the work you do every day as you learn control of your magic," Cecelia said to the trainees as Isadora stepped away from the window. "Continue to do so, for my reputation is at stake as much as yours. Welcome to our family. You are here to do a beautiful work."

Isadora scowled at a half-burnt apron, set a tablecloth aside to deal with in the morning, and left the *lavanda* for the spiraling staircase that led to her small room.

Her weary eyes shut against the fading light that ebbed as the sun sank into the ocean. The vision of the young Watcher, lying on the ground with blood blooming around her, popped back into her head.

Isadora opened her eyes again.

"What am I doing here?" she muttered, rubbing a hand over her face. "Nothing."

The days here had already blurred into a mindless routine. How could she help Lucey while scrubbing the sweat out of East Guard uniforms? When Watchers were tortured to death with whips and fear by Cecelia? There was no information to glean on La Torra. No one visited. Cecelia, despite her own edict, transported in and out. And ever since Isadora had ventured out, unauthorized, Fiona had watched her like a hawk, anticipating when she'd finish laundry. Except for meals—to which Fiona escorted her—Isadora didn't leave the *lavanda*.

Once she shut her bedroom door against a brisk breeze, warmth enveloped her. Her head snapped up.

Maximillion glared at her from the other side of the room.

"You're alive, for one," he muttered. "A hopeful sign."

Candles bounced on the small, round table, revealing an array of food that made her stomach grumble. Good, old-fashioned Central Network food! Warm chicken pie with a flaky crust. Hearty bread with plump flecks of brown—most likely figs. A jug of what must have been mulled cider, if the slight tang of orange in the air meant anything. The scents of home choked her. How did he get cider and figs? And chicken?

She rushed across the room, abandoning her apron.

"You brought me food?" she cried. "Oh, it smells so wonderful!"

He said nothing but pretended to be absorbed in a book titled, *Basics of Ilese and All the Nuanced Details of Learning a New Language*. He looked as imperious as ever—if a bit tired. Isadora sank into a chair, bone weary, and reached for the glass of mulled cider. The delicious *zip* hit her tongue with a little thrill, and she shuddered. A fire crackled in the hearth, warming her.

A chair appeared next to him. He sat in it, back ramrod straight. "Update me."

Isadora tore a hunk of bread free without bothering to cut it. Wafer-thin crackers and soup that tasted like water had left her ravenous after so much physical work. She felt as if she hadn't eaten in years. She ate until her stomach bulged.

Then the words slipped out.

"They killed a Watcher yesterday."

His gaze narrowed.

"Go on."

Isadora fumbled through the re-telling, leaving out her plan to stop the death, and ended it feeling more exhausted —yet also more relieved—than ever. At least the story wasn't just hers now. At least *he* knew.

Maximillion's expression didn't waver. "Of course Cecelia killed her. What did you expect? It's what Defenders do."

Tears stung her eyes, but she blinked them back. "Your lack of compassion doesn't make it less horrible. She was a young woman. She was ... she was my age."

He studied her, his expression all angles and sharp lines, then stood up to pace. He clasped his hands behind his back, drawing out his surprisingly broad shoulders, while striding across the room.

"You can leave anytime," he said. "You don't have to be here if you're going to sulk."

"I cannot leave."

"In fact, I encourage you to come home."

"After that? No."

"I've told you it's not safe, and now you're starting to understand. No one would blame you."

Isadora met his gaze. "I would."

He stared at her for a long time, as if debating what he wanted to say. "While unfortunate, that's precisely the end one can expect to meet when one throws themselves on the mercy of someone like Cecelia."

"What do you mean?"

"That Watcher turned herself in."

Isadora straightened with a bolt of fury. "You already knew about all of this."

"I did."

Somehow, Maximillion and his Advocacy *were* everywhere. Did someone on the staff work for Maximillion? A second, equally stunning thought occurred to her. "Wait. You said she turned herself in. Why? Why would anyone do that?"

"A hope for mercy. A foolish one."

"How did you know?"

He said nothing.

"I could have saved her!"

"And lost your own life in the process. We cannot stop all the deaths until the Eastern Network changes. You'll have to come to terms with that."

His lack of annoyance startled her. She reached for a piece of bread but lost motivation halfway to the bowl. Instead, she turned to him, hating the sound of defeat in her voice.

"Cecelia said something about a *connection* and *matches*. Do you know what she meant?"

"Haven't the slightest idea."

Isadora frowned. A long silence prevailed between them while she mulled over Cecelia's speech. There had been such fervor in her voice. She truly believed she was doing the right thing by murdering Watchers. Isadora glanced up, studying the lines of his face.

"Why am I here if you already know so much?" she asked quietly.

He paused. "Extra assurance."

"I'm not doing anything, Maximillion, and we're no closer to finding Lucey."

"That's your own fault."

"*My* fault?"

"There is information to be gathered."

"Like what?"

"Have you had any other run-ins with Cecelia?"

A flash of irritation pulsed through her at his quick change of subject, but she let it go. "No."

Maximillion frowned. "Have you seen any of the Defenders by themselves?"

"Ah, no? They don't really come to the first floor."

"Are they on a schedule?"

"Not that I can tell." Isadora bit her bottom lip. "I haven't really left the *lavanda* for very long and—"

"You mentioned something about the cooks. Tell me about them. Do you know their names?"

"Er, not really. Ernesto despises me and—"

"Where are their loyalties?"

"Loyalties?"

"Cecelia or the East?" he snapped. "These are not hard questions."

"I couldn't be sure. I—"

"How many East Guards here?"

"Ah ..."

"Sailors?"

"Only on delivery days, I believe."

"When are those?"

"I-I guess I'm not sure."

Maximillion's nostrils flared. The sparks in the grate plumed with bright streaks of green. "What, precisely, are you doing here if not gathering information?"

"How is any of that pertinent?" she snapped.

He advanced, looming, dark, and snapping with rage. "If the Defenders are never alone, that means Cecelia is aware something is amiss. It means they are on alert, or in training, or any number of things. If they have a schedule, we can know when they're gone on a raid. If they're new, we can exploit their inexperience or find an ally who is uncomfortable with the way Cecelia runs her force. If the cooks are loyal to the Eastern Network, they could be persuaded to help us. If they're loyal to Cecelia ..."

He trailed off. She waited, but he didn't finish the thought. The desire to hide under the table nearly swallowed her. Her powers flared, tightening like a vise around her head.

"Aren't the East and Cecelia one and the same?" she asked, putting a weary hand to her face. The threads of this situation spun into a complicated tapestry. How did he track so many things at once?

"No, they aren't one and the same. Do you see my point?"

"Yes."

"Stop feeling incompetent and sorry for yourself, and observe. If you want to help Lucey, you'll find the answer in the details. *That* is how we will get Lucey back and conquer Cecelia. That is why you are here. I may understand large moving pieces, but I cannot see the details and nuance of La Torra. Do you understand?"

"Yes."

"How are your powers?"

She grimaced, feeling a fresh surge of a headache. "Restless."

He studied her, eyes slitted, and a quiet understanding passed between them. She had to do better. His jaw tightened like an overwrought string, as if he'd snap at any moment.

She tilted her head to one side, grateful for an excuse to

turn the conversation away from herself. "Are you all right, Maximillion?"

He looked away. "Fine."

"You don't look fine."

He hesitated. "I would be better if I hadn't just returned from a meeting in the Southern Network."

"Oh?"

"Dante, High Priest of the Eastern Network, is calling for a delegation. A meeting of the Networks." He waved a hand. "They're saying it's a truce, but I don't believe it. This would be a third attempt at peace. Last time, the South overthrew a table, the West promised eternal revenge, and Greta smashed a wine glass. This time, Dante has been muttering something about a pact."

"Think they'd use it as a chance to attack?"

"I don't know."

Maximillion plunged deeper into thought. When he shook his head, some of the vagueness vanished from his eyes, replaced with his usual steely disapproval.

"The West hasn't even responded. Charles, of course, is all for it." Maximillion rolled his eyes. "He naively believes we must foster any chance of peace."

Isadora thought of the young High Priest with a pang of fondness—and fear. The floppy-haired witch without much common sense but a great deal of heart was no leader. The former High Priestess, Greta, had instituted Charles as little more than a puppet. A voice that would never challenge her whims. A witch who, by all accounts, would be best left tending a garden. Now he'd inherited the many messes she'd left behind.

"I take it you don't agree."

"I don't know what to think," Maximillion muttered. "The East hasn't the resources to keep fighting. Except for the West, I don't believe any of us do. Which is why Vasily is erecting that stupid wall around the Southern Network."

Maximillion muttered something about incompetent Guardians and a militant High Priest as he stopped at the door, looking out on the ocean.

"Have you received any letters from my sister?" she asked before he could leave unexpectedly, as he often did. His shoulders tightened.

"None."

"That seems odd."

He reached into his pocket and pulled out a small scroll. His voice was flippant as he studied it. "She's busy right now."

She gripped the chair. "Is something wrong? Has something happened?"

"Many things."

"Like?"

"Nothing you need be concerned over."

"But—"

He sent her a scathing glare. "You trust me, don't you?"

The words swelled between them. Isadora's jaw bobbed for a moment. *Did* she trust him? Could she just ... *answer* that question without weeks of forethought? She finally said, "Yes."

"She's fine. You need to focus on staying alive and integrating yourself here at La Torra. Things at home will sort themselves out."

Isadora pulled a letter out of her pocket and extended it to him. *Sanna* was scrawled across the front. Maximillion glanced briefly at it. Without touching her, he grabbed it and slipped it into his pocket. He stepped back outside with a scowl, supposedly transporting away.

The world had grown dark. Weary from the day, Isadora

sank to her bed and stared at the spot where he'd stood until the sound of the sea rolled into the room, lulling her to sleep.

Sanna bolted upright out of a dead sleep.

Luteis stood in the cave entrance, blocking the dusty light. A scream came from outside, followed by muffled laughter and a tinny, high-pitched sound. Bells? The scent of charred meat drifted into the cave, making her stomach grumble. She pushed to her feet, rubbed her eyes, and fought off a yawn.

"What's going on?"

It appears to be a celebration.

In the camp, several tents had been cleared away, leaving an open spot in the middle packed with witches. At the very center, an elevated platform was littered with dead carcasses. Blood saturated the sand beneath. Four bright torches danced at every corner of the platform, casting light on a dragon egg laying in the middle. Yellowed boulders at least as tall as Sanna's shoulders suspended the platform off the ground.

"A hatching?"

It would appear so.

"Where is Jesse?"

Down there, I believe. Luteis nodded to the right.

Sanna scowled, her eyes landing on a familiar broad, short figure off to the side, speaking with a female witch with bright brown eyes and wavy hair. Sanna reached up and felt the greasy strands of her own braids, then shook her head. Tashi appeared, bells tinkling from bracelets around her left ankle.

"Halloa."

"*Avay*," Sanna said.

"A dragon egg is about to hatch." Tashi lifted a hand and crooked her fingers. "Come. You must try our *sentara* bread. We grind our yellow beans into a paste for it. Delicious."

Despite her longing for home, a sliver of curiosity pulsed through her. Sanna glanced at Luteis.

"Are you going to come?"

His eyes narrowed on the teeming space. The desert dragons remained on the outside, snapping at each other— an oddly friendly gesture for such wild beasts—and screaming back and forth. He lowered his head. Luteis's body would occupy too much space.

No. His tail twitched behind him. *I'll remain here. I prefer to observe. Being in the open that way feels ... wrong. I will be your eyes. Enjoy the other witches.*

She couldn't fault him.

"All right."

Tashi waited a few steps away, a hand shielding her eyes, and motioned to the platform as they headed that way. Outside the tents, meat cooked on spits above individual fires, tended by witches who sat on the ground on dusty, makeshift pillows. Fat sizzled as it dripped into the flames, releasing a sweet, smoky smell. Sanna's stomach growled.

They passed a witch carrying a basket of what appeared to be loaves of round, fluffy bread. The kind that was mostly air when bitten into. All around them, high-pitched shrieks tore through the camp. They set Sanna's hair on edge until she realized they were a form of music. When she listened hard, she could hear the faint chime of bell-like instruments accompanying a repetitive tune.

Tashi drew closer to the egg just as a hushed whisper tore through the festivities. The sounds of revelry ceased. Young children darted through the crowd, working around the adults, until they made it to the platform. Twenty children thronged the egg, which trembled.

"The sand beneath the egg and the rocks supporting it represents its Western heritage. It's about to hatch," Tashi said, drawing Sanna to the side. "See the crack forming at the top?"

Sanna had never seen a forest dragon hatch. They hatched in the quiet, alone, with their mams. Only after the hatchling had eaten, slept, and found their legs did they meet other dragons. Witches might not meet them for weeks—even months. Unless there was an issue with the mam and a witch had to keep the egg warm with fire, which was also rare. The sires usually stepped in. To have it so openly regarded felt strange, like a sacred ritual she shouldn't be invited to.

A hum of excitement rippled through the crowd when the first crack widened. The children ringing the stand were oddly still, expressions impassive. Tashi motioned to them with a jerk of her chin. "The children are here to be chosen."

"Chosen?"

"The hatchling will have its choice of witch or food first. Whichever it chooses decides its fate. If they want food, they will be given it, then raised until they are four in a pen with other dragons, at which point they become independent. If they go to a witch, they are integrated with the child's family immediately, and the bond begins."

"But it's so young."

Tashi nodded. "The ritual has proven itself time and again. If the dragon is witch-inclined, it will be so from the beginning and will immediately choose its witch. If it is not witch-inclined, it will tear first into the food. A food-inclined desert dragon is dangerous to keep in a home."

The egg cracked again. Subtle movements gleamed from inside the egg as fluid seeped out.

"How many choose a witch?"

"Perhaps one in every ten."

"So few."

"To us, it feels as if it's many."

Another crack appeared. Sanna thought of Tenzin. His distant gaze, a bit wild, as if he lacked intelligence inherent in forest dragons. A collective gasp rippled through the crowd when a chunk of egg fell to the ground. Two of the youngest children feinted toward it, but the older ones behind them grabbed them by the shoulder. Tashi grinned.

"The eggshells are said to be omens of good luck. All the youngest children try to grab them, but that could spook the hatchling."

"We use our dragon eggshells."

"Really?" Tashi asked.

Sanna nodded.

"What for?"

"To make dishes."

Tashi made a perplexed humming sound under her breath. Another chunk had fallen away from the side of the egg. Except for the shifting of shadows, nothing was visible yet. The crowd seemed to hold its collective breath.

"When will it come?"

"When it's ready."

All at once, the egg burst apart.

Shards of egg sprayed the children, who scampered away from the thick, gray goop that flew out with it. The older children held their ground. One boy, in particular, didn't flinch, even though part of the egg lay on top of his head, and strands of a grayish substance oozed onto his shoulders.

Standing where the egg had once been was a miniature desert dragon, about half the size of a forest-dragon hatchling, which was usually the height of Sanna's arm. This one would stand only as tall as her elbow to fingertip. It croaked and gazed around. Its sloping nostrils flared. A male, it appeared. With a cry, he spread his tiny wings, fanning them. He tilted his head back and sniffed, then lowered his head to the carcasses that littered his feet. A child made a peep. The dragon startled, then lifted his eyes to the ring of children.

Sanna's hand twitched for her knife. Forest-dragon hatchlings were unpredictable so soon after birth, and *hungry*. Even such a small dragon could kill a witch with a well-placed bite to the neck.

For a long pause, the hatchling locked eyes with the boy with goop dropping off his head. Not a breath moved in the crowd. The hatchling stepped forward once. Then twice. A carcass lay just ahead of him, right between him and the boy.

"Nah," Tashi murmured. "He's going to go for the food."

Something lurked in the dragon's eyes. Something deep, almost ... intelligent. Not as visceral as the wildness she saw in the rest of the desert dragons. The way the hatchling held his head straight—didn't tilt it in surprise— meant something. She didn't know what, but it meant something. There was a savage kind of beauty in the desert dragons, particularly one so small and perfect.

"No," she whispered. "He'll pick the boy."

Right then, the hatchling let out a screech. He hopped over the carcass and plowed into the child, who staggered back. Cries of surprise littered the crowd. The rest of the children melted away without a word or a shriek of protest and left the boy and his dragon alone together. The dragon climbed up the boy's arm—he winced when the talons sank a little too deep—and settled on his shoulder. The boy murmured something, ignoring the ripples that spread through the crowd, and reached for a dead animal. He held it up to the hatchling, speaking all the while, as if they had always known each other.

Tashi glanced at Sanna out of the corner of her eye. "You knew?"

"A lucky guess," Sanna said.

Tashi's gaze narrowed. Something flickered in her eyes. Surprise? Sanna couldn't tell. "Was it?" Tashi asked. "You have witnessed what we call a *molina*. A miracle, in your language."

"What happens now?"

"They will grow together," Tashi said. "Learn to fly. Learn to fight. Learn to defend their own lives and the lives of others. Desert dragons are cursed with simple minds— but raised right, they are loyal and can be trained."

Sanna stared at the hatchling, enraptured by the way it nuzzled the boy just behind the ear. Was it purring? Could it really bond so quickly? Was such a thing possible with forest dragons? Probably not. To try to force something like that would only rile up already-strained relationships.

But ... *maybe* ...

She made a mental note to ask Luteis why most forest dragons hated witches. It seemed to be an inclination they were born with, but perhaps it was just another gift left over from Talis. Perhaps a better relationship could be fostered with the right kind of leader.

Sanna swallowed hard.

The crowd dispersed, breaking into patches here and

there. Sanna stepped back, ready to be away from the crowd. Not only was her skin a different color, but her hair was, too. She stood out like a belua in a stream. The crowd parted to let her and Tashi through. Fires continued to dot the landscape, and the air smelled like sizzling meat and cinnamon.

"Thank you, Tashi."

Tashi nodded.

"It is important that we all see such things. When Selsay broke her promise and began to covet and cherish her dragons, all things fell out of balance. Then the massacre of the forest dragons occurred, and all seemed to crumble."

"Selsay. You've mentioned that name before."

Tashi stopped. "Selsay. The goddess."

"What?"

"The goddesses. Surely you know of them?"

Sanna grabbed Tashi's arm, then immediately released it when Tashi glared at her. "Do you really think I'd ask you questions I already knew the answer to?"

"No."

"Who is Selsay?"

"The goddess of the mountains." Tashi gestured north with a hand.

Sanna's stomach hardened into a rock when she gazed on the distant, craggy peaks. They seemed closer tonight, somehow, as if they had moved since she'd arrived. Shock rendered her speechless. More goddesses?

"I ... I haven't ..."

"Deasylva hasn't told you?"

"No."

Tashi started to walk again. "I'm not surprised. Goddesses, by nature, are protective of the creatures within their care. It is part of their maternal instinct—the powers that give them strength. Perhaps she thought it would protect you to keep you so isolated."

Sanna scrambled to keep up with Tashi as she slipped out of the tent area and back toward the rocks. Glimmers of Luteis appeared overhead, where he flew in a broad circle.

"You said something about the massacre of the forest dragons." Sanna jogged to keep up.

"Yes."

"You knew about it?"

"Of course. The forest dragons withdrew and were never heard of again. Selsay grew greater in her mistrust and jealousy, particularly of Prana. It's why you will see Yushi."

"Prana?" Sanna cried, exasperated. "Don't tell me. Another goddess?"

"Of the sea."

Sanna gritted her teeth. It seemed inconceivable that there should be three goddesses, but no doubt appeared in Tashi's face.

Tashi stopped just outside Sanna's cave. A basket of food lay on the ground, thick with the same sweet, charred scents of the gathering below.

"Get your rest, daughter of the forest." Tashi's eyes gleamed. "Tomorrow, you meet Yushi."

CHAPTER

FOURTEEN

You seem troubled.

Sanna sat at the mouth of the cave, knees pulled to her chest, brow furrowed. Below them, the party still continued, dotting the landscape with fires and the occasional flare of a nearby drum. Night had settled, throwing a thousand stars across the sky like discarded grains of sand. Luteis kept his bright gaze on the horizon. Jesse and Elis were off somewhere, no doubt, drinking in more of the festivities. Even back in Anguis, Jesse had always been more excited about events.

"I am troubled."

The hatching?

"Yes."

An odd ritual, to be sure. Why would one want to be hatched to an audience? You were not birthed with all the dragons watching.

"No, but it's not like the hatchlings know any different. Maybe they don't care."

He thought on that with a low growl deep in his throat. *Perhaps, but it still seems strange to me. What is the plan?*

205

"Tomorrow, we meet with this Yushi witch."

His eyes slitted, and his tongue flickered out. *The desert dragons have been difficult to comprehend. They do not communicate with me at all. It's ... disconcerting.*

Sanna tipped her head back to look into his eyes. "Luteis, why don't forest dragons like witches?"

I was not raised with them. I wouldn't know.

"They've never spoken with you about it or given you any clues? I always thought it was the way of things. But based on the way the witches here are so closely tied to the dragons, I can't help but wonder ..."

Forest dragons are different in temperament and intelligence. They can—and should—think for themselves.

"Yes. But ..."

I'm sure something here ties back to the ancient agreement.

"The ancient agreement made by Gregor?"

He inclined his head. *Forest dragons will be tied to Chatham Castle until Almorran magic is proven eradicated. Deasylva has spoken often of this.*

Sanna had heard the agreement spoken of once before, but Daid had dismissed it. With the only surviving dragons living in Anguis, it had seemed preposterous that such an arrangement ever existed.

"Do you think Almorran magic has been eradicated?"

No. I can feel the weight of the agreement in my bones. I believe that would be gone if the magic didn't exist anymore. It's a terrible tie. Something we can never escape. Perhaps the forest dragons' hatred of witches relates to the obligation. Didn't Tashi say the desert dragons were a cursed race?

"She did, but I don't know what that means. Maybe something about her goddess, Sarena?"

Perhaps.

Sanna gazed back outside for several minutes. She

reached over, putting a hand on his scales, comforted by the touch. "Do you think that witches and forest dragons could ever be as close as the witches and desert dragons?"

He growled low in his chest, a warm, friendly kind of sound. *Have you and I not already answered the question?*

Warmth infused her.

"Yes, I suppose we have."

Even if the rest of the forest dragons do not feel the same as you and I, that does not matter. We will be whatever we need to be. It's up to the dragons—and, in some regards, the witches—to decide what is possible. Based on the dragons' distrust since the massacre, I don't foresee that happening soon. But a new generation is rising already, and you have the trust of Rosy and Junis.

"Yes."

For some of us—he nudged her in the shoulder—*being close to a witch does not seem like the worst fate.*

"Thanks." She managed a wry smile. It faded, lost in the sudden urge to lie on the ground beneath sprawling trees and see nothing but the canopy. No stars. So expansive a sky made her feel lost. She drew in a deep breath.

"I miss home."

I agree. This openness is … unsettling.

"I'm itching to get back. If things are really as dire as they say, we need to speak with the dragons and the Dragonmasters." She scowled. "Especially Finn."

Agreed.

"After we meet Yushi tomorrow, let's return."

Allow me to accompany you to the meeting. Sometimes, with witches, I have found it advantageous to be of greater size.

"Of course." She grinned up at him. "I would never go without you."

❧

S̲anna woke again̲ to the sound of screaming. This time, however, there were no festivities.

Luteis filled the cave door, blocking the light from outside. Elis stood behind him, taking up most of the cave. Before she could gain her feet, Luteis said, *There is an attack.*

"Who?"

I do not recognize them for certain, but they appear to be mountain dragons.

Still groggy with sleep, she crawled up his rigid spine and peered over his shoulder. Jesse already sat astride Elis, grim-faced. In the dim light, she could barely make out his mussed hair. Shadows swooped from the sky like wraiths. In the distance, fingers of sunlight just broke the horizon—darkness still hovered over the city.

Witches screamed. The shrieks of the desert dragons rang above the burgeoning chaos.

"No fire," she whispered.

None.

Something thick and stinging filled the air, however, whispering by with every small gust of wind. It stung the back of Sanna's throat.

"Mountain dragons, indeed," she murmured, recalling that heady stench from when Daid died. "Let's go."

You desire to fight?

"Those monsters killed my daid." Sanna gripped her knife hilt tighter. "You have no idea how much I want to fight."

"We'll go too," Jesse said, meeting Sanna's gaze. "For Rian."

Luteis fell silent.

Shouts called out over the terrified screams. Bodies flashed by the cave as Luteis stepped outside. Sanna tightened her knees around the place where the base of his neck met his body. The magic held her secure, but she felt better with a firmer grip.

Within moments, he was airborne, nearly silent amongst the shrill cries from below. They flew higher. In the waning moonlight, she thought she saw desert dragons darting through the air. Even in flight, they blended in with the sand from above.

We must be careful, Luteis said, likely more to Elis, who flew alongside them, than Sanna. *Night fades quickly.*

Shadows appeared in the air. The mountain dragons. Their transportation ability gave them a distinct advantage, even over the speed of the desert dragons. But Luteis and Elis were almost invisible in the night, and their size would benefit them in direct attacks. Besides, there seemed to be no witches with the mountain dragons.

Mountain dragons and desert dragons battled in the air above the sand, while the scurry of witches continued below. Most hurried toward the caves, leaping into crevices that provided some cover. Mountain dragons flew by the witches, or appeared out of nowhere with gleaming talons. Sanna drew an arm over her nose and mouth. Her throat burned like coal. *Their acid is foul,* she said. *Let's get this over with, shall we?*

It would be my pleasure, Luteis purred. Then he dove.

Wind tore through Sanna's hair, sending it flying behind her like a banner as they plummeted toward the ground. Three mountain dragons, flying abreast, darted toward a group of women running for the hills, slowed by small children.

Luteis—there. The children.

Luteis leaned to the right, changing course toward them. Within seconds, he swooped above the dragons. The middle mountain dragon looked up, shrieked, then disappeared.

The other two crunched beneath Luteis's hind legs.

He grabbed them by their necks, and then unfurled his wings. The rapid descent halted as he pulled them back into the air. Sanna gritted her teeth against the quick change in direction. The two mountain dragons in his claws flailed, gnashing their long, pointed teeth. Could they vanish? It didn't seem so—at least, they hadn't yet. Isadora had said something about not being able to transport if someone was touching her.

Luteis's body jerked back and forth despite his powerful wingbeats counteracting the mountain dragons' mad thrashing. A tingle flared in Sanna's chest, as if heat had just been poured over her heart. It flowed through her arms, all the way down to her fingertips, which warmed like fire. Below, the women and children disappeared into the rocks.

"We're going to crash!" Sanna called.

Luteis curled his talons into the dragons' necks, then reached down with his head, snapping at their wings. The mountain dragons hissed. Something caught Sanna's eye from the side. She turned. Her eyes widened.

"Luteis!"

His head popped up seconds before another mountain dragon—this one almost equal in size to Luteis—slammed into them.

Sanna felt the impact all the way up her spine.

Her teeth jarred. She shifted to the right, clinging to Luteis's back. He bellowed, released the mountain dragons, and lashed out with his tail and fire. The bigger mountain dragon screamed, the muscles of his strong neck taut all the way to his powerful chest. A pendant hung from his neck—

something round. Thin. As if hollowed out of bone. Clouds of yellow billowed from his mouth. Sanna ducked, throwing her arms over her face. Luteis spun, angling her away from the cloud, and absorbed it with the scales of his belly.

Acid! he said. *Don't breathe.*

The strange heat in Sanna's chest expanded, demanding release. But how could she let it go? What was it? The mountain dragon followed as Luteis maneuvered away from the poison. Luteis threw his tail in an arc, but the dragon disappeared, reappearing only a few wingbeats away. His eyes seemed wild, almost lost.

For what felt like an eternity, they attempted to fight. The dragon disappeared, always reappearing in a more advantageous spot. Keeping track of him set Sanna's hair on edge. She reached for her knife, feeling as if her hand were on fire.

What can I do? she asked. *I feel so ... helpless. So itchy. I need to do something.*

Remain calm and protect yourself.

She frowned.

But I want to help! This doesn't feel right.

Wind bore the acid behind them, clearing the air. Sanna coughed, eyes watering. Three other mountain dragons appeared in a semicircle. They looked to each other, as if speaking, then disappeared. Only the largest remained, glittering eyes on Sanna.

Do they communicate? Sanna asked. *Is this their leader?*

It would appear they have some form of organization, although I cannot see any patterns. The rest of the dragons seem ... a bit wild. Not unlike the desert dragons, but obviously, with greater intelligence.

The mountain dragons roved the sky, tearing into lone,

weak desert dragons. Some grabbed at the tents, snapping left and right. Others harassed the desert dragons on the cliffs. The mountain dragons' wiry bodies changed colors with the landscape as they moved, creating a strange sense of motion below.

It doesn't make sense, she said. *What are they doing here?*

One mountain dragon streaked by, shrieking at the top of its lungs. Something wild seemed to possess its eyes, as if it weren't really aware. It continued on, screaming for no apparent reason, before disappearing into the lightening sky. Another mountain dragon flew into the cliffs, slamming into a rock. It fell, wing broken, and twitched on the ground.

We need a plan of attack, Luteis said. *Theirs is madness. We cannot follow suit and expect to overcome them.*

I think we aren't the only ones attacking. Sanna motioned to the ocean.

A cloud billowed out of the water, saturating the air with unexpected moisture. Tendrils of fog slipped over the land, heading toward them. Rain pelted the ground, rolling in with the storm. Waves surged, audible even though a craggy line of sandy rocks separated the camp from the water.

The surge of rain brought the desert dragons out in greater numbers. The mountain dragons hissed, disappearing, then attempting to reappear farther away. The cloud seemed to chase them, spreading in all directions at once.

Two other dragons appeared by the largest mountain dragon, then disappeared. As if suddenly remembering them, the leader climbed toward Luteis and Sanna with surprising dexterity.

Sanna stood up, eyeing the distance to the ground. Several hundred paces, at least. The leader closed in, a glassy expression coating his eyes. Thirty paces away. In just a few seconds, he'd slam into them. The mountain dragon snarled and snapped, shrieking like the others.

They were all *mad*.

If there was anything that couldn't be trusted, a mad dragon was it.

You're confident in your diving abilities? she asked.

Very.

Then don't let me hit the ground.

Before he could argue, she leapt off his back.

Her stomach caught as she free-fell for half a breath before landing on something solid. The mountain dragon shrieked as she wound an arm around his neck, clinging to him, before she nearly fell off the other side. He beat his wings, slowing his flight. They wobbled in the sky. Sanna's right arm flailed with her knife, sliding along the dragon's scales.

You have courage, little one, but not even that knife can break my scales. I am not here to kill you.

The quiet, serpentine voice that filled her mind sent a shock through Sanna—she almost let go. Her knife fell from her hands, clattering to the ground, as the mountain dragon evened out. No magic kept her safe here, which made every subtle shift feel wrong. He drew his wings to their full length, stabilizing them. Sanna paused, heart racing.

"You can speak?"

We are not wild as the desert dragons. I come to deliver a message. Call off your dragon.

Sanna glanced up to see Luteis circling, snapping as he flew. Flickers of fire illuminated the waning night. Below, the mountain dragons seemed to disappear one at a time.

Rain flooded the camp. Fog loomed around them, hiding the ground. Quiet had fallen.

Luteis, she said. *Wait. He's speaking with me.*

Luteis calmed, though his eyes glittered with malice.

"What is your message?" she asked.

Surrender or die.

"A bit dramatic," she muttered.

My goddess, Selsay, demands your allegiance.

Sanna groaned. "Not another one!" He craned his head around to glance at her. Amidst the slivers of ... *something,* she thought she saw sanity. Intelligence. Perhaps even desperation. His nostrils flared, as if smelling her out. He turned around.

You do not respect her.

"I don't have any idea who Selsay is."

Do you fear her?

"Hardly."

Luteis, she said. *Go beneath us, and be ready.*

Subtle as a shadow, he descended. The mountain dragon tracked him. Unlike Luteis, with his expansive back and large body, this dragon had less room for her—and less flying finesse. Her teeth ached from bouncing up and down as he navigated in a broad circle over the field. Rigid spines stuck up from both the bottom and the top of his neck.

If goddesses had a problem with each other, why couldn't *they* figure it out? The fast-growing rain clouds built overhead. The dragon eyed them.

I am Pemba, leader of the mountain dragons. If you do not surrender the forest dragons to Selsay's will, we shall attack.

"I'm sure you will."

You do not take us seriously! Pemba hissed. *You insult the goddess of the mountains!*

"Calm down," she snapped. "Tell your goddess we're not surrendering anything."

If you will not, I shall—

She felt him shifting down before he finished his thought, and took the moment to roll to the side. One of his spines stabbed her shoulder as she tumbled off him, plunging to the earth. A second of perilous free fall passed before she slammed into Luteis. The magic seemed to grab her even before she touched him, anchoring her to his warm back.

If you were planning an attack on the foul creature, he said, curt, *I would have appreciated advance notice.*

Sorry. Last-minute idea.

Luteis plunged into a dive. Sanna grabbed his shoulders, clinging to him. Rain sluiced down his scales, pelting her face. She glanced back to see Pemba just above them in the air, then he disappeared. She frowned. The dive through the now-empty air seemed to do the trick of getting rid of them.

Pemba didn't follow.

Let's go see if we can help, Sanna said. *I'll tell you what Pemba said later. He's their brood sire, I think.*

There was much about that that was odd, Luteis said. *I could not speak with Pemba. Or perhaps he ignored me.*

Or he's dependent upon touch.

Perhaps. There is much we don't know.

They alighted on the ground amidst shrieks and screams. Sanna slid off his back, then paused. Her hands dropped to her sides.

On the ground lay a young Western Network boy and his brand-new hatchling, both stilled in death.

～

Isadora's headache pounded like the tide.

It rippled across her neck, tightening her muscles all the way down her spine. She rubbed her fingers in a circle on her temples. When her eyes closed, she could feel the magic tugging on her.

She opened her eyes and grimaced. Something had to be done.

Soon.

Without admitting defeat to Maximillion.

An almost empty *lavanda* greeted her. All the recently cleaned linens were gone, leaving nothing but cords of firewood, driftwood, barrels, and cupboards. Darkness cloaked the room where the light from her candles didn't reach.

Outside, a gale howled, whipping against the castle, sending rolling waves high onto the shore, which seemed perilously close. The slap of water on the wall sent cold shudders through Isadora. The ocean seemed livid enough to swallow them whole. She wondered if La Torra had ever been engulfed in waves. They didn't seem so far away now.

After breakfast, only a few piles of laundry had awaited her, left over from yesterday. She'd sped through it, sorting with greater ease. Silk. Linen. Cotton. The bubble of boiling water and the scent of a particularly tough cleaning potion had filled her nostrils. The *lavanda* heated up quickly, but she didn't mind the heat.

Two hours had passed before she had all the material stretched on drying racks or hanging from the walls.

Satisfied, she stepped into the hall.

Footsteps echoed to the left, a light, fast staccato. One of Cecelia's maids, probably. But why would she be down here?

Isadora made a mental note of the time. La Torra seemed to purr like a clock. She listened for more, but found nothing. Even that, by Maximillion's standards, meant something.

With a tentative step, she slipped out of the *lavanda* and headed to the right.

Maximillion's voice echoed through her mind as she navigated toward the dining room. *If you want to help Lucey, you'll find the answer in the details.*

The other servants were her best chance of hearing something. From what she could tell, the staff congregated in the dining room throughout the day to talk or complain or make fun of the East Guards. Heated gossip flew around at breakfast—today had been no exception. One of Cecelia's maids had been reportedly sneaking off with an East Guard—although no one could figure out who.

Fiona and Lorenzo sat at the table. Outside, the storm churned the ocean into a fury that sounded even louder here. Thrumming rain lashed the windowpanes. Lorenzo's gaze darted to the window, the table, and back to the window again. He clutched a cup of wine in his white-knuckled hand while Fiona chattered, nonplussed. Outside, her small boat rocked on the waves, seeming no worse for wear in spite of the gale threatening to tip it over.

Isadora stood in the doorway. The *clank* of dishes and jovial singing drifted from the kitchen, as usual. The sharp tones of Ernesto's voice were distinguishable over all the others—at least he wasn't *only* irritable with her.

"Isadora?"

Fiona's questioning voice broke through her thoughts. She stared at her in silent question—or was it astonishment? Isadora averted her gaze.

"I finished all the laundry. I came to see if I could be of assistance some other way."

Lorenzo's eyebrows lifted. "That's very kind of you."

"I enjoy work."

Fiona said nothing, but took a sip of tea. "No. The *lavanda* maid remains where she is. Return."

Disappointment curled in her stomach. It would have been a lovely opportunity to explore more of the castle. Not to mention battle her boredom of that room. The only witch with any *real* chance to explore the castle was Fiona. Even Lorenzo couldn't go onto Cecelia's floor. The maids that worked for her were rarely seen; Cecelia didn't let them leave.

Lorenzo reached over and pulled a chair away from the table. "Sit and have some wine with us. We're just discussing how we'll celebrate this time when the Defenders go out on a raid."

Isadora complied but left a seat between them. "Celebrate?"

"We always throw a little party when they leave." Lorenzo grinned. "There is no one to stop us when Cecelia takes them out. It has been several weeks now since their last raid, so we are all ready for them to go for a bit."

Chagrin flooded her when Fiona turned the conversation. Fiona and Lorenzo resumed their mild chatter—quick and low, forcing Isadora to strain to hear plans about brioche rolls, white wine, and cooked eel. She glanced at the wine they proffered with a sigh, then sniffed it. Less potent than she'd smelled on Pearl's breath on occasion. Thus far, she'd only had water.

She pressed the wine to her lips and sipped. A dark, yeasty flavor flooded her mouth. Not entirely unpleasant, but—

Something slammed into her chest, sending her reeling back. Her chair tipped over, crashing onto the floor.

Isadora gasped.

Her powers whipped into a frenzy.

The feeling of someone grabbing her by her ankles and swinging her around overcame her. She pressed her lips together, attempting to control her response. The disorienting whirl deepened. Several moments passed while the magic ran rampant in her veins, careening through her, demanding escape. It wasn't until she heard the utter silence that she realized Lorenzo and Fiona were hovering over her.

"Are you all right?" Lorenzo asked.

Burning with magic—and embarrassment—Isadora scrambled off the chair. "F-fine. Just ... I'm fine."

"Our wine is good," Fiona said with dry amusement. "But not *that* good."

Concern filled Lorenzo's gaze. He slipped into the common language. "It seemed as if you were hit. Are you sure—"

"Fine. I'm fine. Just a ... slight headache."

"No sick days for the *lavanda* unless the apothecary says so," Fiona said, then frowned. "But I think we have a headache powder if you need it."

"The laundry is all done," Lorenzo said to Fiona, allowing the words to trail away. Isadora opened her mouth to say she didn't need the day off when the magic tugged on her. Darkness crowded the edges of her vision, threatening to take her into the paths right there. Her nostrils flared as she warred with it.

I will not return.

"Are you certain you're all right?" Lorenzo sounded distant, as if through a long tunnel. "You seem—"

No! Isadora cried in her head, trying to imagine the powers under her control. The dining room faded again, transposed with leaves. A tree.

Darkness.

No!

She stomped her left heel into her right foot, then jumped with a yelp. The grip of the magic retreated. Tears smarted in her eyes. The wine must have lowered her defenses, and the magic had come stampeding out. She could barely control it.

"Goodness!" Fiona cried. "Are you mad?"

Isadora shook her head, biting the inside of her cheek. The powers released their hold on her, white hot in her head and whipping around like the frenzied storm outside. She grabbed them, tucking them into her mental closet.

"What's going on?" barked another voice. Ernesto peered out from the kitchen, saw Isadora, rolled his eyes, and retreated.

Peace, she commanded.

"I-I'm fine," she said. "Just tired."

"But your foot!" Lorenzo cried. "Why would you—"

"I ... I thought I felt a mouse."

A voice called from the hall outside, startling Isadora into silence. "Fiona!"

Lorenzo jumped. Fiona whirled around, eyes wide. Isadora's blood turned cold. She knew that voice.

Cecelia.

FIFTEEN

The rustle of an expensive dress entered the dining room. Isadora gulped, eyes trained on the table. Her prickling fear caused the magic to flare again. Lorenzo and Fiona stared at the doorway, both seeming annoyed.

I am safe, she said to the magic. *I don't need you. I am safe.*

Still, the magic bloomed, whizzing through her. She stamped it down. Like a witch dying of thirst, it reached out again. As if it would escape from her very bones and jump to Cecelia. A longing to be in the paths followed. How badly she wanted to enter the magic again!

"Fiona!" Cecelia called again. "Where has Giorgia gone?"

Fiona slipped to the doorway—she never rushed anywhere. "I'm not sure, milady. I haven't seen her today."

Isadora clenched her hands, knuckles white, and forced her mind elsewhere. Who was Giorgia? A maid, no doubt. What kind of maid would risk Cecelia's wrath?

"She was missing this morning," Cecelia continued. "Did you see her when you delivered breakfast?"

"I brought breakfast early and didn't see any of the maids."

"I don't appreciate hunting for those that work for me. Call an East Guard. Have them search for her."

"Right away."

"Once she's found, send her to my office. I shall be preparing for tonight's raid. She couldn't have gone far."

Tonight's raid.

Isadora kept her gaze fixated on Cecelia's shoes, which shone in the muted candlelight. Low light from nearby torches made the diamond bracelet around her left wrist sparkle. She wore a dress made of *linea*, a rare and expensive material that responded to the environment, cooling the person who wore it or, alternately, warming them if needed. Layers of it flowed around her waist, hovering just above the floor in lacy perfection.

The burn of Cecelia's penetrating gaze hit Isadora. "Who are you?"

Isadora lifted her head. Cecelia's eyes were stunningly cold—like flecks of ice. Not a hint of warmth. No smile lines. No cheeky sarcasm. Nothing but cold, hard determination. Fear doused the magic, withering it away inside her. The *Ilese* words nearly abandoned her.

"My name is Isadora." She dropped her eyes again. "I am the new *lavanda* maid."

"You're not Eastern."

"No."

"I've seen you before."

"In the halls, milady?"

"You address me as The Great One."

Isadora suppressed the urge to apologize and simply nodded.

"No," Cecelia continued. "I haven't seen you yet in the halls. Somewhere else."

A pregnant pause grew between them. Isadora's heart raced, thudding in her chest. Would Cecelia have seen her that distant day in the Central Network when an entire mob of hungry witches had swarmed her carriage? No. Impossible.

Cecelia's eyes narrowed.

"No matter. Just remember to be careful with my silks."

Her feet tapped the stone floor as she walked away. Isadora waited until she was well out of the room to look up. Both Fiona and Lorenzo had relaxed. Several seconds passed before Fiona said, "You'd do well to heed her warning."

With that, she left the room.

"An easy encounter with Cecelia," Lorenzo said. "Consider yourself a lucky girl."

Isadora remained alone in the dining room with the wind whipping outside for several minutes. Her mind spun, remembering the young Watcher. She frowned when the magic settled in a pulsing headache at the back of her scalp.

She turned toward the *lavanda*. Her racing blood slowed. Too close. Would Maximillion contact her? There was no way for him to know about the raid—or for her to tell him without magic. She sighed. He'd have to worry about that.

In the meantime, she'd take care of her powers.

Tonight.

DESPITE LUTEIS'S and Elis's warm bodies filling the cave,

cooler air swept through it from a hole somewhere in the back.

Jesse built up a fire, tending it with unusual attention. She suspected it wasn't as much about the warmth as it was about doing something familiar. A few scratches marred his face and hands. He'd been quieter than usual since the attack that morning, when he and Elis had helped protect some of the Western Network witches. The entire camp felt somber. Last count, five witches, three hatchlings, and six adult dragons had been killed.

If more of this was in their future, the desert dragons would have to mount an unbelievable defense against the mountain dragons. A force they had no real hope of marshalling without the intelligence and communication that the desert dragons *should* have had. Yet another way goddesses had been failing their dragons for years.

Perhaps Deasylva wasn't alone in that.

Colorful blue and lavender flames licked high into the air from Jesse's fire. Jesse and Elis had scrounged the shore and the craggy rocks for driftwood, finding some hidden in a smaller cave. Sanna studied the flames, falling deep into thought. Desert dragons. Goddesses at war. Mountain dragons.

Was the world really so big?

She longed to return to Letum Wood, where things were still all-encompassing, but smaller. She felt a pang for Daid and wondered how Isadora could handle so many new things all the time. Didn't she ever long for home?

Luteis leaned over, nudging her with his snout. *You are deep in thought.*

Yes, she responded internally to keep from bothering Jesse. *If this was Selsay's wrath, I'm worried about the rest of the Dragonmasters.*

I as well.

Jesse glanced up in wordless question. Before they could utter another word, someone appeared at the door. Tashi stood there, expression pointedly blank.

"Yushi has come," she said. "I will bear you to him."

Sanna could never have imagined something so *vast*. The ocean stretched across the entire horizon, seeming to fall at the edge into a wild unknown. The horizon blurred into a watery sunrise that washed the sky in rose and butter yellow. In the far south, the sky and ocean met under a dark, churning mass of clouds. A storm had gathered so far away Sanna couldn't see anything but occasional flashes of lightning.

Waves licked the beach with foamy kisses, then retreated with a sigh. Sanna stood just shy of the water. Something about staying out of reach settled the rankled feeling in her chest. The vast expanse of the ocean didn't feel trustworthy. Luteis shuffled somewhere behind her— away from the water, but not by much.

What do you think I'm supposed to do here? she asked him.

Although I cannot make out any plan on Tashi's part, I would imagine we wait for Yushi, Luteis said.

Tashi kept an eye on the skyline and said nothing. Another witch stood next to her. Aki. The High Dragon-master of the desert dragons, who had only briefly introduced himself by bowing his head, lifting a hand to his chin, and touching the tips of his fingers to it before pulling them away. He was a sprawling man with dark shoulders like mountains and arms as thick as boulders. He had glacial blue eyes, as if patterns of frost had been etched into windows. The sand dusted his stubbled cheeks, making his face appear gritty.

She could taste the sand between her teeth as she scanned the cliffs. Where was this *Yushi*?

A hissing sound came from the water.

Sanna whirled around to find a dragon rising out of the ocean in elegant lines, scales shimmering. Pieces of seaweed clung to a robust, lithe body as thick as a tree trunk. He had no wings, no legs, just a long tail with a transparent emerald webbing that ran all the way up his spine. Fangs stuck out from his upper lip, and he stared at her with black eyes. Thanks to his serpentine face, with a wider snout and thicker neck that grew into a stocky body, she could see hints of the other dragon races within him. A gleam of indifference lingered in his studious gaze.

"Your greatness." Tashi bowed at the neck. "It's my honor to present the High Dragonmaster of—"

Sanna stepped forward, cutting her off.

"I'm Sanna."

He closed his eyes, then opened them again on her. "Greetings, daughter of the forest. I am the leader of the sea dragons. You may call me Yushi."

He spoke from deep in his throat. The foamy sea rushed up around him. Sanna stepped back from the surging water. She had to tilt her head to meet his glittering, intelligent gaze. She'd expected *something*, but a sea dragon wasn't it.

Certainly not one that spoke outside of her mind.

For a long moment, they stared at each other. Water dripped down his scales from the top of his neck and back to the ocean, getting lost in the waves.

"Your Greatness," Aki said, positioning himself in front of her. "She is new to our ways and—"

"She has made no insult," Yushi said. "Go."

Aki's mouth opened, then closed. He nodded once. "As you wish."

Aki and Tashi bowed, then retreated. Only Luteis and Sanna remained. Once the others faded from sight, Yushi turned back to Sanna.

"You will not dismiss your dragon?"

"Never."

"Admirable." Yushi's eyes narrowed. "You do not care for the traditions of your allies? They would never conduct business alongside their dragons."

"I don't know anything about the Western Network, and we have no agreement as allies."

"Are all dragons not allies?" he asked.

There was too much levity in his tone for Sanna to think the question genuine. A thousand retorts slipped through her mind, but she gave none of them. Yushi hissed a little. Was it a laugh?

"You fake ignorance but see much," he said. "I know your game, Sanna of Gregor."

"There is no game."

"There is always a game."

"Such as leading witches to practically worship a dragon that isn't even one of their own dragon race?"

Yushi's lips curled in a coy smile. "You believe they worship me?"

"I believe they're terrified of you."

"It is not the same."

She thought of Talis and Drago and silently disagreed. Luteis snarled under his breath and stepped closer until he towered over Sanna. Yushi straightened but barely met Luteis's shoulder. However, his long body seemed to coil forever into the water. There was no telling just how big—or powerful—Yushi was.

I do not like this dragon, Luteis hissed.

Me either, she said. *But maybe we can get some more information.*

"How do you know I don't belong to the Western Network witches?" Yushi asked. "Is it so strange that the Western dragons would ally themselves with a far more powerful race?"

"You aren't the god of the Western dragons."

"You who knew nothing of the gods and goddesses?"

Sanna's nostrils flared. Aki or Tashi must have already spoken to him. "I'm no fool just because I don't leave my forest."

"So you say."

His body slid over the wet sand with ease, closing the distance between them but not leaving the water entirely. Sanna held her ground by sheer willpower.

"You are correct," Yushi continued. "My goddess Prana is not responsible for the vagabond dragons of the West. They have been abandoned and will not be adopted. Indeed, they cannot be. Such is the legacy of the lost gods. Prana welcomes *you,* however. Not only to the ocean, but to understanding."

A wave crashed up from behind him, splashing in a spray of foam. Sanna stepped out of reach of the water again.

"What understanding are you talking about?" she asked.

"Of who you are. How could you understand your power as High Dragonmaster without meeting the other dragons and High Dragonmasters?"

He's playing at something, Sanna said to Luteis. *What is it?*

Yushi's gaze slipped to Luteis. A moment of silence followed before Luteis replied to her.

I cannot tell.

Yushi peered at her again. "You're reticent. You hold your thoughts close, don't you?"

"Yes."

"Wise in certain circumstances, but I must encourage you to see the benefits of hearing out Prana. She is the oldest and most powerful of the goddesses." His tongue flickered out. "And the one most suited to helping you with your little ... problem."

"I never said we had a problem."

A slithering, hissing sound rumbled out of him. Sanna tensed, reaching for her knife. Luteis's wings also tensed. Several seconds passed before she realized Yushi was laughing. Luteis lowered his head with a rippling growl.

Let's leave.

Wait.

"The goddesses are awakening," Yushi said. "So are the old jealousies. Selsay, goddess of the mountains, has made foolish decisions. A fit of madness has taken hold of her dragons, poisoning their progeny and themselves. They cannot function as dragons should. Their minds are nearly lost. Selsay seeks to heal them—"

"Hardly a reason for war."

"—by killing forest dragons and drinking their blood."

Luteis hissed.

Sanna tightened. Of course. Forest-dragon blood had healing properties. Why hadn't she seen that coming?

"Not even you can dispute this," Yushi said, seething arrogance in his voice. "Even you have seen their uncontrollable fits of madness."

Sanna pressed her lips together. All the information slid into place, creating a grisly—but clear—picture. Whatever Selsay wanted, her dragons weren't well. And if Selsay knew of the power of forest-dragon blood, the forest dragons were in even more danger than Sanna had anticipated. She hesitated. Could she trust Yushi?

"Prana has asked me to speak with you." His liquid black gaze flickered over Sanna's shoulder. A hint of disdain colored his tone. "As her emissary, I have been working with the desert dragons in an attempt to create peace with Selsay."

"Has it worked?"

He stared at her with a flat, unperturbed expression. Heat flushed Sanna's neck. Of course it hadn't worked. Why else had there been an attack early that morning?

Sanna clenched her knife hilt a little tighter. "How do we defeat her?"

"Dragons don't defeat goddesses."

"What do they do?"

Yushi blinked lazily. "They defeat each other. According to rumor, a goddess is only as strong as her dragon force, which is only as strong as its Dragonmaster." He drew himself up, blocking the sun with his elegant neck. "If Selsay decides to turn her fight toward Prana, we'll be forced to fight. Dragon to dragon. That is why it is so important that you have come. A war is brewing between the goddesses, daughter of the forest. And you are the only one who can stop it."

No wonder Tashi said the dragons owed you something.

"Then we're in bad shape," she muttered.

Yushi paused, tongue slipping out, before saying, "My goddess desires to form an alliance with you, High Dragonmaster."

"No."

His gaze tapered. "Interesting."

"Is it?"

"There may come a time when an alliance with a powerful goddess could turn the tide in your favor. Indeed, it may be the only thing that can save the forest dragons from ... dissent within?"

Sanna clenched her teeth. "There may also come a time when the Western goddess returns," she said, "but I don't really see that happening."

"Your arrogance will get you into trouble."

"I'll take my chances."

"You truly don't see yourself as High Dragonmaster," he said. "I didn't believe them. What fool would disdain such an honor? And yet ... you stand before me."

"It was forced upon me at a time it was needed, then taken away."

"Greatness often is."

"It's not mine anymore."

"Not if you don't want it."

"If you want to win a war, do it yourself. The forest dragons can't be expected to save you when you did nothing to save us."

"One could hardly have stopped the massacre of long ago," he said. "You blame the wrong species, witch."

Another pause. He seemed contemplative, even intrigued. Then all emotion faded from his expression.

Something strange about the ferocity in his eyes reminded her of the desert dragons.

"If you want back-up," she said, "talk to the forest dragons themselves. I have no right to speak for them."

"Interesting," he murmured. "This means Deasylva is even weaker than Prana expected."

"If the dragons want to fight, I'm no dictator who will stop them. They get to make their own choices now. But things might be a little different in Letum Wood than you're anticipating."

"You're odd," he murmured, "but at least you speak the truth."

She said nothing.

Yushi retreated, taking the ocean with him. Sanna breathed easier once he slid backward. Luteis's tense forelegs eased. Yushi acted as if he didn't notice.

"I'll give you time to ponder this, daughter of the forest." Frothy white waves swept around him. "No doubt Selsay will convince you soon enough just how much you need an alliance. The time will come when you cannot win alone. My offer stands."

With that, he slipped back beneath the waves.

"You're leaving."

Tashi stood at the mouth of the cave, her sheer linen skirt whipping in the breeze. Sanna shoved a hunk of airy bread and a woven bag of seeds into her blanket. She tied it, then slung it over her shoulder.

"We must."

Tashi placidly surveyed her.

Sanna scowled and breezed past her. "Are you going to lecture me on my duty to become High Dragonmaster?"

Tashi swiveled to follow. "Do I need to?"

"I've heard enough. I've seen enough. The last time we had a leader, it destroyed all of our history and could possibly be the reason for the extinction of the forest dragons today. I won't be responsible for that."

"That may happen anyway."

Sanna scowled. "I won't be responsible for it."

"So you think."

"Yushi is a sea dragon that, clearly, has enough power to take care of this problem for both of you."

"Sea dragons cannot fight on land, except perhaps right along the coast where they can use the ocean to their advantage. You see the desert dragons—they pose no threat. Forest dragons, however, *can* fight on land. You are the only force that can fight against Selsay in the mountains. Until she is controlled, she will allow this wild breeding and eventually take over. The consequences extend far beyond dragons, but to the world."

Sanna scowled and headed toward Luteis, perched on top of the cave. His eyes scanned the sky. Elis stood next to him. Both appeared regal in the glimmering, relentless sunlight. Jesse stood with a group of witches—mostly female, which only perturbed Sanna more—a few paces away.

"Jesse," she barked. "We're leaving."

As soon as he saw her, he turned back to the amassed witches, pressed three fingers to his chin, and drew them away. The witches did the same. Young desert dragons hid in the rocks, some buried in the sand with only their eyes peeking out. Both Elis and Luteis ignored them.

"Whatever will happen, will happen, Sanna," Tashi said. "Do you want the weight of that on your shoulders?"

"The forest dragons won't *act*," Sanna said. "Do you not understand? They don't know how. Talis ruled them for the last century and a half. They can't ... they can't even fly or hunt. I've tried, and they don't care. I won't be a tyrant, even if some irresponsible goddess *did* force me into the position of High Dragonmaster at one point. If the desert dragons need us, they'll have to figure something else out."

"They need *you*, daughter of the forest."

"Yushi can figure it out on his own."

"I didn't mean Yushi."

"Fine. The desert dragons."

"Or them."

Sanna stopped. Tashi stared at her, eyes full of expectation.

"The forest dragons?" Sanna asked. "That's what you mean?"

"No. You. Regardless of whether you will help us fight or not, Pemba is about to be your problem. No amount of denying what—and who—you are will stop that. Like it or not, you are the High Dragonmaster of the forest dragons, or the closest thing there is to one. Perhaps you will not fight for the desert dragons, but soon you will be forced to fight."

A grouping of desert dragons soared overhead, drawing Sanna's gaze. She watched them fly, wings outstretched, with a catch in her belly. Even feral, they were regal. Like all dragons, they possessed a sort of unbound beauty.

Sanna turned away.

"Look, the forest dragons are a mess. They're split into groups of two, maybe three by now. There's no solidarity. We're just coming out of a tyrannical, disastrous rule. Leadership—and a goddess who abandoned us to slaughter—isn't really high on the forest dragons' trust list. Even if I *was* High Dragonmaster, it wouldn't matter. They don't listen to me. They blame me for all their current problems."

"For the betterment of the world, you must figure it out," she said quietly. "We cannot stand divided. For centuries, we have tried. If we fail, so do the dragons, with consequences far deadlier than anything we've ever seen."

Sanna turned away, scowl deepening, and approached Luteis's side with relief. The urge to get away bore down on her. She wanted to be back *now*. In the forest. Amidst the trees.

Are you ready? Luteis asked without tearing his gaze from the sky.

Been ready since we left home.

Rustling came from nearby. Clods of tightly packed sand dropped from the cave face, revealing a small collection of hatchlings gathered on top. They slithered backward but stayed within sight. They weren't total cowards, anyway. Their eyes flickered to Luteis, then back to Sanna, then back to Luteis.

Luteis nudged Sanna. *We must be on our way. Storms arise in the south and move quickly.*

"I'm sorry, Tashi," Sanna said. "But there's nothing I can do to help. The forest dragons are scattered. Not even a High Dragonmaster can change that."

Jesse climbed atop Elis, waving to his new friends, while Sanna settled herself high on Luteis's shoulders. Seeing Tashi so far below gave Sanna no comfort.

"May the goddess look down on you, Sanna of the forest," Tashi said, eyes squinting as she gazed up at her. "For all our sakes."

SEVENTEEN

Sea foam lapped at Isadora's ankles.

Stars smattered the sky like an open scroll. A hint of marmalade lingered near the horizon, where the storm had retreated an hour before sunset. In the distance, a spout of water broke from the ocean. The staff told tales of massive creatures beneath the waves—dragons, sharks, whales. Magical fish with teeth as long as her hand.

Isadora shuddered.

The distant clink of armor betrayed Guardians nearby, but they had already passed on their rounds. The laugh of a chef rolled out from the kitchen windows far away. The sound of a distant aquila crying rang in the background, but no flapping of wings followed. Candlelight winked in several windows, as if La Torra were on fire. Another small bank of land lay off La Torra's shores, not far beyond the break of waves, invisible in the darkness.

Isadora tossed her knotted stockings behind a spindly cocoanut tree with a grimace. The bright pink fruit on the inside of the hard discs tasted mildly sweet—she'd take a fallen one back to her room after this.

The magic burned bright, triggering a headache behind her eyes. With the magic acting like a wild thing, she'd never be able to help Lucey. Nor could she leave now—it would take any other Advocacy member twice as long to integrate in, earn trust, and find out more information. And time ticked away. With La Torra mostly empty thanks to the raid, there would be no better time to release her magic.

She glanced over her shoulder before advancing into a hissing wave, intent on the small bank of sand not far away. It would have to do.

The warm water lapped around her shoulders when she slipped into it, the salty taste of the ocean on her lips. Thanks to the frantic flapping of her arms and legs—and a gentle ocean in the wake of the storm—she stayed afloat as she battled the rolling tides. Only a few minutes of treading the warm water passed before she felt sand under her feet again.

Her eyes adjusted to the darkness just before she caught the rocky shore with her toes. A darting movement captured her attention. She looked down.

"What the—"

An underwater world teemed with life beneath her.

Bright sapphire fish glided by with lazy ease. Elegant, flowing tendrils, like bright green fingers, waved back and forth. Beneath it all crawled a network of ... *something* riddled with holes. Tiny fish flittered in and out of the spots nearest her. The surface below felt sharp beneath her feet and stretched as far as she could see in the murky water.

"Beautiful."

A sudden attack of nerves arrested her. She glanced at La Torra, winking with candlelight, then at the sky. No aquilas or East Guards. Despite her fear, the calm atmosphere lulled her with the reassuring swish of the waves. Did she have a choice? The magic careened in her mind, plunging her back into agony. No. No choice. She'd have to hurry. The Defenders could return at any moment. She lay back in the sand and let the water rush around her.

A violent, breathtaking jerk took her away.

The powers opened on their own. She stood beneath the familiar, soaring canopy of Letum Wood again. Light raced through the forest in unbroken streams, so bright she recoiled. Crisp lines infused every leaf and twig with details that hurt her eyes. She shielded her face with an arm. Wild wisps and sharp jerks of the trail appeared. The air itself hummed with frenetic energy. She tried to shove her power free, as if she could bundle it together and dump it all at once.

The chaos brightened.

Frightened, Isadora tried to close the magic. Darkness crept in from the edges of her vision. The magic fought, tugging her back. The light brightened. With a grunt, she pulled free, slipping away from its steel-like tendrils.

Cool water slapped her face.

Isadora shot up with a sputter, nearly submerged in a rolling wave. She shook droplets from her face and blinked. How long had she been gone? Moments, surely. No sound lingered around her except the waves. She braced herself, prepared for Defenders to rush at her with their whips.

Nothing happened.

Her powers overwhelmed her, like a dam breaking again. With a shove, she fell back to the sand and tumbled into the magic. The paths shone with energy and power. Isadora closed her eyes, pushed her fears aside, and allowed the power to unfurl. Her heart fluttered. Her body felt as if it would disintegrate.

Once the initial surge of power faded, she opened her eyes. The forest continued to glow, but without the same manic energy. For several moments she stood there, blinking. Intricate paths heavy with wisps—almost too thick to walk through—awaited her.

She didn't even recognize her own magic anymore.

"Show me only Sanna's path."

A confusing array of wisps popped up. Mountains. Dragons. Sanna, with a heavy frown, on the back of Luteis. None of them made sense, but she studied them anyway, moving from one to the next, drawing comfort from any sight of her sister.

Where was Daid?

Mam?

The other Dragonmasters?

Jesse cropped up in one path. She followed it until she caught glimpses of Mam. Sanna seemed to have left the Central Network. But why? What terrible thing could force Sanna, of all witches, from Letum Wood? Surely, Maximillion would have told her if she needed to be concerned.

Wouldn't he?

Isadora returned to the beginning to find new paths had populated, some occurring in Letum Wood. Perhaps she hadn't left, then.

She frowned. There *had* to be a sense to the chaos, a purpose to a magic as powerful and consuming as this. "What are you for?" she murmured to the still air. "Why do I have you?"

The magic didn't respond.

"Show only my paths."

Wisps disappeared, decluttering the space. For what

felt like hours, she wandered, searching for Lucey. Anything that might happen within La Torra's borders remained blurry, indistinct. She *couldn't* see the future at La Torra.

Interesting.

Somewhat comforted by the familiarity of wandering the paths, she returned to the beginning. The light hadn't ebbed, but her chest felt lighter.

"Show me Lucey's path."

Sanna's paths disappeared, but nothing replaced them. Isadora frowned. She attempted Lorenzo's but couldn't see his either. Too far away, perhaps. Or the suppressive magic of La Torra prevented it somehow.

Frustrated, she turned back to the space where the paths began. Behind her, more forest lingered. Nothing new there. A thousand possibilities for testing the magic occurred to her, but she'd tried them all before. Instead, she sat at the base of the biggest tree. The roots were taller than she was.

She stared into the forest, letting the power flow away from her.

A blast of light tossed Isadora back against the root. Her back slammed into the tree, jarring her teeth. When she looked up, a pillar of light climbed up from the ground like bubbling water. It coalesced into a familiar pair of boots, then broad shoulders and perpetual scowl.

Maximillion.

Isadora clambered to her feet, not taking her eyes away. "Max?"

The wind rustled, as it had before. *Merciful.*

Isadora stopped only a few paces away, eyes narrowed. She'd seen this before—more than once—but this time was different. Bolder. More clear. She could even see the gritty determination in his eyes.

This wisp had appeared on its own. That had never happened before. So why was he here?

"You," she murmured with a shake of her head. "You maddening ... *child* of a man."

The pillar vanished.

Seconds later, it bubbled back up, into a child half the size of Maximillion, but with the same piercing eyes. A split lip, a swollen eye, and a livid scowl graced his young face. Her breath caught.

"Max?"

The young wisp seemed frozen in time, caught in a moment of terrified crisis. Isadora reached out to touch the vapor. It disintegrated and reformed.

"What happened to you?" she murmured. "Why can I see you right now?"

He stared back in perfect silence.

Heart racing, Isadora mused, "If this is you as a child, what were you like as a teenager?"

The pillar collapsed again, scattering like beads until it reappeared. A teenage witch with an indignant expression in a handsome face. His fists clenched at his side. Jaw taut and tilted back, as if in defiance. Maximillion, at about fourteen years old.

"You're livid," she murmured.

For what felt like an eternity, she stared at the fractured boy. The rage in his eyes. A testimony to whatever he'd been through, surely.

Her heart broke.

"Remove him."

He shimmered away. Isadora breathed easier when he was gone, feeling guilty for having seen him at all. She turned away, suddenly tired. The bright lights had ebbed slightly. The once-frantic air cooled. She'd never seen so many facets of a witch before. Why Maximillion?

And *how*?

Weary of the endless search for meaning, she closed the magic and opened her eyes. A gentle lap of warm water rolled past her, brushing her chin. Stars still twinkled over-head. With a sigh, the magic curled up inside her. The tense humming of her body faded.

She stared at the night, her mind reeling, body weak. Her powers were different. Stronger. They'd revealed some-thing new. She'd known she could see an aspect, a facet, of a witch. But ages? Multiple facets? Almost as if, like the Defenders, she also glimpsed the past. Perhaps this magic was something she couldn't possibly fathom.

Was it possible?

Isadora sighed.

THE WIND WHISTLED through La Torra with a hint of sea salt and the promise of another storm the next day. The same bulging thundercloud remained on the horizon. Ahead of it raced meringue-like clouds, bringing wind and pelting rain. White-capped waves crashed onto the beach. Isadora gazed on the piles of washed, dried, pressed, and folded laundry on a creaky old cart. Her legs and arms ached from lugging heavy, wet blankets onto the drying line.

She stopped and held out a hand. Seconds later, a blue, shimmering cloud hovered above her palm. The woven mark of the Advocacy. She tightened her fingers into a fist. It disap-peared. So magic *could* be used at La Torra, even if it seemed to have suppressive effect on the paths she saw of those within it.

Confusing magic or no, she still had a life to save and information to glean. She pinched her arm, shook her head, and forced herself to wake back up.

The lack of unsettled magic gave her a bit more courage—perhaps foolishness. Unfortunately, the need to find Lucey burned brighter than wisdom and louder than the inner Maximillion in her head. Her plan was a foolish one, surely, but there was no going back now. Besides, Fiona was stuck on the third floor with Cecelia, doing who-knew-what. Isadora might never get another chance to find the elusive entrance to Carcere.

Outside, a patrol of East Guards strolled along the outside of La Torra, peering into the windows as they went. She pretended to be busy counting blankets and sheets. They disappeared around the corner, right on time.

She shoved her cart into the hallway.

Maximillion would withdraw her from the mission—or wring her neck—if he knew what she planned to do, but she couldn't wait another moment while Lucey suffered in Carcere. Besides, he couldn't have eyes *everywhere*. She'd caught a few glimpses in the paths the night before and formulated her plan around it. There was hope of it working.

And there was a greater chance it wouldn't. Still, time had passed, and the paths were never the same from one minute to the next.

Isadora trudged toward the servants' hall until she found the door she sought. On accident, she'd observed Lorenzo come out this door with a trolley of cleaning supplies. Instead of stairs, a smooth, spiral surface wound upward, allowing a cart to move from floor to floor with relative ease. She hurried inside and began to push her cart up the steep incline.

Based on Maximillion's map and Lorenzo's gossip, above the fifth floor was Carcere. While it technically occupied two floors on the same floor plan as the rest of the building, rumors said it seemed far larger inside. Whatever that meant.

Her rattling cart quieted when she spilled onto the fifth floor. The spiral path ended here. Isadora parked the linen in the middle of the hall, near a closet.

The hall lay quiet.

No decorative screens up here, just stone walls with an occasional limp torch in an empty, circular hall. Rain plunked against the closed windows. The stone hall lay damp, dark, and forbidding. Isadora shuddered.

A shout caught her attention. She crept across the hall and peered through a window onto the courtyard. Defenders trained in a semicircle with Cecelia in the middle.

What luck.

Cecelia stood beneath a protective awning made of glass on three sides that came to a point at the top, like the windows of La Torra. Rain sluiced down the sides, pouring off the edges and onto the ground. The wind didn't seem so strong within the circular courtyard. Each Defender maintained an expressionless face, as if the rain didn't bother them.

Isadora had woken up to find the Defenders returned, but no gossip reported whether they'd been successful. It rarely did. Lorenzo, Fiona, and the cooks seemed disinclined to acknowledge the Defenders—beyond when they left. The late-night wine party conducted in Cecelia's absence had left everyone subdued at breakfast that morning.

Today, Cecelia wore an elegant dress the color of spun

sunshine. It drifted around her legs in silky luxuriance, floating atop layers of underskirts. Even in the muted light, a thick necklace with strands of gems glittered from her collarbone.

"Sapphire," Isadora murmured as she studied the fist-sized gem in Cecelia's hair. "Coiled in a bun. Lace along the sleeves. Buttons up the back. Thirteen … fourteen … sixteen."

Isadora chewed on her lip as she memorized every detail. With a pit in her stomach, she checked the empty hall one last time, then retreated from the window and murmured a weak transformation spell.

The chill of a rush of ice water trickled down her back, startling her. She hadn't expected it to work. Still, the magic tingled through her. The *lavanda* outfit faded into a sleek, buttery dress that fitted her much-fuller chest like a glove.

Isadora stopped the magic, then slipped back to the window. Two Defenders stood in the middle, eyes closed. Their lips moved, as if they were narrating something. Cecelia stared on, intense as ever. Nothing seemed to have changed.

Isadora backed away.

She repeated the weak magic. This version of the dress was darker than Cecelia's. Nearly too dark—almost orange. Her fingers reached back to find only seven buttons. Her hair appeared too short, and a shade too light, but it would have to do. Unlikely that an East Guard would notice. Most East Guards were frightened of Cecelia, anyway. She couldn't impersonate Fiona or Lorenzo. The Guards knew them too well. Besides, what if she ran into them while they were going about their work?

Her hands trembled when she straightened the gown. Could she impersonate such a frosty personality?

"Just find the door," she whispered. "Find the entrance to Carcere, and get back out. Move quickly. Be confident. No one will know. I *am* Cecelia."

Isadora banished her frightened, squeaking voice and started down the hallway. If she was going to *be* Cecelia, she had to own it. Only three steps later, she paused. The skirt swayed around her legs. Although ample, it was still much too thin to be Cecelia's.

How did Cecelia carry herself?

A moment of panic overcame her.

Stupid girl, Maximillion said in her mind. *You'll never pull this off.*

"At least I'm doing something," she muttered, and pressed on. Attempting to copy Cecelia's walk would only waste time. Better to move fast and get it over with.

A commotion down the hall hurried her on. She tilted her chin back, shortened her stride, and hoped for the best. A back staircase—and a likely route upstairs—waited at the end of the hall. She held her breath as she turned a corner, ignoring the noise at the other end, which immediately fell silent. She forced her fingers to relax, her arms to loosen.

"Just check the stairs," she murmured. "Just make it to the stairs."

With relief, she reached for the doorknob. As her fingers grazed the top, it flew away. She paused, startled by the sudden movement.

A maid appeared, giggling.

"Giorgia!" called a distant voice. "Come back!"

"You'll have to catch me!"

The maid darted out of the stairwell, then skidded to a stop a breath before slamming into Isadora. Her eyes widened.

"Oh, Great One," she cried, dropping her gaze.

The maid rambled, speaking rapid words Isadora had no hope of understanding. *Giorgia.* The name rang through Isadora's mind until she recalled why it sounded familiar.

The missing maid.

Giorgia's eyes remained averted but only barely. Isadora slid her foot back when the stained edge of her own shoe peeked out of the dress.

"Excused," Isadora said in a clipped tone. The less she said, the better, for her voice remained her own.

The maid blinked and tilted her head to the side. "Forgive me, Miss Cecelia, but ... your *pastanda*. Where is it? I will gladly find it for you."

Eagerness—perhaps mollification—laced her tone. Isadora's mind raced. *Pastanda.* What in the name of the good gods was a *pastanda*? Something Cecelia wore, apparently. Isadora avoided the urge to glance down.

"I removed it."

The maid's eyes grew wide as saucers.

"Of a truth?"

Isadora swallowed hard. Had the maid said *of a truth* or *where are they*? The words were too similar for clarity.

"Check my room," Isadora said. Her tongue felt awkward and gluey, nothing like the flowing elegance of *Ilese*.

"Forgive me, Miss Cecelia, but I was just there. Do you want me to search somewhere else? I-I've never heard of you removing it. Won't you need it for your ... ah ... time with the High Priest tonight?"

"No."

Deepening confusion filled the maid's eyes, giving way to something like ... doubt. No matter how deeply she searched her mind, Isadora couldn't recall ever learning *pastanda*. Whatever it was, her ignorance might get her killed.

Wouldn't Maximillion be smug?

The maid's eyes narrowed. "Aren't you supposed to be training with the Defenders right now?"

Isadora's palms began to sweat. "Do you question me?" she hissed. The maid averted her eyes but only for a moment. Her suspicious gaze returned.

"May I see your mark, Miss Cecelia?"

Mark? What mark?

"An impertinent question," Isadora said, nostrils flaring. The girl leaned slightly to the left, but Isadora moved with her. The sound of something clattering in the courtyard, followed by a heavy shout, filled the sudden silence. Isadora forced herself to maintain eye contact. The girl's mouth tightened.

"Are you—"

The door slammed open behind them. A young Guardian rushed through the door, eyes bright. Isadora barely stepped back in time to avoid his broad shoulders and giddy smile.

"Giorgia," he called, laughing. He pulled her into his arms and nuzzled her neck. "I thought I would never find you."

The maid shoved him off with a hiss, angling his body so he could see Isadora standing there.

"Don't touch me!" Giorgia cried, voice shrill. "I don't know you."

His arms dropped to the side. He leapt back, hand on the hilt of his sword. Isadora's gaze moved to his hand, and he released it, cheeks burning. Murmured apologies streamed from his lips, too fast for her to comprehend. The maid trembled, staring at Isadora in a mixture of terror and uncertainty.

"Leave immediately," Isadora commanded. She held out a cupped hand and forced her voice to stay steady. "Give me your cuff links. Transport away and never return."

"Transport?"

Isadora stumbled over the word. Egads, but Cecelia didn't allow it! "I want you out of my sight immediately. I shall inform Fiona of your ... dishonor."

"I-I—"

"Silence!"

The maid pressed her lips together. Her eyes darted to the side, then back. Isadora's heart fluttered like a hummingbird. Would the girl risk it? Would she sound an alarm—and possibly be wrong? Not after being caught in a forbidden love affair with an East Guard, surely. According to the cooks, Cecelia had granted death for less.

With shaking hands, the girl removed her cuff links and dropped them into Isadora's palm. The Guardian glanced up from underneath his brow. His gaze dropped when Isadora glared at him, upper lip curled in the way she'd seen Cecelia snarl before.

"Please," the girl whispered. "Please don—"

"You have done this to yourself. Leave."

"Oh—"

"Now!"

The girl whimpered, cast one last glance at the Guardian, and disappeared in a transportation spell. Isadora's skin prickled. Splotches of her tanned skin began to appear. The weak magic was fading.

Isadora turned to the Guardian, chin high.

"Report to your superior. Confess all you've done—" She stopped when confusion flickered across his face. Had she said it correctly? No ... *confess* wasn't the same word ...

Her gaze dropped to her skirt, and a bolt of panic shot through her. The fabric ruffled as the layers underneath disappeared.

"Milady?" he murmured, brow furrowed.

He knew. The sudden, suspicious gleam in his eyes said everything. He suspected, at the very least, like the maid. The maid wouldn't return, but he? He'd stay. She didn't know Cecelia's power over the Guardians. Could she command them away?

"Report to your superior."

"Yes, Great One."

"Go."

With a clatter of armor, he disappeared back down the stairs he'd come so quickly up. The hall stood empty. Heart still pounding, Isadora let out a long breath. The magic bled free. Cecelia's elegant clothes drained back into her maids outfit, her soft bun at the nape of her neck. The layers of dress fell away, leaving her standing in the hall feeling utterly naked.

A sudden silence caught her ear. She blinked, then spun around and hurried to the window.

The courtyard lay empty.

Isadora darted back to the closet, where she'd stashed the laundry. By the time she'd yanked it out, composed herself, set the cuff links on top of a stack of linens, and started walking back the way she'd come, her control had nearly unraveled. Images of the dead young Watcher flashed through her mind as she hurried around a corner, then skidded to a stop.

Cecelia blocked the hallway.

Isadora's heart leapt into her throat. Defenders flanked Cecelia as they strode down the hall, forcing Isadora to shove the cart to the side or be trampled. Isadora swallowed hard and pressed her back to the wall, eyes averted. She counted their ankles as they passed.

"Felt it here," one murmured.

"Who would do magic here?"

"Who *could* with the *oro*?"

"I'm certain," said another, voice firm. "Magic was in use."

"Transportation, likely. It came and went."

"No, I detected something steady."

Just keep going, she silently begged. *Please keep going.*

Cecelia's black shoes, brightly polished, stopped right in front of her. The endless layers of her gown swayed. Isadora fought a grimace. Her version of Cecelia's dress had looked nothing like the real one.

"Why do you have those, *lavanda* girl?"

Her languid voice—so far from what Isadora had attempted to mimic—felt like ice on Isadora's skin. Cecelia held the maid's cuff links in her slender fingers now. Outside, a roll of thunder broke loose.

The Defenders kept walking.

"A maid, milady," she murmured, allowing her voice to fully shake. Her already-awkward speech came out bumbling, almost idiotic. "Sh-she resigned."

Cecelia frowned. "Why?"

"I-I don't know. She handed these to me and ... transported."

Cecelia sneered. "These are Giorgia's. She must have given a reason."

Unable to speak, Isadora just shook her head. Cecelia

stared hard at her, as if in doubt. The temptation to run nearly overwhelmed Isadora. She forced herself to stay by remembering Lucey.

"Was she upset?" Cecelia asked.

"Yes."

"She used magic to leave?"

"Yes."

If possible, the darkness in Cecelia's gaze deepened. Was it disbelief? Rage? "Take them to Fiona," she said, dropping them back to the sheet. "Tell her I will follow up on this later."

"Yes, Great One."

Five seconds passed before Cecelia continued onward again. Isadora stood rooted to the spot, drawing in deep breaths, until Cecelia disappeared. With one last burst of courage, she checked two more stairwells, saw nothing that led higher into Carcere, and returned to the *lavanda*, trembling.

ELIS TOLERATED the flight back with far more ease.

Luteis took them back to the functioning oasis, where they rested overnight, then pushed them hard all the way back deep into the forest. Both dragons, weary from the near-silent flight, descended into the canopy with relief. Sanna breathed deeply for what felt like the first time. The thick, dense air of Letum Wood soothed her rankled nerves.

"They're back!" one of Elliot's youngest children called. "There's Sanna and Jesse!"

Children ran in circles on the ground as Luteis and Elis descended, landing gently on the forest floor. Sanna slid off Luteis's back with a surge of guilt. She'd hardly thought of

Mam the entire time she'd been gone, and she certainly hadn't explained where she was going. A *thump* sounded next to her. Jesse had leapt off Elis and now soared past her, running as fast as his legs would carry him. All of Jesse's siblings boiled out of the foliage, shrieking for him.

"Jesse!"

"Mam!"

Babs wrapped her thick arms around him with an audible gasp and sob. They'd left only a hasty note for Babs. No doubt she'd been worried, even though they were only gone a few days. Jesse had never been parted from his family before.

Sanna's mind went immediately to Isadora, then Daid. A wave of disappointment crashed over her. No, Daid wasn't here. But she looked anyway, as if a miracle would bring his expectant face to her.

We should have stopped at Anguis, Luteis said. *To make sure your sister hadn't come home looking for you while we were gone.*

He'd read her mind.

Isadora said she'd be gone for a while. I doubt she would have come back. Besides, she'd probably be able to find us if she did.

You miss her.

I'm happy for Jesse, she said, although a pang of loss struck her anew. No one rushed out of the trees to see her. She missed Daid's quiet smile and the gentle way he set his hand on her shoulder. Was Mam well? Did she even realize Sanna had been gone?

The sound of Elliot's reverberating voice broke through her reverie.

"You returned."

Sanna glanced up to see him standing a short distance

away, hands on his hips. They hadn't been gone long, but Elliot seemed even more haggard than before.

"With news."

He drew in a deep breath, then nodded once.

"Come inside. It appears we need to talk."

CHAPTER

EIGHTEEN

An hour later, Sanna, Jesse, and Elliot sat in front of a warm fire outside Elliot's shanty. Babs murmured to the children in the background, preparing them for bed. Every now and then, the cry of a screaming gnome came from far away, and for a moment, Sanna almost felt as if they were back in Anguis. Elliot stared at the fire, blinking. A glazed expression had overtaken his face, as if he couldn't quite believe all they'd told him. Sanna couldn't blame him.

She wasn't sure she believed it herself.

"Desert dragons," he murmured. "Mountain dragons. *Sea* dragons. Who knew?"

Jesse poked at the fire with a long stick already charred at the end. "Apparently, we were the only ones who didn't."

While Elliot brooded, brow heavy, Sanna studied him. His tattered clothes hung off his shoulders. Babs had used black thread to stitch up a once-white shirt—somewhat haphazardly, at that. Elliot hadn't given them many details, but he'd mentioned beluas and a hint of a troll.

Other creatures, he had said. *Never seen them before.*

Dinner had been meager. Stale leto nuts, late winter shrooms, and a couple of overripe falla melons that smelled rank. Sanna's stomach rumbled. She intended to hunt with Luteis later.

None of the dragons had hunted for Elliot.

"I'm sorry, Elliot," she said. "I should have left Elis and Jesse with you to hunt. Without Rubeis ..."

"I'm going to be honest, Sanna." Elliot's eyes cut through the flames and right into her. "It's not what I thought it was out here. Without Finn and all the dragons that went with him, it's far more dangerous. The forest itself feels angry." He shuddered. "I know it sounds like I'm mad, but I can't shake the feeling. Tree branches fall all the time, half-rotted and dead. Sunlight doesn't pierce the canopy except at high noon, and we're always cold. When we had all those dragons here? Didn't seem as bad. But now?"

Sanna swallowed, unsure of what to say.

The forest is angry, Luteis said. *It has been forgotten.*

"Perhaps we should go somewhere else," she said.

He shrugged. "To where? What if it's like this everywhere?"

Ah, Talis, Sanna thought. *The legacy of your reign is still unfolding.* In some ways, they were no better than babies out here. With dragons that didn't know how to fight, hunt, or fly. And the desert dragons wanted *their* help?

"We have to find Finn," Elliot said. "He can't be faring any better than we are with all those dragons to feed. Even if we have to head north with him, maybe it would be worth it."

"You can't be thinking of—"

"I am."

"Elliot, it's only been a few days. We—"

"Exactly. That's all it's taken me to realize we can't do this forever."

Sanna stared at him, at a loss. *How can I ask more of Elliot?* she asked Luteis.

You cannot—and yet you must.

"The isolation out here has almost driven Babs mad." Elliot ran a hand through his hair.

Sanna had seen signs of strain on Babs's usually cheery face. Babs had lost weight. Her skin sagged in deep lines of worry. She startled often, twitching at almost every sound. Mam's neediness didn't help. Mam had hardly said a word when Sanna returned. She'd just stared at the empty air, arms folded over her chest like she was warding something off.

Sanna thought of Isadora and clenched her fists. She was missing *everything*.

"It's not just Babs, either," he said. "It's ... without Rian, I can't ..." He swallowed hard. "The emptiness of the forest can't be easier than life with Finn. Maybe we can convince him with your new information. Maybe the dragons will fight."

"The dragons that followed Finn definitely don't recognize me as Dragonmaster," she said. "They wouldn't listen to me even if I wanted them to."

"Don't you want them to?"

Sanna hesitated, her breath stalled. Did she? Perhaps a small part of her thrilled to the idea. But would they? And if they did, what would it mean?

"I want us to be safe."

"Do you think they're really going to attack?" Elliot asked.

The fiery burn of Pemba's breath, the sudden ferocity in his eyes, replayed in Sanna's mind. Those desert dragons had died. Witches, too. In a carnage as bloody and real as her own daid's death. She certainly hadn't imagined it, even if she hadn't wanted to face it. Did they have a choice now?

"I do," she said, swallowing hard. "I do think they're going to try, at least."

"There's no reason for this Selness—"

"Selsay."

"Selsay to kill all the forest dragons. Maybe she doesn't want us dead. Perhaps she hopes to strike a deal."

"Then she'll have a hard time explaining Daid's death."

Elliot blew out a hot breath, as if conceding her point. Sanna thought of the mountain dragon that flew into the cliffs, breaking its own wing and later dying. There was more than met the eye there. There had to be.

Something wasn't right.

Elliot's expression seemed to waver for a moment, torn between disbelief, fear, and uncertainty. Then it settled into troubled lines as he gazed back at the fire. Sanna straightened, pulling her shoulders back.

"I think we should return to the Ancients," she said. "Maybe Finn will even be persuaded to go."

Luteis lifted his head.

"There are houses and water, and it's safer there," she continued. "Maybe it's our only chance."

Elliot shook his head. "The massacre happened there."

"There was one at Anguis, too."

"Cursed lands," he hissed. "We can't go back! We have to go forward."

"Wasn't *this* moving forward? Does it really feel so much better?" She spread her hands.

His expression darkened.

Jesse reached over and put a hand on her arm before she

could argue. He shook his head softly. Behind him, Elis moaned in his sleep.

"Just ... consider it?" she asked, blowing out a hot, annoyed breath.

Elliot scowled. "Not now."

Talis had assuredly destroyed any hope of unity, not only with his tyranny, but by instilling doubt and distrust amongst witches and dragons. The effective *leadership* Sanna had seen had been nothing but destructive—from Talis to Deasylva. Could the chasm ever be bridged?

She doubted it.

Very *highly* doubted it.

THAT NIGHT, Sanna climbed as high as she could go amidst the decaying trees.

She found a spot on a sturdy branch and settled onto it. Luteis eyed the peeling bark of a nearby tree. *Needs a good torch,* he muttered before laying behind Sanna on their massive, shared branch. His face rested near her back. She leaned against him, grateful to be in the silence, where it was easier to think.

After several hours staring at the underside of the branches overhead and slipping in and out of sleep, the sound of rustling wings broke into her stupor. Jesse leapt off Elis's back and dropped onto the branch. He sat across from her, and a flicker of movement and color told her that Elis lingered nearby. Only forest dragons could be such powerful creatures but maintain such a lithe grace.

With her ankle on her knee and her hands stacked behind her head, she glanced at Jesse. Luteis was settled next to her, his tail lazily curled around a branch, eyes closed.

"You've been unusually quiet since returning," Jesse said. Luteis reached over to hold Sanna's ankle with his tail even though their bond didn't require touch anymore. She appreciated the warm, familiar burn.

Sanna straightened. "I have an unusual amount to think about now."

"You do."

A thousand thoughts whirled through her mind as she watched Jesse flip a smooth stone over and over in his hands. They sat in the dark for several minutes. Sanna soaked in the ambient sounds of the forest. The gentle sigh of the wind. The creak of branches, the chitter of animals.

Why had he come here?

"Are you going to give Deasylva the message from Pemba?" Jesse asked as he crossed his ankles in front of him and leaned back on his palms.

"I tried. She didn't wake up, or whatever. Besides, if she's a goddess, shouldn't she just ... *know* ... somehow?" she asked. "Why should I have to tell her anything?"

He shrugged. "I'm as new to this as you are. I dunno what the rules are or even what they should be. Didn't know she existed until ..."

His voice trailed away.

"Talis died," Sanna snapped. "You can *say* it, Jesse. It's not going to harm you. It happened."

"Calm down," he said easily. "I just didn't know how to finish my thought because I couldn't remember when you told me about her, all right?"

"Oh. Sorry. I'm ... just on edge."

Luteis opened one eye to study her. She tried to relax—but not very successfully. She leaned back against the trunk instead, wishing she could fold herself inside of it. Surely nothing could be more reassuring than the sappy, warm heart of the forest.

"It's good to see my family again, at any rate." Jesse plucked a piece of moss off the branch and flicked it aside with his fingertips. "I didn't realize how much I had missed them until I saw them again. And, we were only gone a few days. Didn't know the world was so big. Now I kind of get why Isadora wants to see so much of it. Want to talk about what's on your mind?"

Sanna shoved her worries about Mam and Isadora aside.

"Not sure you want to hear."

"I do. Because I don't think it's as much about the existence of other dragons as it is about *your* leadership of *these* dragons."

She wrapped her arms around her knees and pulled them close to her chest. "I don't know. I don't know what to think. Everyone out there was under the impression that I was the leader of the forest dragons, but it's not true. There is no leader now. And there can't be. Not with Talis's reign of terror hanging over our heads. Can there?"

He opened his mouth to speak again, then shook his head.

"What?" she asked.

"Never mind."

Sanna fell into silence, grateful he didn't push. Her thoughts lay on a path she didn't want to follow. Luteis watched her closely.

Several minutes later, Jesse murmured, "It's sad."

Sanna glanced up, startled. "What's sad?"

"That Talis is still defining who we are. That his control,

the fear he instilled, is alive and strong, even after his death."

He stood up.

She scrambled to her feet. "I didn't ask for this, Jesse. I wish you could be the leader, or your father. Or—"

A knot in her throat forced her to stop. *Or Daid.*

His gaze softened. "None of us asked for this, Sanna. Not your daid. Not Elis or Luteis or even Talis."

"It was forced on me."

Jesse lifted his hands and gestured around them. "Us too."

Words failed her. She opened and closed her mouth, then looked away with a scowl. She hadn't thought of it that way before. Grief pressed on her shoulders, making her feel like a ghost. The thirst for bringing Selsay to justice—to make Daid's murder mean something—nagged at her. And being the High Dragonmaster meant expectations. How could she possibly handle more right now?

Just as the storm began churning in her mind, a warm tail squeezed her ankle again, sending a soothing sensation through her.

You are not alone, Luteis said.

Her shoulders relaxed.

Jesse drew in a deep breath. "Listen, Sanna, I know you don't want to be the High Dragonmaster. I wouldn't want to either. Daid is also grateful it didn't fall to him. And, I know you didn't ask for it, but we need you."

"Jesse, I couldn't even ..."

Save my father, she finished silently.

"No one could have," he said.

How could she save all of them? How could she lead without being a dictator like Talis that ruined things for everyone? The responsibilities of leadership tripled out, years beyond her. A moment of quiet understanding passed between them. She looked away. Deasylva hadn't saved Daid either. Just as she hadn't stopped the massacre that, by all accounts, she knew was coming. So, why should they trust any of these immature goddesses, really?

"A mantle may have been given to you, but that doesn't mean it has to control you," Jesse said. "We all have to deal with what life sends us."

He grabbed a vine and disappeared. Elis followed without a sound, leaving Sanna staring at empty space. Luteis shuffled closer, his head draped near her. She reached out blindly, pressing a hand to the scales along his face. They were smooth, burnished. Luteis let out a little grunt deep in his throat and closed his eyes.

What do you think it means to be the High Dragonmaster? she asked. He blinked once, his yellow eyes bright against the dark backdrop of Letum Wood.

I think that's entirely up to you.

Is it?

Deasylva had bestowed the title on Sanna, but it didn't mean anything, really. Not unless the dragons let it mean something. That they'd run away from her at their first chance wasn't a mark in her favor. Even Elliot's dragons had been indifferent, perhaps a bit annoyed, when she'd returned. Though, she couldn't tell if that was because Luteis came back with her.

The Dragonmasters before us were leaders, Luteis said, nudging the side of her leg. *Not tyrants. Not like Talis.*

Which makes it even more unfortunate that the dragons blame me for their current predicament.

Do they?

His question rang in her head. Why else would they

shut her out when they knew she was near? Avoid her? Not look her in the eye?

Then the strange, feral ferocity of the desert dragons came back to her. And worse—the mountain dragons with their wild eyes and lack of control. What if that happened to Luteis? Would he even know her? Could she handle such a loss after everything else?

Calm yourself, Luteis murmured.

Her hands had formed tight fists. Pain radiated from her jaw into her skull from clenching her teeth too hard. Sanna forced herself to relax, but it was slow in coming.

"Sorry," she mumbled. "Just thinking."

Luteis nuzzled closer, then closed his eyes.

Sanna stared into the quiet canopy again, more lost than ever. The tangled mass was as unfamiliar to her as the rest of the forest. She longed for the worn paths she knew so well in her own trees back in Anguis. But it wasn't likely she'd ever get them back.

Whispers of another Defender raid—and subsequent staff party—floated through La Torra.

Isadora waited impatiently for word from Maximillion, cataloguing her quiet observations. Numbers of East Guards. Schedule rotation for the cooks. Cecelia's strange silence—no Defender had been training in the courtyard for the past week. No snapping of whips. No breaking of vases. Isadora didn't dare write her observations down, so they ricocheted through her brain like jumping beans.

Once Cecelia and the Defenders left on the raid, an almost audible sigh of relief swept La Torra. While the staff ate crab cakes and drank wine without suppressing their voices—Ernesto amongst the loudest of them—Isadora waded back into the water. They didn't miss her.

In fact, they hadn't even invited her.

Water rushed around her shoulders and gently pulled her in. The swim to the sand bank went faster this time. She lay on her back, eyes taking in the stars as she passed beneath them. The thrill of knowing she'd be back in the magic filled her body. She hauled her body up onto the gritty shore. Except for the ocean, no other sound reached her ears. No Guards. No aquilas. For one delicious moment, she felt entirely alone.

Isadora slipped back into the magic.

Light infused the paths, illuminating strands of ivy, curling flowers, and a ground littered with petals. She held an arm over her eyes to block the brightness as the power pulsed through her body in a euphoric song. She'd expected it to have lessened—her magic wasn't as wild this time— but it seemed brighter than ever.

Her own path, and Sanna's, populated. Just the two. They split into different directions. Isadora's path showed her on the sandbar, eyes closed, with sea foam around her shoulders. Down the trail lingered a glimpse of Maximillion, another of Cecelia. In the very farthest, faintest trail lay Sanna.

Before she lost herself in concern for her sister, Isadora closed the paths.

She lay on the sand again, staring at the velvety sky. No sound. No movement. One quick check reassured her. No one had found her. She closed her eyes and returned.

Letum Wood awaited.

"Show me Lucey's paths."

Nothing showed. She frowned. The wisps disappeared back into the empty forest. She stood there for a moment, reveling in the quiet. Her magic whirled, pleased to be in use again.

"Show me Cecelia."

A wisp of Cecelia bubbled up, a simple recreation of the calculating, flamboyant witch who Isadora so dreaded. Haughty. Lips pressed in a thin line. Gaze pointed down. The expression on her face indicated pain. Isadora waited for the wind to stir, for the magic to whisper a word about Cecelia.

Nothing.

Isadora stared at her in disappointment. She'd expected something like *ruthless* or *murderer*.

"Remove her. Show me the Defenders."

Ten shadows populated in place of Cecelia. They seemed to slam into the space all at once. Her magic tugged, strained. She pressed into it, feeling relief from allowing it to flow, unrestrained. It drained out of her, moving as fast as lightning while the shadows attempted to expand.

Whispers assaulted her on all sides. They grew to a crescendo. Shouts. Distant wails. She understood none of it. Heaviness pressed in on her. Letum Wood darkened. Yet, somehow, the light itself brightened, racing from the trees to the ground at her feet. Dark shadows sprouted nearby, sweeping in with an oppressive weight. Silhouettes crept over the ground, branching off Isadora's own path, to spiral into the forest. The light countered, radiating brighter than ever, as if a battle waged between the two.

Isadora reared back, blinded. "Wait!" she cried. "No!"

More whispers came, as if tripping over themselves. The power continued to tug at her, as if ... as if she were pulling the Defenders into the paths.

No.

Not possible.

Weariness rushed over her. The strange forms began to coalesce. A face. A beard. A hint of blonde hair. They weren't wisps—but they weren't yet solid, either. As if they were trapped in some in-between.

"Stop!" Isadora cried.

The smoky images slammed to the ground, vanishing with a curl of smoke.

The darkness ebbed. The light gained more ground, outshining the shadows as they slipped away. The oppressive air retreated.

Isadora dropped to her knees with a gasp, feeling as if her body had just been entirely emptied, heart and soul. An eerie silence hung in the forest.

Something cold tugged on her, overcoming her in a suffocating wave. Isadora closed the magic and woke back on the beach, choking on seawater. She shot out of the sand as a second wave crashed over her.

A Guardian shouted from La Torra.

"Oy!"

Isadora stumbled to her feet, nostrils on fire. Water drained from her mouth as she coughed. Two Guardians stood on the islet, their arms crossed.

"Stupid girl!" one of them called. "What are you doing? Drowning? Come, now. Whatever you're upset about can't be that bad."

They snickered.

Isadora drew in a deep draught of air as she crawled up the shore. They laughed when she shoved the hair out of her face.

"All right, then?"

"*Lavanda* maids." One shook his head, clucking. "Not very *intelligenta*."

Ignoring their cackles, Isadora swam back to La Torra and stumbled her way toward the *lavanda*. Her body tingled. The risk of attempting such a foolish thing had been too great. Had she just called the Defenders back? Had she ruined everything?

Although she couldn't explain it, something strange had happened.

Something terrifying.

~

Isadora sat on the edge of her bed and drummed her fingers along her cheek. A fire crackled in the hearth, sending out sporadic waves of heat to warm the wet air. She blinked, entranced by the flickering flames before she forced herself to look away. At this rate, she'd fall into a relaxation so deep it would take her back into the paths.

Her gaze darted to the clock.

"Any minute now, Max," she murmured.

I'll arrive at eight, his letter had said. *If I'm not back from the Eastern Network's High Priest's Ball by then, consider me dead. Transport back to the Central Network.*

Four minutes left.

Isadora's legs already ached from pacing—on top of a full day of laundry and suppressing the urge to wander the castle again. She'd need to lay low for a bit after the strange event in the paths last night. Since then, the island had been oddly quiet. The Defenders had returned from their raid surly and empty-handed. She'd heard nothing more about it.

She leapt back to her feet to pace, and then her door opened.

"Maximillion?"

A thin, twiggy man scowled at her, clad in an elegant black coat, ironed to perfection, with coattails hanging halfway to his knobby knees. His eyes were ocean green tonight, his hair blond and subdued. She recognized a few features—Maximillion often maintained his strong brows and thin lips when he transformed.

"You were supposed to be gone by now," he muttered, dusting pieces of fluff off his shoulders, as if he'd rolled in a bath of feathers.

Her gaze flickered to the clock. "You were only one minute over. Why such a strange message?"

The color bloomed again in his face. Pale skin gave way to something infinitely healthier, with a sharper jawline and fuller cheeks. Something heavy clenched in her chest when she realized she was drinking him in, like a starving witch who hadn't eaten in days.

The good gods. Had she *missed* him?

"I was in a perilous situation," he said, drawing her back to the moment.

She waited. When no other explanation was forthcoming, she tried not to roll her eyes. "And?"

"And nothing. It was a ball. I was spying on Cecelia."

"Why?"

"Because it was an opportunity," he snapped. "Since when do you question me?"

"I've always questioned you."

His expression darkened. He didn't dispute her. "Waste of time. The blasted Eastern Network leaders think they're so important. Cecelia didn't even look at Dante once all night long, which makes it difficult to prove my theory that they're having an affair."

"She seems far more discreet than that."

"Perhaps, but she left before I did. No answers, whatsoever."

"But did she really leave?"

"She's returned here, if that's what you wanted to know."

Disappointment overcame her. Not only had she hoped for more from the event, but Cecelia's arrival meant the tension would return to La Torra. The lighthearted environment amongst the staff would be sorely missed. Even if they didn't let her participate in it.

"I see."

He eyed her briefly over his shoulder while he stood with his hands extended toward the fire. She couldn't imagine why he would have been cold at a ball.

"Have you noticed anything unusual?" he asked.

"Like?"

"The Defenders. Have they been acting strangely?"

"Not that I can tell."

He frowned. "Odd. The raid they had last night ... something happened in the middle of it. They ... I don't know."

Isadora gulped. "Oh?"

Maximillion fell into thought, then shook his head. "Never mind. Your powers. How are you handling them?"

"Ah ..."

His head snapped up, eyes narrowed, the moment he sensed her hesitation.

"Ah, they're fine," she said, adding in a mumble, "sort of."

"What does that mean?"

"I've found a safe place to use them."

"Nowhere in the East is safe!" he hissed. "Or have you forgotten how it felt to watch that other Watcher die? Are you mad?"

"I wasn't in the Eastern Network. At least ... not really."

His gaze tapered. "Where in the name of the good gods were you?"

"The ... ocean."

When she explained the almost deadly encounter with Cecelia in the dining room and her unexpected release of magic, his nostrils flared.

"When did you first try such a foolish thing?"

"An inconsequential detail."

He turned his back to her and stared at the wall. Isadora bit her bottom lip. He appeared downright irascible now—which meant it certainly wasn't the right time to tell him about the other side of her powers. The idea that she could see witches—personality traits too, it appeared—possibly pull other witches *into* the paths infinitely complicated ... everything.

When he faced her again, all signs of annoyance had cleared. Instead, he seemed strangely neutral. Was he trying to hide something?

"Have you seen any Defenders in the paths?" he asked.

"Ah ... sort of."

"Cecelia?"

She thought back to the shadows. Cecelia's strange form. She'd *seen* her but hadn't gotten any kind of glimpse into who she was. It seemed something about Cecelia, perhaps La Torra, complicated the magic.

"Not exactly. Anyone in La Torra is vague, undetailed."

"It shouldn't be possible to conjure a Defender in any form with our magic."

"I didn't see her *well*. At least, not as completely as I see others."

"It's still not possible."

"I did it."

He scowled again, but fell into thought. He turned back to the fire. "Well ... stop trying. I don't know what the repercussions are."

"What do you mean?"

"It's possible a Defender could know when you're attempting to see them."

Isadora cast about for a reply but found none. He had a point. They knew little about the Defenders' magic. About their own magic, even.

Maximillion's hair had returned to its usual dark mass by now, as rumpled as ever. They sat there, lost in the silence. Then his shoulders softened, and he seemed a bit more at ease. Light flickered across his skin as he stared into the flames. Isadora turned away before she too deeply appreciated the handsome, sculpted angles of his cheekbones.

"Any updates on the Central Network?" she asked.

"Nothing noteworthy."

"I would like to know——"

"No word from your family."

Her heart sank, but she hid it. Nestled amongst all her other worries were Sanna and Mam and the other Dragonmasters. What were they doing? Were they safe? Was the gradual onset of spring easing their hunger? She committed herself to writing another letter that night and sending the ten she'd already written to Sanna with him.

"I'll check again when I return," he grudgingly muttered.

"Thank you. I have some updates and observations."

With a weary nod, he motioned for her to continue. For the next twenty minutes, Isadora relayed everything she'd seen. From the number of Defenders, to how often they did —or didn't—practice, to the sheer quantity of storms whipping past the castle. She couldn't imagine how that meant anything, but told him anyway. He listened without interruption, but she knew he was filing the information in his head.

"That," she said, "is all I have right now."

He stood. She tilted her head back, wishing she could ask him to stay. The nights were so quiet here—so long and barren without the noises of the forest or the city or Pearl snoring. He opened his mouth, hesitated, then closed it again.

"I'll check on you at some point." He reached for the door, then paused with his hand on the knob. "Tomorrow."

"Tomorrow?"

"Yes," he snapped. "There's another raid, and I thought you'd like to know how it pans out."

Before she could manage a reply, he transported away, leaving nothing but a lonely whistle of air in his wake.

NINETEEN

Weak hints of sunlight filtered slowly through the canopy early the next morning.

Sanna woke before anyone else stirred in the camp. Moments after opening her eyes, she began to climb again. Luteis flanked her without a word, using his talons to dig into the bark. Even though the vines, moss, and fallen branches made navigating slow, Sanna climbed until her chest and legs burned. By the time she made it to the top, sweat trickled down her spine, and moss stained her toes.

Luteis peered over the treetops and launched into the sky alone. Sanna appreciated the elegant angles of his form. A broad wing span. Orange scales glinting in the sunlight.

He dove into the treetops, reemerging from their emerald depths seconds later. Something hung from his jaws. He snapped it in half in mid-air, then proceeded to devour it as he flew.

Sanna rolled her eyes.

Show off.

After they'd returned, he'd spent hours hunting for Cara

and the hatchlings, only providing food for the other dragons if they attempted to hunt themselves. When he returned, bright-red blood glistened on the delicate scales around his jaw. She put a hand over her eyes to shield them from the bright sunlight.

I desire a long flight, Luteis said, curling his head to meet her gaze. *Perhaps to find Finn.*

"Finn?"

We must warn them. They can't be that far away by now.

She shifted uneasily. He was right, but confronting Finn wouldn't be easy. Although, a ride on Luteis would get her away from Jesse and his happy family and the ghost of Daid and Isadora.

"All right."

She climbed onto his back, feeling the magic shift within her like a sigh. He sprang from the branch, his powerful talons carving imprints in the tree. Instead of flying away from the sun, Luteis turned north.

You think Finn went too close to the border and got the attention of the mountain dragons, don't you? she asked.

I think it's possible.

The implications were staggering. Would that place the blame for this mountain-dragon debacle on Finn? Hadn't she warned him not to leave? Her shoulders slumped. No. This wasn't Finn's fault.

It was Deasylva's.

Or Selsay's.

Sanna's braids flapped behind her as they soared over Letum Wood. An hour passed. She lay back, legs draped over his shoulders, her body kept warm by the friendly burn of his scales along her spine.

The sun continued to climb, but the cool air made it difficult to feel it. Her thoughts spun out, and for the first time since they'd returned, Sanna felt free to think. Luteis hung low in the sky, skimming the treetops, his nose constantly assessing. They canvassed several areas for almost an hour.

No water here, he said.

"The canopy is too sparse, too." She gazed down on a patch infested by strickenine moss. "They certainly couldn't live there."

Luteis grunted and flew on.

Another hour passed. They scouted water sources, then flew along the streams, searching for signs of life. Sanna stood up, stretching her arms. Luteis slowed, nostrils wide. *I smell something familiar.*

His nose lifted in the air.

Only the whistle of wind echoed in her ears. But what were the chances that she would hear anything while flying? Then the sound of a shriek jerked her out of her reverie. Sanna whipped around, held firm on Luteis's back by the magic. His head turned to the right.

Did you hear that? he asked.

Sanna leaned forward to gaze over his wing. Letum Wood stretched in an eternal expanse of green, except for a few dimpled, purple mountains in the distance. They were certainly further north here. She swallowed hard.

I did. Could be a screaming gnome.

Another cry came, this one familiar.

Down there, he said, head ducked to study the trees. *I see flashes of color. Fire, perhaps.*

Go.

They dove. The roar of the wind in her ears drowned out all sound. What felt like an eternity later, Luteis slid into the canopy. His descent slowed as he spread his wings, navigating around the sprawling trunks, knots of vines, and fallen branches with impressive dexterity.

I must stop, he said. *I cannot navigate this safely.*

I can. Meet me down there. Stay unnoticed if you can. Let me see what's happening first before you announce yourself.

Sanna leapt off his back and grabbed a vine. Bursts of fire and screams came from beneath them. Her hands burned as she loosened her grip and plummeted down. Screams rose up to meet her. A familiar, tangy burn lingered on the air. Mountain-dragon acid, for certain. Sanna crashed into the ground and pulled her knife at the same time.

Fire exploded across her chest, tearing down her arms. Above her, Luteis screamed, his fire so hot she felt the curls of it on the back of her neck.

"Get back!" she screamed.

All movement stopped. Five mountain dragons loomed in the trees, staring at her with narrowed eyes. One of them thrashed, caught up in a mess of vines that had suspended it several lengths off the ground. Soft sobs sounded behind her. Sanna shifted back, opening the space between her and the dragons. Out of the corner of her eye, she saw several familiar lumps on the ground.

Witches.

Dead dragons.

"Where's Pemba?" she barked. "I want to talk to him."

The mountain dragons shrank back, glancing at each other. One of them hissed, his tongue flickering out. The leader of this group, no doubt, for the others kept looking to him.

Another feinted toward her. She threw her knife, piercing it in the chest. It reared back and howled. Blood spurted around the handle, hitting the ground with boiling blue bubbles. A third reared back on its hind legs.

Luteis dropped from the trees.

With a reverberating *thud*, he crushed the standing mountain dragon beneath him. Sanna ran and yanked her knife out of the gurgling mountain dragon. The leader shot acid at Luteis, but Luteis grabbed the dead dragon beneath him by the throat and threw it. Its body slammed into the leader, toppling him into the trees. Sanna whirled around, skin prickling from an inferno that raged beneath her skin. Three witches stood huddled near a tree, holding a bleeding, unresponsive body.

Finn.

"Run!" she yelled. Something hit her from behind, sending her into the ground. She slammed into the dirt with an *oomph*. The muscles in her chest froze, paralyzed. Acid thickened the air, burning her skin. She ducked her head and tried to gasp. A dragon leg stepped a few paces to the right of her head.

She whipped onto her back and shoved her knife up.

The mountain dragon above her screamed, then reared back. Sizzling blood dropped on the ground next to her. He stumbled away as Sanna regained her breath with a heady gasp, scrambled for her knife, and found her feet again. Luteis, still recovering from the acid, roared fire. Finn's children disappeared into the trees.

A flash caught her gaze. Sanna whipped around to find the remaining mountain dragons grabbing a dead forest dragon. Marbled streaks of mauve ran through the scales. Stellis. The stodgy old sire who had fathered Elis. One mountain dragon wrapped its talons around Stellis's limp neck. The other gripped the tail and a thigh.

They rose into the trees.

Luteis! She stumbled toward Stellis, her eyes watering from the acid, lungs still seizing. Fire flared in her chest again. *They can't have Stellis!*

Luteis snorted, and the acid ignited, burning off his scales. The other mountain dragons had already disappeared. Sanna hauled herself onto his back, and they took off. He struggled through the canopy, the acid on his wings causing boils to rise. Glimpses of the mountain dragons, burdened by the deadweight, appeared every now and then through the branches. Vines, boughs, and leaves moved out of Luteis's way as he climbed higher.

Once they broke free of the canopy, Luteis's mighty wings pumped after the mountain dragons, who flew with surprising dexterity despite their burden. Stellis hung limp between them. Better to be dead, no doubt, than alive and suffering intense pain.

Or was it?

Luteis roared, shooting a plume of fire so hot the flames crackled. The mountain dragons glanced back, shrieked, and flew faster. Luteis gained momentum with every stroke of his wings. He bore down on them in seconds. They swerved to the right, dodging his back foreleg, but he swiped, raking his front talons down the wings of the leader. The sound of a tear rent the sky. The dragon shrieked and released Stellis, then plummeted to the ground with one wing beating frantically. The other dragon jerked down, pulled by the unexpected weight, and released Stellis. It whirled around, spraying acid. Boiling liquid lashed Sanna's face.

She screamed.

Their acid got me!

Sanna wiped frantically at it with her sleeves. The liquid ate into her cloth, burning like coals. She kept her eyes wrenched shut, but it tore through her skin like the hellfires of Hatha. For a moment, her entire being was consumed by pain.

Luteis!

We must go back to the forest, Luteis said. *And heal you.*

The initial pain receded slightly, leaving a burning on top of her skin.

Get Stellis first. She swallowed hard. *I'm ... fine.*

I leave no one behind.

Can you carry him? Sanna asked.

Back to Finn's? Yes. Do not open your eyes.

Luteis dove. Sanna wrenched one eye open. A tangle of vines suspended between two branches cradled Stellis—no doubt Letum Wood had lent aid. With a quick grab of his back talons, Luteis plucked Stellis free. Sanna quickly shut her eye again. Flying on Luteis's back without sight was disorienting, but the wild pain that filled her face felt worse.

Hold on.

His voice was strained. They stayed above the canopy, even if just barely. Daid's death. Luteis carrying Rubeis back. The blood-pumping sense of panic. It replayed back through Sanna's mind, sending dizzying whirls through her body.

What felt like an eternity later, the feeling of sunlight on her skin faded. The burn of the acid calmed in the shade of the forest as they plunged down. Luteis landed, nearly collapsing on top of Stellis.

Sanna slid off his back. "Water!" she croaked. "I need water!"

No, Luteis said. *Deasylva forbids it.*

"It burns! I—"

Something landed on the ground next to Sanna with a *splat*.

Pick it up, Luteis said. *Smear it on your face.*

She dropped to her knees and reached blindly. Her hands thrust into something wet, and she recognized the sweet, saccharine scent of a broken falla melon. The fleshy insides felt cool on her tingling hands. When she pressed it to her forehead, eyes, and cheeks, the burn instantly cooled. She thought she heard a light sizzle as it died away. An awful, sulfuric smell filled her nostrils.

The sound of approaching feet followed. Sanna shoved more falla melon onto her skin.

"Sanna?"

She paused, recognizing Trey's voice. He was Finn's eldest son, six years older than her.

"Trey?"

"What are you doing here?"

"We came to find you," she said. "We've been looking for hours."

Silence. Sanna rubbed the rest of the squishy melon into her skin, relishing the cooling effect.

Now? she asked Luteis.

For now, yes, Luteis said. *You may open your eyes.*

Juice dripped off her face as she wiped it away, opening her eyes. Everything was fuzzy at first. Then she blinked, cleared the rest of the melon off her face, and gently dabbed it with the back of her hand. Her vision cleared.

Trey stared at her.

Tear streaks ran down his face. Blood covered his hands and neck and clothes. Behind him stood his sister, Greata, and their youngest sibling, Hans. Sanna blinked, more juice sluicing into her eyes. With a flash, she recalled seeing Finn on the ground, face slack and body bloody. Cold rushed through her.

"Your parents?" she whispered.

Trey's lip quivered. "Gone," he said, looking away. "They're gone. We …" He paused, blinking again, then seemed to rally some strength. "We are the only ones left."

I can smell their blood, Luteis said.

Sanna put out a quiet call to the dragons, speaking in her mind, but feeling foolish at the same time. None responded. Of course they didn't—she wasn't their Dragonmaster. Or was she? But she heard a shuffle in the brush not far away. She tried again. Luteis sniffed, then slowly moved toward it.

Trey's eyes darted to Stellis, then to Luteis, then back to Sanna.

"What were they?" he asked, lips trembling. He held onto Hans's wrist with white knuckles. Hans, less than five years old, peered at Sanna through wide eyes. Memories of Daid, of the young boy in the West, flooded her mind.

"Mountain dragons," she said in a hoarse voice. "There'll be more where they came from because they didn't get what they wanted. A lot more. Start packing what you can, all right? We need to leave. Now."

"Leave?" Trey cried. "To where?"

"Back to Elliot."

"But—"

"We'll burn your family on a makeshift pyre before we go." She paused at the stricken terror in his eyes. How well she understood how quickly everything could be lost. Sanna softened her expression. "I'm sorry, Trey. But if we stay much longer, they may come back with reinforcements, and all of us will die."

He opened his mouth to protest again, but shut it. His

sister tugged on his sleeve, tear streaks staining her cheeks. Then they turned away. Trey froze when he saw his father's body on the ground, as if he didn't know what to do.

Sanna called after them. "I'll prepare your family. You get what you need."

Luteis reappeared at her side with a low growl in his throat. *This will only get worse,* he said. *Selsay is acting more quickly than I expected. She's taking advantage of our weakness.*

"I know."

Her gaze dropped to the mangled bodies on the forest floor. Finn. His children. Behind them, several dragons in the trees. They were all dead. Vines had already started to crawl over them. The ground shifted as the tree roots reclaimed the fallen dragon bodies. Luteis was right. It was only going to get worse.

What is your plan? he asked.

Sanna gripped her bloody, slippery knife a little tighter. Her entire face ached, as if the skin had been peeled away and then replaced. Her vision blurred again. She closed her eyes, shaking her head. The powerful heat that had filled her body ebbed now, leaving her feeling like an empty shell.

"Go back to Elliot," she said, firm with a conviction that felt surprisingly good. "Then figure it out from there."

I shall use my secundum for Finn and his family.

Sanna sank her teeth into her bottom lip, filled with dread and bitter memories. She pushed the darkest thoughts away—she'd deal with those later.

"I'll gather their bodies."

~

WHEN ISADORA STEPPED INTO THE SERVANTS' dining room the

next morning, the scent of bacon filled the air. She breathed the crackling, crisp scent of pork and missed home.

Fervor infused the room. Isadora sat next to Lorenzo, who smiled as he sipped his morning wine. The accents of the staff were less difficult to work through now—excluding Ernesto, who ensured his words rolled off his tongue as fast as flames when she was near.

"Of course," Lorenzo said to one of the cooks. "I would not miss it."

Ernesto glared at her over a plate of eggs. Next to him, one of the younger chefs leaned forward.

"Sergio is fixing his famous raspberry *plias*," he said to Lorenzo.

"Then you'll roll me back to my quarters."

The table dissolved into laughter. Isadora managed a smile but wondered what *plias* were. As if on reflex, Lorenzo's speech slowed as soon as he addressed her. "Isadora, what will you wear?"

She gave him a puzzled stare.

"Wear?"

"For the party this evening! The long-awaited day has come."

"Of what?"

"The day of Vittoria, of course."

Fiona sat on his other side, studying a piece of toast. She set it aside and said, "Vittoria was the first High Priestess in our Network to come from outside the nobility. The tradition that the High Priest marries a bride from poverty began with her. Vittoria was the poorest of the poor. She was also a *lavanda* maid."

Isadora's spine prickled. She'd never heard of such a tradition—Maximillion hadn't warned her about it.

"Ah," she said, suppressing the urge to ask, *Then why do you hate lavanda maids so much?*

Fiona met her gaze. "You are the *lavanda* maid and cannot attend."

The irony wasn't lost on her.

Everyone continued with their conversations, no doubt purposefully forgetting she hadn't responded. Ernesto spoke with another chef while Lorenzo frowned.

"I'm sorry," he said. "I shouldn't have gotten your hopes up. I had forgotten."

Isadora shrugged but felt relief. She was used to their strange social hierarchy by now and was glad she didn't have to worry about running into Cecelia again. "How do you celebrate Vittoria Day?"

"Wine," he said. "A lot of wine. And silk. You must wear silk."

Her nose wrinkled. She hated the feeling of silk on her skin. Worse—she hated knowing that loads of it would pour into the *lavanda* after the party. She bit back a sigh and scooped a piece of bacon off a serving plate.

The entire staff drunk at a party, however, meant a different kind of party for her.

"Where is this party?" she asked.

"In the courtyard, of course. Where all the parties are. This is the only revelry Cecelia allows all year while she is here."

"I hope you enjoy it."

He grinned, but only for a moment. "Ah yes ..." His mirth dropped. He cleared his throat. "Perhaps it won't be any fun."

With that, he picked up his wine glass, called across the room to someone else, and slipped away. The sound of his laughter rang through the air. Isadora crunched into her bacon with a giddy realization. A party for the servants meant one thing.

She would have the castle to herself.

~

A POWDER, like talc, puffed into Isadora's face that afternoon.

She wrinkled her nose, assaulted by the dry, gritty scent of the soap, and dumped the rest of the spoonful into the steaming water. Hair clung to her neck in limp tendrils, sticky from the heat. Isadora reached for another Guardian uniform with a sigh.

No wonder Pearl hated laundry so much.

I could deliver laundry to the fifth floor again, she thought, then shook her head. *No. No good. I already checked the fifth floor.*

Thoughts of finding the elusive entrance to Carcere consumed her. Tonight would be an unparalleled opportunity to explore, but she had to approach it carefully.

Fourth floor, she thought. *Haven't been there yet. Or the second. That may be a better place to start.*

The first floor would be crawling with witches exiting and entering the kitchens for food and wine, or just out of sheer drunkenness. Smells of a great feast already drifted down the hall. Shrimp dipped in fresh cocoanut milk and fried, for one. Ernesto had been bragging about it all morning.

Disguise myself again? She eyed the pile of laundry on the far side of the room. Cecelia's maids had a few dirty dresses in there, but then she'd be restricted to the third floor. Risky to venture into Cecelia's lair again, although she needed to confirm Cecelia didn't keep the entrance close to her quarters.

Isadora sighed and grabbed another piece of clothing to soak.

A *thunk* sounded in the wooden tub when a pair of pants hit the side. Isadora felt the thick material, then reached inside a pocket. She withdrew a cool, oblong metal object. Her fingers unfurled, revealing a small, round key. Circular at the top, with jagged teeth on the far end, no bigger than her palm. Her brow furrowed. Cecelia's maids constantly left oddities in their apron pockets. Guardians? Never.

It couldn't belong to Cecelia's maids, anyway—all those rooms were protected by complicated puzzle locks. Her gaze slid down the pants, then over to the pile where the pants had come from. These weren't from the outside Guardians—sand always infused those clothes. Rusty-colored dirt streaked down the side. Neither was this from a Guardian working inside La Torra.

This was laundry from upstairs.

Her eyes narrowed. A few select closets aside, that meant this key could belong to Carcere, or something within Carcere.

She closed the key in her hand, then stuffed it into her pocket. With a splash, she plunged the uniform deeper into the sudsy water and began to scrub. Dirt floated to the top of the tub. Her mind spun. She suppressed the urge to slip into the paths. What if she took the key? What would happen—or not happen—if she returned it? The paths would show her possibilities, but sometimes that worked against her. Seeing it all unfurl often provoked anxiety. And likely, going into the paths would open up a trove of other problems.

Like Cecelia.

No, her magic wasn't an option to help her decide this time.

For the rest of the afternoon, Isadora's mind spun. The key weighed heavy in her pocket. By the time she finished scrubbing, wringing, hanging, and ironing the Guardian uniforms—and a few towels and sheets that smelled rotten —the entire afternoon had passed.

Plans continued to populate in her mind. She knew where the entrance to Carcere *wasn't*. Out of sheer luck, she'd seen all the doors in the servants' hall open, and none led upward.

That left one likely place.

The third floor.

Preparations for the party in the courtyard still rang through the hall. Based on a few jovial shouts and the scent of fresh-baked cake, celebrations had already begun.

Isadora finished folding the uniforms and linens and checked her reflection in a glass window. Night had fallen. Only two Guardians strode by outside, doing their last round for several hours before heading to the courtyard, no doubt. If there was any time to sneak to the ramp, it was now.

"Now or never," she murmured. As usual, she thought she heard Maximillion in the back of her mind.

A bloody fool!

Isadora spun on her heels, grabbed a cart of linens, and headed toward the third floor.

CHAPTER

TWENTY

Once they returned to Elliot's, Sanna sank down at the makeshift wooden table, and Jesse sat on a log next to Trey. Descriptions of what happened were brief—the shock on Greata and Trey's face, not to mention Hans' occasional bursts of sobs—did most of the explanation.

After Sanna finished, none of them spoke. They just stared at the long, crackling tongues of fire. A blanket woven out of thick, fuzzy leaves draped Trey's shoulders. He held a chipped mug in his hand but stared at the fire without drinking. Hans slept on the floor at his feet now, his breathing shallow. Greata sobbed quietly in Babs's arms in the far corner. Her soft, hiccuping breaths deepened the ache in Sanna's chest. Mam had retreated, unable to bear such an outpouring of grief. Sanna didn't blame her.

Luteis and Elis had left as soon as Luteis returned with all four witches on his back. One hatchling had been tucked into the underbrush, trembling but still alive. Although Sanna had attempted to communicate with any surviving adults, nothing had happened. Luteis believed at least three or four adults were still alive, likely scattered and frightened, and he hoped to wrangle them together.

Sanna leaned over the table, voice low. "Listen, Elliot, I know you're shocked, but we have to act. Now."

He blinked, eyes glazed, and met her stare. "How?" He looked at his open palms. "How can we ever fight such a force?"

"Now isn't the time to dwell on what happened. We just ... we have to act."

"And do what?" His voice rose.

Trey glanced up from his spot by the fire. Babs shot them a quick glare. Hans stirred. Elliot's shoulders expanded as he sucked in a deep breath. Several seconds passed.

"How can we possibly fight when it's clear they outnumber us?" he whispered. "Outnumber us *with deadly force*. You want these dragons to fight? They can't even hunt." Elliot studied her face. "If those dragons can do *that* amount of damage to your face, what could they do to Babs? To your mam?"

Sanna's nostrils flared. Her face still throbbed. Pinpricks of pain stabbed through her every now and then. Babs had smeared a foul-smelling salve all over the skin, which had soothed it to a tingling numbness. She couldn't imagine how grisly and horrific it looked—particularly because Jesse grimaced every time he looked at her.

"I'll think of something," she said.

Elliot stared at her from beneath bushy brows.

"You?"

"Yes."

"You don't even believe you're High Dragonmaster. Jesse said you haven't even delivered a message to Deasylva from that mountain dragon."

A detail she hadn't forgotten.

Sanna scowled, and the movement hurt her scabbed face. She fought a wince. Was there another option left? The difficulties of their position weren't lost on her. She met his gaze.

"I know."

"So?" he asked. "What are you going to do? We have fewer than ten healthy adult forest dragons, only two of which can fly well. A few others have attempted unsuccessfully, and given up too soon. We have six hatchlings that we must protect at all costs or risk losing the entire race. It's … it's the massacre all over again, only this time strung out. It's like …"

He trailed off, but she could have finished his thought.

It's like we brought this upon ourselves again.

As if they'd feared something so much, they'd actually made it happen. Sanna groped around for something— anything—to say in response. Finding her resolve only took a moment.

"They killed my daid, and now they've slaughtered Finn's family. If we don't do something, it will be all of us."

"Agreed. But what are you going to do?"

"Train the dragons!"

"The mountain dragons could attack tonight! Training will take ages."

"We should have a few days, at least. They have to find us, and they don't like the trees. They found Finn faster because he was close to the North and in an area that's more sparse than here. Here, they'll have to hunt, transport in and out."

"So we have a week?"

"Maybe more. We … we teach the dragons to do as much as we can while we have the chance. Fortify our living space, somehow. Move to the Ancients. We have options, Elliot."

Elliot's brow puckered. "Tell me what to do, Sanna, and I'll do it. But if you can't make this happen within a week, I'm leaving. I'm taking the dragons and getting out of here."

Memories of Daid's last breaths whipped through her mind, along with a vision of Talis's gnashing teeth. His horrific anger. Did it matter who took charge now? Yes. It absolutely did.

Perhaps it always had.

Sanna drew courage from the ferocity of her memories.

"I accept that," she said, then turned her thoughts to Luteis.

Tomorrow, she said to him, *we train with the dragons. This time, they don't have the option to say no.*

~

"WE COULD ALWAYS PROTECT ourselves with fire."

Distant shrieks rang through the back of Sanna's mind at Jesse's suggestion. The trees didn't appreciate the idea, but Luteis seemed to be considering it.

Sanna, Elliot, Jesse, and Luteis stood at the base of an oak tree, glancing out over Elliot's makeshift camp. Trey had constructed a hasty tent out of tree branches and young vines for himself and Hans. Jesse and two of his younger brothers shared a similar dwelling next to them. All the girls slept inside with Babs and Mam. New growth had started seeping down from the canopy—the forest floor always bloomed last. Spring meant more privacy.

And less visibility.

"No fire if we can avoid it," Sanna said. "That will only make the trees angry, and we'll need them to help."

"Can't you ask your goddess?" Elliot asked. "Seems like she should have some defensive ideas."

"I never said anything about her. I spoke of the trees."

"Aren't they one and the same?"

"I don't think so."

In some sense, Luteis said. *They are.*

Every now and then, the trees spoke to her in hushed whispers. She heard their fears, their naive imaginings of a stirring wind or warm breath of sunshine. Like children, really. Few thoughts, simplistic at best, happy just to sing.

In much the same way as Deasylva is to her dragons, Luteis said. *The two cannot be parted. I believe this is true of all goddesses and their creations.*

Sanna remained silent, pondering over what that meant for Selsay.

"Fine," Elliot said. "No fire unless we have to. You think the mountain dragons will come from the sky? Fly in? Or do that ... *appearing* thing you spoke about?"

"We're not entirely sure, to be honest, but that seems to make the most sense. They had a habit of just ... appearing ... in the West. Isadora spoke about it before—it's how she travels home. Called it transportation."

"Magic?"

"Would have to be."

His frown deepened. He growled in the back of his throat. "Huh. Dragons doing magic. Odd."

"Perhaps we should move," Sanna said. "The Ancients would provide at least a little more protection. I think."

"They'd be able to track our scent," Jesse said. "And we'd have to set up defenses. Makes sense to stay and fortify, if you ask me."

"We could probably find something that would hide us better," Sanna countered. "Caves for the witches who won't be fighting alongside the dragons." She shot Elliot a knowing glance. He still had young children, not to mention Babs, Mam, and Greata.

Jesse chewed on his bottom lip. "But that takes away from practice time for the dragons. Getting the adults to fly is the most important priority."

"We just need to stop the mountain dragons," Elliot said. "Not defeat them. If we can stop them, we'll buy time."

"For what?" Sanna growled. "For the rest of them to swoop in and finish us off?"

Calm yourself, Luteis said.

Something fell, nearly striking her in the face. She leapt back just before it crushed her nose. "What is that?" she cried.

A giant melon dangled in front of her face, suspended from a thick vine. Lines of purple and pink decorated the outside of the fruit in bulbous swirls.

"Odd." Jesse's brow furrowed. "It looks like a falla melon."

Sanna tilted her head. "But ... it's ..."

"Swollen."

The melon seemed as if it were about to burst. The rind was tight and three times its usual size, the entire thing far bigger than her head. Luteis lowered his snout, sniffing without touching, then recoiled.

It smells rotten.

Elliot grimaced at the wave of heat that came with Luteis's movement. Jesse straightened, then reached out to touch the melon. Luteis nudged his hand away. Jesse recoiled with a hiss, shaking his hand at Luteis's intense heat.

"Ouch!"

Deasylva says not to touch.

Before Sanna could get the words out, the vine spasmed and tossed the fruit against a nearby tree. The hard, cylindrical pieces exploded. Smoke rose from the inside of the fruit, which slowly ate away at the bark with a long hiss.

"Nice," Sanna murmured.

A tinny, high-pitched shriek sounded in the back of Sanna's head, accompanied by a rush of panic. Sanna grabbed the flake of bark above the decimated fruit and peeled it down. The tree quieted.

"Rotten fruit?" Elliot asked, eyes wide.

"Must be," Sanna said. Whatever remained behind wasn't magical and stank like a belua. The piece of bark in her hand slowly wore away, disintegrating into pulp. Sanna tossed it away and turned to Luteis.

"Is there enough that we could use it, you think?" she asked.

More vines dropped, halting just above the ground, bearing more degraded fruit. *Deasylva speaks,* Luteis said. *She would not offer something she could not provide. The fruit should be thrown by the vines in order to avoid jostling it.*

"The forest speaks," Sanna said to Elliot. Luteis whacked her in the back of the legs with his tail, but she ignored him.

The forest. Deasylva. All the same.

"That decides it, then, doesn't it? We stay," Jesse said. "We need to mount a defense."

He met her gaze with a firm stare of his own. In truth, Sanna didn't know if it would be best to stay or go, and she didn't want to bear the burden of being wrong. They stared at each other, at an awkward impasse, as if no one wanted to make the final decision.

"We stay," she said, motioning to the foul falla melons.

"We'll stand our ground until the adults can fly. Then we'll go west and speak with Aki, the Western Network High Dragonmaster."

Not Yushi? Luteis asked.

Jesse glanced at her, brow furrowed, as if he had the same question.

I'd rather avoid Yushi, she said. *Something isn't right there.*

"Sounds like as good of a plan as we can expect in these circumstances," Elliot said. "Does your goddess have any advice?"

"No."

Luteis nearly knocked her over with his snout. Sanna stumbled at his not-so-gentle nudge. *Admit you haven't spoken with her.*

Not now.

Deasylva speaks to all her dragons and witches, if they listen. If you refuse to acknowledge her, she'll find a witch who will listen.

Will she?

He didn't respond.

I'm busy saving the dragons. I've attempted to give her the message three times. Instead of chasing her, I think I'll try to save our lives.

"Sharpened spears are another good idea," Jesse said. "We can hide them in the undergrowth to skewer anything that comes on foot. Or dragons that fall. If they're the right size, they could snap beneath the weight of the forest dragons without injuring them but still pose an issue for the mountain dragons."

"We could dig down, too." Sanna burrowed her toes into the wet earth. "Find an old tunnel system used by the screaming gnomes. It could serve as a trench, or be hidden so it collapses."

"They wouldn't be large enough to really stop dragons," Jesse said.

"No, but they'd buy time. Maybe injure some, if we put in sharp stakes."

"True."

"You're the one who can communicate with all the dragons," Elliot said. "Can we leverage their help? *They* could dig tunnels far faster than us."

Agreed, Luteis said.

"Possibly," Sanna said, "if I could speak with them. Their voices haven't been in my head since right after Talis died."

Elliot frowned. "Have you tried?"

Her mouth bobbed open and closed. Outside of her attempt at Finn's, she'd largely ignored the issue. "I'll try tonight," she grumbled. "Once I figure out what they can do."

Luteis growled. *You don't ask. The High Dragonmaster decides and commands.*

Sanna glared at him, a hard stone in her stomach. Memories of Talis whipped through her mind. His border. His fire. Burning, burning, burning. The scent of death and char. How could one lead without pain and fire and tyranny? Talis commanded and decided, and look at where that got them.

"Tonight," she said. "For now, let's see if there is a gnome tunnel beneath here and start finding fallen trees that can serve as stakes."

～

Wild stories of Carcere spun through Isadora's mind as she wound up the slippery, slanted path in La Torra. The cart rattled like an old bag of bones, warning her to retreat to the safety of the *lavanda*. So far, no signs of other servants.

Strange magic rules Carcere, Fiona had said one day. *Some Watchers spend their whole lives up there. Rumor says there's no end to the number of cells. Even the Guards who work there don't know how many.*

Isadora seriously doubted that.

More likely that tales were exaggerated to keep witches afraid.

Once Isadora arrived at the third floor, she paused. The sound of revelry rang from the courtyard. Torchlight flickered along the curved corridor despite its emptiness. An expensive use of fuel.

Unlike on the fifth floor, gaudy decorations filled this hall. Elegant paintings cluttered the wall space, leaving no stone visible. On the rare empty spot, elaborate paper, flecked with primroses and curling grass, hid the ugly walls. Tables with claw feet and velvet-cushioned divans littered the floor. Several porcelain statues stood along the inner wall next to mosaic vases housing exotic plants. Here, the hallway was as wide as the trees in Letum Wood, as if it doubled as a ballroom. Despite the open space, the suffocation of *stuff* made Isadora's throat thicken.

She pressed on.

No rooms became visible. She frowned. Nothing but hallway.

The second floor, which she'd glimpsed only briefly, was rumored to have twenty bedrooms. Its hallway was a quarter this size to accommodate the guest quarters. Despite hundreds of paintings ranging from the size of her fist to larger than her whole body, the third floor seemed ... empty.

Her nerves felt as taut as a violin string as she walked,

trolley ahead of her, waiting for a maid to call her out. Her teeth ground together painfully. The hallway narrowed ahead of her, giving way to what must have been several rooms—or one large apartment. Then she saw a door on the right and the left.

Isadora slowed.

The distant sound of laughter still rang from the court-yard. To her left, ornate double doors covered with stained glass glinted in the flickering torchlight. She studied the glass—a tree with sprawling branches stretching over both doors, winding paths twisting out from its base. Several panes of darkness surrounded the tree, interspersed with beams of light.

Next to the door stood a table with a piece of parchment and a vase of flowers as tall as Isadora. She peeked at the scroll. Names. She frowned. *Fiona. Giorgia. Serafina.* Times were scrawled off to the side. A visitors' log?

Definitely Cecelia's quarters.

Abandoning the laundry cart, Isadora slipped further down the hall. A few more stained-glass doors here and there—no doubt extensions of Cecelia's apartment. Her quarters took up nearly half of the third floor, eventually tapering back into the wide, ballroom-like area.

Isadora returned, then gently put her hand on the first doorknob.

Locked.

Her maids would be inside, no doubt. Was Cecelia? Isadora didn't dare look into the courtyard for fear of being seen, even by a drunken servant. She rushed to the next door. Locked.

All of them.

Except for the servants' staircase and the twisting ramp, no other access to the next floor appeared. She stood in the hallway, hands on her hips. It had to be here. Her gaze darted to the outer wall, then the inner wall. Whatever kept Carcere's magic suppressed could be hiding the entrance, but more likely it was a matter of logic. The magic couldn't both suppress and create at the same time, could it?

And how did Cecelia manage to use spells to protect her quarters, anyway?

Isadora shook the questions off.

The inner walls of La Torra had no external protrusions —all staircases were on the outside of the castle. Which meant the entrance to Carcere must also be along the exterior wall. She might have missed the entrance on the fifth floor, but she didn't think so.

"You're here," she murmured, stepping back into the staircase, "aren't you?"

The spiral staircase stretched above and below. Bare, wet walls here. Suppressing the urge to step into the paths and *see* what was possible, she reached her fingers out to touch the chilly stone. She paused, waiting. More shouts from the courtyard. The distant roar of the waves.

Then a gentle, subtle shift of the air.

For a second, a breeze rushed past her, stirring her hair, as if a distant door had been opened. Her hair fell again, limp on her shoulders. Her eyes narrowed.

Two cracks crawled up the wall, running along the edge of several stones. They widened, revealing a jagged outline. Isadora ran her fingers over the stone, tracing it high overhead, then followed it across with her eyes. A door. Short, jagged, and thin, but a door. Definitely.

Hidden doors could require any number of things to open, from spells, to certain words, to amulets, to potions. But an ancient castle like Carcere, with a leader who wouldn't tolerate magic and rotations of East Guards who had to come in and out? Likely it was a matter of pressure in the right place. Potions, magic, spells, and words were too volatile. Too messy. They could be forgotten from one witch to the next, then the prison would be lost to the world. Cecelia seemed to focus on killing Watchers, and the rest ran smoothly.

Now, where would the hinge be?

Isadora pressed around the stones. Nothing. She patted on the left, felt along the subtly thicker openings along the edge of the door. No movement. She ran her entire palm along the edge without success. Frustrated, she slapped the right side of the door with a scowl and felt it give way, then swing open toward her with a grating sound.

She leapt back, eyes wide, and stared into a thick, dark chasm.

CHAPTER

TWENTY-ONE

The darkness of Carcere seeped through the cracks in the walls.

It crawled down the staircase with cold fingers. Isadora's hair shifted again. The door paused, open only a few paces wide. She hesitated only a moment, then bent down, untied one shoe, grabbed the Guardian uniforms off the trolley, and stepped inside.

The door slid shut behind her.

For one terrifying moment, Isadora couldn't breathe. Pure, unrestrained darkness pressed on her, as if it would choke the life right out of her. No flicker of light interrupted the solid wall of black she'd stepped into.

The good gods! she thought. *Why didn't I grab a torch?*

A distant sound—a cry?—caught her ear. With a heavy swallow, she held out one hand, felt the wall, and shuffled forward. Her toe collided with stone, and she rose up a first step.

The air chilled as she moved, one step at a time, up into the pervasive darkness. No windows along the stairwell.

The stuffy, oppressive air pressed on her lungs. She staved off the claustrophobia by sheer willpower, realizing only after minutes had passed that her powers had retreated. They stirred, limp and weak. Being without them afforded some relief.

And anxiety.

Another muffled sound caught her ear as she groped her way along the dark, narrow passage, clutching the uniforms to her chest. The darkness, so deep, awoke paranoia deep within her. Did she see a flicker of light? Was that just her eyes, seeking what they wanted but couldn't find?

Was Lucey stuck in such a suffocating space?

What felt like an eternity later, the seemingly straight hallway curved beneath her groping hands. She followed, then reared back, blinded by a sudden burst of light. The uniforms dropped with a *thud*. Two Guardians stood there.

"Allo?" called one, advancing like a bull. "What are you doing here?"

He spoke rapidly—she'd startled him. Isadora held up a hand, but her eyes quickly adjusted. He stopped moments before plowing into her. His heavy brow drooped over his eyes. A deep accent from an unfamiliar region of the East colored his tone. Frantic, she parsed his words.

"You shouldn't be here," he barked.

"I-I've come to replace the linens and uniforms. I just forgot my torch."

"Who gave you permission?" he barked.

"F-Fiona."

"She would never," said the second, coming up behind him. He had long hair tied in a neat ponytail. The dim torchlight cast menacing shadows across both their faces.

"She did," Isadora said, forcing strength into her voice.

"It's Vittoria Day. Do you think she wanted to run the laundry around tonight or tomorrow?"

A flicker of hesitation, for just a moment, lingered in the first one's gaze. He glanced at her and the pile of clothes, and jerked his head down.

"Leave them on the floor."

"On the floor?" she cried, scuffing the ground with her toe. "I spent the whole day cleaning them!"

"No one cares about the poor *lavanda* maid."

"I care."

"I don't."

Her nostrils flared. A bead of sweat trickled down her back. Something foul lingered in the stuffy air. "I'd like to take them to the closet, if you don't mind."

"No."

"Besides, I have more to bring in. If I don't, Fiona will have my head."

"Don't care," he snarled. "Get out of my prison."

"*Your* prison?"

"Out!" he shouted. The noise rippled behind him. Isadora stepped back, feigning terror. Behind the Guardians waited more darkness—and a distant torch. So the hall continued. Half-moons of disorienting, pitch-black space hovered to the left and right as well, meaning *more* halls. Egads, Carcere really was a complicated maze. Not even the wide walls of La Torra could accommodate this kind of cavernous space. Somehow, Carcere suppressed magic yet also actively used it.

Isadora drew herself up. She underestimated this place.

"I will go as soon as I've completed my errand. Won't lose my job because of you. Besides, the *lavanda* is hot, and I'm letting it cool down."

The other Guard snorted. "Hot as *troita* up here, and you don't hear us complaining."

"You just did."

"Did not."

The first, a burly witch built like a wall, stared at her with glittering eyes.

"Go."

No translation needed there. Isadora put her hands on her hips. "Might I at least instruct you on the proper way to hang these so all my hours with the iron aren't wasted?"

"No."

She paused, as if annoyed. "But—"

"Get out of here already!"

"Sorry," she stammered, ignoring the other Guard's silent chortle. She reached into her pocket and pulled the key out, holding it in her palm. "If you would have been friendlier, I would have helped you out. I suppose you ungrateful wretches don't want to keep your heads."

The first Guard rolled his eyes, but the second took the bait. "What are you talking about, *chit*?"

Ignoring the implied insult—a *chit* was a hysterical chicken in the *Ilese* language—Isadora stepped back, using one hand to smooth down one of the uniforms. "Oh, nothing. By chance, you aren't missing a key, are you?"

The first Guard reached out and snatched her arm, jerking her close. Isadora screamed. "By Drago!" she shouted. "What's wrong with you?"

Her words echoed down the halls, rippling one at a time.

Drago. Drago. Drago.

"Where's the key?" he growled.

"You should be nicer, and I'd tell you!" she shouted

back. An unnatural stillness echoed after. She strained to hear.

C'mon, Lucey.

A flush colored his cheeks. "Give me the key, or I'll throw *you* in a prison cell."

Isadora's heart thrilled. Now there was an idea. She shoved that off and met his gaze. Fortunately, no witch was more terrifying than Maximillion.

"No wonder you're edgy," she said. "You lost a key, possibly to something—or someone—important in here, and now you want it back?"

He tightened his grip on her arm. Isadora screamed again, injecting a shrill note of terror in it that was sure to carry.

"Give it to me now, and save your own life."

She scowled, then shoved away from him. He released her. Isadora fished in her right pocket, then her left. She patted them, frowning.

"Where is that key?" she murmured.

Both Guards glowered.

Silence from Carcere.

"Come on!" the Guard shouted, meaty hand outstretched. "How many pockets could you have?"

Isadora reached into her dress pocket and extracted the key. She held it out to him. "I found it while doing the laundry. I'm assuming it's the key to the linen closet, eh?"

The Guards exchanged glances before the burly one snatched it from her palm. "Erm, yes. That's what it's for."

"The linen closet," said the other.

Liars, she thought. Good. That meant the key opened an important door.

"Is this gold?" she called, reaching out to touch the veins of color that ran through the wall, sparkling in the torchlight. The first Guard grimaced and rubbed his ear. The smaller of the two snorted.

"It's *oro*," he said. "Fool's gold."

"What's that?"

"You don't know?"

She shook her head. "I'm not from here."

"Obviously," he muttered.

The burly Guardian tilted his head back, chin jutting into the air. "Suppresses all magic. No spell needed."

"That shouldn't be possible."

He shrugged. "It is. It's one of the things that makes Carcere special."

Special was one word for it.

Isadora held out a palm. With a silent spell, she attempted to create a flame. Sparks sputtered in her hands, crackling just above the skin without forming a real flame. Both Guards advanced on her. She closed her fist just as the burly one slapped her across the wrist.

"You fool!"

"Sorry!" she cried. Her skin smarted. "Just wanted to see."

"You'll call the wrath of The Great One!"

"How would she know?" Isadora asked. "Wouldn't the *oro* suppress her ability to sense it?"

Both Guards stared at her quizzically, buying her precious seconds to listen. No sound followed. Drat! Lucey must have heard her—or else Carcere was bigger than she thought.

The larger Guardian narrowed his eyes, as if he sensed her thoughts.

She forced a smile.

"*Oro.* Good for a prison, no?" she asked, loudly. Her voice rang down the hall with a slight echo. In the lull, she strained to hear. A drip. A cough. The squeak of a mouse. Nothing but a reverberating silence stretched through the hall.

"What do you know about prisons?" barked the first Guard. "You're done here; now go!"

"Not very kind," she muttered, pushing a strand of hair out of her eyes, "to someone who just saved your head."

His scowl deepened.

"You're wasting our time. Leave!"

She splayed her hands in front of her. "I will, I promise. But … are there any, ah …" She snapped her fingers. "Ah, what do you call it? Ghosts? *Sprutto?*"

The smaller Guard laughed.

"*Spettros?*"

"Yes! Do you have *spettros* up here?"

The startled expression on the larger Guard told her she'd hit her mark. "What?" he asked.

"*Spettros.* Do they live here? I-I've always loved to see spirits and—"

"No *spettros.* Go away. You annoy us."

"Ask your prisoner!" she cried, just a *touch* too loud. "She'll tell you about the ghosts. You know, the *spettro* the whole staff talks about."

Isadora paused, listening again. Nothing. The smaller Guard paused, eyes darting to his superior.

"Tell us what?" he asked.

"Silence! Don't fall for her stupid questions."

"The *spettro* of the old Watcher." Isadora turned to the smaller Guard. "An old man, I hear, who was tortured to death many years ago and haunts those who persecute his kind. You haven't heard of him? Even I have, and I'm from the Central Network."

Both Guards frowned.

"He lived in Carcere for sixty years." She straightened, pulling her shoulders back, and letting her voice roll through the tunnel. "He's particularly fond of birds. Forests. He loved to go on long walks and tell tales about dragons."

The smaller Guard gulped.

C'mon, Lucey, Isadora silently pleaded. *Make a noise.*

"Now you *are* annoying," the Guard said, advancing with a scowl. "Leave, *lavanda* wench."

She held up her hands, backing up before he could touch her. "Fine! Fine. Don't believe in *spettros*. Let them haunt you for being here and interrupting their mortal journey. It's the risk you take."

The smaller Guard shifted in place, casting a glance back into the encompassing darkness. Isadora shuffled back a step, her mouth opened for one last attempt, when a distant note, like the trill of a bird, so faint it could have been a whisper of wind, sounded through the hall to the right.

Her heart thrilled. She knew that bird. A ribbon lark. Found only near Anguis. One of Lucey's very favorites.

Only one thing left to do.

Isadora smiled and backed up, pulling her shoe with the untied lace closer. The uniforms lay in a pile on the ground, abandoned. She wagged a finger. "Have a good day! Don't you dare mess up my hard work on those uniforms!"

When she spun around to head toward the stairs, she tripped on her shoelace and flew into the wall with a cry of alarm. Her head struck the stone. She closed her eyes and flopped onto her back, her body slack.

She slipped into the magic.

It was sluggish, bringing her into the paths slowly. A muted forest met her gaze. Darkness instead of trees.

Shadows instead of detailed leaves. Tepid light sliced through the darkness, then faded.

Is this what Maximillion sees in the paths?

Still, a few faint paths sprang to life at her feet, the edges blurred. Seven paths—or was it six? Three for her and the Guards. That left three or four Watchers close by.

"Show only Lucey's path!"

Slowly, the darkness gave way. She remained in the black for what felt like an eternity before four faint, glimmering wisps leapt to life off to the left. That meant something. At the least, Lucey was here. A stinging sensation spread across her face. Isadora closed the magic, satisfied at the confirmation, and returned to the dungeon.

The smaller of the two Guardians hovered over her, tapping her on the cheek with the back of his hand. Isadora tucked the magic farther into herself than she'd ever locked it before. It disappeared without a fight, no doubt ushered there by the suppressive effects of the *oro*.

She slowly opened her eyes, as if groggy.

"Miss!" he shouted. "Awake!"

She pressed a hand to her forehead, eyelids fluttering. "Oh, I'm sorry ... I didn't ..."

"You are in pain?"

"A headache. Did I ... did I fall?"

He motioned to her shoe with a wave of his hand. "Your shoelace."

She straightened, breathless, then added a theatrical grimace. "How silly. I'm so sorry. I'm ... quite well, thank you. Please don't bother."

"I will walk you to the door."

"No! No, really."

"You struck your head."

"I'm fine."

The Guard looked back. Isadora fluttered her eyes, feigning lightheadedness. With a growl, the burly Guard nodded toward the fathomless cavern behind her and muttered, "Get her out of here." Before she could form another protest, the other Guardian hauled her into the pitch-black stairwell.

Isadora let him take her, weak with relief.

Lucey was still alive.

LUTEIS FACED a semicircle of reluctant dragons that kept peering up in the canopy, then back at him.

One must strengthen the wings, he said. *That can only be done by flying, even if you drop almost immediately to the forest floor.*

Sanna sat on a root, hands braced behind her, watching the first flight lesson begin. Six hatchlings and six adults filled the space, which wasn't expansive. Cara slipped in and out of the trees, nudging hatchlings that grew bored, growling at those that tried to slip away.

A body settled onto the root next to Sanna.

"How's your face?"

Jesse tossed his hair out of his eyes as he made himself comfortable on the mossy pillow beneath them. Sanna sighed, gently probing the skin of her forehead.

"It hurts."

"The skin?"

"My head. The light hurts my eyes. Yes, the skin too. It pulses."

He glanced over at her. "It's scabbing. That's a good sign, Mam says."

"Think I'll get a scar?"

Jesse grinned. "Probably. Can you still see?"

"Thanks to Luteis and that falla melon."

Luteis had spaced the dragons out by several wingspans, which wasn't easy in such a small clearing. Two of the adults had to peer around tree trunks. Luteis's instructions rang through Sanna's mind.

Your wings are weak. Your focus must be on strengthening them before we can truly teach you the dynamics of flying and being one with the wind.

"What is he saying?" Jesse asked.

"He's explaining that their wings are weak. They have to strengthen them first. Is Elis doing all right?"

A shadow crossed Jesse's face momentarily. Sanna thought back to Stellis, when the mountain dragons attempted to bear him away.

"He's all right. More shocked than mournful, I think. Dragons don't seem to grieve like witches. Elis seems to fear more for the future than in losing his sire. They weren't close, anyway."

Alis, the hatchling that came from Finn's, leapt onto a trunk and scrambled up the nearest branch, which was parallel with Luteis's head.

You may proceed, he said.

The hatchling hesitated, her eyes focused on the ground.

Don't look at where you'll fall, he said. *Look at where you want to go. Where your eyes go, so does your body.*

Alis quivered, then stretched her wings and sprang from the branch, wings spread. She flailed, flapping awkwardly as she dropped like a stone. She crashed into the forest floor with a screech. Instantly, three other hatchlings surrounded her, Rosy included. Junis watched from a distance, then snorted fire, as if bored.

Amusement laced Luteis's tone. *A promising start for a hatchling. Next.*

Jesse gave a low whistle. "If she crashed that hard, can you imagine what it's going to be like for the adults?"

"They have greater wingspans," Sanna said.

"And heavier bodies."

Another silence fell when a second and third hatchling ascended the tree. One of the adults shifted his weight from one leg to another. The once-plump dragons, fat from feasting on the carcasses obtained by the witches, had grown gaunt, almost ghastly, in their thinness. Their scales lacked luster. Luteis's edict that they must attempt flight had met with little resistance—Alis and her tales of the mountain dragon attack, no doubt, had convinced them of the necessity of them working.

A hopeful sign.

The two hatchlings, together, plummeted to the ground. Their wings tangled halfway down in their desperate thrashing. Their heads knocked together as they fell to the earth. Sanna winced. Jesse sucked in a sharp breath as Luteis commanded them to try again. He turned to the adults and motioned to a much-higher branch.

"Is this hopeless?" Jesse asked, frowning.

Sanna hesitated.

Of course it *seemed* hopeless on some level, but she couldn't bring herself to say it. Adult dragons that had never attempted to fly in their life could hardly learn in time to fight a force like Selsay. Forest dragons might have size on their side, but without flight they lost a great deal of their advantage.

She'd been thinking about it constantly. Were they wasting their time? Or was there some advantage in taking action? She hadn't decided. In light of a firm answer, she kept going with their current plan. Doing something seemed far better than nothing.

"No," she said. "It's not hopeless."

He studied her face, then nodded.

Sanna tilted her head at the sound of crackling leaves. Elliot strode toward the dragons. He stopped thirty paces away, hands clenched at his sides, and pulled in a deep breath.

"No way," Jesse murmured.

Sanna straightened, one arm lifted. "Ell—"

Jesse grabbed her arm, stopping her. "Wait."

Elliot stepped into the circle near Luteis. Luteis glanced at Sanna in question. Before she could open her mouth, Elliot turned to Luteis and said, "I want to learn to fly."

He must merge with a dragon first, Luteis said, glancing back at the dragons. They all shuffled.

Dragons, Luteis called. *A Dragonmaster awaits a merge. This will strengthen you for flight and give us much more advantage in any conflict. Together, you are stronger.*

Alis stepped closer, nostrils flaring as she sniffed Elliot's direction. Sanna's brow furrowed. *Can a hatchling merge?* she asked Luteis, eyeing Alis. Though she was small for a dragon, a hatchling of ten years could easily bear the weight of a witch like Elliot, particularly while he was so gaunt. But it did seem odd.

It is not recommended.

She lifted one eyebrow. *How do you know?*

Luteis's gaze tapered. He'd grown up in isolation—raised by the forest after his mam was killed by the tyrant Talis. Until he'd saved Sanna, he'd never met another dragon.

It is not recommended by me, he hissed. *They aren't prepared for the responsibility or the power.*

Sanna fought off a smile when his tail twitched danger-ously close to her right cheek, whistling past her in warn-ing. When she turned, Jesse was staring at her with a strange expression.

"Luteis says he doesn't recommend a hatchling merge," she said, her amusement fading back into concern.

"Why not?"

She shrugged.

"He won't force another dragon to merge with Daid, will he?" he asked.

"No."

The word came out more forcefully than she'd expected. Sanna cleared her throat. "We don't force dragons to do anything. That's Talis's game."

Luteis glanced back, then snorted her direction. Elliot's hand twitched. He must have heard her. Right then, Gellis, a female in mid life at eighty years old, stepped toward Elliot. Sanna had always known her as forward, but calm. The perfect dragon for Elliot.

Elliot stood there, frozen.

"Lift up your hand," Sanna hissed to him as Gellis approached, gazing on him with curiosity. "Let her touch it with her snout."

A trembling hand rose in the air. Gellis pressed her snout to it. Elliot sucked in a sharp breath, held his hand there for a pause, then pulled it away with a wince. Sanna hid a smirk. Gellis would be ready to mate soon, which made her burn hotter than usual.

"Wh-what next?" Elliot asked under his breath.

"Do you want to merge with Gellis?" Sanna asked.

Elliot paused, met Gellis's deep eyes, then nodded.

"Exchange of blood is next then," Sanna said, sounding

more confident than she'd expected herself to sound. "That initiates the merging."

Gellis looked at her with an assessing gaze. Sanna held it. After what seemed an eternity, Gellis turned back to Elliot. She scored her own leg with a talon, allowing blood to rise to the surface. Elliot, with a knife pulled from his pocket, nicked the side of his thumb. When he pressed his skin to a drop of Gellis's sizzling blood—which could have half-filled a bucket—he shouted.

Sanna held her breath. What would happen next? Would Elliot be overcome with power, the way she had with Luteis?

Elliot's brow furrowed.

"Yes," he said, not taking his eyes off Gellis. "I can hear you."

A success, Luteis said.

Why was it so different from ours?

I don't know.

Gellis slipped back a few steps, head flailing slightly, as if she were upset. Elliot turned to Sanna, panic in his gaze.

What do I do? he seemed to be asking. Sanna fought off a smile.

"Let her go," Sanna said. "The merging is ... a big step. Give both of you time to get used to it."

With seeming relief, Gellis disappeared back into the trees. Elliot stumbled over to Sanna and Jesse. Jesse clapped him on the shoulder with a grin.

"Good work, Daid."

Elliot mumbled under his breath as he sat next to them. "Odd feeling. In my head. Didn't expect ..." Sapphire blood still stained the skin of his hand and wrist.

A hopeful sign, Sanna said to Luteis.

Indeed.

She looked to Jesse. "See?" she mouthed. "Hope."

He grinned.

The dragons continued to move toward the branch Luteis wanted them to jump from. It stood over ten times Sanna's height, and twice theirs. The hatchlings scrambled upward fearlessly. One of Elliot's adult males, Torrelis, sank his claws into the tree but climbed only three arm spans off the ground before he fell on his backside with a ferocious growl. A second later, he tried again.

Another dragon made it halfway, began to fall backward, and abandoned the tree. Her wings flailed as she plummeted, crashing into the ground on her back legs. She howled. Luteis's tongue flickered. More dragons crashed, growling and throwing flame at each other when each attempt failed. The hatchlings peered down at them.

Sanna opened her mouth to say something to Jesse but closed it again when she saw Trey lingering just outside the open spot, watching. He looked so much older than she remembered. Haunted, even. Burning his family on a makeshift pyre had made her vomit several times in the bushes, but Trey had stood strong and silent.

Jesse tilted his head back. "Maybe Elis could help."

Luteis spun around to stare at them, eyes tapered into thin yellow slits. Jesse held up two hands in a gesture of peace.

"I'm not trying to make you angry. I'm trying to be efficient."

It's an excellent idea, Luteis said. *I would be happy to turn this over to Elis. We need to patrol, anyway.*

You just want to fly.

I want eyes on the enemy.

Sanna turned to Jesse. "It's a good idea. Would Elis do it?"

"Gratefully."

A body lumbered out of the trees before Sanna could ask him. Elis nuzzled Jesse. Sanna heard a whisper, a stirring, in the back of her mind. Before she could turn her attention to it, it faded. Luteis's voice replaced it.

Elis will take over from here. I want you to try another spot, Luteis said to the dragons. *Jumping from boulders and extending the wings will also strengthen them and be an easier start. Follow Elis and the witch boy Jesse.*

Come, Sanna of the Forest. We fly.

THREE CHILDREN SCAMPERED past Sanna the next evening, giggling as they ran.

Scraps of old material tied Elliot's youngest daughter's hair into a bramble-filled messy bun at the back of her head. Hatchlings dropped from the trees, some of them flying, a few still falling—at least at first. Most of the hatchlings had quickly progressed to gliding. Rosy had long shown talent above all. Luteis often took her on longer flights with Junis. He pushed their endurance every day.

She slipped through the trees, seeking Jesse, a half-sharpened spear in her hand. Smoke rose from a deep hole in the ground where embers sizzled when forest-lion fat dripped into the fire. Mam stood, rotating the meat on a spit, staring at the orange and red flames with glazed eyes. She turned it so slowly the fat dripped into the flames instead of coating the meat. Sanna sighed. Mam seemed to be anywhere *but* in the forest.

"*Avay*, Mam."

Mam glanced up and blinked. Seconds passed before recognition flittered across her face. "Sanna," she said.

A breath of relief slipped from Sanna's lips. Mam remembered her, at least. What of Isadora, though? Did anyone remember her? It seemed ages ago that they'd last seen her.

"Smells good."

Sanna settled on a rock not far from the fire. In the background of her mind, she heard Luteis's voice as he hunted with Elis and two of the older hatchlings. He spoke about beluas and forest lions and the differences in their scent. Although beluas had proliferated in the forest, particularly north of here, the meat was tough and gristle-filled and smelled foul.

For once, she felt better having her feet on the ground.

"*Avay*," Mam said.

She turned the spit, and fat sizzled as it landed on the logs below. Sanna resisted the temptation to stretch out on the ground, the way she did when it was just her and Luteis. Mam probably couldn't handle her lack of propriety. Even in the middle of the forest.

An awkward silence stretched between them until Sanna asked the question that had been burning in the back of her mind all day.

"Have you seen Isadora?"

Mam shook her head once. Her lips pressed together. "No."

"Oh. Ah ... not at all?"

"No."

"Letter or ..."

Mam shook her head. Sanna frowned, her frustration deepening. What now? When would Isadora return? Daid had been gone for weeks now, and Isadora didn't even know.

"That's not like her."

"We're gone." Mam shrugged. "She may have tried."

Sanna thought of going back to Anguis with Luteis, but banished the notion. She couldn't leave with one of the two competent dragons—not for more than patrols, anyway. And how would they even find her? None of them knew anything of Isadora's world.

Their first mistake.

"Perhaps," Sanna said. But she let her worry go. Clearly, Isadora had taken care of herself so far. She'd have to continue to do so.

"How are you, Mam?"

Mam pressed a weary hand to her forehead. "Tired. Hungry." She tilted her head back, shuddered, then closed her mouth, as if to cut off something else she wanted to say. Sanna waited, but Mam ventured no more.

"It's been good to ..."

The words died on her lips. *To see you again,* she wanted to say, but didn't know how. Instead, the air between them grew tense. *Was* it good to see Mam again? To remember Daid—the horror of his death? Her distance from Isadora? The strange shell of the woman who resided in Mam's body?

Sanna kicked at some pebbles on the ground. Mam turned the spit and frowned. The crease lines in her forehead seemed to burrow deep.

"Mam, are you okay? Really?"

The question came out on its own. The moment Sanna heard herself speak it, relief flooded her. How badly she'd wanted to ask. Mam's gaze met hers for a brief moment, then flittered away.

"Talis cared for us in so many ways," she said. "He provided. He kept us safe. Your daid wouldn't be dead if Talis were alive."

"Wouldn't he?"

Mam closed her eyes. "I don't know. It's all so confusing. Aren't you confused?"

"I was."

"Talis clearly crossed the line, didn't he?" Mam asked. Her fingers toyed with the edges of her tattered dress. "He ... he killed witches. That's wrong. It's wrong, right? Even for Talis. And Drago. Yes, of course it's wrong. But if we were to do wrong and bring it upon ourselves? No, because Drago doesn't exist ..."

Mam's voice trailed away, anguish in her eyes. She lowered herself to a log, her face pale. Sanna stood and turned the roasting meat. No wonder Mam always seemed exhausted. Was she constantly running through this mental dialogue?

"Talis killed other forest dragons, too, Mam. And may have initiated the downfall of the forest-dragon race."

"Yes. But ... don't you feel afraid without him?" She glanced at the canopy with distrustful eyes. "There is so much that could harm us. I never felt this way with Talis. And then your daid ..."

There is so much more than this, Sanna thought, grateful Mam didn't know the extent of what they faced.

"These other mountain dragons could attack at any moment," Mam continued. "What's to stop them? Talis would have."

Mam stared at her, as if lost. Sanna scrambled for reassurances but had none to give. Mam continued, speaking more than she had at one time since Talis died.

"Why haven't they attacked? It's been three days. It's awful, waiting. Fearing. Thinking that we could ... but then, your daid ..."

Sanna couldn't tell if Mam felt hope at the possibility of

death, or fear. In death, at least they'd see Daid. Or would they? Was Halla real? Or did Daid just not exist at all anymore? Perhaps that thought comforted—or motivated—Mam. But she seemed terrified. Distraught at the very idea of another massacre.

Sanna couldn't blame her. She felt it, too, all the way to the tips of her fingers. There hadn't been a single sign of the mountain dragons yet. Not even their daily reconnaissance missions made her feel more at ease.

She tried to remind herself that while the mountain dragons could be looking for them, Letum Wood was expansive and disorienting. The mountain dragons hadn't yet moved close enough to be dangerous.

At least, not that they could tell.

"Still," Mam said, shaking her head. "Now that Talis is gone, and we're doing this without his rules and without ..."

She trailed off, but Sanna knew exactly what she would have said.

Without Daid.

"I can't help but ... it's like there's something inside me that's remembering what it was like before I came to Anguis and handfasted your father. Something I felt once."

Sanna chose her words carefully—Mam never spoke of life before the dragons. Never. Maybe she had feared Talis's wrath, or just didn't *want* to remember the past.

"What is it?" Sanna asked.

"Never mind. I ... I miss Anguis. I miss your daid and Isadora and a time when things made sense."

Tears pooled in Mam's eyes. Her lips trembled. One hand clutched her heart, and Sanna doubted she was even aware of the gesture.

"Mam, about Da—"

"Stop." The firm command rang through the air. "I can't talk about him anymore, Sanna. I'm not ready."

"I just—"

Mam stood up and strode into the trees without another word. Sanna watched her disappear with a sinking feeling in her chest. She reached up, touched the acid burns that still smarted on her face, and let her hand drop.

"I miss you, Mam."

TWENTY-TWO

Isadora frowned at the waves.

They frothed in a lacy ribbon along the edge of the shore, a white backdrop to the churning sky. The sun had just climbed above the horizon, painting the expanse in a wash of tangerine orange. In the distance, the slate cloud still lingered—a dark smudge in a beautiful globe. It never disappeared. What did it cover? Lightning streaked from it, darting to the water.

Isadora's mind spun with questions about Lucey and Cecelia and the Defenders. How big was Carcere? Were there only two Guards? She'd only seen a breath of the gloomy prison, but it still felt expansive. Endless.

The temptation to slip back into the paths nearly overcame her. She winced against a restless surge of power. She'd need to vent her magic soon. Despite the triumph of seeing Carcere, her mind kept slipping back toward the paths. To Maximillion—as an adult, a child, and a troubled teenager. To the night she felt she'd pulled the Defenders into her magic. Why did the magic show her so much of Maximillion when he wasn't here, but not Lucey? And how could she see him as a child? That would be the past, and the Defenders saw the past.

Why did she feel like she was missing a piece of this puzzle?

Thoughts of Maximillion shot a tight pang through her chest. She had so much information now—when would he come? Getting Lucey out actually seemed, for the first time, at least slightly plausible. There was the question of getting Maximillion into the castle, finding Lucey within the intricate maze of Carcere, extracting her, and getting off the island ...

... but they *could* do it.

If only Maximillion would show up, already.

A commotion from the hall caught her attention, drawing her from her thoughts. Fiona stood in the doorway, frowning.

"Cecelia requested her bedsheets be changed," she croaked. "Better do that first today."

Fiona's bloodshot, red-rimmed eyes were bleary, but Isadora knew better than to ask why. The Vittoria Day party must have gone longer than anticipated. The castle had been quieter than normal this morning.

Isadora frowned. Cecelia had never requested her linens changed before. Besides, they had just been washed two days ago.

"The extra set should be in the closet."

"Cecelia requested the *lavanda* maid do it. Don't ask me why." Fiona flicked her wrist as she fought off a yawn. "Don't know. She must have had one of her usual ... ah ... *visitors*." Fiona frowned. "Seemed odd, at any rate, that her maids aren't taking care of it."

"Where are they?"

Fiona shrugged. "She said they're gone for the day."

"Recovering?"

Fiona mumbled something incoherent under her breath. Isadora decided not to press her luck.

"Of course I will do as Cecelia has requested, and right away."

Satisfied, Fiona moved on, still grimacing as her skirts swished. A prickling suspicion nagged Isadora, tingling up the back of her neck. This wouldn't—couldn't—have anything to do with her trip to Carcere, could it?

No.

Absurd.

Still, she wondered.

~

NOT A SINGLE MAID GREETED ISADORA.

The third floor lay as hauntingly empty as before, except the double doors to Cecelia's apartment stood ajar, spilling light into a rectangular entryway. A glittering chandelier hovered overhead, its half-melted candles seeming to hold their breath. Small rooms that likely housed the maids branched away from the entry.

Not a single sign of life stirred. No sound, not even the ocean.

Isadora paused on the threshold, sheets draped over her arms. Her neck prickled. What now? Could this be a test? Blast Maximillion for instilling her with such paranoia. Her magic stirred, and she wondered if it could sense her fear.

She hesitated a moment longer before advancing a step. A sliver of light peeked out between two doors—similar to the ones in the hall but decorated with a glass mosaic instead of stained glass. One of the doors moaned at a little shuffle of wind, swinging open another half-pace. Isadora paused, heart pounding. The temptation to throw the sheets down and run nearly overcame her, but she drew in a deep breath. Perhaps it was good she hadn't gone into the paths. Courage felt far more difficult when she knew what she faced.

Her knuckles tapped on one of the doors. She poked her head in.

"*Allo?*"

Light infused a sprawling room, falling over the furniture and illuminating the stone floor. A four-poster bed the size of Isadora's entire room stood against the far wall. Elegant tapestries lay on the floor, depicting sprawling trees. Winding paths of darkness and light. Circular windows of stained glass dotted the top of the outer wall with varying designs of magnolia flowers. A gentle sea breeze caressed her face. The entire room felt ... oddly bright.

"What is wanted?"

At Cecelia's voice, Isadora whirled around, nearly dropping the linens—which she'd ironed twice just to be sure. She clutched them to her chest, barely maintaining her hold by sheer luck.

Cecelia stood in front of a mirror, hair tucked into a complicated maze of braids that wove into a bun at the back. A dove-gray dress hugged her arms, leading to lacy cuffs around the wrists. Pearls were strung around her neck, and from her ears hung diamond earrings. Her eyes flickered briefly to Isadora, hardly long enough to register her, and then back to the mirror.

Isadora dropped her gaze and bowed.

"I'm bringing the new bedsheets you requested."

"You may proceed."

"Yes, Great One," she choked out.

Isadora shuffled toward the sprawling bed, mind racing. The powers swirled, but she forced them back into their quiet spot.

Not here, she said. *You're not needed.*

They careened through her chest anyway. Isadora lay the sheets on the bottom of the bed, studying five layers of decorative pillows. No doubt Cecelia had rules regarding her bed's appearance and what length the sheet should be on either side. If Isadora put the pillows on the floor, would Cecelia throw her off the balcony?

Deciding a lack of confidence would be more detrimental, Isadora started to stack the pillows. Only the crashing waves rang in the background.

"Forgive my lack of maids," Cecelia said, casting herself a cursory glance in the mirror as she patted her hair. "I find myself short-staffed due to a recent loss."

Then Cecelia stared into the mirror, eyes tapered, lips thin, as if she wanted to extract answers from herself.

Setting the pillows aside on a window seat and starting at the top corner, Isadora turned down a silky, garnet bedspread. She folded it in layers and set it on a thick cedar chest infused with gems at the end of the bed.

"It's odd," Cecelia murmured, "that Giorgia, one of my most loyal maids, should just up and quit, don't you think?"

Not so loyal, she wanted to say, *if she was fooling around with an East Guard.*

There was a long silence before Isadora realized that Cecelia meant for her to answer. She paused, meeting Cecelia's probing gaze through the mirror. After a few moments' perusal, Isadora turned back to the bed.

"I wouldn't know anything about her reasons."

Cecelia spun. "You were there. I remember seeing you in the hall. You gave me the cuff links."

"Yes, milady."

"Tell me again what happened."

"I was returning recently washed linens to the closet."

"Which is against my rules. The *lavanda* maid stays in the *lavanda*."

Isadora met her gaze. "I know, milady."

Cecelia's eyebrows rose. "You knew?"

"Yes. I was tired of being in the *lavanda*."

Cecelia's eyes tapered. Something, wispy as smoke, moved through them before disappearing.

"Continue."

"The maid appeared to me, crying. She gave me the cuff links and said to give them to you."

By sheer force of will, Isadora held Cecelia's damning gaze. Only months of working with Maximillion could have prepared her for such intensity. Perhaps the aggravating man knew what he was doing after all. The hair on the back of Isadora's neck stood up when Cecelia tilted her head to the side.

"Interesting," Cecelia murmured. "Because the whole story was quite odd and unexpected. Naturally, I looked into it. My Defenders found Giorgia at her home. She told a *very* different story than you."

Isadora curled her toes under her feet.

"Milady?"

Cecelia's gaze didn't waver. "Giorgia claims that I spoke to her. I fired her. She claims that I didn't seem to be myself. That something was off. In fact, I wasn't wearing my *pastanda*." She reached up to touch her right earlobe, where a fourth diamond sparkled at the very top of her ear. "Something I've never taken off. Do you know anything about that?"

"No, milady."

"You see, one of you is lying. It couldn't have happened the way Giorgia suggested. I was in the courtyard with the Defenders, you see. Since you were the only other witch in that area of the castle at the time, I was hoping you could shed more light on the subject."

Perhaps, had she been any other witch, Isadora would never have noticed the subtle shift of magic that filtered into her mind. She'd have mistaken it for terror, perhaps. Or a desperation to live. But the gentle tension in her thoughts was anything but fear.

"And I do hate liars," Cecelia said. "My castle is my home, and I protect it with my life. Rituals protect us, you see. Systems. Rules. Castes. They create stability."

Magic swelled through Isadora's brain like a cloud. It wound into her chest. Her bones. She fought the urge to unfurl all her power. The paths. She *wanted* the paths. She needed the paths—craved them like a dying woman. Just for a moment.

A simple, single moment.

"Milady," she whispered, "I have no reason to lie to you."

"Neither did Giorgia, supposedly. It's up to you to convince me."

Something flashed in Cecelia's eyes. Isadora had seen that look before, somewhere. Only a few seconds passed before she recognized it. The same look Cecelia had right before she killed the young Watcher in the courtyard. A cat with a mouse. The triumph of a woman who thought she had all the power.

But she didn't.

Isadora strengthened her voice. "She was having an affair with a Guardian, milady. I think that makes it fairly straightforward."

Cecelia glanced to the balcony, as if considering.

"Repeat your story again. I want to be sure I haven't missed any of the most important details."

Isadora said the exact words she'd used before. She knew Cecelia's game here—Mam had tried to catch Sanna in a lie often enough by the same means. Nuance in story always led to the lie unraveling. Once Isadora finished, Cecelia made a noise in the back of her throat.

"Interesting. Why do you think Giorgia would break my rules of loyalty and allow herself to fall in love with a Guardian?"

"Desperation."

The word came out immediately.

Cecelia's gaze cut to Isadora. "Who would be desperate for love?"

"Everyone."

Cecelia snorted. "Sentimental, are you?"

The movement of magic through Isadora continued, stirring her desire to run away yet again. She could protect herself in the paths—at least for a little while. All she needed was a moment in the magic. If she collapsed, Cecelia would call for help. Isadora could duck into the paths, draw a breath, and return. It was a matter of leaving the paths at the right time, before Cecelia caught onto the game. Wouldn't the paths show her when to return? Hadn't she been successful in Carcere?

Isadora pinched her own arm.

Not only was Cecelia a murderer and her sworn mortal enemy, but a cunning manipulator. She clearly knew Isadora's secret.

"Oddity, aren't you?" Cecelia asked.

Sweat beaded Isadora's forehead. She maintained eye

contact by sheer willpower. Why wasn't Cecelia trying to kill her?

"Most here are quite odd," Isadora whispered. A lie detection spell—this had to be. They were well known for forcing a witch to spill the truth they hid. If Isadora could act like there was nothing to tell, she may get away with it.

But how could Cecelia use magic?

"Not feeling well?" Cecelia asked. Isadora blinked, feeling as if she were headed down a foggy tunnel that ended only in the paths. Something had taken hold of her.

"I'm fine."

Cecelia's head tilted back. Her eyes tapered further. "You don't look fine. It's difficult to resist, isn't it?"

"There's nothing to resist, Great One."

The magic zipped away. Isadora came back to her own mind with a jolt. Cecelia continued to watch her, so Isadora made no sound.

"Silly young girls think it's a good idea to fall in love," Cecelia hissed. "A terrible idea. Guardians and Defenders don't *have* love. They don't care about stupid maids beneath their rank. Which is why it's so horrible that Giorgia lied. She crept around behind my back, stole my time, and pretended to be a loyal servant. She broke the vow of service I swore her into. I cannot tolerate such a thing, now can I?"

A pair of curtains gusted open at a sudden burst of wind, drawing Isadora's gaze. She stifled a scream. Giorgia lay on the porch, a bloody knife protruding from her back. Blood pooled around her limp body.

Isadora stumbled back, her spine colliding with the wall. The magic flailed. Black dots stole across her vision as the paths threatened to pull her under. For a moment, she thought the powers would overwhelm her. Cecelia hadn't left her mind—she'd only made it *seem* like she had.

Isadora clawed her way out of the raging magic, clutching at a morsel of control. She clamped down on a piece of restraint, then another, and another, until the magic became her servant again.

Cecelia's lips thinned.

"Silly little girls," she sang. "Never doing what they should. Always wanting what they can't have. Always fighting for the witch who won't love them back the way they deserve. I've done Giorgia a favor. Now, get out of here, you imbecile, before you join her."

Isadora spun on her feet and ran. Cecelia's laugh followed her, ringing in her ears until she skidded to a stop at the *lavanda* window, leaned out, and vomited onto the sand below.

With relief, Sanna settled against a trunk, nestled between two deep grooves on a branch as wide as she was tall. Subtle slants of moonlight pierced the upper canopy and fell around her like splashes of rain. She held out a hand, watching the shift of light play across her palm.

"I thought I'd find you up here."

Jesse dropped from the branch just above, landing with perfect balance on his bare feet. Sanna lifted an eyebrow.

"You're getting more confident up here."

"Elis likes the trees."

Most dragons do, Luteis purred through her mind. She wondered where he was but could only sense that he was near. Sanna clutched her legs to her chest to make room for Jesse. Instead of sitting in front of her, he plopped on the branch at her side and leaned back against the trunk. His shoulder rubbed hers. She swallowed hard.

"I needed a break," she said, then gently touched her face. "All the dust from making those spears is getting into my wounds."

Jesse snorted. "I've never worked so hard in my life. Daid and I only slept two hours last night, but we finished the underground cave between that root system. It'll be perfect for your mam and the kids to hide in until it's all over. The roots will keep the ground from collapsing. It'll be dark and damp and cramped for a while, but better than facing fire."

"And acid."

The fatigue showed in his red-rimmed eyes and drooping shoulders. Still, a light infused him when Elis's tail appeared from nowhere and nestled close by.

"So?" she asked, inching to the side. "How is it being back with your family?"

He grinned. "Beautiful. I don't know how Isadora does it."

"Does what?"

"Being gone so long. Just being in the Western Network was hard enough, and we were only there a few days. Hardly enough to really miss them, you'd think. But I did."

"Did you miss your family or the forest?"

"Family," he said immediately. "Probably the forest, eventually, but not like my brothers."

Sanna thought of the deep, exhausting yearning she'd felt to be back under the canopy. To soar through the forest on long vines. To feel the familiarity of Letum Wood sing in her veins.

"Oh."

He glanced at her. "You?"

"Forest."

"You don't miss Isadora?"

Sanna hesitated. She missed Isadora, but that didn't explain the surge of rage and disappointment that accompanied thoughts of her. Isadora was *gone*. So was Daid. Now Isadora would never see him again, never know how much they'd struggled. She had her own life now.

"I miss her," she said, but her voice was flat.

"Your mam?"

"Desperately," she whispered. She missed the mam she'd known growing up. The familiar mam, not this ghost who lingered in her place.

Jesse propped his forearms on his bent knees and stared into the trees. Some hair had fallen into his eyes again. He blew at it. Sanna tried not to wish that he'd go away. She wanted to want him there, but ... she didn't.

She just wanted Luteis.

"Sanna?"

She jerked out of her thoughts to find Jesse staring at her, only a breath away. The movement of his breath felt hot on her cheek. His gaze flickered from her eyes to her lips, then back.

"I ... can I ..."

His eyes closed. He leaned forward, bridging the gap between them. Sanna gasped and reared back, tipping over the side of the branch. Before she could fall, a black tail snaked out and grabbed her by the shoulders. She dangled upside down for only a second before Luteis set her safely back on the branch, facing Jesse. Jesse's cheeks flamed bright red.

"What in Halla was that?" she cried.

"I don't know!"

"Were you trying ... did you want ... you were—"

He glanced behind, then stumbled back. "J-just forget it happened."

"I can't!"

"I-I need to help Daid," he said, snatching a vine. "I need to go. I just ... sorry, that ... it'll never happen again."

Before she could say another word, he plummeted into the foliage. The gentle, subtle rustle of branches from the next tree over followed. Elis, no doubt. Sanna whipped around to find Luteis looming over her, a condemning glare on his face. Heat radiated from him in shimmering waves. His lips closed over what had been bared teeth.

What event just transpired? Luteis asked. *I didn't like it. You seemed to not have enjoyed it either.*

Her shoulders relaxed. She glanced back at the branch and resisted the urge to touch her lips. Jesse had definitely wanted to kiss her. The thought made her upper lip curl. Kiss *Jesse?* One of her only childhood friends?

That kind of thing was for Isadora.

"I think he wanted to kiss me."

What does that mean?

"I don't know."

Is it a form of attack?

"Uh ... not really, I guess. Most witches probably like it."

What is done during this ... kiss?

This time, Sanna's cheeks flared. She turned away, grateful that shadows had fallen. "You touch with your lips."

He snorted. *I cannot see the purpose.*

"Me either."

She sighed. How desperately she needed Isadora. Isadora always knew what to do in situations like these. Surely this would change ... *something* between her and Jesse. How did one kiss, anyway? Isadora had once mentioned something about tongues touching, but that seemed too revolting to be real. Surely it wasn't that strange of a practice. Mam and Daid had always been so reserved around them, like the other Servant couples, that she'd never seen much affection.

I did not like him so close to you. Shall I be on defense against future attempts?

"No. No, it's fine. I can handle it."

But should you? Perhaps he will not try if he knows that I stand between your lips and his.

Sanna rolled her lips together to keep from laughing. "Perhaps. I don't want to talk about this anymore. Can we fly?"

I was hoping you'd ask.

Sanna crawled onto his back, settling into the juncture between his wings with relief. By the time he burst into the night, the sun had sunk in the far horizon. Darkness crept along the top of the forest like a bruise. She leaned into the heat of his neck and sighed.

Your heart seems heavy tonight.

"It is."

Your daid?

How could she explain that it wasn't just Daid that made her sad now? But Mam? Isadora's absence?

Everything?

At least the dragons showed continual improvement. Not only did the hatchlings power increase every day, but the younger adults had mostly progressed to gliding. Perhaps, should Selsay still be seeking them, they had a chance.

Luteis tilted to the right, spinning them in a low arc over the trees. They never flew high anymore, choosing the murky backdrop of the forest to provide cover for them.

Moonlight cast long shadows that even mountain dragons could see. She preferred staying close to the trees.

She turned her thoughts away from Daid and watched the horizon. No signs of dragons, though Luteis had seen hints of them a few hours away that morning. Luteis shifted to the left, taking a new course, as he did every night.

"Tashi mentioned Halla when we were in the West," she said. "What do you know of the place dragons go after death?"

I saw it briefly, when I died after fighting Talis.

She straightened. "Really?"

Very briefly.

"What is it?"

A place much like Letum Wood, only very different at the same time. I find it difficult to explain, wasn't there long. For the time I was there, I felt a tugging, as if pulled between two places. Then I returned to you.

Disbelief swelled within her. He'd never mentioned this before.

"Why didn't you tell me?"

You did not ask.

"Did you see your mam?"

Perhaps, but I cannot remember.

"Was ... was Deasylva there?"

Of course. She escorted me to that place and prevented me from going entirely in. A gift, really.

Sanna snorted. "How?"

I know it exists for certain. I have seen a portion of it. Now I will never fear death and will always trust my goddess, for I know she does provide for us in the afterlife, as she has promised.

"Is it for witches as well as dragons?"

Do you think we would be parted?

"I hope not."

Me as well.

Sanna couldn't help but notice that he didn't answer her question. Not really. But she realized there wasn't really an answer.

Luteis's body rippled beneath her, skimming the tops of the trees as they soared. His scales were warm to the touch. They normally comforted her, but tonight, something itched deep inside her soul. Below them, Letum Wood lay in quiet repose, nothing but the lush—sometimes bare— trees rustling below them in a soughing dance. The blank sky, holding only stars, remained empty.

Something doesn't feel right, she said. Speaking out loud felt too abrasive in such encompassing silence.

Why?

I'm not sure. I just … it's been so quiet. The mountain dragons attacked Finn days ago, and we've seen nothing.

They likely don't know where we are.

Perhaps.

Quiet is good.

Is it?

It is more desirable than battle.

Or a precursor to it, she said. *What if we're focusing too much on this? What if Selsay's pursuit of the blood of the forest dragons is just a distraction from a different … thing?*

What else could we fear now?

I don't know. That's just the problem. None of this fits together.

Luteis fell silent. Sanna's thoughts wandered to Finn and the attack. Her face flared with fresh heat, as if the wounds recognized her memories. The burn of acid in the air. The way the mountain dragons seemed to just appear, then disappear.

If Selsay was truly the wrath-filled goddess that she seemed to be, she should have attacked by now. Should have been more ruthless in *some* way.

Maybe she wants us alive, Sanna said.

The massacre of the Dragonmaster family and your father would suggest otherwise.

Sanna scowled. He had a point.

Can we go in a different direction? she asked.

You want to go North.

Yes.

He hesitated. *It is my wish as well. It will be a risky flight.*

We've done risky before.

Though their usual rounds varied every night, they'd begun to travel farther and farther from Elliot's camp. Sanna wondered, but didn't dare ask, if Deasylva had some part in protecting them. In that convenient way that she helped some and not others.

While the moon hid behind a bank of clouds, Luteis used his mighty wings to climb higher. His energy seemed unflagging these days, as if being around other dragons had energized him again. Sanna ducked closer to him as the air thinned out, cooling. He flew above the clouds, turned to the left and leveled out.

It will be several hours before we reach it.

Sanna burrowed closer, warmed through by his heat and the lull of his wingbeats. *That's all right by me.*

The hours slid by, lost in snatches of sleep and thought and the warm burn of Luteis beneath her. Every now and then, he dipped below the clouds, providing a brief glimpse of the landscape below. For much of it, trees unfurled as far as the eye could see. The distant horizon remained dark until it slowly changed, trees giving way to chunky black mountains.

By the time they passed over the last of the thinning forest and into the rolling, rocky hills, Sanna's legs were cramping. Even Luteis's breath was a bit strained.

Ahead, she said. *Do you see the movement on the horizon?*

Teeming dots flittered here and there in the moonlight. Luteis darted above the cloud cover, going higher. His breath huffed, as did Sanna's. She shivered in the bitter cold even as she pressed her body against his burning spine.

Mountain dragons, he said.

There are so many.

They pressed on, cutting through the quiet air. The farther they crossed into the rolling hills and toward the sharp, craggy mountains, the more mountain dragons appeared. They seemed to dance in the air with unusual ease. Even more congregated amongst the rocks below. Sanna peered down at them in surprise.

"There are so many," she murmured.

How do they eat? Luteis asked. *Can there be enough food in such hostile terrain?*

She thought back to Pemba—who had seemed healthy enough—and the other mountain dragons. They had been thin, certainly. Nothing like the thick, muscular bodies of the forest dragons.

The rocks here were sharp. Barren. It was an exposed life, no doubt creating tougher creatures than any Letum Wood sustained. Even the scariest mountain troll seemed less formidable than anything this desolate world could produce.

They're strong, she said, watching several mountain dragons whirl in an airborne dance, snapping at each other. Despite their ferocity, she couldn't deny something magnificent about their sharp way of flying. The angles of their wings, their studded necks.

Smaller in size, he mused. *Size may be one of our only advantages, outside of fire.*

Something glimmered in Sanna's fingertips, then faded. Despite watching them soar through the hills, Sanna couldn't track the mountain dragons. Just as she'd catch a glimpse, they'd disappear.

They take on the color of the night, she said, pointing. Four dragons that had been soaring side by side disappeared against the mountain backdrop, then reappeared against a cloud. Their color seemed to fade into the wisp.

The color of their surroundings.

Or they just disappear and reappear.

Perhaps both.

Her stomach dropped. This wasn't good. Thousands of mountain dragons must live here, and who knew how many places they congregated? Growls and bellows rippled through the air, reaching them even at their considerable height.

Luteis, she murmured in her mind. *We cannot defeat this many.*

We may not ha—

Something hard landed on Sanna's back. Luteis screamed fire. The thick burn of acid filled the air, stinging her face like a thousand needles. Claws wrapped around her body and snatched her into mid-air. She scrambled for Luteis, flailing.

"Luteis!"

The word had barely left her mouth before his head whipped around with a livid shriek and snarl.

Sanna was whisked away.

CHAPTER

TWENTY-THREE

Hours after confronting Cecelia, Isadora's hands still trembled.

Maximillion stood in front of the fire, arms folded. His broad shoulders pulled his jacket tight, making them appear wider than ever. Curls of chocolate hair gleamed in the flickering firelight. Isadora forced herself to look away, sniffling. Tears lurked in the corners of her eyes. She banished them.

Maximillion's office wrapped around her. She'd transported back to the Central Network as soon as she'd regathered her wits.

It didn't feel any safer.

Her mind whirled with questions. Was this her fault? Had she inadvertently killed Giorgia in her attempt to save Lucey? What did saving one witch mean if others died? That maid had no less worth than Lucey.

"She knows."

Maximillion's words shattered the quiet, drawing her attention away from her miasma of grief, terror, and rage. Isadora glanced up from the teacup she'd been staring into, unable to muster the strength to sip it. She untangled her thoughts slowly, coming out of the haze.

"What?" she asked.

"Cecelia knows."

"What does she know?"

He frowned. "She knows you're a Watcher, for one. And ... she knows something we don't."

He hadn't yelled at her. Yet. Hadn't even raised his voice when she'd quietly confessed all that had happened, from finding the entrance to Carcere to hearing Lucey's whistle to impersonating Cecelia. A small part of him seemed resigned, as if he'd known this would happen.

As if her disobedience had been expected.

"Of course she knows *something*," she muttered. "She's ... odd, Max. Frighteningly so. And there's something about her that's wrong."

He snorted. "Everything about her is wrong."

"No. No, that's not it."

"Then what is it?"

She shook her head, brow furrowed. "I don't know. But she let me live. I think she knew I was a Watcher, and she didn't even try to stop me. That means ... something."

"Precisely. It means I have to get Lucey out tonight. There's clearly no alternative."

Isadora's eyes widened. "What?"

"Go home."

"*I* am doing nothing of the sort," she snapped, shooting to her feet. "I will see this through."

"Not if you're dead."

"Maximillion, you can't! We've argued about this so many times now th—"

He spun around, all cold, glacial lines. The frost in his eyes sent a chill through her. She quieted.

"I can't?" he purred.

She reached out to touch his arm. "Please, Maximillion. I—"

He wrenched free with a growl. "Never touch me!"

"Let me make it right. I-I shouldn't have transformed into her."

"That's big of you. You really think you could cause all this?" he demanded.

She shuffled back a step, cowed by the sheer power of his annoyance.

"This is bigger than you, thank you very much."

"I did more than you have!" she cried.

He stilled so completely Isadora feared he'd leave. Something churned in his expression. Something wounded. Something like …

Pain.

"I … I'm sorry, Maximillion. I just meant that I … I'm just not sure about—"

The momentary window into his soul closed, his expression resuming its usual stoic, subdued rage that burned in the background of his disdain. "You've done admirably," he said, flicking each word off his teeth. "You managed to find an entrance I couldn't. We may even know where Lucey is in Carcere, at least generally, which is no small feat. But now you're finished."

"We can't abandon Lucey."

"I'm not."

"Please," she pleaded, her voice ragged. "Don't make all of my work mean nothing."

"Don't blame me."

It wasn't until that moment that Isadora realized how close they stood. If she reached out, she could place both of her hands on his chest. Something crackled between them

—a tension she'd never comprehended before. Maximillion's nostrils flared. He glared at her.

"Go home. You don't belong here. You wouldn't survive Cecelia a second time."

"I would."

"Demmed arrogant witch. Leave before you're hurt!"

He grabbed her wrist and yanked. Her chest slammed into his with a *thud*. His lips pressed hard into hers, sealing off her reply. His touch burned like a poker against her mouth. She threw her arms around his shoulders. He lifted her off the ground, grabbing the back of her neck with a hand. Isadora tilted her head, forcing him to deepen the kiss. All the terror, pain, and uncertainty faded. She knew nothing but Maximillion. Felt every hard angle of his shoulders. The sweet taste of peppermint lingering on his tongue.

When she couldn't bear another moment of such strange, exquisite agony, he was gone. She stumbled back onto a chair, stunned. He stood halfway across the room, his back to her. His hand trembled against his lips. Several long, drawn-out moments passed.

"Leave immediately."

"No." She straightened her shoulders, her voice shaking. "If you're going in after her, I'm going with you. You can't take Cecelia on alone. No one can. Besides, there must have been a reason she let me live."

He hesitated, staring at her through slitted eyes. If they hadn't had that heated kiss—if things weren't totally, unexpectedly, frighteningly different—he would have refused her. Forced her to leave. He would have taken this beast on by himself, the way he always had.

But now, a flicker of uncertainty lingered in his gaze.

She stood.

"You need me. You need me to help with the intricacies of the castle and Carcere and Cecelia's apartments."

"It's a suicide mission."

"It has been from the beginning."

"You could die."

"So could you."

"I don't know why she let you walk away, or what it means. We could discover something you don't want to be part of."

"You can't scare me, Maximillion. I've been living this."

He stared at her, hard, as if trying to get her to back down by the sheer force of his intimidating stare. She met it. If she could face down Cecelia, she could face down Maximillion. Besides, something in his gaze had shifted.

A new angle she hadn't seen before.

"Get ready," he said. "We're breaking her out tonight."

MAXIMILLION STOOD ACROSS THE ROOM—AS far away from Isadora as he could manage—when he extracted something from a pocket deep in his coat and sent it to her with a spell.

"Here."

She accepted it, recognizing it as a knife only after she grasped it. She didn't have to ask what it was for. She strapped it around her left forearm, then pulled her sleeve down to cover it.

He watched with one eyebrow raised.

"Sanna," she said. "She always carries a knife. Daid insists."

His expression darkened. He turned away. Firelight

flickered across the room. Isadora thought of Sanna, then Letum Wood, then the paths. Would there be—

"There's no time for you to see your sister. Don't look into the paths," he said. "Never before a big confrontation." Before she could protest, he met her gaze. "I'm serious."

She nodded. "I know."

He opened his mouth, then closed it, as if he hadn't expected her to acquiesce. The urge to let the eager magic loose surged through her, but she tucked it back down.

Soon, she promised.

This time, it calmed.

Maximillion went to the window and glanced out. With a murmured incantation, he conjured a gauzy bird. Although she strained to hear, Isadora deciphered nothing of his message. The bird winged away, disappearing into the darkness. He stared out several more seconds before he patted his chest, as if searching for something. His chin lifted. He pulled something from an inner pocket. *A bundle of letters?*

Isadora frowned.

"What's that?"

"For you." He tossed them on his desk. His face had become all lines again. Hard. Angular. Unreadable. Isadora reached for the letters, bound by twine. The haphazard paper and smeared handwriting looked like a bird attempting to wield a quill. That could only mean one witch.

Sanna.

"Letters?"

"From your family."

Isadora felt them with her thumb. "You ... lied?"

"I did."

"But ..."

"I had to. You have been in grave danger for weeks. You needed to focus."

She clenched the letters tighter. "You're a rat," she hissed. "I could have used these for some courage."

"I've never been in the business of caring what other people think of me. I kept you alive."

Behind her disbelief and rage lingered a niggling doubt. Would it have been easier to cope with her mission if she knew Sanna had written? Did the letters contain good news or bad news? If bad news, then no. It would have been harder to be in the East. If good news, it might have only made her more homesick.

Isadora let her arm drop to her side.

"Fine. I will ... I'll read these later, then."

"Fine," he muttered. His eyes glittered with unfettered malice. "Let us be off. We have one witch to save and one to subdue."

Isadora followed his transportation spell as he disappeared, shuddering as she wondered just what he meant by *subdue*.

THE WHEELS of the laundry trolley squeaked with every turn.

With an irate Maximillion hidden in the bottom compartment, draped with a sheet, it certainly wasn't the easiest thing to push. The uphill track near the servants' quarters only intensified the strain.

Isadora huffed and puffed her way up, attempting to be as quiet as possible. La Torra lay in quiet repose. Likely, no one had even noticed she'd left, even though the temporary use of magic may have caught someone's attention.

Outside, darkness had fallen. Torchlight illuminated the

castle halls, oddly still in an usually breezy world. The crash of the waves sang through the air, wrapping around Isadora as she walked. In the distance, lightning crackled.

Her stomach churned as they reached the third floor. She parked the trolley, panting, then glanced around. No sign of Lorenzo or Fiona. After she tapped the trolley with her toe, Maximillion extracted himself. His hair was tousled when he straightened, but his eyes were sharp. He sent her a questioning glance as he straightened his shirt.

Isadora nodded. She led him to the stairwell entrance several steps away. Getting Maximillion *to* the staircase wasn't the difficult part.

Getting him *inside* was.

She stopped by the thick, hidden door, linens in her arms, and pressed against the hinge. As before, it creaked open. They stepped hastily inside, then forced it shut. Darkness surrounded them. Maximillion's arm brushed against hers then jerked away—a reassuring accident.

"Feel your way up behind me," she murmured. "They shouldn't know we're coming."

He said nothing as she crept forward, searching blindly with her toes for the first step. Every now and then, he reached out, felt her back, then reared away. They said nothing in the seemingly endless dark.

Once the telltale flicker of light—and low voices—appeared ahead of them, the quiet shuffle of Maximillion's feet paused. Isadora pressed on, heart in her throat.

A familiar scowl met her. The same East Guards waited at the intersection of the three tunnels. The smaller of the two sat on the ground, legs sprawled out. He scrambled to his feet once she moved into view. The burly one pushed away from the wall.

"You again?" he muttered. "What do you want?"

She held up the linens. "To deliver these."

"We didn't send any down."

She frowned. "Really? Because they smelled awful and took hours to scrub."

The burly Guard glared at her. "They aren't for here. Get out!"

"But—"

The Guardian collapsed to his knees with a grunt, then fell flat on his face when a heavy rock slammed into his forehead. The second let out a shout, but Maximillion advanced from the shadows. Despite his usual elegance, he moved fast as lightning, using the smaller Guard's surprise to his advantage. After only a short scuffle—and one hit to the jaw that drew a grunt—Maximillion subdued the Guardian, tied him, gagged him, and straightened up.

"You're sure there's only two?"

"That's all I've ever seen."

"Let's go," he hissed, yanking keys from the burly Guard's belt. He wound a rope around the Guard's wrists and ankles, then gagged him as well. The East Guard groaned.

Maximillion grabbed a torch. Something uneasy flickered through his eyes as he glanced around. Although it was intangible, Isadora felt it too. Something was ... *off*. Whether they were walking into a trap, or Carcere just felt heavy, she couldn't tell.

"Where to?" he asked. Isadora peered into the passages, chewing her bottom lip. Lucey's birdsong had been faint.

"Ah ... to the right, I think."

"You *think*?" he hissed.

"I'm almost positive."

He pressed his lips together as if suppressing a thought, then growled and stalked into the darkness. Her steps were quick as wingbeats, mimicking her terrified heart, as she followed. Knowing they were finally closing in on Lucey sent a thrill through her.

Within steps, their pace slowed. Torchlight flickered off damp walls hung with irons, manacles, and ropes. Moldering benches lined the hallway. The foul air seemed to fill her throat, making it difficult to breathe. She put a hand over her nose.

"Disgusting," she murmured.

Maximillion grimaced, as if he'd sucked on a sacran coin, but said nothing as he continued on. Every now and then, cells popped up. All of them empty. Everything was silent. What if they'd moved Lucey? Or perhaps she'd heard wrong?

When the passage began to twist and turn, branching like blackened arteries, Isadora stopped. Empty prison cells populated around her. She'd certainly had underestimated the powerful magic of Carcere. The space here expanded far beyond La Torra, encompassing entire meadows in places, it seemed.

"An illusion?" she asked Maximillion, reaching to touch a damp wall. In the distance, a rat squeaked. There had been no rats in Ernesto's kitchen in La Torra.

"It's ..." He trailed away.

"Otherworldly," she whispered.

The sensation of someone walking past her sent a chill over her skin. A vague outline of Maximillion's shoulders and body breezed by—even the torchlight seemed to dim in the bleakness.

"It's meant to be confusing," he said. "Security reasons, no doubt."

"How will we find Lucey?"

"With a prodigious amount of luck."

Maybe at the cost of our lives. Could they wander forever and never find the end? Surely, it *had* to end somewhere.

She hoped.

Isadora lifted the torch a little higher. Light glowed off the shimmering walls. *Oro.* Her eyes darted over the wet stone. *Oro* ran thick here, like trickling, golden rivers. Must and decay thickened the air.

Several moments of silence passed. Maximillion's attempts to renew an invisibility spell met with failure. Isadora reached out and ran her fingertips along the *oro*.

Something shuffled behind them. Isadora whirled around, wielding the torch, but Maximillion rolled his eyes.

"A rat," he muttered.

Rats on an island that had never seen them before? Or was Carcere that strange? Feeling marginally better when she saw Maximillion in front of her, Isadora followed, waving the torch from side to side. Very little changed, but she had the sense that their direction had. They didn't branch into the smaller hallways but seemed to move toward the farthest reaches of Carcere.

If there was such a thing.

A faint sound caught her ear. "What is that?" she whispered.

He shook his head. Their pace flagged. The sound grew in strength as they stood at a small intersection from which three thin hallways branched. Maximillion hesitated, then turned into the one on the right. Isadora held the torch out, past the empty cells and dank stone walls, to see a strange sight.

Dozens of eyes.

Isadora leapt back, stifling a scream.

"Light!" a voice cried.

"Redemption!"

"We're saved!"

"Another prisoner," whispered another.

"Haven't had one in a while."

The words—spoken in the quiet, garbled tones of the common and *Ilese* languages—assaulted Isadora all at once. Maximillion threw out an arm, halting her. They stood at the top of a stretch of prison cells. Waste and mold overpowered the air. Isadora fought back the urge to vomit at the fetid, toe-curling stench.

The eyes that peered back at her recoiled from the light but continued to stare at it from behind raised arms. Men. Women. One teenager, it appeared. Long, anemic faces, gaunt with years hidden from the sun, stared at them.

"Maximillion, what—"

A second cacophany of voices followed.

"They aren't Guards!"

"It's the Advocacy!"

"Praise be to the goddess mother Prana!"

A cold wash pulsed through Isadora's body, starting at the top of her spine. "No," Isadora whispered.

If they knew the Advocacy, that meant ...

Maximillion murmured, "Watchers."

An excited murmur rippled through the hall and all the way back, into unknown cells. Voices lifted. Some shouted, screeched. A sob rang through the air.

Isadora's heart seized. She grabbed Maximillion's arm —for the first time, he didn't pull away.

"Max," she whispered, "we can't possibly—"

"Silence," he barked in the common tongue. The room quieted. "Who are you?"

A man to their right moved out of the shadows and into the circle of torchlight. He had the cell closest to them. Knobby fingers—the knuckles swollen—clung to the metal bars of the door. Strings of hair hung from the side of his head. His eyes, bloodshot and rheumy, had a spark of fire.

No, rage.

"We are the ones she fears the most," he said in *Ilese*. "The ones she considers to be most dangerous."

Maximillion's gaze sharpened. "Watchers?"

The man nodded. Something in him, perhaps a glimmer of insanity, kept Isadora's attention. Desperation swelled through the air here, but this witch was different. The magic stirred in Isadora's chest, then faded away. She attempted to open it but failed. The witch's eyes snapped to hers. She didn't waver.

He frowned and looked away first.

Maximillion glanced around, eyes darting all over the place, no doubt trying to calculate how many were there. Within the ring of light, Isadora counted ten. The thin stalls were barely long enough to lay down in. There could be any number of witches here.

"How long?" Maximillion asked.

The man shrugged. "Does time still exist?" He jabbed a thumb at the wall behind him. "Made a notch for each dinner they brought."

Isadora swallowed hard and lifted the torch higher. Thousands of marks covered the wall. "The good gods," she whispered. She bit her bottom lip, banishing the urge to call out for Lucey.

Maximillion swore under his breath. "And how many of you?"

"Thirty-four."

"Impossible. I've watched Cecelia for years now. There haven't been that many ..."

His words trailed away, and his expression darkened. Isadora bit back her horror. At least some of these witches had been imprisoned since before Maximillion had started the Advocacy. Cecelia had found more Watchers than Maximillion had known. Had she been playing this game all along? Staging certain raids to be caught?

A long stretch of silence passed. The man shifted forward, leaning into the bars. "Are you the Advocate?"

"No," Maximillion said, "but I work for the Advocacy."

She glanced at him but saw no lie in his eyes.

Isadora ventured farther down the hall. Eyes peered out from everywhere, drawn to the light like desperate moths. Hands gripped the metal bars. A girl who appeared to be a teenager stepped out of the shadows nearest Isadora. Isadora reached out and put a hand on her face. The girl flinched, then leaned into it. Her cheeks were cold, her eyes soulful.

The man's voice carried down the hall. "Are you here to save us?" he asked Isadora, pressing his face to the bars. His eyes bulged out of a too-thin face.

Silence fell. For the first time, Maximillion had nothing to say. He gazed at them, eyes as calculating—perhaps as afraid—as ever.

Isadora whirled around, faced Maximillion, and said, "Yes. We're here to set you free."

TWENTY-FOUR

Sanna flailed hundreds of paces above the ground.

The craggy, rocky mountains of the Northern Network passed below her, swift as eagles. She tried to spin around, pummel the claws of whatever had her, but to no avail. A deep chuckle froze her blood.

Not so feisty when you're not the one in control.

She scowled. Pemba.

A familiar scream came from not far back. She ducked her head to see mountain dragons surrounding Luteis in the air. He sprayed sheets of fire, some of it his secundum, to drive them back as he flew. Fire as hot as his burned in her hands—again—but soon faded. Sanna watched as dragons appeared on top of Luteis, as if from nowhere, weighing him down. He flipped on his back, scoring them with his talons and flame.

I'm well, she said to him. *Save yourself.*

They will not have you! he growled, then disappeared under another horde of dragons. Fire burst from between them. One mountain dragon plummeted downward, tongues of flame consuming his wings as he attempted to recover. Haggard mountain dragons streamed toward the fray in the sky.

Sanna slammed into the ground.

She landed hard on her left shoulder and rolled across a dusty rock. Breath escaped her; her lungs froze. Bits of rock skidded across her skin, bringing blood to the surface. She moved with the momentum—just like when she rolled off a tree—and eventually slowed when she hit a rock wall inside a cave.

The moment she stopped, Sanna leapt to her feet, crouching low. She bared her teeth, growling when she saw Pemba glaring at her from the entrance of the sprawling cave. Her shoulder and face pounded.

You have come to see us, he drawled. *What a delightful turn of events.*

She studied him. So he could speak into her mind without touching her? Was it part of their magic? She straightened up, scowling.

"Don't flatter yourself."

Why are you here? Bringing a message from your goddess? She is a hard one to communicate with.

"I agree."

He blinked.

"I haven't even delivered the first message, if you want to know."

Odd.

His eyes closed. She fought the urge to grimace. His acidic breath made fire dance across her eyes, blurring her vision until she blinked to clear it. She forced her mind to clear, fighting the distraction of the pain. As if he sensed her distress, he snorted her direction.

She turned away, grimacing.

His laugh filled the cave, rolling like peals of thunder.

He slipped back into the air like a ghost, giving her a glimpse of his profile. His *thin* profile. The edges of his body had begun to turn slate, the color of the rocks.

Sanna scrambled for the edge and skidded to a stop. A ledge only two paces wide jutted out ... leading down a steep precipice and nowhere else.

The world seemed to turn to ribbons below. Her heart slammed in her chest. A flying knot of dragons soared in the distance. She felt as if she hovered in the air, rocks and rills flowing away from her in all directions. Letum Wood was nowhere in sight—they had flown farther inland than she'd thought. No sign of Pemba remained in the sky.

I'm fine, she said to Luteis. *I'm fine. It was Pemba.*

I cannot land. I am only able to evade, and only barely. They are tracking me. The lower I attempt to go, the more come.

Get away. Find some water. Get some rest. I'm in a cave and can't get out. There's no reason for both of us to be captured.

I will not leave you.

Of course you won't. You're preparing to help me when it's advantageous. I don't think they're going to kill me.

A long hesitation filled her mind as she studied the sky, identifying where he was by the sight of fire. Pemba had flown much faster than she'd expected. After a silence so long that she feared the mountain dragons had overcome him, Luteis said, *Very well. I will be close.*

Thank you for trusting me.

Do nothing foolish.

When do I ever?

Precisely.

～

Sanna glanced up hours later, pulled from her reverie by the *thunk* of a rock tumbling down the mountainside, skidding past her. It fell, plummeting into the air and disappearing without a sound.

She observed the mountain life teeming in the fading moonlight below, revealed only by the bleakest slants of sunlight from the horizon. She shivered, cooled by the chilly mountain air. Dragons flew like armies in the sky. Perhaps Selsay had ordered them to congregate to give Sanna a false belief of just how powerful she was.

Or maybe there were just that many in the area.

But where were the hatchlings? The females? All of these seemed to be the same—slender, masculine dragons half mad and too thin. A few larger mountain dragons drifted into sight every now and then, mere glimmers against the slate clouds. She never saw them long—their camouflage seemed more powerful than that of the smaller ones flitting around, snapping at each other. They all seemed so uniform. So perfectly, strangely similar. No variation in face, wing structure, or size. Few of them flew close, but those that did were thin.

Sanna blinked, startled out of her thoughts again. Pemba appeared. He hovered in front of her, shattering her contemplation. His broad wings kept him impressively steady in the air.

Climb.

She stood.

"To where?"

He motioned to the left with a jerk of his head. Sanna peered around the edge of the cave. There was a small enough space along the rocks for her to shuffle sideways. It disappeared into the smooth, slate wall.

"To my death?" she asked.

You are not so lucky. Go. The path will appear.

She scowled. "And if I don't?"

Acid filled the air, thickening it. She recoiled, feeling as if flames were consuming her face. "All right!" she snapped. "I'll go."

A chuckle rumbled deep in his chest. As if he could hear her distress, Luteis's voice filtered through her mind.

You are well?

Pemba is back. We're climbing.

I have found sustenance and water. Whenever you need me—

I'll let you know.

I shall have to trust you.

You stall, Pemba hissed. *Climb!*

"I'm not a fan of heights," she muttered.

You lie. You are the High Dragonmaster. We have seen you in the high trees, nearly tall as mountains, fearless.

"It's different." She stepped carefully onto the ledge and reached a hand out, pressing her palm against the cool surface of the rocks to shuffle forward. Pemba was right— the way did seem to appear. At first she thought it was magic, but then she realized it was little more than the twists and turns of the rock. The ledge remained thin, precariously so, but she clung to the side and made her way along it.

Eventually, the path opened onto a different trail that meandered amongst boulders twice her height. No moss or lichen grew up here—this world seemed deserted in every way possible. Dragons seemed to be the only life in this vast, barren expanse. She half-turned, pausing to catch her breath, which was strained and ragged. The thin air brushed past her in a brittle wind.

Keep moving, Pemba snapped.

Sanna ignored him, attempting to stuff as much air as possible deep into the crevices of her lungs. She pointed down the hill.

"What is that?"

A caravan of what appeared to be witches trekked up the far mountainside, mere specks against the rock. They were so far away they looked like ants, but Sanna could just make out bright swaths of fabric, wagons, and what appeared to be piles of dead creatures. The growing sunlight, though weak, continued to build. She preferred the dark. Heights this barren and exposed rattled her bones.

Tributes, he hissed with pleasure. *They were almost late. It is not wise to be late. Continue.*

Tributes. Some form of offering. Even though the witches brought quite a few dead creatures, there was no possible way these bleak mountaintops could feed all these dragons. She kept walking.

Where are you? she asked Luteis.

Close enough to see you.

You're safe?

Safer than you.

Sanna suppressed the urge to look at the sky. Moments later, the rock wall she had been ascending gave way to air. She stood on top of what appeared to be the tallest mountain in the area—though purplish peaks in the distance jutted so far into the sky that they pierced the clouds and disappeared. She struggled to catch her breath for more than one reason.

It's a strange kind of beauty up here, isn't it? she asked Luteis as Pemba alighted on a rock nearby. She turned her back to him.

Bleak, he said. *But powerful. Mountains cannot move.*

Sanna let out a long breath. A rumbling voice entered her mind, shaking her like an earthquake. It was deep and thick, oddly feminine in a husky way, as if just woken from a long slumber.

You are the only witch to have spoken with two of us.

She whipped around. No one stood anywhere near her —not even Pemba, who had fallen to the rocks, his face pressed to the dust in prostration. Even though Sanna had been sitting at the mouth of that cave for what felt like hours, memorizing the layout of the land, watching the habits of the mountain dragons, she saw nothing that could belong to the rumbling voice.

An odd thing to happen, the voice continued, *for a witch with so much animosity to the goddesses.*

Sanna crouched and pressed her palm to the cold stone. The voice seemed to reverberate into her bones, all the way through her skeleton, as if it originated from the very mountains themselves.

Selsay.

"Forgive me if I feel less than honored," Sanna said. She thought she felt a quiver of movement beneath her palm.

You do not fear me?

"I didn't say that."

I appreciate your honesty.

"I appreciate my freedom."

A long pause. Sanna held her breath. The wind whipped by, dragging strands of hair out of her braids and across her face. Had she imagined such a thing? No. Why would the goddess of the mountains speak to her?

The voice returned.

My dragons are ill. I require the healing properties of the forest dragons to heal them, so I can continue mounting my defense.

Something cold crawled up Sanna's back. *Mounting my defense?*

"Don't you mean preparing for world domination?"

Ah. You also are subject to the lines Prana feeds.

Three mountain dragons tangled in a knot in the air not far away, teeth gnashing. Blood arced into the air as one bit into the neck of another. It fell. Both uninjured dragons darted after it, snapping for the first bite.

Madness filled their eyes.

Or was it?

Sanna frowned.

"You want to murder all of the forest dragons so your crazy dragons can keep breeding to make your army?"

You mistake my intention. I never spoke of murder.

Despite her keen intelligence, Selsay's voice had a soothing quality to it. Almost like a purr. Or a gentle land-slide. Sanna peered around again, but like with Deasylva, no physical form appeared.

"Murder *is* the right word. Your dragon murdered my father, my dragons, and some of my fellow Dragonmasters. There was no need to kill them."

It would serve my purpose to have all the blood of the forest dragons, yes. The mountain dragons are many in number—they must be. But until they can be healed, it will mean little. Your daid's dragon was supposed to be an experiment to prove that the properties of forest-dragon blood can heal my dragons. You have gotten in my way. Twice.

"But it wouldn't serve *my* purposes," Sanna snapped. "And I don't really care what you want."

Spoken like a true forest witch and servant of Deasylva.

"I never said anything about Deasylva."

As if the forest were the only part of the world that mattered, and forest dragons the only creatures with powerful abilities. You know so little of the world you inhabit. I'd feel sorry for you if you weren't so vile, so bent toward the precipice of extinction. All things considered, I fight for you as well as my darlings.

"I don't serve Deasylva. I serve dragons and witches and trees."

Spoken like a leader.

Sanna growled. "Leave us alone, and we won't kill you and all the dragons you send against us."

Brave words for one so scared. You have no allegiance to the goddess who gives you life, magic, and power? And yet you think you can win against the forces that are coming? What army shall Deasylva marshal that could possibly defeat—or even harm—my dragons?

"Wouldn't be that hard," Sanna said as two other mountain dragons collided into each other in mid-air. "All things considered."

All is not as it seems, arrogant witch. There is more at work than what you see. The power of my dragon armies will be the only thing that saves this world.

"From what?"

Prana.

Sanna rolled her eyes. "Seriously?"

The rocks shuddered beneath her. Pemba glanced up with a narrow-eyed glare that Sanna ignored. *Your disrespect is astounding,* Selsay said with a voice of thunder.

"I could say the same. So far, I have no reason to believe goddesses are anything more than catty teenagers."

Assume what you will. I brought you here for answers. What is Deasylva doing to prepare for battle against Prana?

"Why don't you ask her?"

Who says I haven't?

"She doesn't respond to you either?"

A long pause followed. *Do you plan to fight me with Deasylva's magic?*

"She can keep her magic. All I want is peace."

Impossible. I have existed for all the ages and have yet to find peace.

"Sounds like you should stop murdering innocent dragons, then."

A deep rumble rolled beneath Sanna. She pitched to the side, striking the wall with her shoulder. Her ankle slipped off the ledge, but she scrambled back to safety. Several boulders loosened along the cliff, pounding down the mountain in heavy chunks. She coughed in the billowing dust, palms pressed into the rocks to stay stable. The movement stopped.

Do not test me.

"Then we *do* understand one another."

There was another long, unbearable pause, just like when she spoke to Deasylva. Luteis had once posited the idea that goddesses, in their power, existed differently than witches and dragons. Moved slower. Lived longer. Selsay seemed to prove the idea.

Around and around twirled the dragons overhead, wheeling with wings outstretched in a circular dance that nearly took her breath away. Their agitation seemed to have burgeoned since Selsay started to speak, and they'd moved closer. Perhaps her voice drew them in. Sanna braced herself when the mountain shifted yet again, sending a spray of rocks over the side. A wave of vertigo passed through her with another burst of chilly wind.

Give me the means to conquer this illness, and I shall fight your battles. Just the way Deasylva expects, no doubt.

Something cold tingled through Sanna, followed by the

flash of heat she still didn't understand. She looked at her burning hands.

"I'm not giving you my dragons," she said.

I don't want all of them.

"You're not very persuasive."

It is owed to me, although Deasylva will not recognize the debt. Perhaps you will, as her High Dragonmaster. If any High Dragonmaster still has honor, of course.

"Don't *you* have a High Dragonmaster? Isn't that a rule, or something?"

No.

"What debt are you talking about?"

Our past goes far deeper than you could imagine, into things you know nothing of. If Deasylva would not explain it to you, then I shall not either. Perhaps she has grown out of her strange love for you weak creatures and realized how unreliable witches are. If you do not give me what I require to fight Prana, I will take it by force. Our time runs short. The powers of the ocean are agitated, and Prana will not stay her hand for long. Once she attacks, all will be lost.

Sanna's mind sped back to Yushi, the ocean, and the Western Network. Who was right? Yushi claimed Selsay to be the dangerous one, yet Selsay said the same of Prana.

There is a war brewing between goddesses, daughter of the forest, Yushi had said. *And you are the only one who can stop it.*

Sanna pulled her shoulders back. "No. You can't have my dragons."

Give them to me!

The wild reverberations struck her like a slap. Sanna braced herself again as the mountain moved beneath her, but she managed to stay on her feet. Selsay's voice whipped through her like a torrential wind. She was not unlike her dragons, Sanna concluded.

A bit mad.

"Why do you ask my permission?" Sanna snapped. "Why don't you just take what you want? If you're such a powerful goddess, anyway."

Do you not understand the power that Prana wields? We have no time. You have subverted my dragons twice now. Your dragons will listen to you if you command them here.

Sanna laughed. "*Mori*, but you're going to be disappointed."

You're either very brave or very foolish.

"The two aren't far apart, are they?"

I tire of your attitude. Give me your strongest sire, all but one of your mams, and no fewer than three hatchlings.

Terror struck Sanna, nearly robbing her breath. Give up the mams? Of course Selsay wanted the mams. She would try to dilute the madness of her lines, or even worse, have the mams breed hatchlings for bloodletting. History had seen such atrocities before.

"Or what?" Sanna snarled.

I take them myself, leaving none behind. I am willing to leave you one mam to rebuild the race.

Sanna grabbbed a rock and hurled it at the mountain. "You can try to take them!"

Pemba snarled from behind her. She ignored him. Something shifted slightly to her left. Sanna paused, watching an oddly smooth rock from the corner of her eye.

Like all witches, Selsay said, *you are a fool.*

The rock twitched again—but it wasn't a rock. It was too round, almost uniform, with a few sweeps of dust curling off it in the gusty wind. Beneath a layer of stone dust, it ... glowed. Sanna shifted to the left a step, as if to regain her balance when Selsay rumbled again.

"I will never give you my dragons."

Then you shall die with them.

"It would be my pleasure."

Continue in your arrogance if you must, weak High Dragonmaster. Without Deasylva, without magic, and without a leader, you have no hope of defeating me or my innumerable dragons.

"You don't even care about your dragons, do you?" Sanna asked, motioning to the wild things flailing around her, some of them kept away from Sanna only by Pemba's snarling presence. How odd that Pemba should be protecting her. She stumbled to the left again—only an arm's length from the faintly glowing oval orb. "You just want to beat Prana."

If life will continue in Alkarra, yes. Her madness infects the land—even the witches can feel it. I must defeat Prana to save all you ungrateful fools, and you stand in my way.

I am coming, Luteis said. *Something else stirs in the North. I hear unfamiliar cries. You are not safe.*

I have a plan, she said, edging toward the ledge.

My astonishment is almost exceeded by my fear. I am almost there.

"You'll never get my dragons," Sanna hissed. "Not even if you should kill me."

We shall see, Selsay said, her voice rippling with terrible majesty.

The ground trembled. Sanna pitched to the left, grabbed the strangely oval rock, and wrapped her arms around it. It warmed beneath her touch, glowing with greater intensity. As she'd suspected—an egg. If Selsay were truly attempting to build an army, every egg would be precious. Pemba unleashed a roar of fury that made her bones quake. The mountain began to split, sliding down the ravine in sheets. Sanna threw herself off the ledge, turning in mid-air. Pemba followed, wings unfurled, fury in his eyes.

Sanna pitched the egg toward him as she fell.

A dark shadow appeared from above, dropping fast. Pemba's descent faltered as he scrambled for the egg. Just as Pemba snatched the egg with his back talons, a familiar claw grabbed her out of the air. Bearing the egg back drew Pemba away, allowing Sanna and Luteis to glide free.

Mountain dragons broiled overhead, darting toward them. Selsay's voice no longer rang in her mind, but the slide of rocks and crash of mountains told her everything she needed to know.

Luteis's broad wings beat above her like a reassuring heart.

Hold tight, he said, tossing her onto his shoulders. She slid into place just as a curtain of black covered the sun, descending toward them. *They're here to kill us.*

"Lucey isn't here. Or, if she is, I can't find her."

Isadora made the announcement in a whisper, only a pace away from Maximillion. The lone torch cast a weak light—which made the heavy darkness even more suffocating. He glanced up with sharp annoyance, even though he didn't seem surprised.

"It would be too simple otherwise," he muttered, running a hand over his face. His lips formed a thin line, and his jaw tightened. Isadora gazed past him to the faces staring at them with rapt fascination and fear. How awful that they should bring any hope to this dark hell.

"I looked in each cell." She tore her gaze away. "There are thirty-four. None have seen any sign of Lucey."

"The question," he murmured, "is where is she?"

"And why not here?"

He paced down the narrow hall, lending a frenetic energy to the already-tense air. He shook his head, muttering to himself. Every now and then, he winced, then growled. Instinctively attempting to access his powers, no doubt, and unable to. Isadora reached out for hers but found nothing there. It left a strange, ringing emptiness in her mind.

"They haven't accessed their powers—or been able to do magic—in upwards of ten years," Maximillion said. "That's something we need to consider."

"Can the magic build?"

"Does yours?"

Her torchlight waved, a little weaker now, but still lined his face with shadows. She didn't answer—didn't need to. The power, if strong before their imprisonment, could either be dead after so long an imprisonment or so blindingly powerful.

"How are we supposed to save thirty-four Watchers who may not be able to use magic, on an island, in the ocean, and still get them *and* Lucey away from Cecelia?" he murmured.

To her surprise, no malice hung in his tone. Nothing but a question, as if he were puzzling through the challenge without fear. Maximillion wouldn't leave these witches to die, but the weight of the task before them piled up to dizzying heights. In truth, he couldn't save *all* of them. Several seemed a day or two from death. Returning to life, to sunshine, to their *powers*, after such a duration could kill them.

"There's no going back," he said. They couldn't leave without the Watchers now. The bound-and-gagged East

Guards wouldn't be that way forever. Carcere's magic alone prevented them from returning for the Watchers—Cecelia would change her defenses. La Torra would tighten down until it was impenetrable. Perhaps she would simply slay all these Watchers, even though she hadn't yet.

"We remove them one at a time?" she said.

A flurry of hushed voices echoed around them in a wave again. Exclamations of joy. Talk of food. Family members. Children. None of the prisoners spoke very loudly, but even so, the stone walls seemed to echo every breath.

Maximillion shook his head. "No time."

"We let them all go at once and flood La Torra. They outnumber the staff and the East Guards?"

"And what?" he snapped. "Think this weak lot, who haven't had sunlight or magic for years on end, would be able to rush any Defender and win?"

Isadora opened her mouth, then closed it again. She met his gaze. "No. You're right. It's dark out now. That's to our advantage and theirs. We activate the Advocate community. Have them come, help us take these away to safety."

"In the East?" he scoffed.

"Do we have a choice?"

Maximillion's nostrils flared. His hand dove into his pocket, where the keys they'd taken from the East Guard rattled. Even as they spoke, their time waned.

"No."

"This could be a trap, you know," Isadora whispered. "Cecelia could be waiting for all of us to come out."

Maximillion sighed. "It's most assuredly a trap, which is likely why she didn't kill you. As we deduced before, she wants something of us."

Isadora bit her bottom lip. If the Watchers didn't die

trying to leave, they'd waste away in here. Eventually. A swift death at the hands of the Defenders seemed more merciful. She thought of Sanna, Mam, Daid and swallowed hard.

No, she couldn't think of them right now.

"Then we walk into it," she murmured. "We face Cecelia's trap head-on. If we can't do magic, she can't either. It'll be a battle of strength."

His eyes met hers. "Then we fight it."

Isadora snorted, surprised by the rush of warmth that slipped through her at his rueful tone. "I thought all you wanted was peace and quiet?"

"I may only find it in my grave. Are you in, or are you not?"

Isadora nodded once. "We walk into it."

For a moment, his eyes darkened, brewing into a storm. For half a breath, Isadora thought he'd kiss her again, but it passed. A grudging respect lingered in its wake.

"Fine. We walk into it." He pulled his hand out of his pocket and pulled out the keys he'd taken from the Guards. "Start unlocking. I'll group them in the hall and help them out. Move quickly. We need all the time we can get."

"What about the Advocate community?" she asked. "How will we get ahold of them without magic?"

"You let me worry about that."

With that, Isadora spun on her heels, approached the first cell, and shoved the key into the rusty lock.

THE WATCHERS SHUFFLED out of their cells, eyes delirious, bodies bent. Some of them were frantic. Desperate. Twitchy, even. Others were slow. Wary. No quantity of

Isadora's murmured assurances could pierce their paranoia.

One woman, likely in her thirties but who appeared to be sixty, wrung her hands together and mumbled under her breath. Another wouldn't look at her. A third threw his arms around her with a muted sob.

One by one, they spilled into the hallway as Isadora moved down the row, breathing through her mouth to fight off the piercing, horrid smell. Maximillion assisted the weakest in forming a line against the stone wall. Behind her shuffled the sound of the other witches embracing, sobbing.

Isadora unlocked the cell of the male witch they'd spoken to first. He watched the door swing open, then blinked.

"*Gratsi*," he whispered.

He didn't move.

Isadora let her hand fall back to her side. Her gaze flickered to the notch-covered wall. "You've been here the longest, haven't you? Years. Maybe tens of them."

Something burned in his gaze. "Yes."

"How have you survived so long?"

"Rage."

With that, he stepped out of the cell. Isadora watched him as he reached out to help lift a staggering witch. After a breath, he disappeared into the throng of bodies.

Isadora turned to the last cell nearest the hall, on the left.

A young girl had tucked herself into the back corner. The bars on the cage rattled when Isadora jimmied the lock open and swung the door out. Sable eyes peered at her through a curtain of dark hair, waist long, limp, and hopelessly tangled.

"Allo," Isadora murmured in *Ilese*. She extended a hand. "You're safe. We've come to help."

The girl didn't budge. Her cheeks were ruddy, eyes wide. Only a few seconds passed before Isadora realized that the girl trembled—possibly from fever.

"You're safe," Isadora said in the common language.

Maximillion appeared behind Isadora. "Are you ready? We must go now."

"I can't get her to come out. I don't want to scare her."

"Come," he said in perfect *Ilese*, softening his naturally sharp tone. "We're here to help."

He motioned to the others limping into a single line against the chilly stone wall. The girl, eyes wide, trembled. Her teeth chattered. A chill rushed through Isadora. Why did the girl stare so strangely? Why wouldn't she move?

Something wasn't right.

The girl's eyes darted higher, then back. Isadora followed her gaze. This cell had a higher ceiling than the others. The shadows behind the girl were darker—deeper. As if there was more space back there. Isadora straightened, lifted the waning torch higher. The stone wall appeared freshly chipped where the metal door met the stone—as if someone had recently put this door here. Hastily, too. Slash lines cut through the grime to the base of the stone.

"Maximillion," she murmured, gesturing to it. He frowned. Isadora took one step forward. More light fell on the girl's anemic face and stretched into the darkness behind her, as if there were a boxed-in alcove or forgotten staircase.

Isadora froze. In the darkness lurked a figure.

"Max—"

"Maximillion," a cold voice said. "I really shouldn't be surprised to see you, of all witches, here."

His spine stiffened. "Cecelia," he said, pushing Isadora behind him. "As expected."

Cecelia shuffled out of the darkness. Isadora stepped to the side, placing herself closer to the girl, who flinched when Cecelia's velvet, blood-red cloak brushed her arm. Despite the filth on the floor, Cecelia advanced with her unusual energy, like an elegant bull plowing into an arena.

Even in an enclosed space, she was larger than life. Jewels glimmered from her neck, ears, and wrists. Bracelets so heavy they surely weighed her arms down. A simple bun, bedecked with diamond-studded pins, pulled her hair away from her face.

"*Am* I expected?" she asked.

Isadora inched to the side. The Watcher girl tucked her head into her arms with a hiccuping sob. There were only two or three paces between the girl and Cecelia. Images of the last Watcher in Cecelia's power spun through Isadora's head. She wouldn't stand by again.

"Stealing into Carcere was easy enough," Maximillion said. "Getting back out wouldn't be so simple. I assumed you had something to do with it."

Cecelia's gaze flickered to Isadora, then back to him. "I shouldn't have let her live."

"Not if you wanted to be subtle."

"I don't need to be subtle. How long have you been the Advocate?"

"I simply work for them."

"Them, eh? Won't even assign a gender? You're a stunning liar, Maximillion. I'll give you that much. Do you sleep easier at night pretending that the organization isn't yours?"

His cold eyes pierced hers. "I may be many things, but don't insult my honor. I am no liar."

Amusement lingered in her tone. "Indeed? Then who is the Advocate?"

"Someone who wishes to remain nameless, of course."

Isadora inched to the side, through a layer of dried human refuse, moldy straw, and the tattered remnants of what must have once been clothing. Cecelia ignored her. With a low murmur, Isadora crouched next to the girl. She'd tucked herself into a tight ball against the wall. When Isadora touched her arm, she shrank away with a cry.

"It's all right," Isadora murmured. "It's just me."

The girl peered at her, eyes wide.

"Of course you are the Advocate," Cecelia continued. "No witch can be so cold, ruthless, and powerful without some sort of purpose. Too bad you're a manipulative wretch who toys with fate at the same time. Exactly how powerful are you, Max? Tell me—how many paths do you see? How far into the future can you gaze?"

He gritted his teeth. "I accept your compliments."

"I'm not here to play games."

"I beg to disagree. Isn't this whole set-up a game?"

"Fair," she said. "You're right. It's more elaborate than normal for me—visiting the Central Network, setting up an execution date for one of your heathens, and allowing your little girl here to work in my castle. But yes, it was all a ruse. I knew your Watcher from the beginning."

"As I knew you would."

"Then why send her?"

He spread his arms. "Why not?"

"Arrogant, aren't you?"

"There's a pot and a kettle in this situation."

"Indeed."

"I'm quite flattered, Cecelia. All of this to draw me in?"

"Who said I did this for you?"

Isadora's head whipped around. Maximillion didn't take his eyes off Cecelia, but his fists tightened.

"Give me my witch back," he said. "Set these Watchers free. I'll spare your life only on those terms."

Cecelia chuckled. "You're brilliantly funny, Maximillion. Stupid, but at least good for a laugh. Surrender to me, and I'll let *you* live long enough to talk to your idiotic High Priest before I have you burned at the stake. He should know what kind of scum he works with."

"Never."

"Very well. Death with no explanation it is."

A shout from down the hall filled the space. East Guards.

Isadora grabbed the girl and pulled her to her feet. Cecelia's gaze flickered to them as Isadora hauled the girl out of the cell.

"Where's my witch?"

Isadora put an arm around the girl's shoulder and helped her limp into the hall. The girl let out a cry. Her knobby knees and toothpick-thin ankles couldn't bear much weight for long. Heat radiated from her body. Fever, no doubt. Sores riddled the bottom of her feet, putrid from infection and coated in a greenish film.

"You're doing beautifully," Isadora murmured in her ear. "Keep going."

The rattle of East Guard armor rang out from the main hallway, approaching fast. Freed of their cells, the Watchers scrambled to find makeshift weapons, but there were none. Their frantic voices grew louder. One Watcher collapsed. Another cried out, ducking back into her cell. Isadora handed the girl off to another Watcher before rushing back to Maximillion.

"Lucey, my witch, never was here, was she?" Maximillion asked Cecelia.

"She was, but she isn't now."

"With you?"

Cecelia shook her head without an ounce of emotion. "No. I'll never tell you. You think you know so many secrets? You think you know so much about how this world works? Child's play. You haven't even scratched the surface of what Watcher and Defender magic can do."

"Do enlighten me."

A pained, dark smile lingered in her eyes, then quickly disappeared. "You're not the only one with someone to answer to."

"I have no doubt. Dante, right?"

"Tell me about your Advocate first."

He smiled. "We can play this game forever."

"Your *Lucey* is on her way to her early death. But because I do love a good tragedy, I'll delay her burning at the stake so you can burn together. Fitting, even if she doesn't have your evil powers."

"Halt!" East Guards shouted. "Insurrection!"

"Uprising!"

"The prisoners are free!"

"You're going to die." Cecelia's voice rose. Her eyes widened. "The Defenders will win, as we always do. Fate *always* wins, no matter how much you Watchers try to play with it. You cannot manipulate inevitability forever."

Two burly bodies surged out of the darkness behind Cecelia, rushing into the cell. "Max!" Isadora called.

She flung the torch to him. He caught it with a snarl, holding it between himself and Cecelia. The two East Guards paused. Bright, fresh torches caused the prisoners to cry out and shield their eyes. The East Guards surged in, mowing the Watchers down.

Maximillion turned back to Cecelia.

"If I'm going down, you're going with me."

He tossed the torch onto the ground at Cecelia's feet. The floor caught flame. Fire burst to life with a crackle.

"Good luck, Maximillion," Cecelia called over the roar of fire. The fire slid off her dress—as if it repelled flame. As if she somehow used magic in the depths of Carcere.

Two Defenders behind Cecelia ran at Maximillion. He ducked, swinging an arm into the stomach of one and absorbing a blow to his back from the other. Isadora grabbed the keys between her knuckles and ran, jamming them into the neck of a Defender. He screamed. East Guards flooded the hall now, shackling Watchers in the chaos. Cecelia frantically studied the Watchers as she backed away.

"Find him!" she called above the chaos. "Find that miserable cretin and kill him before he escapes Carcere!"

Isadora didn't have long to wonder who Cecelia meant. She ducked an East Guard, then lunged for Cecelia. Cecelia stepped away from her hand before Isadora could get a grip on her skirt. Cecelia disappeared.

Isadora reached for Maximillion, who struggled to push the other Defender off his chest. "Max!"

"Run!"

Something slammed into the back of her head. She dropped to her knees with a cry.

Darkness consumed her.

TWENTY-FIVE

The mountain dragons dove.

Despite Luteis's arrow-straight body, his wings in, his neck sharp, with Sanna burrowed into his spine, the mountain dragons gained on them. Wind whipped past her face. She swallowed hard, her knees tight around his neck.

I know where we can be safe, Luteis said.

I trust you.

A pile of rocks loomed before them with frightening intensity. They wouldn't be able to pull up in time at this rate. Still, he pressed on. Closer.

Closer.

Sanna sucked in a sharp breath as Luteis pulled out of the dive. The *thud* of the closest mountain dragons slamming into the rocks, killing themselves instantly, followed. She grimaced and glanced back. Heat rose in her throat. An entire horde still pursued them, the dragons pulling out of the dive just in time. They seemed to flood the air.

Keep going!

Luteis plunged into the forest at the bottom of the mountain. The mountain dragons screeched, attempting to get away. Trees swayed, pulling aside their branches to make way for Luteis, who navigated the thick boughs and small spaces with practiced dexterity.

Hold on, he said.

They tore through a short thicket and smashed into the ground. Sanna rolled off, slammed her shoulder into a rock, and collided with a tree trunk. She gasped to collect her breath. With a groan, she turned onto her side.

Luteis shoved off the ground, leaving a small crater where he'd landed. He whipped around with a snarl. His tail soared over her head, covering her. The mountain dragons that made it into the forest immediately disappeared, screeching. The trees waved back and forth, smacking into those unlucky enough to get tangled in the branches.

Sanna sucked in a sharp breath when all the mountain dragons finally disappeared. Luteis, crouched, eventually relaxed, then turned to look at her.

"Are we safe here?" she whispered.

Deasylva's dominion reigns everywhere trees live, he said. *They will avoid the forest unless absolutely forced.*

"That didn't answer my question," she mumbled, pushing herself back to her feet, thinking of Finn and Daid. Her side ached, bruised from the landing. Luteis's wings folded into his back. Several scratches ran along their length, racing with bright-blue blood.

The forest was sparse, its trees covered with thin needles, oozing sap, and willowy tendrils. She'd never seen such branches. Old needles littered the desolate ground. The trees here were taller than Luteis, but only barely. It seemed young here, but perhaps most forests were this ... short.

You are well?

"So to speak. Thanks for the catch."

He turned his gaze back to the almost-naked canopy. Beyond them, mountain dragons screeched, flapping overhead. Sanna glanced around, brushing dirt off her palms. Light filtered into the forest, shining all the way to the ground in dappled puddles. She'd never seen so much before.

"We need to get back," she said, eyeing him. "I've definitely angered Selsay. Pemba may already be on his way back to Letum Wood. Can you fly?"

We walk through here, he said. *We must stay in the safety of the trees, then take flight when full light comes and we are closer to the border.*

Sanna sighed.

"We better start running, then. I have my doubts Selsay will wait to unleash her wrath."

Let us hope.

Wind rushed through Sanna's hair as they cut through the early morning light, far above the forest. The safety of Letum Wood unfurled beneath them in shadowy clusters. The crisp scent of her ancient trees settled Sanna's prickly nerves. Luteis, weary now, though he wouldn't admit it, stayed close to the canopy.

So bleak and barren and desolate up there, Sanna said, too tired—perhaps afraid—to speak aloud. *And there were so many mountain dragons. How can we fight a force so strong?*

We must. I flew farther to the north to get rid of them and saw more dragons in the distance. Bigger ones.

Think they're different?

Perhaps stronger. Maybe not so inclined to madness?

Is it madness? Or ... something else?

I think she's protecting the larger dragons. Perhaps these smaller ones are more expendable in a war. If she truly wants to fight Prana—for whatever reason—she'll need as many dragons as possible.

Sanna paused, thinking back to Yushi, to her discomfort at the edge of the water. Selsay seemed certain, perhaps a bit desperate, when she spoke of Prana. Did they have bigger things to fear? Yushi had spoken of Selsay's arrogance. Her desire for power.

Who spoke the truth?

Would staying safe from Selsay only put them in the path of a greater enemy? Sanna shook those thoughts aside for later. Selsay would gladly kill the race of forest dragons to suit her own purposes. They had to stop that first. As to Prana, they'd have to figure that out later.

Their madness, Luteis said, *cannot just be from inbreeding.*

What else would cause it?

Did you observe that they have no High Dragonmaster?

Sanna snorted. *Selsay made her disdain for witches abundantly clear.*

Precisely.

What are you trying to say?

Their madness may also stem from being too close to their goddess. From lacking the use of magic. Didn't Talis begin to go mad? Did you not see it in his eyes?

Sanna paused in thought. It seemed possible. If Selsay had been without a Dragonmaster for hundreds of years, perhaps it could drive the magic into stranger effects. But they knew so little of the magic to confirm such a thing ...

Or hunger, she said. *How could they possibly eat enough up there?*

Selsay has disrupted the order of things by not having a High Dragonmaster. Perhaps this is the result.

She frowned, rolling the idea through her mind still. Selsay didn't trust witches, which meant she may have purposefully removed the High Dragonmaster and never replaced them. If a High Dragonmaster *were* part of the natural order of things ... that would explain that *something* was different. But madness?

It would explain Deasylva's distance, he said.

Bringing Deasylva into the conversation made Sanna squirm. Her reluctant goddess couldn't possibly be helping them by allowing so many unwarranted murders, so much pain.

Either way, Sanna said, *the mountain dragons can transport, which is something we can't do.*

Something that works against us in many, many ways.

They seem to hate the forest.

But not enough for it to deter them entirely.

A thousand questions whirled through Sanna's mind. Had Deasylva known about this? What good could come from a war between goddesses? Selsay spoke about life continuing in Alkarra only if Prana were defeated, but what did that mean?

Either way, it seemed at least one dragon race would be decimated. The forest dragons or the mountain dragons, all because of the goddesses' strange ways. If the dragons and goddesses were so inextricably linked, what would happen, then?

I think she'll come soon, Sanna said. *Tonight, even. Time isn't on her side, I'm willing to bet.*

Luteis twisted his head back to glance briefly at her. *Our dragons aren't ready.*

They don't have a choice.

He soared over a tall tree, taking them past a section of forest consumed by strickenine moss. *Perhaps not.*

We'll talk to Elliot as soon as we get back and initiate the plan.

I shall confer with Elis and the dragons from Finn's camp. They may have insights we have not yet explored. Have you considered that you know the most of all of us? You will have to lead this battle.

The thought had occurred to her, and it made acid rise in the back of her throat. She was no leader. No Talis. It could not fall to her to take them to an assured defeat, for how could they—witches who couldn't do magic and dragons who couldn't fly—possibly win against such a force?

I know, she said.

Sanna let out a long breath that turned into a yawn. She lay against Luteis's back, tucking her arms against her chest to keep the cool wind from chilling her. Then she closed her eyes and fell into a troubled, restless sleep.

ELLIOT STARED AT HER, his skin pale as death.

Next to him, Jesse rubbed a hand over his face and stared at the ground. Elis hovered not far away, his attention mostly on Luteis, who would speak to the dragons.

"Tonight," she repeated. "I'm confident they'll attack."

"We knew it would be difficult," Elliot said. "But this sounds nigh unto impossible."

Sanna couldn't disagree.

"Not only does Selsay have obvious pride issues—which we surely offended by escaping—but her dragons are insane. Maybe starving. They're attacking each other, even. She needs the forest-dragon blood now before she mounts an attack against Prana. Regardless of who is the greater foe, Selsay is the immediate one."

"But she hasn't found us yet," Babs said, chiming in from the back of the room. "Maybe she doesn't know where we are."

Babs paced, taking long strides as she wrung her thick, reddened hands together. Mam sat on a rock, hands folded in her lap, gaze fixed on a cluster of purple mushrooms. Her entire body had paled and remained rigidly, oddly still, as if she weren't even breathing.

"If she didn't, she likely does now."

"Not again!" Babs said, jerking her head back and forth. Her voice thickened. "We cannot go through this again! First Talis. Then Anguis. Then Finn. This is ... this is unbearable."

Elliot caught her by the arm.

"Calm yourself, *amo*. We'll figure it out."

"There is time to get away!" she cried, voice high. "We can escape. Find a way out. What if we—"

"Babs may be right," Elliot said, glancing at Sanna. "If we leave now, we have a chance of outrunning them. Hiding, at least. If they hate the forest so much ... "

He trailed away. Sanna clenched her teeth, forcing patience into her tone. "We couldn't flee far enough. Those dragons can fly and transport, and we cannot. Besides, Selsay has strength to spare. She'll swarm us with her mad dragons and let them kill us to get to the mams."

"We can't just stay!" Babs cried.

"We must. We've already prepared for this."

"Yes, but now it's upon us!"

We can't hide from them forever, Luteis said. *It would be foolish to stall.*

"We fight, Mam," Jesse said. "There is no alternative. They're probably already on their way."

Trey stood. Greata and Hans sat on a log next to him, clutching each other, staring into the crackling fire. Strength born from adversity and pain filled Trey's entire body. He trembled from the force of it.

"I won't run again."

"With what army will we fight?" Elliot said. "It was fine to plan for a fight before we had all this information, but now we know we cannot win. It isn't possible! Our dragons can't fly! We can't do magic. The dragons won't even let us ride on them if they *could* fly. This will be another massacre."

A clamor arose all at once. Greata shot to her feet, standing next to Trey with fire in her eyes. Hans started to wail. Jesse pulled two of his younger brothers away from them. Babs tried to silence everyone. Off by herself, Mam remained silent, as if she hadn't noticed the rise of voices. In the distance, dragons roared.

Something in the chaos, the screaming voices, sent Sanna reeling. Back to the trees of Letum Wood. To the sound of screaming. The smell of blood on the air. Daid draped across Luteis, dead, blood flowing from his body.

The chaos had split them apart and led to this.

Perhaps they had no chance. Maybe there was no way to win. But they couldn't run again. Running wouldn't preserve their lives—they couldn't work on flying lessons or construct shelter or weapons while fleeing. It was just another way to die.

Without honor.

In standing, they had a chance, however small. But not if they were divided.

The voices behind her turned piercing. Shouts broke out between Elliot's family and what remained of Finn's. Sanna gazed between them, thoughts churning. If they continued like this, they'd fracture. Break like the thin sheets of rock in the North. They'd never recover.

You can stop this, Luteis whispered. *Indeed, it is your place.*

I know.

Sanna shot to her feet.

"Silence!"

The cacophony of voices abated. Sanna grabbed a vine and scrambled upward, dangling over them. Silence flooded the forest. Not even the distant call of a bird rang from the trees. Sanna felt heat building in her body, tingling in her fingertips, the way it had in the West when they'd first faced Pemba, or when Finn died, or Pemba took her.

"We will not panic," she snapped. "We will not run. Running won't buy us an advantage. If we run, we weaken our chances of protecting the mams. It's exactly what Selsay wants. We're going to stay, and we're going to fight. Right now."

Sanna turned to Jesse.

"You and Elis are in charge of the adult dragons. They may not be able to fly, but they can fight from the ground or use their secundum. I want everyone fed, positioned where they can hide, and readied for battle."

Jesse nodded.

Sanna spun. "Mam, you're in charge of protecting the children. I suggest all of you head to the hollowed-out shelter underground now. Luteis will burn the ground behind you to erase your smell, just in case. Take the two eggs with you. Babs, if you're willing, I want you helping out here. Mam can keep the children safe." Sanna met Mam's gaze. "I know you can."

Babs's nostrils flared. She opened her mouth to protest, but Elliot put a hand on her shoulder. He shook his head. Babs swallowed hard, then nodded once. Mam gave no agreement until Babs touched her arm, then she nodded.

"I will be in charge of the hatchlings," Sanna said.

Rosy snorted from nearby. Junis shuffled out of the trees. Even Alis advanced.

"Rocks," she said to Luteis. "Tell the dragons to find boulders you can carry that, when dropped from a great height, will break wings. Make piles in the tree limbs. Put them high, so you can grab and drop them."

Rosy, Junis, and Alis took flight and flapped away.

"Luteis will be in charge of ..." She trailed off for a breath. Luteis's gaze never wavered. "Of ... getting the exploding melons."

You mean working with Deasylva.

Whatever.

"Elliot, we need your oldest boys to check the perimeter," she continued. "Make sure the spears are still standing and ready to go. Once they're done, have them climb into the trees and hide near the pile of rocks the hatchlings are getting." She pointed upward. "Give them knives. Your boys can cut the vines and let the melons fall on the mountain dragons."

Greata stepped forward. "I want to help."

"Good. You gather baskets or anything we can use.

Then ride a hatchling and hide up in the branches to help throw rocks."

Another long stretch of quiet hovered amongst them. Sanna's mind spun. She cast about to make sure she hadn't forgotten anything. When a tingle swept through her scabbed face, her gaze hardened. There was nothing more they could do now.

"They will have a leader," she said. "You'll know him by his size and attitude. He wears a white pendant on his neck. His name is Pemba. He's mine. Now, go. We don't have a lot of time."

CHAPTER

TWENTY-SIX

The ocean churned, overtaken by sable clouds on the horizon.

The furious sky thickened the air as wind whipped past Isadora's face, wakening her from her stupor. Pain surged in her wrists and then thudded from the back of her head all the way through her body. Someone moaned. It was her.

She blinked, staring at the horizon, wondering why it seemed so close, yet so distant. Her blurry vision sharpened.

Several moments passed before she understood that she was outside, on top of La Torra. The ocean spread around her like a sapphire skirt. Her shoulders were pulled taut. Something rubbed along her arms. The wet wind, tinged with sea spray, had woken her. In the distance, several aquilas released piercing screams.

Another groan—this one not her own—came from next to her. She glanced over, neck still throbbing.

Maximillion.

And Lucey.

They were both tied to a star-like structure, arms and legs bound. Lucey sagged, skin pale, eyes closed. She slumped downward, as if her legs couldn't hold her. Maximillion blinked through a bleary daze, a purplish bruise on his forehead. Isadora squirmed. She was also tied to a star structure, arms extended straight out.

Isadora sucked in a sharp breath, slapped by recollections. Carcere. Cecelia. Watchers. They'd been captured after all.

Egads, but she hadn't expected this.

"Well," Maximillion muttered with a wince. "This is what happens when you go and get caught, Lucey."

Lucey didn't respond. Her hair drifted next to her in the wind, tossed by the growing tempest. Her eyes were closed, her head hanging low.

Isadora swallowed hard. The sounds of shuffling movement and cruel voices came from below. Out of the corner of her eye, she saw dark Defender uniforms move in the courtyard. Preparing for something.

A celebration, she'd wager.

"This is certainly not the way I imagined my own demise," she whispered, her voice hoarse.

A dry chuckle came from Maximillion. "Then you didn't search your paths far enough."

"Perhaps I have," she murmured, gazing out on the rippling ocean, feeling as if she'd seen this before. Her questions about the paths twinged in her mind. Why this magic? Why her? If she could see possibilities for the future, but not the future itself, why even look?

Despite her impending death, no panic infused her. No sense of terror at her own ending, no fear of the pain Cecelia would surely force them to endure. Would Isadora have to watch Maximillion die slowly?

Her lips, the back of her neck where he'd grabbed her, burned.

"Any last-minute escape plans?" she asked.

"That," he said, "isn't up to me."

She frowned. What could that mean?

"You could try transporting," he said before she could ask. "But I doubt it would be safe, what with *oro* so close."

"No," she murmured. "I shall stay with Lucey, as I assume you had already planned."

Shouting came from below, drawing her attention. Isadora craned her head far enough to the left to see a witch in an ornate dress, skirts so full they stuck out almost horizontally, disappear inside. The Defenders' heads tipped back, staring up at them. A cold shiver graced her spine.

"She's coming," Isadora whispered.

Maximillion's nostrils flared. "Then let her come."

"I'm going into the paths," Isadora said, warmed by the stir of magic in her chest. It beckoned to her in a gentle whisper. An easy movement. A reassurance.

"I would highly advise you not to," he said drily.

"I am. If I'm going to die, I want to say goodbye to the magic. Besides, they already know we're Watchers. What more can they do?"

Maximillion said nothing.

Isadora closed her eyes, opened the magic, and slipped into Letum Wood.

Light unfurled through the forest. The strange, new brightness, or the feeling of something being different, sent her reeling. A surge of strength didn't overtake her or demand her attention this time. The magic purred, as if waiting.

As if it knew something.

Isadora stood at the base of the same ancient trees and

watched countless paths expand outward. Her own. Sanna's. Maximillion's. Defenders'. Cecelia's. Lucey's. Their wisps blurred because of the sheer enormity of possibilities expanding through the forest in never-ending branches. Isadora paused, feeling the air.

"I always tell you what to do," she murmured, reaching out to touch a tree trunk. Light grew from her fingertips in wide circles. "Maybe it's time for you to show me what you can do."

Several beats of silence passed. Nothing happened. She waited, finding peace in the solace. If she were going to die in moments, she'd at least carry the magic with her. It could not—would not—abandon her. A whistle caught her ear. Light. Airy. Almost gauzy.

The chirp of a bird.

She whirled around just as a black bird with burgundy feathers winged by, circling her. It settled on her shoulder in a familiar way. Isadora had seen this bird before. One of Maximillion's messenger birds. Outside of the magic, the birds always appeared empty. Mere puffs of smoke. Here, the bird seemed to be a living thing.

"Well." She held out a finger. "What are you doing here?"

The bird preened, peering at her with intelligent eyes.

"You're magic," she said, reaching to touch its silky feathers and robust chest. "Is that why you can be here?"

Its beak opened up, trilling a song that faded into a whisper. Then the bird flew away instead of disappearing into a puff of smoke. The wisps drew her gaze by shifting, fading into different, newer forms. New trails populated; others disappeared. The constant shifts of fate normally left her puzzled. Today, she studied them, filled with the uncertainty and desperation the last several months had gifted her.

"Why?" she called, tilting her head back to look at the canopy. "Why does this magic even exist, and why in me?"

Light bubbled up from the ground, banishing the trails. It showed her form as she had seen it before. Firm countenance. Shoulders back. Chin high. Determined gaze. Isadora stared at a courageous representation of herself. The wind whispered by.

Powerful.

Her figure disappeared. Another bubbled up to replace it. Sanna. Tears filled her eyes. How she longed for her sister! Just as she reached out to touch her, Sanna faded away. Light burst up in a fountain.

Maximillion.

He disappeared. Pearl replaced him, all spectral, flowing lines of light and magic. Isadora frowned. Pearl? She disappeared before Isadora could really get a look at her.

Baylee came next. Then Charles.

Then Mam.

Daid.

Fiona.

They popped up one at a time, fading only to reveal another witch. Then another. Another. She stopped recognizing the witches. Didn't have a clue who they were, just watched the endless parade of faces. Something tugged at her, as if to pull her back to reality. Isadora ignored it, remaining firmly rooted in the magic.

Finally, Maximillion returned, first as a young boy. He grew into a troubled teenager. Then the merciful man full of fire and annoyance she knew so well.

"What are you trying to say?" Isadora murmured,

reaching out to touch his face. The magic shied away, then formed again. The forest seemed to hold its breath.

Isadora's mind stirred. The paths of future possibilities weren't solid—not like the Defenders. If all magic had a perfect, equal, and opposite counter the way Lucey had told her last summer, that meant Watchers had to have a way to *know* something solid, the way the Defenders did.

Isadora's gaze narrowed.

"That's it," she murmured. "The paths aren't the most important part of the magic, are they? It's not understanding the future that's so important. It's understanding *witches.*"

The magic stalled, leaving an empty forest that stared back at her. Waiting. Expectant. There was something she *wasn't* seeing. Some missing piece that ...

She sucked in a sharp breath.

"Cecelia," she said. "Show me Cecelia as a child."

Cecelia's form burst out of the light. A young girl, at first. She cowered, arm held up as if to protect her face, her teeth clenched in a grimace.

Frightened, the magic whispered.

Young Cecelia grew into a teenager. A girl hidden in grimy, ill-fitting clothes, with a bruised cheek. Beneath the layers of resentment in her eyes, Isadora saw a gleam of determination.

Frightened, the magic whispered again.

Finally, she grew into the woman Isadora knew now. Elegant clothes. Perfectly curled hair. Not a speck of dirt or poverty or filth to be found. Still, something burned in her eyes. Isadora recalled the moment in the dungeon. She'd fled, eyes wide. The Defenders fought for her. Had Cecelia ever been on a raid herself?

Never.

"You're scared of us," Isadora whispered. "What happened to you? Who is she so frightened of?"

The wind rustled by, sweeping her hair off her shoulders. Something cold trickled through her. Light bubbled up from the ground again. The male witch from Carcere—the one who had survived for so long. Isadora stared hard at him.

Why him?

Memories whipped through her mind, sliding together like puzzle pieces. She saw herself as the magic saw her. *Powerful.*

Cecelia as a child and adult. *Frightened.*

When Cecelia visited Maximillion's office, she'd asked how many paths Max could see. The day the Watcher died in the courtyard, Cecelia had spoken of *connections* and *matches.*

Still, Isadora's mind churned. Pulling Defenders into the paths by accident while venting her magic. The male witch in Carcere. *We are the ones she fears the most,* he'd said. Isadora's eyes widened. Understanding flooded her.

"Of course!"

Mind spinning, Isadora whistled a three-note tune. The bird soared out of the trees, alighting on her shoulders again with a ruffle of feathers and a gentle squeak. Isadora reached a finger out, caressing its soft underbelly.

"I need you to do me a little favor," she whispered.

The bird bowed its head. Isadora whispered a message. The bird winged away into the trees. Another tugging, more insistent this time, accompanied a burst of pain.

She closed the magic.

〜

Sanna stood on a branch, facing one of the oldest trees in this section of the forest with a feeling of trepidation. Although she was alone, she hesitated before reaching out to touch the trunk. Moments passed before something stirred, as if the tree were responding to her skin. Her hand fell away when a telltale silvery glow illuminated a flowing script in the bark. A breeze stirred up, whispering.

Sanna.

The scent of honeysuckle followed. Sanna's shoulders tensed.

You have come, the words on the tree said. Sanna stared at them, unsure how to respond. She'd only half-expected Deasylva to speak. There had been plenty of failed attempts in the past.

"You let Daid die."

Heat raced through her body once she let the words go. The tree quivered, leaves rustling. The old letters and words faded into the bark, replaced by a new response.

You are angry.

"No, I'm livid."

I can sense your fear.

"Why did you let him die?" she snapped. "Why did you let Talis take over and destroy everything? Why do you let all these bad things happen? We are good witches!"

Thirty seconds passed before the previous words bled away entirely, and another half minute before the new response appeared. Deasylva's replies were as slow as sap.

Do you want me to have utter control?

Images flashed through Sanna's mind of Talis's reign. Fire. Restrictions. Anguis's borders built as high as a dragon's shoulder. Talis *had* maintained control. Now Daid, Finn, and others were dead. The dragon population had been cut in half, and the threat of extinction loomed too close for comfort.

"No."

Your daid has served honorably and rests in the halls of Halla. This life is not all you have, daughter of the forest. You are meant for more.

The long sentence appeared in chunks, forcing Sanna to wait. She drank in each letter. Her heart thrilled, then slowed. Deasylva was only as real as the words on the trunk—but even the small hope that Daid still lived *somewhere* rang deep in Sanna's chest. No matter how difficult it had been to trust Deasylva, Sanna desperately wanted it to be true.

As if on reflex, she reached out to touch the tree again.

"The mountain dragons are coming," Sanna said. "I expect them any minute now."

Yes.

"Do we … can … how can you—"

The words faded quickly this time, replaced by a bright response—the brightest so far. *I trust you, Sanna of Gregor.*

Sanna scowled. "What does *that* mean?"

You are the High Dragonmaster. I trust you with my dragons.

"I have no idea what I'm doing! If I'm the only leader you have, we're all dead! Besides, the dragons don't listen to me. Their voices aren't in my head anymore. Daid was supposed to be the High Dragonmaster."

I trust you.

"Then you're a fool!" Sanna muttered. "I don't know how to lead! I won't be like Talis. I can't. I can't be a tyrant."

Was your daid a tyrant?

"No."

Luteis?

Sanna's brow puckered. "No."

Leadership is not tyranny.

"Then what is it?"

A long pause followed, so long Sanna thought Deasylva had left. If leadership wasn't taking charge and telling others what to do, what could it possibly be? What did Daid and Luteis have to do with it?

It's trust.

Sanna's heart seemed to slow. Talis didn't have trust. Neither did Selsay, who didn't trust witches. All the leaders she feared becoming lacked the very thing she lacked of *her* supposed leader.

Four shimmering words appeared in the trunk, one interminable letter at a time.

Do you trust me?

Sanna opened her mouth to protest, but stopped. Deasylva had saved her life several times. From drowning shortly after she met Luteis. From a pack of forest lions. Through the forest, she'd provided the falla melons to help when the acid stung Sanna's face. Perhaps more. But she hadn't saved Daid, or Finn, or prevented the massacre. How could she trust a goddess?

"I don't know," she whispered.

You will when the time comes. Just as you will know who you are, and how that can save you. You are a powerful being, Sanna, daughter of the forest. It is time you learned for yourself.

"Learned what?"

Who you are.

The last word, so faint she almost couldn't see it, barely touched the surface of the trunk. The gentle breeze stirred one more time, then disappeared. Sanna stepped back. Deasylva had retreated; she would say no more. Sanna's mind spun. Deasylva trusted her. Deasylva, the unreliable goddess.

Or was she?

Sanna let her hand drop from the trunk. "I'll try," she whispered.

Luteis waited behind her, eyes glowing.

Are you ready? he asked.

Sanna set her jaw.

"I am."

No matter what happens—

She reached out, touching his snout. "We'll be together."

He nudged her with a gentle motion, nearly sending her to the ground. Sanna grinned, then climbed on his back.

"Let's go, Luteis. My chance to avenge Daid may be falling into our laps."

~

SANNA GLANCED up at a silent canopy. The distant screech of something rang through her mind, not witch and not dragon.

The trees.

The mountain dragons are here, Sanna said to Luteis so he could tell Elis. Elis would tell Jesse, who would inform his brothers who waited in the trees with Greata.

Sanna turned and waved her left arm once. Elliot made the same movement from across the way, then tucked himself back into his hiding spot. The sign would ripple from one witch to the next until everyone knew. Sanna leaned farther back against the tree, into the grooves of the trunk, and waited.

The branches above them began to sway. She gripped her knife tighter.

Are you ready? she asked Luteis.

I have been for many days.

The mountain dragons wouldn't be able to see them from their current flight path. Nor was it likely they'd just appear—Isadora had once said something about using transportation to appear only where you'd been before. No doubt the mountain dragons had never been to this specific spot in Letum Wood, but they'd be able to smell the forest dragons. No, they'd descend.

Sanna waited on a branch closer to the ground. Elliot, Jesse, Babs, and Trey were concealed in the roots, crevices, and branches of several trees on the forest floor, where they couldn't fall onto the hidden spikes.

Sanna's nostrils flared as she braced her legs, crouching. Letum Wood lay still. After an hour or two of rushing around and preparing, waiting at their designated spots felt interminable. The hatchlings and the older children would pop out during the battle to throw the rocks and then hide again. The rest of them would be exposed. Most of the fighting would likely happen on the ground since the adults couldn't fly.

Sanna swallowed hard.

The sound of a *conk* broke the silence. A mountain dragon fell, limp, from the branches. It crashed into the ground, eyes closed. Sanna glanced up.

A rock from a hatchling, Luteis murmured.

Rosy? she asked.

Yes.

The inability to speak directly with the dragons had become more than inconvenient—she wondered if Luteis had tired of relaying messages. She didn't know how to bring that ability back.

More branches rustled, drawing her attention back. The sound of something, like a low roar, descended. Then, all at once, like falling rain, small mountain dragons filled the forest. They screeched, thrashing, spittle dripping from their teeth.

Vines flew from the trees, entangling them. Boulders dropped from above. None of the witches would venture out until the hatchlings had finished throwing their stones.

Tell the dragons to hold their secundum, Sanna said to Luteis. *Until we must have it. They shouldn't tire themselves.*

The mountain dragons flew in circles, some slamming into trees, others appearing perfectly lucid as they sniffed the air, eyes searching here and there. They couldn't see the forest dragons yet, because the forest protected them in that uncanny way it had.

Sanna settled in, grim-faced.

As some mountain dragons fell, more arrived. Rocks descended from the heights, pelting them in the head, wings, body. Several screamed and fell. Hidden forest dragons snapped for them. Injured mountain dragons began to pool on the ground.

Melons! Sanna commanded Luteis.

"Now!" she shouted to the witches.

Elliot, Babs, and the older children released the ropes that held their rocks aloft. Melons dropped from the canopy with light whistles, landing with a *thud thud thud* on the ground. Explosions of rotten fruit burst over the injured mountain dragons and burned those flying overhead. One melon landed on the head of a younger mountain dragon, knocking it unconscious. He crashed into another dragon, taking them both down.

The invading dragons screamed, turning away from the sizzling rinds and acidic flesh.

"Second wave!" Sanna shouted. She climbed away from the tree, scrambling for Luteis's tail from where he hid behind the trunk.

It is a start, he said, watching the chaos. *But I can hear the rest. They are coming. These are the weakest. They are almost all mad. An easy sacrifice, no doubt, meant to weaken us.*

How many, do you think?

I cannot number them.

Tell the hatchlings to release the next baskets but leave a few behind.

Luteis complied. More melons and rocks fell. While the mountain dragons screamed, a thud roared overhead. More dragons streaked through the branches—these larger and more lucid. The smaller mountain dragons impaled themselves on the spears. Sanna pulled a cloth over her mouth and nose as the air thickened with acid. Her face burned.

The fall of melons began to slow.

They are almost out of rocks as well, Luteis said.

Then let's go.

Luteis sprang from the branch where they waited, hidden in the shadows. Screeching mountain dragons flew with greater strength now, uninhibited. Sanna stood on his back, knife in hand.

Tell the dragons to make themselves known. Preserve their secundum and strength where they can, but fight for their lives.

This would be a far simpler plan if you told them yourself, Luteis muttered, dodging the sharp wings of a half-crazed mountain dragon.

I agree. Then, with a gulp, added, *I'm sure Deasylva will give me the power to talk to them again soon.*

He cast her a startled glance, but said nothing.

Fire shot out of the forest in random tongues of flame. Unsuspecting mountain dragons, some of them teeming on top of the pile of their own dead, whirled around. Several caught on fire. Luteis soared through the chaos, blowing fire and smoke ahead of him. Four mountain dragons attempted to drop onto his back, but he darted away. Sanna slashed at them. Blood from their scored wings dripped onto Luteis's scales.

Where is Pemba? she asked.

Luteis dodged a larger mountain dragon just as it tore a branch off a tree and dropped it to the forest floor. While skimming away, Luteis grabbed another with his talons, tearing its wings.

I have not seen him.

"Pemba!" she shouted. She ducked when a mountain dragon—eyes half wild—attempted to slash at her from above. A rock fell, pelting the wing. The crack of a bone followed. The dragon fell.

Light burst from the forest floor. Sanna spun around just as Elliot darted away from the makeshift shelter. Not far from him, Babs threw buckets of water at any dragon that approached. Flames engulfed the shelter, sending mountain dragons reeling back.

Elis slipped into the forest, out of sight except for the *whack* of his tail as it slammed a mountain dragon into a tree. Several mountain dragons reared away from Cara's flames, plumes of acid halfway out of their mouths. The acid caught fire, engulfing them in a fireball that sent them reeling back. Cara dodged when more mountain dragons fell toward her.

Luteis's wings pumped as he climbed higher, snatching mountain dragons out of the air as they flew. Still, they poured down with wild intensity, appearing out of thin air or descending from the canopy. Sanna hacked at anything she could reach, nearly retching from the acid and the pain in her face. Chaos unfurled around them.

Luteis, she said, coughing. The metallic taste of blood rose in the back of her throat. *The acid is overpowering. I can't ... breathe in this.*

A moment, Luteis said. He landed on a branch not far away. His tail flickered around, sapphire, sparkling drops of blue covering the end.

Drink.

Your blood?

A taste is all that's needed. It is the only way to heal you.

Had there been any time to think it over, Sanna would have recoiled, possibly vomited. Instead, she slid her hand along an open wound along the edge of his tail, then sucked the blood free. A horrible taste exploded in her mouth—like iron and loam and the worst mold all combined—but the pain in her chest abated. Luteis had already whipped around to assess the battlefield from his bird's-eye view.

The battle teemed below. Cara screamed as five mountain dragons advanced on Marelis, whom she fought next to. Despite the attempts of the hatchlings to pluck out mountain-dragon eyes with their talons, Marelis collapsed beneath the weight of the invaders. Sanna watched in horror as the mountain dragons surrounded him, teeth gnashing. She slid off Luteis's back.

There is no sense to this, Luteis said. *We are simply fighting for our lives. We will never win if we don't fight together.*

Go to Marelis.

Luteis darted toward him, roaring. Alis collapsed on the branch next to Sanna, gasping for air.

"Alis!" Sanna cried. She dodged the edge of a mountain-dragon wing and put her hand to Alis's chest. A gash three inches deep cut through her glimmering scales. Thick, sapphire blood flowed out. Her eyes, dimming, met Sanna's.

"Alis, no!"

Her chest bucked, then stilled.

"Alis!"

Alis's body went limp, head slackening against the branch. Heat built up in Sanna again, tripling through her chest, arms, all the way to her fingertips. It made her tremble as it grew hot, hot, hot in her chest.

Mountain dragons darted past her, headed for the carnage on the forest floor.

Forest dragon. Mountain dragon. Adult. Hatchling. The mountain dragons were destroying and eating all of them. Their madness had reached a bloodlust frenzy—it seemed all they craved was more death.

Sanna stood up, knees trembling. Luteis fought amongst the forest dragons, his secundum the only thing keeping him, Cara, and Junis alive now. Marelis lay on the ground, eyes shut.

Was this the end?

Had her ancestors felt this way during the massacre?

Sanna clenched her fist, which burned as hot as dragon fire. The heat flooded her body again. It rushed through her, oddly buoying. A scream filtered through the chaos, winding all the way to her ears. Sanna glanced down just as Elliot ran, slid through the blood-drenched dirt, and grabbed an oddly still Babs in his arms.

"*Amo!*" he screamed.

Sanna opened her fist, looked at her burning hand. Deasylva's words slipped back through her mind.

You will know when the time comes, Deasylva had said, *who you are.*

A thousand things whirled through Sanna's mind. Daid. Finn. Isadora. The Western Network dragons. Selsay. Pemba. Prana. Life in the trees when Anguis was still very much alive. The unfolding chaos here was what happened when there was *no* leader. Talis's regime happened when there was *too much* leader.

Which meant there was a middle ground.

Maybe she didn't ask for this, but neither had Elliot or Babs or even the mountain dragons. It didn't matter if it was thrust upon her or someone else, the Dragonmasters *needed* a leader. If she truly loved the dragons, she would be what *they* needed.

Not what *she* needed.

"I am Sanna of the Forest," she whispered. The heat grew in her chest. She looked at the canopy. "I am the High Dragonmaster."

Luteis flailed below, buried beneath a pile of mountain dragons, attempting unsuccessfully to throw them off. His secundum had begun to waver. Cara was no longer visible. Only mountain dragons.

Endless mountain dragons.

The heat grew in Sanna's body until she couldn't control it anymore. Her frame shook. Her heart would be consumed if she let it.

She released the heat.

CHAPTER
TWENTY-SEVEN

When Isadora returned out of the paths, the wind whipped her hair with angry lashes across her eyes. Two Defenders stood in front of her, scowling. Her cheek prickled with pain—they'd struck her, no doubt.

"Go for a lark, did you?" Maximillion hissed, his bottom lip split in half and oozing blood.

"I can get us out of this," she whispered.

"You've been hit in the head too many times."

"Do as I say."

"*Silencio!*" one Defender screamed, slamming a fist into Maximillion's stomach. Maximillion doubled over, wheezing. Isadora forced her surge of rage to calm as he gasped for breath. Lucey still hadn't stirred. Had she lost her mind in Carcere? Was she a shade away from death already?

Was she faking?

With Lucey, one could never tell.

Torches and candles illuminated La Torra under the darkening sky. The brightest concentration of light came from the courtyard, where the sound of amassing

Defenders rang out. The Defenders had no swords or phys-ical weapons—not even their whips—but Isadora felt the sheer terror and exhilaration of their situation all the same. Then Cecelia appeared from a set of stairs in the floor, slowly, elegantly, in her usual coiffed perfection.

The magic whipped up inside Isadora.

Cecelia strode through heavy silence, right up to Isadora. Maximillion gave a wet-sounding cough.

"So," Cecelia said, "you are finally mine."

The layers of haughty elegance bled away, fading into a picture of a little girl. Isadora swallowed hard, confused by the strange dichotomy. Was Cecelia a terrified girl or a horrible monster?

Or both?

"You set this up to bring *me* here, didn't you?" Isadora asked.

Cecelia's gaze registered surprise.

"This wasn't about Maximillion. You captured Lucey. Went to Maximillion's office. Allowed me to work here in the *lavanda*. That day in your room—you were in my head, testing me."

"In a way, yes. All of my raids are designed to find more Watchers."

"But you weren't looking for *any* Watcher."

Cecelia swallowed. "No."

"How long have you been searching for me?" Isadora asked.

"Long enough."

"I'm not *your* match, am I? I'm matched to someone else."

The edges of Cecelia's lips twitched. She tilted her head back. "Fortunately for you, you're not."

"What"—Maximillion spat, attempting to hit Cecelia

with his spittle but failing—"in the good gods are you talking about?"

"Matches," Cecelia said, gazing at him. "Or don't you know? No, of course you don't. The truth has been hidden from Watchers for centuries now. Only the Defenders *really* know how it works."

Maximillion's nostrils flared, but he said nothing. Next to him, the wind stirred Lucey's hair. Her head bounced slightly, as if twitching.

Cecelia turned back to Isadora.

"It's part of the magic," she said. "Every magic has a counter-magic. For every powerful Watcher, there is an equally powerful Defender."

"Matches," Isadora whispered. "*Connection.* The magic forms a connection between the two matching witches, doesn't it?"

Cecelia sneered. "Unfortunately. Some would say that the match augments the power, although it also allows a weakness. Rumor has it that your match may join your paths. See what you see. May *betray* you. Murder you. Use your own power against you, even. It is the legacy of Watchers everywhere." Her eyes flickered with pain. "Betrayal."

"What a delight," Maximillion muttered. "Please tell me you aren't mine."

"No," she snapped. "You don't have that honor."

"You're seeking my match," Isadora said. "Aren't you?"

Cecelia smiled. "That's the question, isn't it? I have always had the greatest power amongst Defenders—until I sensed you. I thought myself safe, but clearly there is one greater than I."

"When did you first sense me?"

She gestured to Lucey.

"On the raid."

Wind whistled past Isadora's ears, buffeting her with the wrath of the white-capped ocean. She had accessed the powers on the raid. Cecelia hadn't been seen on the raid, but she'd likely attended. Watched. Let the Defenders do the work. Cecelia's hair billowed around her shoulders. She stared with a steady, alarming gaze.

"You want my match," Isadora murmured.

"Yes," Cecelia hissed. "Your power exceeds mine. Indeed, your power exceeds *any* Watcher I've ever detected before." Her gaze flickered to Maximillion, then back. "In more than just magic."

"How would any Defender know they were my match?" Isadora asked.

"We can feel your magic," she said, forming a fist over her heart. "We can feel the connection, perhaps before you can, because you didn't even know it existed. Every time you use your magic, you bring us closer and closer."

Isadora thought back to the evenings in the water. The sheer amount of power she'd poured out would have been an eternal beacon.

"Fool," Maximillion said. "You'd call a more powerful Defender here, through her, with no hope of defeating them should they also be a power-hungry dog?"

"Who said there was no hope?" Cecelia asked lightly. "Defenders," she called without removing her eyes from Isadora, "prepare your torches."

Cecelia turned away.

"Your match," Isadora called out. "You've already found your match, haven't you?"

Cecelia stopped. Her shoulders stiffened.

"But you haven't killed him," Isadora continued. "I met

him in Carcere. He's still alive. He rivals you. Why haven't you killed him?"

Cecelia remained silent, hands balled in fists at her side. Isadora's mind raced. Her mouth rounded.

"Because if you kill him, you might also die," she murmured. "Equal power. Your match might be tied to your own life."

Cecelia spun, rage in her eyes.

"Silence!"

"Or do you not know either? But you don't want to risk it? You don't want to allow a Defender to connect with their match to find out. The Watchers you've killed have been weak, haven't they? Their matches unknown. But the Watchers you kept—they match your Defenders. You haven't killed them because you don't know. Or because that means someone *else*, someone unknown, then becomes the match."

"You know nothing."

"I know I'm more powerful than you," Isadora said, warming to her courage now. "I know that you're terrified of me. Of Maximillion. Of all Watchers. That's why you're always surrounded by Defenders. That's why you have to be the strongest, why you live where Watchers can't access their magic easily. You're terrified."

Her eyes brightened in a terrible, majestic rage. "What do you know?" she shouted. "What do you know of the horrible power of Watchers? The pain they inflict? The control they assert? You see what *may* happen, then twist fate to suit your own desires. Who protects free will? Who protects fate? I do! Defenders! Kill them now."

The magic beckoned.

Isadora returned to it.

The forest appeared in deep shadow and teeming light.

Beams of luminescence ran along the forest floor, darting this way and that, infusing leaves, forming trails. Darkness wound alongside each speck of light.

Isadora poured her powers out, unleashing their coiled tendrils. The moment she let them loose, the air changed.

Someone screamed.

A dozen paths bubbled to the surface, all originating in fields of darkness. With this much of her magic turned loose, thousands of wisps, extending into what seemed like eternity, appeared. The darkness intensified, growing as thick as the light. Wisps disappeared at an alarming rate. A war outside of her influence raged around her.

She advanced into the chaos of light and darkness.

Wisps popped up everywhere, detailed to a degree she'd never known before. A few of them moved, only for a couple of seconds. Still, she analyzed them from a distance. They could mean many things—or nothing at all. Wasn't that the true downside to this power? For as much as it revealed, there was more it must hide in the sheer number of variables it presented.

"Remove my path."

Letum Wood remained alone, infused with the struggle of light and darkness. Something else tinged the air. Pain, was it? Yes, but more than that. Longing. Unadulterated, rabid *need*. Swept away by the desperation, Isadora closed the magic and opened her eyes.

Cecelia stood only a pace away.

Something wild had overtaken her. The same frenetic spirit that had revealed itself in the paths. Both worlds seemed to collide. The wind whipped Cecelia's hair, stirring it in a torrent. Out of the corner of her eye, Isadora glimpsed the courtyard.

Defenders stared up at them.

Thunder boomed in the background.

"By Prana," Cecelia whispered, clutching a hand to her chest. Her skin blanched white. "Your power is deep."

"You're wrong about Watchers."

Cecelia physically jolted, as if brought out of her own shroud of magic. Isadora tugged on the magic, pulling it onto La Torra.

Paths raced through the ground at Cecelia's feet, intermingling darkness and light. Leaves sprouted. Vines grew. Isadora tapped into a reservoir of power she didn't know existed—light flowed through her, whirling in an eddy of darkness and light around each Defender. The Defenders recoiled, crying out. Isadora pulled, tugging them farther in. Letum Wood began to overlay La Torra. Isadora didn't know if she brought the forest here, or if she pulled them there. It didn't matter.

The war surged.

"I'm never wrong," Cecelia hissed. Her eyes darted around, taking in their new surroundings. She backed away a step.

Isadora's left arm was numb, the bones in her wrist aching from the ropes. The whipping frenzy of the wind faded into the calm of Letum Wood.

Darkness crept along the stones beneath Cecelia, crawling toward Isadora's light. The two wrestled, tangled, bringing the war of the magical world into this one. Isadora let out a cry—what had she done? Had she created a bridge between the two worlds? Fatigue threatened to overcome her. She couldn't maintain this for much longer.

The darkness pooled around Cecelia, as if cradling her. Isadora pushed one last burst of energy into the light.

With a jolt, La Torra disappeared.

Sanna released the heat in her body all at once.

Luteis's bright-orange secundum billowed like a wave, tripling in size, ripping through the crowd of mountain dragons assaulting him. The viscous fire—almost like a burning liquid—attached to the mountain dragons' wings and burned through them. They screamed, flapping away. Luteis crawled out of the pile and looked up.

"*Mori*," Sanna whispered.

Voices populated through her mind, mere whispers at first.

My hatchlings. Where is my Rosy?

Marelis!

They continue to fall from the sky!

The dragons' voices were back? An expansiveness had opened in Sanna's mind again—similar to before, but more … open. Powerful. As if last time were an accident and this was on purpose.

No more! called another dragon. *We cannot win.*

I need help!

What's happening?

The witch, Babs, has died.

Amongst the voices, she could just make out Luteis. *You are changed,* he said. He peered at her from the forest floor, through the fighting.

I am.

Sanna, perched high, surveyed the battlefield below. Mountain dragons fell from the sky or appeared out of nowhere, but most of them weren't focusing on the forest dragons. They were attacking … everything. Not far from Luteis pulsed another teeming pile of mountain dragons. Winks of a ruby color appeared beneath it.

Marelis.

Fire, Sanna said to Luteis, somehow directing it to him in her mind. *I need your fire. Throw it toward Marelis.*

Luteis didn't hesitate. As soon as the flame left his mouth, Sanna let go of the building heat in her chest. Luteis's secundum roared to life again, flaming over the mountain dragons like a blanket. They screeched, whirling away. Sanna reeled the internal heat back in. The torrential flow of fire from Luteis's mouth stopped.

Sanna looked at her hands, still burning as if a thousand candles lived within them. The strange, pulsing power grew and coalesced again. What was this?

Magic?

You are the High Dragonmaster, Luteis said, anticipating her question. *And now you have accepted it. This is part of your birthright in battle. We are stronger together, are we not?*

She sucked in a sharp breath. It *was* magic. More dragon voices filtered through her mind. She'd never communicated with them on purpose. She didn't really know how it worked, or how to start. After several pointless attempts at calling for Marelis, she reached into the strange void at the back of her mind, seeming to slip inside it.

Marelis, she said quietly.

A strange silence followed, at odds with the rampant chaos unfurling around them. Sanna watched the mountain dragons streak by. A slight pause followed.

Yes, High Dragonmaster? replied Marelis.

Her breath caught.

Climb free of the mountain dragons as quickly as you can, then find Cara. She's to your left. There's a small hollow in the trees there where you can take a minute to recover. She can lay down flame to protect you if any mountain dragon comes to attack.

Thank you, High Dragonmaster.

Cara? Sanna asked.

I will.

Elis, she said next, throwing his name into the void. The word hung there like a breath. Waiting.

You requested me, High Dragonmaster?

Sanna frowned. The way his voice rang, as if in a cavernous space, meant something. That others were listening, perhaps?

Junis needs help to your right. Come up from behind, and the mountain dragons won't see you. Pick up a dead mountain dragon to throw at them as you go.

Yes, High Dragonmaster.

A screech caught her ear. She turned to see several mountain dragons snapping at a determined Rosy, who was attempting to fly away.

Rosy, drop.

Rosy glanced up, startled.

Stop flying, Sanna said.

After a moment's hesitation, Rosy obeyed. She pulled her wings into her sides and fell. The mountain dragons slammed into each other and, snarling, began to tear at each other's wings. Rosy collided with another mountain dragon about to attack Laris, the youngest hatchling.

Recover, Sanna said to Rosy. *Fly again to the top of the canopy. Scout for me, will you? Let me know if more are coming. Be stealthy, if you can.*

Levity entered Rosy's tone. Perhaps relief. *Yes, High Dragonmaster.*

Yes, Sanna realized. She *could* lead because the dragons trusted her. Somehow, they really did. Sanna turned back to the battle below, her body tingling with this newfound power. With her eyes, she guided each dragon. Coordinated and amplified their fire. Prevented attacks. The fearful chatter she'd first heard settled down into a quiet space, filled with her commands and their responses.

The tide began to turn.

Mountain dragons drew back, flying higher in the trees, scales and bodies burned. They hesitated instead of plunging forward. Forest dragons amassed in intentional rhythms, throwing fire in coordination, protecting the witches, creating a field of flame that stopped the mountain dragons in mid-air.

Then the air shifted.

Something changed.

The solid *thud thud thud* of descending wings sent acidic air flying at Sanna. The skin around her eyes flared with pain. She threw an arm up, recoiling.

Ah, drawled a familiar voice. *How typical. A forest witch cowering from a mountain dragon.*

Sanna's toes curled.

Pemba had finally come.

PEMBA HOVERED in the air next to Sanna, staring straight into her eyes.

"Coward!" Sanna snapped, eyes watering from his acidic breath. "Showing up only after all your advance dragons have died. Some leader you are."

You who will not even acknowledge her goddess?

The rage that had burned deep in Sanna's chest surfaced again. "You better believe it," she snarled, throwing her shoulders back. "These are *my* dragons, this is *my* forest, and you will never defeat us. You can burn in the hellfire of Hatha. I'll never give my dragons to you."

Are you finally willing to claim leadership now that your entire race is on the verge of extinction? You who care so much that you wouldn't act until you had to?

With a guttural shout, Sanna ran, leapt, and threw herself into the air. Luteis swooped up, catching her as he threw fire at Pemba. The heat coiled out of her with true fury. Luteis's fire expanded, nearly consuming the mountain dragon.

Pemba disappeared, only to reappear out of Luteis's reach. He roared, flinging his wings open.

Sanna stood up.

You shall die! Pemba screamed.

Sanna's vision blurred again, her eyes watering. With another growl, she ran, threw herself off Luteis's back, and landed on Pemba blindly.

Sanna! Luteis cried.

She grabbed her knife from her belt and slammed it into Pemba's scales. The sharp blade glanced off his hard scales, not even drawing blood, and plummeted to the ground. Pemba spun. Without magic to anchor her, Sanna flew off his back. Her body slammed into a tree trunk, then dropped onto a branch. Her ribs cracked. Her breath stalled.

Luteis roared. Coppery flames shot through the air as he soared right at Pemba. The two collided in mid-air with deafening screams, talons engaged. Blood sprayed in bright arcs around them.

Sanna gasped, crawling away from the edge of the tree branch. Pain spiraled through her ribs with every breath. Her face felt like it was on fire.

Rosy's high-pitched cry preceded another *thud.*

High Dragonmaster! More are coming. They are large and fill the sky with their swarms.

Pemba's acid made the air shimmer—Luteis turned it

to fire. They darted around each other. Sanna peered over the edge of the branch, gasping.

The battle raged amongst the adult dragons. Cara crawled over dead mountain dragons—at least thirty of them—to stop a living one from taking down Junis. Another hatchling fell, screaming when a mountain dragon attempted to wrench its wing off. Bellis tried to throw fire, but nothing came out. Mountain dragons swarmed her, eyes wild with madness.

What now? Rosy asked, turning to Sanna in sheer terror. *What now?*

Sanna's chest heaved with pain and fire and horror. They'd been doomed from the moment Talis died. Even if she could grow the fire of the forest dragons, they had run out of energy. She didn't know the magic well enough to do anything but throw flame. Junis's voice broke through Sanna's mind and the cacophony of dragon voices that filled it.

High Dragonmaster! he shouted. *Look out!*

The edge of a wing hit Sanna from behind.

She dropped to her knees on the branch, stunned. Her ribs tightened.

Sanna gathered her breath back, banishing the black spots from her eyes, to see a mountain dragon attacking Rosy. Rosy screamed, but her fire gave out. Rosy ducked, but the wild beast grabbed her neck with a talon. Sanna scrambled for her knife, but it wasn't there. Rosy feinted, taking out the dragon's leg.

The mountain dragon fell off the bough, taking Rosy with him.

"*No!*" Sanna screamed. Junis leapt off the ground with a livid bellow. Rosy dropped into the teeming melee below.

∾

Isadora stood in the paths with Cecelia, face-to-face, as if she wasn't tied to a ready-to-burn star back in Alkarra.

In the magic, there was no flamboyant dress. Nothing but Cecelia without adornment or facade. A woman who appeared haggard and deeply terrified. Cecelia rushed backward with a cry, slamming into a tree. Isadora hadn't realized it before, but in the paths she wore a simple dress with elbow length sleeves and a pale, ivory material.

"What are you doing?" Cecelia screeched.

"Watchers aren't here to disrupt fate," Isadora said. "You're wrong."

"And yet you do! Let me free."

"Some do, maybe. We can't avoid evil … but interrupting fate isn't the purpose of the magic. Even *I* didn't see that until now."

Cecelia scowled. "Oh, really? Then what is your noble cause? Why does the magic give you the ability to control, to inflict pain, to interrupt what will be with what you want?"

"Show me young Cecelia," Isadora said quietly.

Off to the left, a familiar pillar of light rose from the ground. A little girl, flinching, eyes squeezed shut. Cecelia saw it and fell to her knees with a cry. Her mouth opened in wordless question.

Isadora stared at the little girl, brow furrowed. The wind stirred again.

Frightened.

"Someone hurt you, Cecelia," Isadora murmured. "A Watcher?"

Cecelia's nostrils flared. Another piteous cry escaped her.

"My brother," she whispered.

"He was a Watcher?"

Her eyes closed. For a second, Isadora considered asking the magic to reveal him, but she thought better of it. Could Cecelia handle such a thing?

"A vile witch," Cecelia muttered, staring at the girl, transfixed. "Cruel in his use of the magic to control me. To force me to bend to his will." She swallowed hard. "To do awful things for him. *To* him. No one protected me from him. No one."

The little girl changed, growing into the defiant, impoverished teenager. Cecelia's terror hardened into a grim, flinty expression. She straightened, shoulders pulled back.

"When he died, I was fifteen. My own power awakened then, too late, almost like a cruel joke. Freedom," she whispered, reaching for the wisp. "Not only had I been given freedom, but the chance to make sure that no Watcher ever had power over me—or others—again."

"You went too far."

Cecelia's fingers dropped from the gossamer wisp. "I did what I had to do to protect others." Tears filled her eyes. "From what I endured."

Silence swelled between them. Isadora quietly commanded the magic to recede. Cecelia's form disappeared, dropping to the forest floor in prisms of light. Cecelia stared at the spot where it had been.

"I will not let you continue this," Isadora said. "You cannot persist in your relentless pursuit of murder. We are not your brother."

Cecelia straightened to her feet, eyes flashing.

"You cannot stop me."

Letum Wood began to fade. Stone replaced the earth. Sky replaced the canopy. Instead of light, darkness. The howl of a tempest filled Isadora's ears. When she gave into the closing magic, she collapsed.

Someone had freed her from the stake.

Chaos reigned. Maximillion stood in front of her, bellowing. Defenders advanced. The wind screamed by. A familiar burly body and dark head of hair—Ernesto— fought next to Maximillion, using a heavy frying pan. Lucey lay on the ground in a crumpled heap. Prickles raced up and down Isadora's legs and arms as she attempted to stand. East Guards amassed from below, heading toward the stairs.

"Kill them all!" Cecelia screamed, only a few paces away.

Flimsy little Sera appeared on Ernesto's other side, waving two torches. Defenders skittered back, out of reach of the bright flames. Overhead, an aquila with burnt-orange and red feathers swooped out of the air, plucked a Defender off the top of Carcere, and carried him away. Another aquila came.

Then another.

Cecelia inched back.

"You may have so much power over me!" she called. "But you have yet to meet your match. Your match will be as powerful as you, strong in all the ways you are not. Do not underestimate us. We hold the power of the past. We know you better than you know yourself. The uncertainty of fate is no match for the certainty of the past. Your match will find you, and if they care anything about the Defenders, they will kill you."

Behind Cecelia, a shadow shifted. Seeing it, Isadora drew her shoulders back.

"That's where you're wrong."

Cecelia turned to flee into the staircase, but stopped. A

witch stood there. A thin, beaten, pale witch with fire burning in his eyes. Cecelia skidded to a halt, a scream stuck in her throat.

"Eighteen years, four months, five days, thirteen hours," he ground out, advancing one halting, weak step at a time. "That's how long I endured without sunlight. Without fresh air. Without the comfort of my Lissa. Without my son. Without *anything*."

Cecelia shrank away. "No," she whispered. "Don't."

"You imprisoned me," he cried. "You took away my life. For what? Because my power equalled yours? So you could prevent me from harming you?"

Cecelia stumbled back, tripping over her elaborate skirts. The witch tilted his head back, staring down at her.

"For the first time in nineteen years, I can feel it. My power returns. It fills me so deeply I almost … I almost cannot endure it. And now, because you feared it, it will be the final thing you know."

Isadora stepped back. Light cut from him in a dazzling arc, swooping through the air. Cecelia soared back, tossed away. Several Defenders fell over the side of La Torra, plunging to the sand below. Those not thrown clear scrambled to their feet and ran.

Cecelia dropped to her knees with a scream. The muscles in her neck became rigid. Her fingers curled. Magic flowed from her match in unrestrained lines of power. It infused the stones. Illuminated the top of Carcere. Only the lightning flashing in the distance competed with the brilliance of his light. Isadora turned away, momentarily blinded, to see an astonishing sight.

Beyond Carcere, along the shore, were ten small boats. Witches moved back and forth, carrying limp bodies with pale faces and gaunt expressions.

The Advocacy had come.

Aquilas continued to soar overhead in a circle, as if patrolling the castle. Defenders disappeared from the top of La Torra. Cecelia groaned. She rolled onto her side, hitting the wall. The male witch fell to his hands and knees. Agony etched Cecelia's features as she looked at Isadora.

"I will suffer in fear no more," Cecelia said. "No more."

With one swift move, she hooked an arm around the wall, heaved herself over the top, and plunged to the courtyard below. A sickening *thud* followed. Isadora turned away with a cry.

The darkness abated, and the light retreated. Within seconds, only the flicker of the torches in the courtyard illuminated the night, plunging them back into the tempest-induced darkness.

The battle on top of Carcere ebbed. East Guards and Defenders disappeared. Maximillion stood a few paces away, panting, staring at Isadora with unease in his eyes. Isadora met his gaze.

"Lucey," he whispered, eyes widening.

Unable to bear the terror she saw in his gaze, she turned away. Maximillion scrambled for his friend just as the male witch collapsed. Isadora hurried to his side, crouching next to him.

"She's gone. You don't have to suffer anymore."

He breathed heavily, peering up at her. The rage had dissipated into a foggy in-between, as if he straddled this world and the world of magic. He reached up, touching her face.

"I can be at peace," he whispered, staring past her at the smattering of stars overhead. "Ah, the stars. I see you again, my old friends. Fi-finally."

"Your name?" she asked, grabbing his hand. "I will tell your sweet Lissa that you still loved her."

A faint smile crossed his lips.

"Francesco Mal—"

The words faded off his lips. His head went slack as he turned his face away.

Wind soared past them. Isadora looked out at the final boat retreating into the stormy waters. Magic would protect them, these sea-faring witches getting the Watchers to safety. Maximillion would live. Hopefully Lucey.

Isadora felt like a husk. A burnt-out, empty shell, scorched by the power of the magic.

Her view of the stormy ocean blurred.

Isadora collapsed.

TWENTY-EIGHT

S anna screamed.

"Rosy!"

Rosy and Junis disappeared in the flood of mountain dragons. Sanna couldn't even see the ground anymore. Couldn't direct their movements. Forest-dragon voices rang through her mind with sheer panic. Luteis and Pemba still fought in the air. Pemba's quick transportation left Luteis in a perpetual scramble. Sanna tightened her fists.

There must be a way.

Luteis sent a spray of weak fire into the air. He, the strongest of all the forest dragons, was running out of energy as well. She could see it in his eyes. In his frantic, less-graceful movements. His wings beat the air as mountain dragons whirled all around, confusing him. Pemba controlled their movements from overhead, his white pendant flapping with every movement. There wasn't even a Dragonmaster for her to fight, to speak with, to reason with. How could one face such a wild, untamed force mad with magical power they couldn't use without their High Dragonmaster?

The fury built up inside Sanna, fueled by memories of Daid, Anguis, and all she had lost. The magic—whatever it was—tingled as it soared through her veins. The acid in the air was so thick she could barely breathe. Her throat felt raw. Her face burned. They couldn't fight the mountain dragons by sheer numbers. The only thing the forest dragons had that mountain dragons didn't was ...

Her.

A sinking feeling made her chest heavy. Suddenly, it was so clear. Why hadn't she thought of it before? There was no choice. She didn't know much about magic, or how to be the High Dragonmaster, but she at least knew one thing.

She wouldn't give up.

Luteis, she said, eyeing Pemba across the way. *I have a plan.*

Yes, he said, voice strained, *High Dragonmaster.*

When I tell you, grab Pemba. Hold him however you can.

Luteis, still battling the sheer number of mountain dragons that surrounded him, grunted. He was three wingspans away from Pemba. *I will try.*

Elis? she called. *Can you help?*

I will try, High Dragonmaster.

"Pemba!" she shouted. "Your fight is with me."

He turned, eyes glittering. *You bring this upon yourself. You should have submitted.*

Perhaps I am not the one who should submit.

Pemba snarled.

She drew in a deep breath.

Forest dragons, she called, *we are stronger together. We can win as a brood. Witches and dragons. The gap is not impossible.*

Fight with me, and I will fight for you. If you trust me, give me all your fire. Whatever you have left.

Weak flames flickered in the air in response. Luteis in the air. Cara on the ground. Was that Junis? Marelis? Elis? Sanna drew from their strength, then unleashed the building heat inside of her. The flames expanded. She sent more. More of herself. More of her heat.

More of her magical soul.

The flames strengthened. Heat flowed out of her, feeding the fire. Pockets of acid made the flames grow— Sanna coaxed them bigger. Faster. Hotter. The fire climbed through the air, racing like vines, all the way to Pemba. She felt as if all the blood had drained from her body. Sanna dropped to one knee.

A little more! she called, gasping for air.

The growing fire reached Pemba, nearly engulfing him. Pemba wheeled back just as Luteis approached. Elis, coming from the other side, grabbed Pemba in his talons, preventing him from using magic to get away. Pemba shrieked, attempting to correct with his wings. Sanna struggled back to her feet.

Hold him right there.

With shaking legs, she sprinted across the branch, leapt off the side, and launched onto Pemba's back. She jumped through the wall of fire that held the other mountain dragons at bay and grabbed Pemba's shoulder. He bellowed.

She slipped, grabbing hold of the ridge along his back at the last second. The ridge pierced her palms, wetting them with blood. With one hand on his wing and the other flailing free, Sanna flapped like a rag doll.

What is happening? Luteis asked. *You will die!*

Trust ... me.

With her free hand, Sanna reached over, grabbed the white pendant around Pemba's neck, and yanked it free. The fire wrapped around Pemba. Luteis swooped beneath them.

Sanna dropped onto his back.

Flames ensconced Pemba, wrapping him in tongues of fire. He shrieked. His wings burned. Acid flew out of his mouth, but the fire only pulsed hotter. Mountain dragons peeled away one at a time. One wild glance of Pemba's eyes was all that remained before he fell to the forest floor, consumed.

Luteis landed on a branch, chest heaving. All the mountain dragons had scattered, flocking to the branches, eyes trained on her.

No, on the *pendant*.

Sanna opened her fingers one at a time. A chiseled piece of bone lay in her bloody, trembling hand. A snarling mountain dragon. Like the egg in the North, it glowed from within, opalescent. She stared at it.

Luteis's quiet voice broke through the odd silence of her mind.

Do you see? he asked.

Sanna looked up, and her breath caught.

A spiral of mountain dragons surrounded her. They fanned in the air, on the trees, staring at her from the darkening forest. Their eyes were full of expectation.

One dragon advanced, broad wings flapping. He looked just like Pemba. A new voice hissed through her mind.

High Dragonmaster, he said, his tone strangely subdued. *We are at your service.*

Luteis's head whipped over to face her.

"Luteis," she whispered, clasping the pendant again. "Please forgive me."

YOU HAVE SACRIFICED MUCH.

The words appeared on the old tree trunk, even though Sanna didn't expect them, several days later.

Deasylva's words were dimmer this time, as if even she felt weary. For a split second, Sanna thought of pretending she didn't see the glowing writing or smell the honeysuckle in the breeze. She dismissed the temptation.

The time for ignoring their problems was over.

"Yes, well, you tend to ask much of those that ... that trust you."

As I give. Your heart has always been that of a leader. You have not seen it.

"Ah ... thanks. What now?"

The great war of the goddesses is coming.

Sanna tried to conjure up surprise, even anger, but could muster neither. She had known since she met Yushi that this wouldn't be simple. What other inevitable end could there be?

She let out a long, weary breath. The skin around her eyes prickled, and she rubbed it.

"I met Selsay."

I know.

"Really?"

We have our ways. Selsay and I do not agree on much.

"Prana is the problem, isn't she?"

As you say.

Weariness still rang through Sanna's body, even four days after the great battle. Smoke from the pyres still lingered in the air. Babs's body had been burned. The forest had already claimed Laris, Bellis, and Rosy back to itself.

Her heart ached for her dragons—and the piles of mountain dragons yet to be burned.

"We're going back to the Ancients," Sanna said. She gazed past the old tree. No one had even questioned her when she'd made the declaration. Whether they were simply too stunned, too tired, or too scared to care, she didn't know. Perhaps they also accepted her as leader now, and simply went as she commanded.

Perhaps it was trust.

"It's safest there. At least there are homes and water and greater protection from the forest itself. We'll ride the hatchlings. It'll take a while, but I'm going to make all the dragons fly. Or attempt to. Even the older ones." Despite herself, speaking her reasons out loud felt better. At least for the moment.

You have my trust.

Sanna let out a long breath and rubbed her aching eyes. The writing grew fuzzy. She needed sleep. The gentle wind, and scent of honeysuckle faded. Slowly, one letter at a time, the writing faded. The sound of a twig cracking snapped behind her. She glanced back. Was it Jesse? Only when he approached did she recognize his weary expression and drawn face.

"*Avay,*" Jesse said, trudging closer.

"*Avay.*"

The words disappeared entirely before he stepped too close. Sanna turned to face him, feeling a resurrection of the awkwardness that had been so strong before. He kicked a rock out of his path, cheeks burning.

"Listen," he said, "I'm sorry about trying to ki—"

"Don't."

He glanced up, as if startled, then managed a wry smile.

"I expected you to make me grovel. I never thought … I guess I just needed to know."

Sanna snorted in amusement. "Although it has a nice ring to it, you didn't do anything grovel-worthy. If anyone should … I mean …"

This time, he stopped her.

"No. It's fine. I just had to know. And now I know. I always thought that the dragons had your true allegiance, you know."

Sanna stared at him for a long time, aware of the ages that seemed to pass. She longed again for Isadora, who would know the exact right thing to say right now. She felt as if she were back at Anguis, at a fork in the trails high above the ground. One seemed so obvious to take. One, so dim. She could reassure him. Tell him there was hope for the two of them in the future.

But that would be a lie.

Sanna knew that there would never be anyone, aside from Isadora, more important than the dragons. It had to be that way. The forest had made it so—infected her very blood, and she had welcomed it.

Her shoulders relaxed back. "I'm sorry."

He waved it off with a half-hearted smile. "I get it. You never really did fit in, did you?"

This time, she cracked a smile. "No."

He drew in a deep breath. "So," he said. "We're going to the site of the Great Massacre."

"Yes."

"Odd, isn't it, that we should go back there, now, of all times?"

Sanna said nothing but didn't love his implication. There had *almost* been another massacre.

Almost.

Jesse peered into the distance, as if he hadn't expected a response. Then he nodded.

"Well," he said. "I think we're almost ready if you are."

"Thanks. I'll be there in just a moment."

A dark cloud passed overhead, casting a dim shadow on the ground. The undergrowth rustled as Jesse strode away, fading into the trees.

You are very still, Luteis said. He appeared at her side. She held out her hand, gazing at a beam of light that fell from the upper canopy onto her palm. Her hand blurred. The tips of her fingers. Sanna's entire body turned to ice as she narrowed her gaze on the dimmed forest beyond her.

Dimmed.

Why dimmed?

Pain flared through her face. Her eyes swam. When she looked at Luteis, the tiny scales around his eyes blurred together. Beyond him, the canopy lacked clarity.

"Luteis," she murmured, rubbing her eyes. "My vision."

What is wrong?

Sanna blinked, but the picture didn't clear. Something cold rippled through her, ending in a knot in her belly. She locked eyes with him, mute at first.

"I think," she whispered, swallowing hard, "I'm losing my vision."

CHAPTER

TWENTY-NINE

Isadora stared over the vast ocean.

A tepid breeze blew over the churning whitecaps. La Torra lay silent beneath her, a puddle of stone and sand and horrible memories. Ever since Cecelia's demise, the strange air of the place had receded, as if the wind had taken it away. La Torra seemed like a limp rag. Worn out. Gray. Lackluster.

Isadora closed her eyes, enjoying the spray of the salty air. All of the staff except Fiona and Lorenzo had been dismissed, leaving an empty chasm in their wake. Only two East Guards patrolled the perimeter here and there; Carcere lay empty. Blocked doors had been thrown open, spilling light into the dank shadows. What Defenders still lived had escaped. No sign of them had been seen since Cecelia's death.

"It's beautiful, no?"

Isadora spun around to see Fiona standing there. Isadora managed a weak smile and nodded.

"Yes. Beautiful. I believe I'm going to miss the ocean."

Fiona's nose wrinkled. "You have your strange forest at home, I hear."

Isadora's heart thrilled. "Yes. I do. My forest. My family." Her mind ran to memories of Sanna. The canopy. Mam. The smell of Daid's pipe. Although Anguis was gone, her family was not. What would Daid have to say about her description of the ocean? Could she bottle it up and take it back to them? No. Even if she could, there was no way to appreciate the vast expanse of the sea, the magnanimity of it, without witnessing it themselves.

But Lucey would be there. She'd understand.

"Ernesto asked me to bring this letter to you from your friend Maximillion. He is meeting with Dante, our High Priest, today, to report to him what happened."

Isadora's stomach caught. Maximillion meeting with Dante for any reasons created political tension for the Central Network, but considering he fought East Guards and the Ambassador died while Maximillion was there meant even *uglier* implications. Would the East declare war, just when things had possibly turned toward peace? She doubted Charles went with him. Her mind trailed to their kiss, the horror in his gaze after she'd used her powers to battle Cecelia. The burning tingle of her lips sank all the way into her belly.

Had she imagined the passion behind his kiss? The fear in his eyes once she returned? Now he would know precisely how much power she had.

"Thank you," Isadora said. Her pained heart took her by surprise.

Fiona studied her. "You seem better," she said.

"I feel better, thanks to your help."

Two days had passed while Isadora remained in her stupor. Maximillion had assisted Lucey back to Letum

Wood. The Advocacy had already sent the imprisoned Watchers to various safe houses in the Central Network. Efforts to track down their family members were underway, inhibited by a new edict from the Eastern Network High Priest that prevented travel across the borders.

"Take your time here," Fiona said. "We are in no hurry for you to leave."

"Will you stay?"

Fiona gazed over the ocean. "Yes. La Torra is in me. *Solo coraggioso.*"

Isadora's lips twitched in amusement. The sign over the servants' hall.

"Only the courageous," Isadora whispered.

Fiona disappeared down the stairwell with a wry, parting smile. Isadora cast one last look at the ocean. She would miss its wild vastness.

Not the laundry.

Overhead, the sky remained empty. The famed aquilas had been Advocacy members after all, which explained how Maximillion had been able to transport in and out— he'd simply transformed into the bird. That sort of magic, expected by Defenders, went unaccounted for. Isadora peered at the empty sky, wondering how many times the aquila had been Maximillion, checking in. No wonder he knew so much.

A splash of white in the crook of her arm caught her eye. Sanna's letters. She'd nearly forgotten that Maximillion had given them to her. A thrill zipped through her, all the way to her toes.

Home.

With no one chasing her away from La Torra, she sank onto the parapet and removed the twine from around the bundle. Her lips twitched in a smile as she shuffled through the envelopes. Sanna's handwriting had always been horrid. How she missed them!

Isadora's brow furrowed. The handwriting became more and more hasty until it was nearly illegible. She looked back over the pile. Considering how much time had passed, there weren't as many letters as she'd expected.

The pit in her stomach grew.

She tore through the first one, skimmed it, and felt a growing horror. "No!" she cried.

With fear, she tore into the next. Tears filled her eyes. Her hands trembled. She read each letter once, twice, then crumpled them in her hands and transported away with a soft cry.

FREEDOM

A SNEAK PEEK FROM THE 3RD BOOK IN THE DRAGONMASTER TRILOGY

The ruins of Berry lay in charred waste against the backdrop of Letum Wood.

Although over a year had passed since the attack from the Western Network on the sleepy town, the wound felt fresh. Only a few witches had attempted to rebuild their pillaged homes. Most of the lots lay empty, filled with the fallen boards of what had been. In some cases, nothing remained. It lay underneath a constant, gray cloud that beckoned winter with gray fingers, wrapping the barren landscape and choking the life out of it.

A cold wind whipped by, whisking Isadora Spence's thoughts with it. She shivered, tightened her cloak, then slipped back inside a broad tent.

Dirty canvas tents formed a sort of city in the main meadow of Berry. The High Priest of the Central Network, Charles, had set up a refugee camp here only a few months before. Those not brave enough to take their chances living in Letum Wood, but had been uprooted by fire, pillaging, rape, and other atrocities, came here.

Witches injured from battle streamed in from attacks on the borders, or worse. Most of the witches that came for healing died. Those that stayed here were mere shells. Lost in their memories, fear, and pain.

Outside the collection of tents were eight larger apothecary tents that formed a protective circle. Witches bustled in and out in familiar frantic movements.

Isadora headed for the apothecary tents again, intent on finding her friend, Lucey. Defender attacks had virtually stopped on normal Watchers since Cecelia's death months ago in the East, leaving Lucey with nothing to do for the Advocacy. She volunteered most of her time here, attempting to help however she could. Isadora often joined her.

An upswing in the war, with increasing violence and pressure on the borders now that the East had completely isolated themselves, meant that Advocacy volunteers couldn't do much anyway. They were either dying, or too busy trying not too.

The sharp smell of a cleaning potion assaulted Isadora's nose when she pushed aside the flap for the surgical tent. Light leaked through the thin canvas, which spanned wide as a house and tapered at the ends. Witches lay on the dirt floor, moaning. Blood stained their shirts. These were the wounded that were able to transport away from the battles to receive assistance. The most severe were tended there.

Isadora, used to the coppery smell of blood after her eight hour shift, gently stepped past.

"Is Lucey here?" she asked a passing apothecary. He shook his head before tearing away without a word. Isadora frowned, then moved to the next tent. Not there, either. Only the stench of death, blood, and putrefaction in two other tents.

"Where are you?" she murmured.

"I shouldn't be surprised ta see ya here. Although, maybe with blood on ya. Formidable, eh?"

A familiar voice caused Isadora to whirl around, heart leaping into her throat. Behind her stood a familiar witch with shocking red hair and lips like a butterfly. Her heart-shaped face and suspicious eyes betrayed her almost as quickly as her hair.

"Baylee?" Isadora whispered.

Baylee smirked. "It's only been a year," she said. "Not like I'd change that much. What are ya doing here?"

Isadora closed the space between them, clasping Baylee to her chest. Baylee stiffened until Isadora pulled away. She immediately inspected her friend, holding her at arms length. She hadn't seen Baylee since the attack on Berry. The school they'd both attended had all but disintegrated afterward.

"Baylee! Tell me you aren't hurt."

"Nah." Baylee waved a hand, stumbling back. "I'm fine. Just takin' care of some business."

She held a scroll in one hand, her fingers curled protectively around it without crushing the fragile paper. Her hair, wild around her shoulders, was nonetheless full and healthy. The rest of her—pinched, too thin, and clad in threadbare clothes—appeared the same.

"Business? What kind of—"

"Did ya go back to the forest after the fire?" Baylee asked. "Or have ya been here the whole time?"

"Both."

"Ya don't seem so good yaself," she said. "What happened?"

"My father," Isadora whispered. "He was . . . murdered in Letum Wood."

"Demmet," Baylee said without wavering, something like experience in her gaze. "That's nasty. Ya angry yet?"

Angry that a dragon had murdered her father and plunged her already weary family into deeper chasms? Angry that his death had create a gulf between her and her sister? Angry that nothing seemed to go right?

"Filled with it."

Baylee stared at her, seeming troubled. "I was . . . I was worried about you."

A hint of a smile softened Isadora's expression. "I've thought of you often too. While in Chatham City, I looked for you a few times."

Baylee's teeth flashed a light yellow when she smiled. "I'm impossible to find, and for good reason. Chatham is where I belong. Lots of work there to keep an orphan busy and food in her stomach."

"The other girls?"

Miss Sophia's School for Girls, where she'd first met Baylee, had been a ragtag group of girls sent away from parents only too willing to be rid of one more mouth to feed. The laughably pathetic school system in the Network had been dwindling since the wars cut most funding. Now, education was all but extinct.

"Most I don't know," Baylee said, a pained expression crossing her face. "Some of them went home, or ran away somewhere else. A few found benefactors."

Isadora's brow furrowed. *Benefactors.* Witches in higher society that would occasionally take on a younger girl for baser interests. A different kind of whore house that was almost impossible to track down. But a valid option for a girl on the street only a breath away from starvation. Baylee said it with the ease of someone that had lived on the streets her whole life, as if the inevitable end only surprised Isadora.

"You?" Isadora whispered, her voice tremulous. "Did you have to find a benefactor?"

Baylee recoiled. "No, ya daft idiot! Think I'd lay with a man for any amount of currency? Too much work in the alleys for that, if ya can handle it. No, I found me a boss." Her fingers tightened ever-so-slightly around the scroll. "Good one too. He's sworn me to secrecy, or I'd tell ya more. I'm here doing his business. I can't stay long, but saw ya, and wanted ta say hi."

A thousand questions rushed to the tip of Isadora's tongue, but she quelled them all. Baylee's shadier dealings were no surprise—she'd been a scrapper her whole life.

"It's good to see you," Isadora said with a rush of conviction. "Really."

Baylee grinned. "You too." Her brow furrowed. "But what are ya doing in a hell hole like this?"

"Looking for a friend," Isadora murmured, remembering Lucey again. "We need her in the surgical tent. I come and volunteer with her when I can. She's an apothecary here."

Baylee's gaze snagged on something behind Isadora. Her face scrunched into an instant scowl.

"Oh, no," she muttered. "Not him. I'm out of here."

Without another word, Baylee disappeared. An unexpected, imperious male voice made Isadora's spine rigid.

"I half expected you to be hiding with your sister in your beloved forest."

Maximillion.

She tried to breathe through a bolt of revulsion— hidden beneath a sudden thrill—that consumed her. She didn't turn around. Why gratify him? She could feel him standing right behind her.

"I tear myself away," she muttered.

Unable to bear it another second, Isadora whirled around, stopping a hair's breadth away from a very familiar chest. The smell of vetiver nearly overwhelmed her as she stepped back, staring into a pair of frosty eyes. Her heart skipped a beat, then resumed at a race. Maximillion glared with all the power of a thousand suns, looking haughty, irritated, and magnificently attractive.

He lifted an eyebrow.

"Max," she whispered, forcing it through her rage-thickened throat. "Always a pleasure to see you."

His nostrils flared. "Maximillion," he snapped. "I've come to have a word with you, if you have a minute to spare."

A thousand emotions rushed over her all at once, but she shoved them aside. For months she'd daydreamed—no, plotted—what she would say when she saw him again. The blistering words of hate and regret and anger that would finally spill out, letting him know *exactly* what effect his indifference and cold personality had on the world.

Not that he would care.

She set her jaw, tilting her head back to meet his gaze. In the folds of ice and frost, she thought she saw a flicker of something. It disappeared, easing into the glacial depths. They hadn't spoken a word since she found out the truth about Daid's death over six months ago. Aside from a few messages with assignments from the Advocacy that she'd ignored, he hadn't even sought her out. Perhaps he'd forgotten the heat behind their unexpected kiss. She certainly had.

Or tried to.

"I don't want to speak with you," she said.

"The feeling is mutual. I assure you, I come on business that is not my own."

Suddenly, Isadora's strength flagged. Hating him required too much effort. The day had been a long one—passing slowly as she worked amongst the wounded streaming in from a battle near the Western border. All the more slowly because she feared each young male would be him, caught in the madness as he went to check on the Guardians there.

She faced him with a jolting stomach, filling her with something hot and cold at the same time.

"What do you want?"

His gaze met hers, pinning her. Under the power of his colossal indifference, she'd always felt pegged. Strangely seen and understood and naked and thrilled at the same time. There was no challenge in this world quite like him. She stopped breathing, arrested in silence. Just when she thought he wouldn't answer, he broke the spell.

"I have an update from La Torra."

"Oh?"

Six months ago, she'd battled the Eastern Network Ambassador, Cecelia Liam, on top of the strange island prison Carcere. Cecelia had been the first witch and Defender Isadora had pulled into the paths, something she hadn't known was possible. Afterwards, the power had doubled.

Then tripled.

She thought of Fiona and Lorenzo and the other band of misfits that had somehow gathered into a strange friendship on that island in the East. After spending months there, she found herself missing the sandy beach. The vast sky. The briny smell of the ocean breeze. She rubbed her arms. The warmth. Although it was only the end of summer, winter had already intruded.

Maximillion's gaze narrowed on something in the distance. "Carcere has been officially closed by Dante as of yesterday. The workers have been forced to evacuate, and the castle closed up in exile. Even the Guardians have been removed for now."

"Oh."

"It's not likely to be real," he muttered. "Nothing with Dante ever is. The man is all smoke and mirrors. No doubt he's scheming something he doesn't want anyone to witness, and using Carcere as his cover."

"What does that have to do with me?"

"I thought you cared."

"About Fiona and Lorenzo, yes. Because witches are important."

"No one said otherwise," he muttered. "Forgive me for wanting to keep you informed on your friends."

Her gaze narrowed. "That cannot be why you're here. Months have passed without a single word from you. What do you want, Max?"

He hesitated for half a second. A sudden wrinkle in his impenetrable armor made her thoughts soften. Images of Cecelia and the filthy, dank stench of all those Watchers, locked in the magical prison for decades, whispered back through her mind.

She looked away. He *had* gone to almost impossible lengths to save all of the Watchers, and had succeeded.

"If I never saw La Torra again," she said, swallowing hard, "it would be too soon."

A hollow silence rang in the air following her declaration.

"I had no choice, Isadora."

She sucked in a sharp breath, instantly knowing what he meant. She wanted to scoff. No choice? He had no choice but lie to her about Daid's death? To withhold information and her right to mourn until the moment that best served *his* interests? Daid had been dead for weeks before she found out. Maximillion had flatly lied to her several times, hiding letters from and to her family. Seemingly without regret.

"You were held at knife point, were you?" she asked icily.

"It happened after you'd fled to the East and taken over the position—something I never asked of you."

"You had ample opportunity to tell me after that," she snapped. Heat ignited in her chest. She let the fire build, enjoying the way it wrapped through her bones and zipped around her body. So much easier to feel than the heavy weight. The guilt. The questions. The feeling of utter and total betrayal.

He grabbed her arm, slamming her chest to his. His breath hit her cheek in a hot caress. Isadora paused, momentarily stunned.

"I kept you safe," he whispered. "I did what I had to to protect you."

On fire from his touch, she wrenched her arm free.

"Don't touch me."

"You were living under Cecelia's nose and insisting you were an adult," he said, eyes burning. "What was I supposed to do? Distract your attention by telling you about your Daid so you killed yourself and all those relying on you to do a job?"

"No! I-I mean . . . you . . . you should . . . that was *my* decision to make."

"It wasn't."

"You should have . . ." All those words, spinning through her head all those nights, failed her. It has been so clear to her before, but now the waters muddied. Suddenly, she didn't know what to say. "You should have—"

Nothing more came from her lips. She stood there, paralyzed by his closeness.

"What?" he insisted impatiently. "What should I have done?"

"Told me!"

"I did!" he growled. "The moment I felt it was right. The moment I felt it was *safe*. When I gave you those stupid letters, that was the safest you had been. You had been sleeping for days after your confrontation with Cecelia. Could you have saved Lucey if you had known your Daid was dead? If the anguish you're feeling now was distracting you from understanding exactly what was happening on La Torra, could you have faced Cecelia and won?"

Her rage lessened as she recalled that awful, strange night. Lucey, half dead. Maximillion strapped to a star next to her, both of them slated for death by fire within moments. The way that Cecelia's eyes burned with hatred and the darkness she brought with her.

Isadora, forced into questions she'd purposefully not answered when they rose in her own mind, couldn't escape now. Could she had saved them that night if she'd known about Daid?

No.

She snapped her mouth closed, then opened it again. Ages seemed to pass before she summoned her response.

"That wasn't your call to make."

"Forgive me, but I disagree," he hissed. "You worked for the Advocacy, over which I have considerable responsibility. If I hadn't withheld that information until it was safe for everyone, your death—and all the others that would have resulted—would have been on my hands. You're a selfish cad if you think this is just about you."

"It's not just that, is it?" she snapped. "It's . . . it's everything that I'm dealing with now because I wasn't home. Because you didn'ttell me. Sanna hates me. We hardly speak, except to argue. So many Dragonmasters died while I was gone. They suffered, and I haven't been here to help. Maybe I could have prevented Babs death or . . . or Daid's! I lost my *family* with no chance to say goodbye. Now, I . . . cannot atone for being gone." Tears filled her eyes. "I lost my home, Maximillion. Because of you, I lost everything."

She met his gaze. Beneath all she said lay something deeper, something laced with infinitely more pain that she didn't dare touch, like a hot, white, consuming light. The real pain stemmed from the truth: he had been frightened of her that night on Carcere. She'd seen it in his eyes. After what happened, he'd left without a word. Not a single word. He, who had never feared anything, had shied away from her.

Her lips tingled, recalling his heated, passionate kiss earlier that fateful night. The burn in his eyes. Even a longing in his scant, avoidant touch.

"I . . . I'm not sure I ever can forgive you," she whispered, looking away, leaving the most important part unsaid.

Maximillion straightened. "Well," he said, chest lifting with a deep breath. His expression, steady as glass, betrayed nothing. "I believe that says more about you than me, doesn't it?"

He disappeared, taking her heart with him.

～

Did you love that?! I hope so! If you want to read the rest, visit www.katiecrossbooks.com and type FREEDOM paperback into the search bar.

Or you can buy it at online retailers.

Thanks for reading!

—Katie Cross

ACKNOWLEDGMENTS

Give me an intense fantasy world, multiple conflict strains, a massive word count goal, and a fast deadline, and I'll gladly tackle that without fear. But put a blank acknowledgments page in front of me, and suddenly, my brain is empty.

Because *so many people* assist in the making of a great book.

First off, to my amazing support team that deal with a lot of late night calls and frustrations when the magic just *won't come together!* Stephan, Kelsey, Brandy, Ta-rah. You support a girl like rockstahs. Thanks.

My production team: Jenny, Kella. Stephanie / Catherine, Chris, Kristen, and all the people in between—thank you SO much for all that you do. Your books are beautiful, and I couldn't do what I do without you.

To my launch team, without whom I would never be able to enjoy launching a new book so much, and who set me up for ultimate success. Thank you for caring, for connecting, and for helping. I wish I could name all of you individually. You all have places in my heart!

For my fans, who read, email, and are the worlds best people ever—thanks. Connecting with you is the reason I write YA Fantasy.

Husband, Little Man, and Warrior Princess—love yer freaking guts. Thanks for being my inspiration. To those I may have missed: I adore you all, and I totally blame baby brain.

About the Author

Katie Cross is ALL ABOUT writing epic magic and wild places. Creating new fantasy worlds is her jam.

When she's not hiking or chasing her two littles through the Montana mountains, you can find her curled up reading a book or arguing with her husband over the best kind of sushi.

Visit her at www.katiecrossbooks.com for free short stories, extra savings on all her books (and some you can't buy on the retailers), and so much more.